All That Glitters

by Dawn Reno Langley

Published by Rewired Creatives, Inc.

rewired creatives inc.

Dedication

For my sister, Candace Lee Cioffi, to feed the happily-ever-after fantasy

Acknowledgements

My thanks go to all the people who answered questions, specific and otherwise, with regard to this story. I am especially grateful to the customs officers of Vermont; the Boston Police Department; Attorney Robert P. Davison, Jr, of Stowe, Vermont; Attorney Michael Kelley of Everett, Massachusetts; Jay Shanik of Shanik's Gun & Sport Shop in Enosburg Falls, Vermont; Chris DuRona and her sister, Louise, for providing information about Paris; Fred Bass for sharing stories about driving through Europe; and to the many travel agents who provided brochures on specific areas.

I also would like to offer my appreciation to those who read the manuscript at different intervals, offering comments and support — Jena Bartlett, Sue Breeyear, Bettie Curboy, Susan Herner, Leslie Kominsky, Allan Nicholls, Susan Sanders, Sue Yuen, and all the folks at the Stonecoast Writers' Conference. And special thanks to Dottie Harris, as well as to Milly Marmur.

In addition, thanks to Ashley Butowski for helping me prepare the new cover and other materials for the second edition.

Prologue

Boston, August, 1991

On any other afternoon in August, chic Brahmin women meandered down Newbury Street, gazing with consternation into boutique windows filled with reed-thin plaster models dressed in the latest fashions. But today, Boston lay deadly quiet. Thick exhaust fumes rose from a long line of stalled cars as Diana Cole wriggled her way around them to reach her shop. Even after living here for thirty-five years, she still wasn't used to the smell. Today, it was like liquid gas.

In spite of the heat, she smiled as she spotted Terence waiting for her in the window, his hands lovingly wrapped around what looked to be a Gorham teapot by the slim, elegant lines of its spout. Manager of Amaryllis of Boston, the smallest, yet busiest of Diana's international antique shops, Terence Pellican could always count on a few of those Brahmin women to wander in to ask his advice about decorating. Their conversations were his springboard for a sale, and clients never failed to take the bait—one of the reasons Diana found him invaluable. Though he was thirty-seven, almost two years older than she, Pellican's thinning blond hair and the half-glasses he soberly wore centered on his straight and narrow nose made him look like a much older, stodgier gentleman. But he known to put a few too many beers away, occasionally finding himself in one of Boston's many barrooms flinging darts like a professional and joining the South Boston laborers and cab drivers in a verse of "Tipperary," his crackling tenor voice dipping and swaying like a drunken sailor's. Another reason Diana adored him.

Set on the upper level of Newbury Street, the shop Terence so efficiently managed was conservative and unobtrusive, the only indication of its trade a muted gold-trimmed sign in the front window, decorated simply with a red amaryllis and the word ANTIQUES. Diana still felt a thrill of pride looking at it. Years ago, she had rightly thought that people who had the wherewithal to purchase something at Amaryllis didn't need a neon sign to show them in.

"Damn!" Her Gucci pump sank in the soft tar against the street curb, its two-inch heel pulled in as if the street were quicksand. With her pocketbook thrown on the curb beside her and the white bowler atop her glistening black hair threatening to fall off, she pulled angrily at her ankle. "The hell with it," she growled, pushing the heel of the other pump into the melted tar as well. Stepping out of both

3

shoes onto the hot sidewalk with a grimace, she marched up the stairs to her shop.

She entered in a whoosh, barefoot and still mumbling to herself. Terence had retreated to the rear of the shop—a wise move, she thought, as she quickly glanced down the aisles to see if any customers were about before pulling her hat off and whipping it into the seat of a Queen Anne wingback chair. Within moments she had slipped on a pair of flats and called Terence to her desk to begin reviewing the day's sales. Both the recession and the heat were working overtime—even Terence's salesmanship hadn't succeeded today. Two sales, both under $1,000. She groaned, but continued checking mail and messages.

When she paused, Terence looked up quizzically. She chewed absently on the side of her full bottom lip, trying to remember if she had entered the morning's auction buy into her laptop on the flight home.

"You didn't get the Gauguin, did you?" he asked.

She ran her fingers through her hair, her brows locking slightly. "Tyrone was there, bidding for Streisand again, and he decided I wasn't going to beat him' on this one. We'll get Barbra the next time I talk to her in L.A. Besides, he paid far too much. I made sure of that. And he didn't know that the painting had been retouched, so I'm not terribly heartbroken." She sighed quietly, trying to collect her thoughts. "Anyway, I'll go to London next week and bring the Monet with me. Sotheby's has some Impressionists going up on the block that'll make the trip worthwhile. Oh, before I forget, we really should restock the Beverly Hills shop, so I'm going to have to plan a trip to the Southwest soon. Check my schedule and call the airlines, will you? And for God's sake, Terence, please don't put me in that little roadside motel again. They didn't even have any ice last time, and there were cockroaches in the bathroom. Before you make the reservations, call that little place in Santa Fe—know which one I mean? — and see if the Hopi kachinas they had last month are still there."

Shuffling through the pink phone messages, she pulled one out and waved it in the air. "I'm going to check on the South American container myself. Dr. Reeves wanted five pieces of pottery from this shipment, and he's leaving for Greece tomorrow. If I can't get my hands on it. I'll have to make excuses to him again. We'll lose him as a customer. And you know what *that* means, ol' boy."

The Amaryllis dynasty had succeeded for many reasons—but first and foremost because she hadn't lost a single customer. No need to start now. It wasn't often that she was so harried and she felt badly about it. Though she realized her manner was always clipped and businesslike, she usually had a smile for Terence, a funny story about her nephews to share, or a comment about an upcoming auction. Not today, and no time to feel guilty about it, she decided. Terence would understand. He always did.

"Oh, before I forget, did Maryann call?" She turned, her eyes a little warmer, her tone softer, less strident than it had been only seconds before.

Terence shook his head. "I thought you had gone there already. Never thought you'd decide to work today." She shrugged and reached for the phone with a sigh. Why did the shipment have to be delayed today, of all days? All she wanted was a dip in the pool, a romp with her nephews, and some gossip with her sister-in-law over a tall, cool glass of iced tea. Was that so much to ask?

"Mr. Walters, please." Her foot tapped impatiently and loudly, the rat-tat-tat graphically reveling her mood. "Harry. Diana Cole. What's happening with my shipment? It's two days late."

"No sign of it, yet, Ms. Cole." The gruff voice on the other end sounded as tired and hot as she felt. "Some guys were here this morning, though . . ." "Thanks, Harry," she whispered into the phone before placing it back into its cradle. The pounding of her heart echoed in her ears like an out-of-control freight train. She dropped her head to the desk for a brief moment, trying to consider all the possibilities. There were so many—and *none* was welcome. "This is no time to feel sorry for yourself, babe," she said aloud as she whipped out of her chair and pulled open her desk drawer. "Terence!" Her voice was thin and high. She didn't turn around nor did her pen stop moving. "I need you immediately. Come! You have to help me . . ." At that instant, the shop door swung open, its silver bells tinkling lightly, then it slammed—hard — and a pair of men in Levis and T-shirts strutted around the corner of the Louis XIV china cabinet at the end of the aisle. Diana slid the telephone into its receiver.

"You Diana Cole?" The man had blond hair swept to the side the way Mick Jagger had worn his in the Sixties. He pulled a slim leather wallet out of his back pocket and whipped it open in front of her face. "I'm Detective Cottrell and this is Detective Deluca. We're from the Boston Police Department." He slipped his badge back into his pocket.

She fought to remain calm, to maintain some sense of composure, but her traitorous hands curled tightly around the edge of the desk. "What can I do for you, gentlemen?"

"I'm afraid you're under arrest, ma'am, for transportation of illegal substances."

"Illegal substances?" Her cool voice seemed a stark contrast to Terence's involuntarily loud gasp of disbelief from the back room.

"Cocaine." The officer grinned sardonically as he raked his eyes over her body, his attitude already pronouncing her guilty.

Diana flushed, her control breaking slightly. "Might I ask where the cocaine was? If I remember correctly, my container was supposed to be full of antiques, not drugs."

Cottrell ran his index finger along the throat of a cloisonné vase on a Sheraton side table. "All we had to do was crack open some of those red clay vases you had shipped back from Colombia. You got through customs in Miami and everything. Must have paid off a lot of people. Pissed *someone* off, though. Pissed them off enough that they wanted you caught . . ."

"I'm not . . ." Stopping abruptly, Diana's eyes widened. "You cracked open the vases? My *Mayan* vases?"

Terence slid in quietly behind her. Reaching forward, he squeezed her arm warningly. She looked up at him, allowing him to see the repressed fear in her eyes.

"That's enough, Greg." With the apologetic stance of someone who knew his friend's behavior reflected on him, the dark-haired cop stepped in front of his partner. "You're going to have to come with us, Ms. Cole."

Diana shuddered in sudden awareness of her situation. She looked frantically from Cottrell's impassive face to Terence's sympathetic one, then toward Deluca. "Where are we going?"

"We've got to book you, then, if you can't make bail, we'll take you to the Massachusetts Correctional Institute in Framingham," Cottrell answered. "Now, c'mon. We don't have all day." The blond shifted from one foot to another, shooting puzzled glances at his partner, who casually leaned against a Philadelphia Chippendale highboy.

Diana took a deep breath and reached for her pocketbook with trembling hands. "No handcuffs, please. I ... I really don't want this to be messy. It hasn't been a good day."

As she ducked her head, she squeezed her eyes shut against the onslaught of tears. This couldn't be happening. This couldn't possibly be happening, she kept telling herself. But when she opened them, the silver frame which held a picture of her nephews was directly in her line of sight. "Can I take this?" She reached for the photo.

Both officers automatically reached for their revolvers. Pellican took a shocked step backward. Diana froze, feeling, as though she had suddenly been thrust into a poorly-made cops 'n' robbers' movie. She fought a hysterical urge to giggle.

"Hey, lady," Cottrell said, "don't move so fast! We don't need to make things any more difficult."

"What are you going to do? Shoot me, right here in Amaryllis? For reaching for a photograph?"

"Greg, ease up." Cottrell's partner straightened <u>and</u> put his gun back in its holster. "Ms. Cole wasn't going to do anything. We don't have to overreact here." Reaching over the desk, he pulled the picture out from behind a Tiffany dragonfly lamp. "Cute kids. Yours?" He gazed questioningly in Diana's direction.

"They're my boys ... my n-n-nephews." She turned her head when Deluca's intense gaze threatened to cause her to lose her composure once more.

"Can I make a phone call? I'd like to talk to my sister-in-law so she won't worry when 1 don't show Up for dinner tonight." Lifting her head, she swallowed hard and confronted the two cops, her face a silent plea for sympathy.

"Well, we usually don't do things that way," Detective Deluca said quietly.

"Listen, let me call now and I won't use the call I've got coming to me at the station. I *do* get one, don't I?"

"Well, I guess it's okay. Just one, though."

As she dialed Maryann's number, Deluca read her rights and she smiled at Terence, though large, rolling tears shed like renegades between her lids.

"You men obviously have the wrong woman," Terence blurted. "Where did you get your information? Who gives you the right to be here? I demand to speak to your . . ."

"Terence Pellican!" Diana put her hand over the telephone receiver. "Save it! There's nothing you can do except call Amie. Tell him what's happened and get him to bail me out. He's the only one who can get money out of my account. We'll talk about this later."

Embarrassed, he stopped talking. The warning look on Diana's face told him all he needed to know for the moment, yet she could tell he was already thinking ahead. Who could he contact if Amie Goldstein could not be reached at his State Street office?

"Maryann, honey, it's me. Take the boys to the cottage for a while, okay?" Diana spoke swiftly, yet loudly enough to let the detectives know she was not making any escape plans. "Don't ask me any questions. Just trust me. I'll talk to you in a couple of days and tell you all about it. Just do as I say. I'll talk to you later and, Maryann . . ." She turned her back on the bevy of men who stood around her desk. "Kiss the boys for me. Tell them I don't intend to miss the Red Sox game next week."

As Diana gathered her belongings, she turned slowly, surveying her shop one last time with a slow, sweeping glance as though she might never see it again. "Take care of everything for me, will you, Terence? Make sure everyone knows I'll be back soon, but don't tell them what happened. And try not to make too much of it, will you? Don't get nervous, okay?"

She gave him a quick hug. He returned her gesture fervently and couldn't stop a tear from slipping from his eye as she turned to walk, straight-backed and proud, out the door and down the steps of her shop. Curious eyes stared at her from behind elegantly-decorated windows. The shopkeepers' faces, usually closed up tight like a Cape Cod house after Columbus Day weekend, were openly inquisitive.

Just as well that most of Newbury Street's residents were gone for the day, she mused as she bent to pull her pumps out of the gutter where she had left them . . . was it only moments ago? It seemed like years.

"C'mon, lady. Jeez, what're you doing now?" Cottrell's grip on her arm tightened.

"These are my shoes. I'd rather wear them than these flats."

"With tar all over their heels?"

"That's okay." Diana straightened up, lifted her head, and let the men lead her into the sedan parked against the curb, a blinking blue light on its roof.

Chapter One

Boston, October, 1968

At four o'clock in the afternoon, it was already dark on Orleans Street in East Boston. Thirteen- year-old Diana Colucci glanced up and down the street, alternately yelling her brother's name and "If I catch you, Robert Colucci, I'm going to kill you!" She knew he was out there somewhere, yet it almost never failed—when she finished cooking their supper and came out to call him in, Robbie was seldom around.

She slapped her hands together and blew into her palms. The November sky, gray and moody, promised snow before the evening was over. On one side of the street, a line of brick tenements stretched up to the corner and beyond like an endless three-story wall. The buildings completely blocked the sun so that, even in the winter, the kids played in the middle of the street—the only place which received a few welcome rays of solar warmth. Each tenement was separated from the one next to it by a five-foot alley. Diana and Robert kept their bikes or sleds in theirs, though in recent years most of the buildings' owners put doors at the end of the alleys in order to curtail thefts of bikes, car tires, and other items the residents stored there.

Open lots, where grasshoppers abounded in summertime, attracted the neighborhood kids throughout the city. Diana's father had often fished a Skippy Peanut Butter jar from the trash, punched holes in its lid, and handed it to her with a whispered "Don't let your mother see the bugs. She'll scream." Chasing those grasshoppers was the closest Diana ever got to spending her summer vacation on a farm.

The wind gave a lonesome whistle. Her thin blue cotton dress and worn cardigan were a meek attempt at warmth, and she began to wish she had thrown her wool coat over her shoulders.

Across from the Colucci apartment, the bubble gum factory sat quiet and empty, the sickeningly sweet smell—usually present in the dead heat of summer—now noticeably absent. She was never sure whether the owners purposely planned their gum-making production by the season in order to irritate the residents with the smells arising from the tall chimneys, or if the stench just dissipated more quickly once the air cooled off. Robbie often wandered into the lot behind the building —"Just catchin' 'hoppers," he'd tell her. Today she had already checked the lot. He wasn't there.

Damn you, Robbie, she thought, turning the corner from Orleans Street and heading toward the grammar school playground. How the hell am I going to get anything done when you do this to me? Couldn't you cooperate for once in your life?

Late-afternoon shadows shivered on the sidewalk before her. A wind tunnel caused by the closeness of the buildings threatened to make the holes in her sweater even larger. Shivering, she wondered, once again, why her parents had chosen to live in East Boston.

"Is just like home," Papa Colucci would explain to Diana when she was sitting on his knee. "In Sicily, we live all together, all like a family. No one has to worry 'bout if they gonna eat or whether someone will help take care of their sick mama. When we get off the boat by that Lady Liberty, we go with our friends to Little Italy, but Mama and I, we don't like New York, and when Gino tell us about Boston, we take the train and here we are. 'Course, is a lot quieter then. No Logan Airport. No planes."

Each time he told the story, he laughed, throwing his chubby arms up in the air and tossing his head back so far that she could see every tooth in his mouth. She'd slip a little off his lap when he started chuckling, but he always caught her. Then he'd hug her tightly and slide her off his knee with a pat on the behind. "No more stories, now. You go help your mama with supper."

The tenements sprang up by the dozens in those early years. Churches were planted and schools built to accommodate immigrants like Anthony Colucci and their growing families. The tiny grocery stores, integrated into the corner buildings on the main streets, stocked Italian canned goods, cannoli, linguine, and sausages to satisfy the cravings of the neighborhood. In their windows hung long yellow cylinders of cheese and pink squares of cured ham and capicolla next to reddish-brown sticks of salami. Like other ethnic neighborhoods, the signs on the store windows were in both Italian and English, the mixture of languages one might hear upon stepping inside. Outside, on the sidewalk, were a couple of kitchen chairs, where neighbors could sit and gossip and the store owner would take a break now and then.

Diana grew up with the smells of those stores and with the sounds of the city's streets. She saw women dressed in black dresses, stockings, and kerchiefs; they spoke little or no English and roamed that portion of Boston which had been transformed into an American version of their Sicilian or Neapolitan villages. Her mother. Rose Colucci, was one of those women, never learning the language of her adopted country, always letting her husband, Tony, do the learning for her.

She shivered as the wind went up the bottom of her dress and slid under her too-large cotton underwear. Our Lady of Mount Carmel loomed before her, its gold-trimmed door and white spires in stark contrast to the ugly brick tenements surrounding it. Without thinking, she made the sign of the cross and genuflected before turning the corner to the playground.

The wind seemed even colder on Gove Street and she found herself damning Robbie again and again. She never thought of damning her father, though she often had a nagging curse in the back of her mind directed at her mother. If Mama had been a little stronger, a little more adapted to the ways of the United States, maybe she wouldn't be out in the cold looking for Robbie.

Diana remembered her mother as a diminutive Sicilian with large dark *eyes* who had once possessed enough energy to cook lasagna for a crew of fifty hungry workmen without any more effort than it took to feed her family of four. Feisty and quick, she had been raised to believe children were to be seen and not heard, so she always kept a wooden paddle hanging off one of the knobs to her kitchen cabinets, reaching for it whenever Diana or Robert misbehaved. Later, she would follow them to their room, sitting on the edge of the bed, a tear in her eye, then would reach for them, to cuddle her bambinos against her full bosom.

Rose supplied the family with love, discipline, and nourishment mid she took pride in her work, seeing that her two beautiful children were scrubbed pink for school each day and making sure they said their prayers before climbing into sweet-smelling sheets every evening. Diana had thought it would always be that way, never realizing that the training she received in her mother's kitchen would be the education she needed in order to continue her mother's job. Overnight Diana lost her status as a child being cared for and became, instead, the caregiver.

When Tony's crane, overloaded with steel rods, crashed down upon him, Joe Petrone, Tony's boss, called Rose immediately and tried to explain to her, in his Americanized Italian, that her husband had had a horrible accident. Petrone had barely hung up when Rose rushed into the Bethlehem Steel building, having talked one of her neighbors into driving her. She arrived even before the ambulance and watched in shock as the workmen used torches to remove her husband's shattered body from the wreckage. From that day forward, she had firmly refused to accept the tragedy God had thrust upon her, leaving her children to fend for themselves while she retreated from the world.

Now Rose no longer cooked for her children, nor held them after she disciplined them. There was no more discipline, no more love, no more volatile conversations in the Orleans Street apartment. She simply sat at her bedroom window hour after hour, day after day, waiting in vain for her dead husband to come home. She spoke little to her children and had seemingly forgotten how to cook. She could not remember her relatives or friends and often forgot her own name. Occasionally, Diana thought she saw a glimpse of hope or recognition in her mother's eyes, but when she would go back for a second look, it was gone. Mama's expression would be vacant once again.

Like her mother, Diana wouldn't have dreamed of asking for

help, nor would she have had any idea how to go about asking. So she took her responsibilities in stride, remembering everything her mother had taught her, continuing with her life as though Papa's death had never happened. If she had let down her guard and given in to the grief she felt on a daily basis, she was sure she would end up like her mother.

Those memories of the Colucci family when it was whole and healthy were what the teenager held close at night, when the apartment seemed dark and foreboding, when every noise sounded treacherous, and when she was sure she could no longer hold the shrinking family together by herself. Those memories got her through to the morning and were what made her strong.

"You're my beautiful *cara mia*" her father had once said. "My lovely, smart little one. You'll make some nice American boy the best wife in the world."

Not a wife. Papa, Diana would think as she clutched her pillow tight to her chest. I'll never be a wife.

Now, the sheets were often left on their beds for a week or two at a time, and Diana often wondered how her mother had kept up with all the work that had to be done in the five-room apartment.

Rose Colucci's illness was kept secret by the two children, or at least they thought so. Though the neighbors were kind enough not to interfere once they realized Diana didn't want any help, they continued to keep an eye out for the two dark-haired, blue-eyed Colucci children. After a while, convinced that Diana was more resourceful than any of them had given her credit for, then once again became involved with their own families. The children were left alone.

Robbie continued to play, as any normal child in the city did. His bike became his transport into imagination, a way to escape the realities of his life, to become Captain Marvel or Superboy. Though the little two-wheeler was too small for him, he could make its wheels turn faster than any other bike's in the neighborhood, winning every race, leaving the others far behind, his face turned into the wind as though riding fast might bring his young world back to normal. No one but Diana knew about the nightmares he had night after night. She had no doctors or teachers she trusted enough to confide in, so she simply held her brother tightly while he cried, whispering the words she had so often heard on her mother's lips.

"Shhh, Roberto, bambino. Shhh. I'm here. I won't go away. We'll be all right, little one. We're going to be okay."

Standing at the door of his room, looking down at his young, innocent face, tears would stream out of her eyes and silent sobs would shake her shoulders. "I can't do this," she'd whisper to the silence. "How am I going to do this?" Overwhelmed with the fear that her mother would never be the same again, she'd slide to the floor, bringing her knees to her chin to sob uncontrollably against their hard warmth.

One morning, Diana, up before Robert and her mother, stood at the stove, absentmindedly stirring hot oatmeal. Robert's dreams had been particularly bad the night before and she had gotten little sleep. When the phone rang, she jumped, leaving the oatmeal on the stove.

"Is this Mrs. Colucci?" the female voice on the other end of the line had asked.

"No, this is her daughter. Can I help you?"

"I need to talk to your mother, dear. It's about your brother. This is Mrs. Steele at the school."

Diana hitched in a breath, then stood, staring at her mother who had gotten out of bed to sit in the chair at the window. Rose's room, right off the kitchen, was the only one which faced the small back yard where Papa had often tried to grow a small crop of tomatoes.

"Mama?" Diana whispered, hoping, as she often did, to get an answer. "Mama, Robert's teacher is on the phone. Mama, can you talk to her?"

No answer. She shook her head in frustration. What did I expect? she thought bitterly. With a deep breath, she cleared her throat and lifted the phone.

"Yes?" she said, in a deeper, more mature voice. It was a game she often played with creditors and other such people who called asking for her mother. Up to now, she had been able to keep the school at bay, though they often sent notes home requesting that Mrs. Colucci come to the school. At first, she had panicked, but, after a while, impersonating her mother seemed the easiest way to deal with the situations that continued to crop up time and again.

"Mrs. Colucci? This is Mrs. Steele, Robert's teacher. I'm calling to ask you to help us with a little problem we're having with your son . . ." Fifteen minutes later, Diana sank into one of the kitchen chairs, her hands shaking and her heart beating so quickly she thought she would pass out. They wanted to keep Robert in third grade! They thought he wasn't smart enough, wasn't keeping up with the rest of the class! By pretending to be her mother, she had bought a little time with the teacher, promising to give him extra help at home, but she knew it wouldn't last long.

The oatmeal had burnt and both children were already late for school when she dialed Arnie Goldstein's number.

"What're you doin', Di?" Robbie asked sleepily from the kitchen doorway, still in his pajamas.

She glanced at him, noting that the childlike roundness of his cheeks was beginning to change. He looked more and more like Papa every day.

"Go back to bed, honey. I don't think we're going to school today."

"We're not? Allllllrrrrright!"

Still holding the phone to her ear waiting for Goldstein, she listened as her brother made the appropriate noises for the Matchbox cars he played with night and day.

The only person who knew what the little family was going

through was Arnie Goldstein, Tony Colucci's lawyer and long-time friend. When Tony died, Arnie had attempted to console Rose. However, the young lawyer was not fluent in Italian and was soon lost in the crowd of dark-haired, olive-skinned mourners monopolizing Rose like a screaming flock of crows.

When he saw Diana and Robert standing to one side, totally ignored by the adults, he took the time to sit with them, to talk to them about everyday things and to take their minds off what was happening. Before he left, Arnie handed Diana one of his cards. "Call me if you need anything. Anything at all. Okay?"

Diana took the card, stared at it, turned it over, then looked back at the lawyer. "You were Daddy's friend?"

Arnie nodded.

"He talked about you a lot. Called you his *paisan.*" The lawyer nodded again and the young Italian studied him for a moment with incredibly stunning blue eyes framed by long, black lashes. "Are you the one who paid for the funeral?"

"Your father's insurance policy paid for his funeral, honey." Goldstein blinked madly, making a heroic effort not to cry. She touched his arm gently, seemingly surprised to see a man whose emotions were so close to the surface.

"I'm the one who has been taking care of his money, though," the lawyer continued. "Your father wanted to get a house for his family. I was going to help him find one and finance it. Now, I have to talk to your mother about it." He had turned to find Rose, but Diana caught him by the shirtsleeve.

"Not my mother," she said quietly. Her somber eyes offset the resolute balance of her chin, the squared pride of her shoulders, as if a vision had stolen over her young mind. "Talk to me."

Her desire to care for her family bothered the twenty-eight-year-old lawyer, but he had made a commitment. Not until several weeks after the funeral did he discover that Rose had taken to sitting at the window in her bedroom off the kitchen, overlooking the back yard and its dying tomato plants.

Goldstein had asked to speak with Rose regarding some papers she needed to sign in order to receive Tony's social security check. Diana had hesitated. With the quick intuition necessary for a good lawyer, Arnie canceled his appointments for the rest of the day to travel to the Coined home.

Though Diana tried to hide it, the lawyer could see that the children got no reaction from their mother though they tried desperately. They talked to her about their schoolwork, shared neighborhood gossip, and asked questions about how to cook that evening's meal of veal cacciatore and artichokes. Nothing they did caused their mother's expression to change.

Robert stood with dirty hands stuffed into his jean pockets, staring wordlessly at his mother until Diana finally pulled him away.

"Mama's thinking of Daddy right now," she told him, looking over the boy's head at Arnie standing in the middle of the kitchen floor. Then, with a sudden smile of self-assurance, she said; "Don't worry. She still loves us."

The lawyer, with a modest amount of sensitivity and tact, took control. Lifting the old black phone receiver on the kitchen wall, he proceeded to dial the hospital, only to be stopped when Diana gently pushed down the button.

"What are you doing?" she asked.

"I'm going to call the hospital for your mother."

"She doesn't need the hospital. She's fine. She's staying with us." As she spoke, the fear vanished from her face, leaving it composed and mature beyond her twelve years.

Arnie looked down into the girl's blue eyes, saw the strength and determination behind them, and hung up the phone. Against all sensibility and caution, but compelled by the confidence and will shining in that piquant figure, he said, "Diana, you can't take care of your mother and Robert and still go to school. She's sick, honey. Can't you see that? She needs help."

"What about us?" she said quietly, stealing a glance at her eight-year-old brother, sitting on the parlor floor playing with his fire engines.

Arnie took a deep breath. He hadn't thought about that. How could he tell her they would become wards of the state?

She cocked her head to one side, a look of apprehension and a trace of sadness flickering across her face. "Can't you let us work this out ourselves? I don't want Mama to leave. Please? If you call someone, we'll never see each other again. I can take care of us. Please."

The lawyer clasped his hands in front of him and leaned his mouth against his knuckles, softly rubbing them with the hardness of his teeth as he always did when faced with a problem. Opposite him, her plaid school dress prudently below her knees, her hands holding the edge of *her* seat, Diana leaned forward to peer anxiously into his face.

"Please?" she repeated, her voice taking on an edge of determination and passion. "1 know how to take care of the house and how to cook. Our neighbors will watch after Mama during the day. You can't take her away. Please don't call the hospital." Though she had little idea what being a foster child would mean, Diana's intuitiveness had told her nothing could have been worse and she held her breath waiting for the lawyer's decision.

He thought for another moment, then unfolded his hands with a long sigh, telling himself he was all kinds of a fool, yet he could not resist her, could not resist the eloquence of her plea. He imagined what it would have been like if his parents had died and left him, a desolate youngster with even younger siblings to care for. And Goldstein, a dedicated and hardened attorney, captured by the courage and persistence in young Diana Colucci's eyes, found himself saying, "All right. But only for a month. If it doesn't work out, we have to get her some help. Okay?"

She nodded, bright eyes shining, a note of triumph in her suddenly straight and strong shoulders.

From that moment on, Amie was a hero in Diana's eyes. He took care of all the Coined bills, using Tony's social security check to cover their meager expenses, sending her a check for the miscellaneous food and household goods she might need during the month, and keeping track of Papa's insurance money by investing it wherever he felt the money would be safe. He allowed her the dignity of dealing with her mother, though he talked with the teenager on a regular basis, teaching her how to balance a checkbook, and doing his best to protect her against what he considered to be "people who take advantage."

Like her father, she became willful, tenacious, and resolute. Rose and Tony would have been proud of their eldest child if they had seen her diligently bent over the checkbook every Saturday afternoon when the rest of her friends were at the movies or outside playing stickball. Her teachers never knew that her sudden interest in business math came about because she had to run a house, or that the reason she signed up for typing classes was because she felt it might help her to get a better job.

No longer was she the little girl Tony had tossed into the air when he got home at night.

To Diana, Arnie became the family she had lost, though she did her best to keep her distance, intuitively knowing that if she got close, she might lose him, too. Arnie appeared to understand her need for privacy and respected it, though he often mentioned it saddened him to see "you youngsters forced into adulthood so early."

"Arnie?" Diana forced herself out of her two- year-old memories, but her hands still shook and her voice lacked its usual strength. "The school wants to keep Robbie back. How am I going to stop them from doing that?"

Goldstein sighed like a man twice his age. Diana knew another lecture was coming. "You know, they're lucky they don't know what's going on at your house," he said, a note of frustration in his Brooklyn accent. "You kids would be right in a foster home.

"I know, I know. You've told me a million times before. But I don't need to hear it again, Amie. I need to know how we're going to get him promoted."

"So what if he stays back, Di? Maybe he needs more help, more time. For God's sake, he lost his parents. Don't you think he needs some time to salve the wound? The teachers can't help him if they don't know what's going on, so you're just going to have to back off and understand that if he *does* have to stay back, it might just be the best thing for him."

Kicking at a dust ball on the floor, she pondered the fact that Amie had tried to be as much a part of the little family as humanly possible. But' at times like these, she wanted someone else to take care of everything.

Though his mother, Sadie Goldstein, often urged him to bring the children over for dinner, more often than not Diana stubbornly shook her head. They had to stay with Rose. Finally, Amie conceded and stepped away from his law books at least once a week to have dinner with the Coluccis. Sometimes he played basketball with Robbie, telling her later that he was amazed the boy never talked about his parents. Nothing Arnie did or said could bring the youngster out of his shell, though he continued to offer his time and companionship to the boy.

She heard an exasperated cough on the other end of the line. "Okay, okay. I'll call the school. You just better make sure he does his homework. There won't be too much more I can do."

Though it had happened over three months ago, her conversation with Arnie rang in her mind as she walked closer to the playground and heard the sounds of children screaming and playing. In the distance, a siren sounded. Diana lifted her eyes, curious as to where it was going. Did old Mrs. Giannelli have another heart attack? Was there an accident up on Meridian? The kids always drove too fast when they were heading up that hill, often driving two abreast, not thinking of what might be turning the corner up ahead.

The siren's wail came closer. Its flashing red light passed by the end of Gove Street. She forced her feet to move faster and called once again for Robbie, though the sound was lost in the noise of the street. As she ran into the playground, her arms no longer cold, her mind no longer full of the hourly worries which placed her, she saw the ambulance pull in the other side of the playground. It headed for a group of children gathered in the northeastern corner, near the swings.

She stopped. Robbie's bike lay up against the fence, its tire twisted, its red brake light shattered. Her heart leaped into her throat, pounding unmercifully. Feeling like she was in a dream, unable to make her leaden muscles move to pump her legs, she slowly lifted one leg, then the other.

The crowd parted as she flew into their midst. Her eyes were drawn to the little body on the ground in front of her. The sneakers, red and blue, their bottoms full of tiny holes, just like Robbie's. Closing her eyes, she reached for the St. Christopher medal around her neck and uttered a quick prayer. "Please don't let it be him. Please make it be someone else."

The medics reached the boy before Diana, surrounding him so completely that she couldn't see beyond their white shirts.

"Please let me in!" she screamed at them. "It's my brother. Please, let me see him!"

One of the white shirts turned, giving her a clear view of the boy on the ground. A red gash along his forehead dripped blood onto the cement next to him and almost obliterated his blond hair. Blond.

"He's going to be all right, girlie. Just stay back so we can get him into the ambulance, okay?" the white shirt said.

Rooted to the ground, she stared at Tommy Talese as though he were a ghost.

"Your brother hit my bike," he said weakly, glaring at her with a little boy's angry frustration. "He broke the fender and ran away. You better tell him I'm going to get him for this."

The blood rushed back into her face. Once again she felt the biting November air against her legs. "I'm sorry. Tommy," she managed, before turning to search the crowd for the rumpled black head of hair she knew as her brother's.

After a few moments, convinced he wasn't among the crowd that had gathered in the playground, she took his battered bicycle off the ground and wheeled it slowly back to the apartment. Robert sat on the front stairs, his head buried in his lap.

"Robbie, you jerk!" she started, though relief flooded through her body. "Why do you always have to start trouble? Do you know Tommy has to go to the hospital? Probably has to get stitches, you know. God, sometimes I don't know what I'm going to do with you."

He lifted his head slowly. From his dirt-stained cheeks Diana knew he had been crying, and she immediately felt contrite. A miniature male version of his sister, he had inherited the coal black hair of his Sicilian ancestors and eyes as amazingly blue as Diana's. His nose had been bumped and scraped so many times there was a permanent ridge across its middle, and his mouth, missing a few teeth, often curved into a crooked smile. Like Diana, his clothes were well worn and shabby, but his revealed the normal abuse of childhood wear and tear, while hers were threadbare because she had borrowed them from her mother's closet. His corduroy jacket wore the patches of several baseball clubs, and his red and blue sneakers were untied and dirty. Resisting the impulse to bend and tie them as she had so many times before, she forced herself to remember Tommy's face.

"I'm going to have to put you on punishment," she said sternly over her shoulder as she wheeled the bike into the front hall. "You're just going to have to learn."

"I didn't do it on purpose, Di. Honest. Tommy and I were playing chicken and he just ... he just ... got in the way, I guess." His high, squeaky voice was nervous. She reminded herself to be firm.

"And how dare you run away when you hurt someone like that?" she continued. "If Papa ever knew you ran from a friend who was hurt, he'd . . ."

"Dad's not around anymore."

She stopped and turned to see her brother's small frame filling a tiny portion of the tall door-, way. Unable to see his face, she knew he could see hers and forced herself to retain control. Taking a deep breath, she said, "No, he's not, but I am, and I'm telling you what you did was wrong. I want you to go to Tommy's house after supper and apologize. Hear?"

The small figure nodded and followed her up the dank hallway where many years' worth of smells, both good and bad, hung in the air.

Robbie's feet dragged on the stairs. Though the apartment was still home to her, she knew it hadn't felt that way to him in a long time. She chose, however, to ignore his feelings, trying her best to make their life as family-oriented as possible.

"C'mon, Robbie. Supper's probably cold by now."

Diana had left the door open. Shutting it quietly, Robbie stepped into the long hallway which connected all five rooms in the dark apartment. Straight ahead was the east-facing kitchen. The only other room in the house with windows which brought in the sun was Rose's, right off the kitchen. He didn't want to see her right now. She scared him.

To the left a large bathroom, complete with a white porcelain claw foot tub, was once Rose's pride and joy. Before moving to America, she had never had the luxury of hot running water, and it was the first thing she had asked for when Tony rented the apartment. One of Robbie's earliest memories was of being immersed in the warm, bubbly water of the tub. Maybe that was why he hated to take baths. They reminded him of his mother. The way she used to be. Normal.

To his right the door leading to his and Diana's rooms stood ajar. Two years ago, they had flipped a quarter to see who would get the room facing the bubble gum factory—right before Papa died. Diana won and seemed to spend most of her evenings at the window gazing up at the stars which lined the black canopy over Boston's skyline.

Lately, though, she spent all her time reading— those sickening love stories. At any time, Robbie could find a pile of Harlequin romances on the table beside her bed. If he felt daring, he would pick one up and find what he and his friends called the "juicy" parts. She had caught him one day and paddled him, but that wasn't the reason he had given up looking at her books. The room depressed him. It reminded him all too clearly that his sister was no longer a child. No longer a friend, but yet another person who wanted to tell him what to do. An adult.

Diana had decorated her room with old furniture she and Robbie had rescued from the trash man on Wednesdays. They never did that anymore. One more thing they didn't do together anymore.

They had made a game out of gathering items for the room, often trading with the trash man for choice pieces he found. An apple pie for the pineapple poster bed leaning precariously up against the wall. They traded two old dresses that were too small for Diana, but just right for the trash man's daughter, for the oval mirror. A tablecloth declared unusable by Mrs. Scotti, who lived on the third floor, was rescued and used as a swag curtain on the room's one window. Pictures of razor-thin models with long, straight hair shared wall space with black-and-white photos of the Beatles, the Beach Boys, and the Rolling Stones. Even his bike, Robbie's prized possession, had been rescued from the junk pile—paid for with a home-baked cheesecake the trash man couldn't resist.

Diana's room was her haven and he had learned to respect her privacy. But, if anyone had asked, he could tell them about the nights she cried herself to sleep} or about the romantic stories she made up about the pictures on her wall. No one did, so he faithfully kept her secret.

Slowly walking down the long dark hallway to the kitchen, he clenched and unclenched his fists. He hated this part of the day. He wanted to be anywhere else . . . anywhere but 36 Orleans Street.

His sister was at the stove, stirring a pan of simmering tomato sauce. His mother's slouched form filled a chair at the far end of the red Formica- topped table. Rose looked at him with blank eyes; she didn't recognize him. As usual, he thought, slamming his body into one of the naugahyde-covered chairs around the table.

"One meatball or two?" Diana asked, begging him silently with her eyes not to make any trouble.

"Two," he muttered, sliding into his chair and leaning forward, both elbows on the table.

"Get your elbows off the table," his sister said mechanically, as their mother had a million times before.

Diana chattered gaily throughout dinner, trying to keep up the facade as she had for the past two years. Robbie drove the meatballs around his plate, up and over the rigatoni, using the long pasta as tunnels or roadways and the meatballs as sports cars. He ignored his mother, who sat on his right, paying little or no attention to the fact that the majority of Rose's rigatoni decorated her lap and the red tomato sauce was smeared all over her chin. Diana tried to feed her mother a number of times, but the woman pushed her daughter's hand away so violently Diana soon gave up.

As soon as he could, Robbie left the table and locked himself in his room, playing noisily with his Matchbox cars while his sister washed their mother's face and cleaned up the supper dishes. Within moments, he was far away from the East Boston apartment, pretending to be racing the Indianapolis 500 and winning a trophy as big as he was.

Diana tucked Rose into the double bed, then walked on tiptoe to Robbie's door. The nine-year-old was curled into a fetus position on the floor, snoring loudly against the tire of an upended Fisher Price tractor.

Tenderly, she lifted the sleeping boy, put him into his bed, then turned on his nightlight. tucking in the sheets, she felt him turn over and looked up to see his bright blue eyes on her.

"Diana," he said in his quiet tremolo, "the kids make fun of me because you act like my mother. They say you dress funny and that it's because we're poor and Daddy isn't here no more. Isn't Daddy going to come back, Diana? Are we going to have to take care of Momma all the time? Huh, Di, huh? And I can't ride that little bike anymore, Di. How come I can't have a big one like the other kids?"

"Don't worry about those other kids and what they say. They're just being mean." She took a deep breath, wondering if she should answer his constant questions about their parents. It was late. She was tired. Too tired to reassure him. Or even to reassure herself.

"We'll fix the seat, Robbie," she said, tucking in the sheets. "We'll make it higher tomorrow. I know Papa has a wrench around here somewhere. Don't worry, we'll make sure the kids don't make fun of you. Just remember I love you. Okay?"

A few moments later, she stood at the door, looking down at his sweet, innocent face, the tears streaming out of her blue eyes, silent sobs shaking her shoulders. Suddenly overwhelmed with the fear that she would never be able to replace her parents, never be able to be all he needed, she slid to the floor, sobbing uncontrollably.

Am I doing the right thing? she asked herself in desperation. Should I call Amie and tell him to find a nice home, a good family, for Robbie? Did I do something wrong, God? Is that why all of this is happening? Please tell me what to do. Please help me do the right thing.

Chapter Two

Boston, November, 1970

Bending over once more, Diana felt her clammy face drain of color as a new onslaught of cramps wracked the stomach she held with both hands. Trying to breathe normally, she tried to force herself to remember what she had learned in Health class last semester, but the only thing going through her mind was that she was miserable and wanted to go home.

Moccasin-shod feet appeared under the stall next door. She fought with herself before yelling out, "Annette? Is that you?"

"Yeah. Why? Who's that?"

"It's Diana. Diana Colucci. You wouldn't happen to have a pad on you, would you?"

"Why? You got your period?" A chuckle came from the stall before the toilet flushed.

Clenching her teeth, she grimaced. "Yes. Would you please either lend me a pad or get one from the nurse? I really can't do it . . ." She moaned as another cramp made her legs feel like jelly and brought a cold sweat to the back of her neck.

The door to the girls' bathroom slammed. Whispered voices filled the air with jumbled words and giggles. They greeted Annette, and Diana heard more whispers and giggles. The small crowd probably consisted of some of the girls on the cheerleading squad, the same ones who always pressured her to give them answers to exams so they could get high enough grades to assure them a space on the squad. Early in the school year, Diana had let them know she didn't believe in cheating. Ever since, they had made sure her life was miserable, making fun of her old-fashioned clothes and teasing her about being what they termed "a-goody- two-shoes-brain."

"Hey, Colucci!" a voice yelled jubilantly. "Guess you and that goofball, Vincenti, aren't foolin' around after all, huh? You got the curse?"

Hot tears burned down her cheeks. Even if she found the strength to get angry, there was no place to go. She was trapped. An overwhelming urge to go home, climb into bed and pull her knees to her stomach, shutting out the world and its ignorant people, crept over her like a blanket.

"Can someone *please* get me a pad?" Her voice was full of tears she normally would not let anyone see.

More laughter came from the other side of the green steel wall which encased the line of toilets, then suddenly, from three different directions, rolls of white toilet paper flew over the top of the stall, falling in streams over her head and shoulders, covering her legs and landing haphazardly on the dirty gray cement floor.

"There you go, fancy pants," jeered the girls. "See if you can make a pad out of that!" The bathroom door slammed amid more jeers, shouts, and loud laughter. She was alone once again. Fighting the sobs that threateningly welled in her throat, she rolled some toilet paper into a wad and stuck it between her legs before pulling herself together to make the long, uncomfortable trip down the hallway to Nurse Wallace's office.

For two hours, she endured the cramps and headache, her only relief the two aspirin the nurse could supply. Her head swam, her legs tingled, and she wafted in and out of consciousness until the final bell rang, signaling the end of the school day. It relieved her of making any more excuses for her mother not answering the phone at home.

At times like these she missed having someone else to lean on, yet she was angry at herself for cursing her mother's inadequacies.

Last year when Robbie had the flu, the school would not let him go home without a parent there waiting for him. They didn't even bother trying to reach Diana or Mrs. Scarlatti. When Robbie stumbled home that afternoon, his temperature was over 103, his thin body shaking uncontrollably.

For three days, she sat by her brother's bed with wet facecloths for his feverish forehead, trying to feed him warm minestrone and keeping a prayer in her heart that she would be able to take care of him.

Like all little boys, Robbie was out and about the next week, terrorizing the neighborhood with his bike and newly-learned Tarzan screams, while his sister lay in bed battling the same flu. Though Arnie's mother telephoned arid sent him over with some chicken soup, giving him orders not to leave his youngest client until she was back on her feet. Diana still found herself calling out for Rose in the middle of the night. She didn't understand why her calls weren't answered until the morning sun came out and reality set in once more.

Vito Vincenti, otherwise known as Marcus Aurelius—in honor of the ancient Roman philosopher, he said—stood outside East Boston High's swinging glass doors. Shifting his books to the other hip, he adjusted his black-framed eyeglasses on his abnormally large nose and grinned at Diana. The grin quickly faded as she came closer, and he fell into step beside her.

"What's the matter? You look awful."

"I'm not going to be able to go to the dance tonight," she replied quietly. "I'm just going home to bed."

"Are you sick?"

She nodded silently, letting him take her books away from her and gratefully leaning against his shoulder.

"Is there anything I can do?"

"Take care of Robbie," she said, forcing one foot in front of the other.

Without asking any other questions, Marcus put his arm around her. Together they walked home, past tiny clusters of people outside the delicatessens and drugstores on East Boston's street corners. Diana struggled to keep one foot in front of the other and to stop small gasps of pain from escaping her lips. She wished she had the energy to tell Marcus how much she appreciated him, but all she wanted was to get home into bed.

Once in the apartment, she stripped off her sweaty, stained clothes and crawled into a warm flannel nightgown, closing her eyes with pleasure. She heard Marcus in the kitchen talking to Rose as if the woman could hear and understand him. She admired his persistence. Not many boys would have understood what it was like to have a mother like Rose, nor would they deal with it in such a calm, patient manner. But Marcus told her many times that he did it because he respected her decision to remain in control and that he would help her in whatever way he could.

"Diana's going to bed for a while, Mrs. Colucci," he said. "I'm going to take Rob out for an ice cream, then we'll come back and make supper. Don't you worry about me calling my mother. She's probably off on one of her toots anyway, and Dad's working at the bar, so it won't be any problem for me to stay here and take care of you guys. Here, now, are you comfortable?"

Sliding between the sheets with a grateful smile for the boy with whom she had begun to fall in love, Diana closed her eyes and fell into a sound sleep.

When she awoke, it was dark and the apartment was quiet. Mercifully, her cramps were gone, but gnawing hunger pains had set in. She realized she hadn't eaten anything all day.

The kitchen linoleum was cold against her feet as she rummaged in the cupboards for some dry cereal and a banana. Once her bowl was on the table, she peeked into her mother's bedroom and found Rose sitting on the chair in front of the window as she knew she would. A strange smell permeated the room, making Diana's nose crinkle with disgust.

"Oh, not now. Mama," she cried. "I can't take care of you and myself, too." With a sigh, she dragged the mop from its corner and spent the next fifteen minutes cleaning the floor beneath her mother's chair, washing her withered body and changing her soiled clothes. When she finally finished, her cramps were back, and she had no appetite for the cereal she had left sitting on the table.

Shuffling down the hallway back to the sanctity of her bed, she heard the downstairs door close and noisy, joyful voices coming up the stairs. The apartment door swung open and Robbie flew by her with a quick, "How you doin', Sis?" before slamming the door to his room behind him. In her bedroom doorway, Marcus stood quietly, his glasses slightly askew, his messy mop of hair plastered to his forehead.

"I must look awful," she said, grinning sheepishly and pulling the quilt up around her neck.

"No, you just look kind of pale. You couldn't look awful if you tried." He handed her a small bag. "Here, we brought you some ice cream. Didn't know if you wanted it, but I thought it would make you feel better."

She smiled at him. "That's so sweet of you, Marc. You're so good to me." As she sat cross-legged on the bed, eating the ice cream with relish, Marcus entertained her with stories of Robbie's ice-cream-eating spree, then talked of his own day in school.

"I don't mind only getting a B in Algebra," he said, a look of resignation in his warm brown eyes, "but I really think I deserve an A in Astronomy."

"So do I," she agreed between mouthfuls. "But you know what Old Scarface is like. He's going to make you work for it because he knows that's what you want to be. Just don't let him get to you. He really is a good teacher and he knows you're smart. Think of dl you can learn from him."

"Yeah, I guess you're right. I just wish school was easier."

She laughed. "What can be any harder than what we go through day after day? Jeez, high school is a piece of cake when you compare it to home. Think of it as building character."

"Yeah, like we need it!" He smiled back at her, his evenly spaced teeth changing the whole look of his face. She loved it when he smiled and always tried to encourage it. He had a handsome face and was a gentle, intelligent being, someone she could talk to about anything. Her only friend and confidante. The rest of the kids at school saw him as a weird, square, mad-scientist type whom they didn't understand. Little did the others realize that Marcus could have been their best friend if they had just learned to let go of their prejudices.

That'll be the Twelfth of Never, she thought ruefully, remembering what had happened to her earlier in the day.

"Aren't you supposed to be getting home? It's almost ten." She wrapped up the empty ice cream container in the brown paper bag and licked her lips one last time.

"Nobody's home. You know that. No one's going to miss me."

"Aw, c'mon, Marc. You know your family loves you."

The pimply-faced teenager raised an eyebrow and made a hissing sound between his teeth. "Yeah, they pay attention to me about as much as your mother pays attention to you and Rob."

The comment, true as it was, brought a silence between them and for a moment each was quiet with thoughts of the families they had learned to live without.

With a sigh, Marcus got up from where he sat at the bottom of the bed and stretched his long, thin form toward the ceiling, fingertips touching the cracked paint. "Someday we'll both be rich and famous, then we won't have to worry about this anymore."

"I can come to your observatory tower in Arizona," she chimed in, continuing the game they played whenever they were alone, knowing all his dreams by heart as well as he knew hers.

"Then I'll fly back to Paris with you, and we'll tour the vineyards in Southern France . . ."

". . getting drunk on cheap champagne and floating down the Seine."

"The Seine's in Paris."

"Who cares? We'll float down whatever river goes through Southern France. Hell, we'll float down the Nile! Then you'll come back to Paris for my latest fall fashion show . . ."

". . . and I'll tell everyone about how I knew you back in Boston when you were still sewing on a treadle machine . . ."

They shared a final laugh, then Marcus leaned over and gently pecked Diana on one soft cheek. "We'll show 'em," he whispered. "We'll show 'em all."

For a moment, he stared into her eyes, smiling gently, and she knew there would never be another person who would know her as completely as Vito "Marcus Aurelius" Vincenti did.

"Hey, Rob, you going out for Halloween?" Tommy Talese skidded to a stop, throwing sand up in front of his bike, and grinned.

"Naw, that's for little kids." Robbie opened the gate beside his house and got out the tire pump, pretending to repair his back wheel, hoping that Tommy would leave him alone. It wasn't that he didn't want to go out for Halloween. He had no costume and no money to buy one. But, maybe, just maybe, after Diana was asleep, he could sneak out the back door ...

Tommy was off his bike, on bended knee next to him. "We're gonna egg the school. Maybe even get Randall's window. Wouldn't that be cool?"

His interest piqued, Robbie stood up. "Egg the school?"

"Yeah!"

"That might be pretty neat. What time you going out?"

"Around eight. Whaddaya think," Colucci?"

"I'll see. If I'm not at your house, I'm not coming."

Tommy tore down the street, rounding the corner at the same time as Marcus's new carl "Hey! You got it!" Robbie said as he ran his hand over the fender reverently, whistling softly. "Cool!"

"Want a ride?" Vito pushed his glasses up on his nose, unable to keep a proud smile off his face.

"Yeah! Oh, wait. Di's home. I got to tell her where I'm going." He flew up the stairs and in the apartment door screaming, "Di! Marc's got his new car! We're going for a ride."

From the kitchen, he heard the sound of running water stop abruptly. "He got it? Wait a minute. I'll come, too."

Shit. Never failed. He couldn't get to do anything first. "Can't you wait till later? You have Marc all to yourself. Let me be first!"

His sister came out of the kitchen, pulling her arms into an old sweatshirt. "No. I want to see it, too. I've waited all day."

"Aw, Di . . ."

She pushed him in front of her. "No arguments. Go. We'll be back in time for supper."

"Ma asleep?"

"Yup."

"Why do we always have to do ever3^hing around her?"

"Robbie!"

Opening the front door, they halted. Marcus stood outside the car, arms folded. The afternoon sun gleamed just right, brightening up the chrome fenders, giving the windshield a certain kind of luster. Even the hubcaps glimmered. A dream car, Robbie thought. And someday I'm going to have one just like it.

Within moments, they were out of East Boston, past the airport, heading toward Winthrop and the beach. Vito drove cautiously, proudly, one arm out the open window, his hand on the mahogany ball handle of the shift. From the back seat, Robbie could hear him giving Diana a lesson in how to drive a standard. Running his fingers over the white leather seats, he wished lie was in front. Driving. Fast. Really fast. Race car fast.

They were home too soon. Marcus left them at the door, yelling to Diana that he'd be back later; he had to show his brothers his new car. Robbie stood on the sidewalk as long as he dared, even after Diana had called him in to supper three times. She saw him, he knew. But she didn't understand. No one did.

Tommy was already waiting outside his house when Robbie screeched to a halt, lifting his front tire off the ground.

"Got the eggs?" Tommy asked as he mounted his own bike.

"Shit, yeah. Whaddaya think? Robbie lifted the package he had been holding gingerly under his T- shirt. Now that he realized what he was about to do, his heart began beating quicker. The adrenaline ran through his veins like an aphrodisiac. A line of sweat broke out on his forehead. He clutched the box as he went over the curb and headed up Gove Street, following Tommy as closely as possible.

No one stood on the corners at this time of night. Most lights in the apartment buildings lining the street were off. The loudest sound was the whir of his bike's wheels.

Tommy skidded to a stop in front of Mr. Randall's house. Robbie put on his brakes, too, almost losing the eggs. "Jeez, Talese, take it easy, will ya?" Rob looked up at the math teacher's apartment and swallowed hard. A small yellow light burned in the right hand corner window. A dark form sat bent over what appeared to be a desk. Mr. Randall correcting papers? Robbie's fear was almost palpable.

"Hey, Coined!" Tommy hissed. "Are we gonna bomb it or are you pussying out on me?" Swallowing hard, Robbie knew that to let Tommy see he was afraid would be the end of a great reputation. With one leg still wrapped over his banana seat, he whipped open the box and grabbed an egg. "Beat this, asshole," he said as he hurled the egg straight at the dark figure in the window.

He was already halfway down the street, letting loose with a series of Indian whoops, when the window flew open and Carleton Randall spotted Tommy Talese in the middle of the street. Alone. A box of eggs on his lap.

Chapter Three

Boston, November, 1971

"That's the Big Dipper, Di. See it up there? And the tip of Orion's belt is right there. Jeez, I wish we had a telescope, so we could see the planets." Marcus's face was alight with wonder, his arm loosely tossed over Diana's shoulder.

"You will, Marc. Maybe we can both save up and get one by Christmas."

"It'll be too cold then."

"So? We'll put on jackets. What's a little cold when you have a show like this?"

From where they sat, on the rooftop of the tenement, they watched the church clock on Gove Street as it ticked away the hours, counted all the planes flying over their heads in and out of Logan, and fantasized about where they would travel once they were old enough. They spied on the Italian families below them as they ate, fought, or made love. And they were free from the problems of the world. It was a position both loved to be in, and it was on the rooftops that they explored each other as eagerly as they discovered new patterns in the nighttime sky.

Sometimes one of them would bring a treat, a candy bar or some leftovers from that evening's dinner. They would spread out an old tablecloth and have a moonlit picnic. Nothing mattered in their little world, neither passed judgment on the other, and their friendship grew deeper as they spent their evenings together talking about the way they wished their lives could be.

Marcus clung to the desire to study the stars, to have his own telescope and to be able to spot comets, meteors, and new planets. Diana, on the other hand, wanted to explore earthly lands, to travel to Europe, to ride a camel over Egypt's deserts, to venture into ancient Mayan temples, to smell the exotic foods and spices in the markets of Hong Kong.

When they were far above the city sounds, the teenagers were no longer just Diana Maria Colucci and Vito "Marcus Aurelius" Vincenti. They were movie stars or free-flying birds. Rich world travelers. Or simply old enough to go outside of East Boston. Anywhere else. When they were on the roof, they weren't poor nor did they have to listen to others teasing them, mimicking their way of talking, calling Marcus "the big-nosed pimple" or Diana "the queen of the slums."

With a noisy cough, Marcus loosed his arm and pulled away from her, still studying the sky though she knew he had her in his peripheral vision.

"What're you thinking of?" she whispered in his ear.

"Nothing." Shrugging his shoulders, he gave a shiver, his cotton madras shirt rippling with the movement.

"Don't give me that. I know you inside and out. You've got something on your mind."

"I was just thinking of Jimmy Magnanti."

"Oh." She joined him in a silent salute to the latest of East Boston High's seniors added to the list of Vietnam casualties. Her eyes were returned to the sky as she thought of the news bulletin she had on Channel 5 the day before, a bulletin which was the first ever to strike so closely to home. Perhaps she wouldn't have been so affected if the school's halls hadn't seemed quieter during the past couple of months. Perhaps she wouldn't have been so worried if Robbie had been less involved in war games of his own. He had taken to riding his new second-hand ten-speed up and down the streets, his face painted with black shoe polish—that was extremely difficult to get off, she had found out— and screaming words like "Get the Gooks! Kill the goddamn slant-eyes!" At twelve, her younger brother had become uncontrollable.

"I don't believe in war," she finally said quietly, her pale cheekbones and chin in side profile to Marcus.

"Neither do I," he admitted, intently studying his long, tapered fingers. "Sometimes I wonder why we're over there, but then I think of what my father did in Korea and about yours in World War II, and I think we gotta continue taking care of this country."

"Not in Vietnam, Marcus. God, that's not our country, not our responsibility. We shouldn't even be there." She stood and straightened her red wool mini-skirt, her latest creation. "I don't want to sound like one of those people from Berkeley or anything, but I really hate hearing about our friends dying over there. You saw Mrs. Buckley the other day. They had to take her out of school when she found out about her son." She took a deep breath and closed her eyes. "I never want to have to go through that again."

He reached for her hand and held it tightly, wrapping his fingers in and around hers and stroking them with his thumb. Around them, the sounds of the city—squealing tires, police sirens, yelling children—pulsated. The heart of their lives was here, their families, their society. Their future was in East Boston, though neither one of them wanted to face it.

"I've been thinking of something for a long time, Di." Turning toward her, he took her in his arms. "We're not kids anymore. Maybe it's time for us to go steady."

Her heart seemed to skip a beat; her hands started to shake. For months she had wished she could brag to the other girls that she was going steady. Perhaps it would finally make her belong. But Marcus had never mentioned it, and she had finally resigned herself to the supposition that he didn't believe in making commitments. After all, he would be going to college in a couple of years, and she knew how strongly he felt about being the first in his family to get a degree.

Swallowing hard, she said, "Are you sure you want to do this?"

"I wouldn't ask you if I didn't." His gentle hands took her by the shoulders, pushing her away so that he could see her face. In his eyes, she saw hope and love, but, most importantly, a young man who understood. A friend. A companion. He smiled, a thin, determined smile which grew to a wide-mouthed grin, making her forget the war, her brother, her mother, and the dirty streets below them.

"Look!" he cried, pointing upwards. "Our first falling star!"

The glistening stream of blue-white lit the black night as it raced through the center of their universe. She closed her eyes tightly and made a quick wish that nothing would ever change between them, that they'd always be together, sharing their dreams, their lives.

When she opened her eyes again, Marcus was still looking upwards. As the sky returned to normal, he turned to her, suddenly shy.

Without a word, he slipped off his high school ring and gave it to her. As she fit the ring onto her middle finger, her heart beat rapidly against her chest. Dismayed, she watched it slip lazily to one side.

"It's too big," she said, afraid he would take it back.

"That's okay," he replied. "We'll wind some tape around it. Then it'll fit."

When he bent his head towards her, she could see her breath fogging up his glasses. She was about to throw her arms around him and kiss him full on the lips when the roof door slammed and heavy footsteps sounded across the tarpaper floor. "Di? Marc? Where are you?"

"Over here, Robbie," she called, with an apologetic smile at Marcus. "What do you want?"

"Gets pretty lonely down there. 1 was wondering what you two were doin'. Wanna play Scrabble?" Shrugging her shoulders, she arched an eyebrow at Marcus, leaving the decision to him.

"Your timing is great, buddy," he grinned and winked at her before walking over to Robbie. With a hand on the younger boy's shoulder, he steered him toward the door. "Now what's this about a game of Scrabble? You know you always lose. I'm a much better speller than you."

Twirling the ring around her finger, she watched the two boys go through the door. Before closing it behind them, Marcus turned. "You coming, Di?" "In a minute."

When all was silent once again, she turned an ecstatic face to the sky, searching for the falling star she knew was no longer there. Wrapping her arms around her, she twirled lightly on one foot, laughing softly.

During the weeks after becoming steadies, Diana and Marcus strode the hallways at school with a new confidence everyone noticed. Together they felt invincible. Every night, they compared notes on their rooftop, agreeing that nothing in the world could harm them now. Everything had changed. No longer did the taunts and jeers of their class-mates matter, and once the other teenagers realized they could no longer bother Diana and Marcus, they turned their evil, sneering words to someone else.

Now Diana was more interested in knowing what crepe de chine felt like against her bare legs, and her mother's old treadle sewing machine kept Robbie up half the night as she—swearing and grunting-struggled to make a mini-skirt or a loose-sleeved peasant blouse. It amazed Arnie Goldstein that she could stretch the meager $200-a- month budget to allow enough money for an almost completely new wardrobe. Little did he know that she waited for fabric sales, buying three or four yards of slinky, brightly-colored silk for less than half of what she would have spent on new jeans.

Dressed in bright colors and soft fabrics, with light scents on her throat and dangling earrings in her newly-pierced ears, she twirled in front of the mirror in her room and saw a new personality. She learned to use Maybelline mascara to accentuate her long lashes, spread blue shadow on her lids, and experimented with Vaseline on her lips. The face that peered back at her rivaled those she saw on the cover of *Glamour*. She brushed her blue- black hair until it shone, then let it fall straight on either side of her face, happy that she had never had the courage to cut it. Now she was completely in style. For the first time in her life, the other girls in school looked at her with envy and the boys' eyes followed her slim, full-breasted figure appreciatively. Her confidence grew by leaps and bounds. She was invincible. Nothing seemed impossible anymore.

"Di, are you going to quit foolin' around and make us supper?" Robbie would ask day after day. "What the hell is in that mirror anyway?" With the aplomb of a pre-teen, he would come into the room, look in the mirror, stick out his tongue, and yell "Yeeecccchhh!" But even his derision didn't bother her.

To see the light in Marcus's eyes when she met him in the hallway dressed in one of her new creations, to feel his arm over her shoulders holding her close to his chest when they sat on the rooftop together, was all she lived for.

Miraculously, Marcus, too, went through a transformation. Almost overnight his pimples disappeared and his voice deepened. The love he felt for Diana created a new sense of pride and power within him. The years he had spent afraid and alone, the times on the streets or in his father's barroom had been strengthening ones, character building years for the young Vito Vincenti, though he had not known it then. Though he kept telling Diana the changes in his personality were due to her, she knew better. They had both been forced into adulthood early. It was only natural that they should mature together.

Now, with Diana at his side, he pretended less and less that he was Marcus Aurelius, the strong and intelligent Roman philosopher. As Marcus, he had hidden from his problems; as Vito he learned to deal with his mother's alcoholism and his father's long absences. His new philosophy was to accept reality.

Yet he still held onto his dream about being an astronomer with the innocence of a child^ as Diana clung to hers of travelling the world.

October, 1972

By the time they entered their senior year, Vito knew all of Diana's innermost secrets and she knew his. Robbie was used to coming home from school to see Vito's GTO parked in front of the house, and the couple often invited him along for a piece of pizza or a Dairy Twist when they cruised Revere Beach in the summertime. In the winter Robbie would go tobogganing with them on Mount Hood in Medford or, when they could get Mrs. Scarlatti to keep an eye on Mama, they would travel even further north to the White Mountains in New Hampshire.

Despite their differences in age, the three of them had one major thing in common: they were charter members of that class of orphans whose parents were still alive. However, they rarely talked about their families; it was a subject too painful to discuss during the happy times they spent together.

If Robbie thought it babyish to spend so much time with his sister, he never showed it. Though he had a life of his own, trying to deal with the confusing feelings of turning into a teenager, he spent every moment he could with Diana and Vito.

School became increasingly difficult for the handsome young boy whom the teachers labeled "trouble." It didn't make any difference that his grades were always A's and B's or that his sports abilities had begun to attract the coaches' attention. Time after time, Diana had to call Amie to intercede when Robbie "accidentally" hit one of his friends or stole a car for a joy ride.

Though Arnie advised her to take him for counseling, Diana stoically refused, continuing to be sister, mother, and friend. If she took him, she knew "they" would take her brother away. And the last thing she wanted was to lose the shaky family unit she had struggled for so long to keep together.

"His anger is exploding all over the place," the principal, a white-haired schoolmarmish woman, told Arnie one sunny October afternoon after the fourteen-year-old had attempted to hit a teacher who made the mistake of calling the boy "silly." "I really like Robert. You know that. But 1 can't seem to get it through his head that he can't skip classes or run up and down the hall terrorizing the teachers and continue to get away with it. He's testing, testing, testing, all the time. If he wasn't such a good student . . ."

"I know. Miss Callahan," Arnie replied, rubbing his nose thoughtfully, feeling more like a disgruntled father than the successful lawyer he had become. He thought of his new, contemporarily-furnished office on State Street and all the work sitting on his desk and sighed. "You know Rob's had a tough life. He just needs some patience and extra attention. I'll speak to his mother."

The principal sighed, putting her coffee cup down on her desk. "The mother should come in once in a while. Maybe we could discuss the boy's problems a bit easier. You know he really has some deep-rooted need to go to the very limits, sometimes to the point of almost killing himself. Remember that bike accident last year? I'd really like to talk to his mother directly about all this. We'd find someone who spoke Italian to translate for her."

She sighed again, seemingly at a loss for words or for a solution. "If only he was like his sister. Such a sweet girl. He has her eyes, you know. But his are mischievous and that grin ... you can tell why all the girls follow him around. If I were that age, so would I." Pursing her lips, she gave Amie a direct stare. "Make sure he knows how close he came to being expelled this time. And make sure his mother understands I can't keep talking to you, passing messages this way."

Gathering his briefcase and files, Arnie rose, happy to have done his job once again, but tired of trying to keep up with Robbie. The kid was more than he had bargained for. But a promise was a promise. He would keep it until the day he died, if necessary.

Diana met him outside the principal's door. She stood, impatiently tapping her foot, and looked expectantly into his face.

"Aren't you supposed to be in class?" he asked.

"What happened?" Diana ignored the question, falling into step with her attorney. "Is everything all right?"

Stopping by the front door, he raised his eyes, pointedly looking out the window instead of at the striking teenager who stood next to him. "It is for now," he replied with a grimace. "But you'd better have a talk with your brother. I can't keep coming to school for him, Diana. He's got to straighten out or I'm going to give up. He's old enough to realize that. You really need to think about what I said about getting him to a shrink. Before he goes off the deep end and takes you with him."

With a twist of his short body, Arnie walked out the door.

It often struck Diana that Rose Colucci was blissfully innocent of the lives her children were leading. Had she been aware of her daughter's moonlit moments on the rooftop or of her son stealing kisses from girls with breasts barely big enough for training bras, she would have whacked them on their behinds with a wooden spoon until their howls could be heard above the roar of the airplane engines constantly passing overhead.

But the little Italian woman remained in the corner of her bedroom, staring out the window, getting smaller and smaller as the years went by. Her lucid days were few and far between now, extending only so far as being able to recognize Diana as she fed her mother her evening meal.

Robbie was a stranger. That was fine with him. In fact, he seemed to prefer it that way. Rose had been a pathetic, vacant-eyed, shadowy figure for so long that, if asked, he probably could not have

35

told anyone what she had been like before. He still spoke of his father as a god-like figure, larger than life and twice as invincible, but he refused to believe that the shrunken, silent woman with the empty eyes was his mother.

When Robbie got home from school, Diana was working at the kitchen table, tapping a pencil rhythmically against the book which was open in front of her. She didn't appear to be reading, but seemed to be waiting for him. Immediately his defenses went up. Another lecture. Another warning. He was sick of it. Sick of Diana. Sick of Arnie. Sick of school. Sick of everything!

"What's up?" he said, walking down the hallway toward his room.

"Don't bother changing your clothes. I want to talk to you." Diana's voice was flat, controlled. She sounded sick of everything, too. Good, they had something in common.

"Oho, Callahan must have really gotten on Arnie's case, huh?" Opening his eyes wide in mock shock, his knees started to shake. What now? Couldn't everybody just leave him alone? "Am I out of there?"

"Not quite, Robert. But you could be shortly. It's not fair to me, you know. You keep on skipping through school like it's not important while I run behind you picking up the pieces and putting them back together. You do the same thing at home. Everything's a game with you. You never seem to think about the consequences. Don't worry about it," she sing-songed his favorite expression. "Di will make everything better. Well, I'm not going to do it anymore. I want you to get your act together and do it now."

Her voice, strident and strong, filled the little kitchen. Robbie filled his mouth with a cookie he stole from the package on the table, avoiding her eyes.

"Close your mouth," she chided. "You're fourteen years old, Rob. I shouldn't have to take care of you anymore. You ought to be starting to help me around the house, taking out the trash, helping with the dishes. I've let you get away with this for too long because I felt bad for you. Well, what about me? The only life I have is when Marcus comes around."

"Vito," he corrected, sullenly putting his feet up on the table.

"Okay, Vito. That's not the point. The point is: I think it's time you grew up. Get your feet off the table!"

He let his head slump further and further into his chest and slouched in the kitchen chair. If she lifted his chin, Diana would see the tears that welled so easily in his eyes. He would have blinked them back if anyone but her had been in the room, but there was no need to hide. In fact, tears were a good weapon when she started in lecturing. They had always worked before.

"I'm sorry, Di," he mumbled. "I try, you know. Really I do. But I just want to have fun. I don't mean to hurt anyone. Have I hurt anyone?" He lifted his chin, knowing his eyes glistened, hoping

Diana would not be able to resist the dejected look on his face. It was getting easier and easier to fool her. Sometimes he hated himself for doing it.

"God, what am I going to do with you?" Her voice softened as she leaned over and put her forehead up against his. "What are *we* going to do with you?"

They sat for a long time, head against head, their arms around each other's shoulders. He thought of his father and gritted his teeth. Thinking of Rose only made him sick. He couldn't even call her Mother anymore. Diana was his only family. The only one who would love him no matter what. No matter what. Diana and Vito. And nowadays he wasn't even sure about them. They never paid attention anymore either. No one did.

Finally, he pulled away and stood, straight and defiant, in front of his sister.

"I'm going to make you proud of me, Di. I promise." At that moment, he meant it with every fiber of his adolescent body, mind, and soul.

Chapter Four

Boston, February, 1973

Instead of looking into Diana's expectant eyes, Marcus stared at the worn linoleum on the hallway floor. She had finished her latest creation that afternoon and was especially proud of this particular skirt because the zipper lay just right, with no bumps or valleys, closing and opening perfectly. Finally, she was getting the hang of working on the new machine Mrs. Scarlatti had given her, and she wanted to dance in circles in front of him to show off.

"Marc, are you all right?" She leaned down a little to peer up into her boyfriend's face. "Your father didn't yell at you again, did he? I told you that you should have come here straight from school."

"You're going to have to learn to call me Vito again, Di," he said quietly. Hands down at his sides, his eyes, averted from Diana's, were beginning to fill with tears.

"Wh . . . Wh . . . Why?" An alarm sounded somewhere deep in her mind. Suddenly she didn't want an answer to her question.

"I leave for basic training next week and they're using my real name because that's what's legal, so you'll just have to get used to it."

"Basic training?" No, she thought. Please tell me I've heard wrong.

"Yeah, in Texas." The boy, once again lost for words, pushed by her and headed toward the kitchen where Robbie sat at the table doing his homework.

"What's for supper?" he asked, lifting the lid from a pot simmering on the stove, then reached for a spoon. Diana's hand stopped him.

"The roof," she said quietly.

"But, it's too cold . . ."

"The roof." Though she hadn't raised her voice, she knew he was well aware she would not take "no" for an answer. Silently he followed her to the back porch.

As she climbed the ancient stairs, he tried to tease her from behind, tickling her long, bare legs and pretending to look Under her skirt. She slapped his hand sharply without looking back.

On the roof, the February cold bit through her thin blouse, knifing its way up her skirt, making her feel as though she wore no underclothes. Behind her Marcus shivered, his teeth chattering. They stood facing each other for a moment in an uncomfortable silence.

"Come here," he said softly. Wiping away the huge tears rolling down her cheeks, he wrapped her closely in his arms, and pulled his jacket around them both so that they could share its warmth. It was only lately that he had seemed comfortable holding her. Each time they were close his whole body came to an erect attention, and he would begin to cover her face with light, loving kisses.

"I'm sorry I didn't tell you before," he began. "I never meant to hurt you, but when I got my draft notice, I didn't know what to do. I tried to get exempted. Honest. I even went to the eye doctor to see if he could tell them my eyesight isn't too great. But they're taking just about everyone, Di. I have no choice. I have to go."

"I don't understand. We've always talked everything over and I thought we agreed. . . ." She spoke between sobs which shook her shoulders so hard Marcus had trouble standing still. "Why couldn't you wait? You can't *go! I* don't want you to go. You know how I feel about this stupid war." She lifted her face to his, allowing him to gently kiss the salty drops off her cheeks and lips, and took refuge in the affection he so freely gave her. "God, Marc, if you go now, you won't even graduate from high school. They can't force you to go before you finish school. Can they? And what about college? What about astronomy?"

She took a deep breath and tried to still her sobs, desperate to make him see that what he was doing was wrong. A ball of fear formed in her abdomen. She didn't want to think of what it would be like without him around. He had found the lobe of her ear and warmly sucked on its tip. She tried to ignore the way it made her feel. "What about us?" she said.

With a sigh, he pulled his head back to the soft hollow of her shoulder. "I've made my decision, Di. I can't turn back now. When I get back, we can get married. I'll be able to get a college loan from the Army and we'll *both* go. You can study dressmaking, become a designer, and I'll study science. We can even help each other with our homework." Though his voice was determinedly cheerful, Diana could see through it, recognizing the torment he was going through, his anguish at leaving her alone with her brother. He had always promised her that they would conquer the world together, now he was going to fight it alone. Why how? she thought, her head whirling, her mind momentarily refusing to think of anything but herself.

Realizing her own selfishness, she pulled him against her swelling breasts and held him tight. If she held him as tight as she could, maybe she could stop time. Maybe he wouldn't go. Maybe this was all a bad dream. He nuzzled her neck in answer, dropping little kisses over the places he knew to be her most sensual, gently lifting the heavy blanket of hair that smelled so sweetly of baby shampoo.

"Let's sit over by the chimney." His voice was husky. "It's warmer there and I think our picnic blanket is still there from this summer."

Taking her by the hand, he watched her face closely. He knew she'd be angry but he hadn't expected her to be afraid. Somehow her fear sparked his and the war suddenly seemed all too real. Nightmarish. The nightly news broadcasted clips of the war flashed through his mind. Kids his age, moaning in pain, the back flash of mortar fire in the distance, Vietnamese families crying. He tried to concentrate on Diana's devastated face. They settled against the brick edifice, and he pulled the girl he teasingly called "Wonder Woman" close to his side, adjusting his jacket so that she would get some of its warmth. She snuggled into his chest as she had so many times before.

"You fit just right," he murmured into her hair. "No one else will ever fill that space under my arm."

Giggling nervously, she lifted a hand to wipe the wetness from her pale pink cheek. "Thank God you use Arrid Extra Dry."

The joke was an old, familiar one with them, yet it didn't seem to make her feel any better. A new sob escaped from her throat. She buried her face into the Hi-Karate smell of his jacket. "Marcus, how can you go? Who's going to help you with your math? Who's going to drive me to the grocery store on Fridays?" Her voice faltered, dissolving into choked, painful cries.

It tempted Vito to think of staying in East Boston, marrying Diana and having children, raising them on the streets where they themselves had grown up, but she meant more to him than that. He knew of her long-lived wish to visit Sicily and to meet her mother's family. If she were to get married, the babies would come instantly; her beauty would fade and her dreams as well. He couldn't do that to her. He also knew that he, too, would be stifled by staying in Boston. More than anything else, more even than his love for Diana, he wanted to fulfill his own dream of becoming an astronomer.

Despite their faults, his parents had not reused a stupid boy. It was obvious to him that the only way he could afford college was to enter the service and take advantage of their financial aid programs. That thought had been uppermost in his mind as he bent over the forms the recruiting officer had handed him. Pushing his glasses up on his nose, he had had a brief moment of indecision, a fleeting glimpse of the girl he had loved for more than five years, before he took a deep breath and picked up the pen to sign himself into the Army.

He crushed her to his chest, covering her face and hair with hard and desperate kisses. Though she cried out against his roughness, he pulled her still closer and held her quivering against his body.

"Please, Marcus. Be easy." Her muffled cry came from deep within his jacket. His heart beat against his chest, almost as quickly and fervently as hers. The feeling scared him, yet it was one of exhilaration. Everything had changed. Nothing was as it had been before. His time for growing up had run out.

"Vito. Call me Vito." He ran his tongue over her slightly open lips, wetting each corner with a pointed lick, tasting the salt of her tears over the slickness of her lipstick. "You're going to have to get used to using Vito on my mail you know, Di." He continued to kiss her between mumbled words, his fingertips exploring her thin, delicate shoulders, his thoughts so jumbled he barely comprehended feeling her young body yield to his. "You *are* going to write to me, aren't you? I don't think I'd make it through all this if you refused to write to me."

"Of course, I will. Every day." Her eyes wide open, she clung to his strong shoulders, feeling the warmth of her love for him surge through her body, bringing heat down each of her limbs and into the cheeks of her face. The only thought in her mind was that there would be no more nights on the roof. No more long, understanding talks with the only boy she had loved. No more warm, searching kisses. "I'm going to miss you so much," she cried as his lips sought hers once again, pulling them open to his moist mouth, his tongue seeking hers to commune in a silent dance of passion.

Though the temperature on the East Boston rooftop hovered right above freezing, in less than a moment they would have sworn they were in the midst of a Jamaican summer. She forgot the Army, Vietnam, the promises they had made to each other, and was totally caught up in the moment.

With trembling fingers, he explored the long throat above the buttons on her peasant blouse, then tentatively reached lower to where the swell of her breasts began. This time she did not stop his hand as she had so many times before. Hesitantly, he pushed the blouse aside, revealing the creamy skin of her chest. His breathing became irregular as he let his eyes feast on the porcelain softness of her young, perfectly-formed breasts.

Shivering slightly, she held her breath as he investigated the roundness of her body. Now squeezing gently, then pulling lightly on her already-erect nipple. Her stomach contracted as his fingers lightly touched her skin, exploring the heavy orbs which he had previously only touched through her clothes. A warm, rushing sensation began in her face, spreading its way over her chest, down her stomach, and into the mound between her thighs. She leaned her head back and took a deep, quivering breath.

With a hungry moan, he bent his head, taking her virgin breast in his mouth. The delicious warmth rekindled between her thighs, opening her entire body to the new sensation. She relaxed, leaning back against the wall, mouth slightly open, heart beating ferociously as she luxuriated in the rough, ravenous caresses she had denied herself for so long.

Gently she stroked the back of his head as his teeth pulled at her pebbly-hard nipple. Her fingers tightened around his chin-length hair as his hands slid down the curve of her back to cup her firm, small buttocks. Instinctively, she pressed her body against his. Beckoning. Pleading.

This is it, she thought, her head swimming with the realization that two decisions had been made tonight—Marcus's—no, Vito's—

to leave East Boston, and hers, to give herself to him. I'll have this, she thought. No matter what happens, I'll have my memories of this night, of him, of our love. When he's gone, I can lie in bed and remember what we had, of how wonderful and right I felt, and be safe until he comes home.

In a sea of whirling passions, she took the almost imperceptible step from teenager to woman. Fear did not even enter into her mind—she was so sure of her actions, so positive nothing else would ever be the same. All she thought was that someday they would be able to share their love night after night in a warm, comfortable bed, whispering their hopes and dreams to each other, nestled in the safety of a relationship like no other. Marriage had never before entered her mind—she had not wanted it, had thought living together would be enough—but the thought of Marcus leaving was simply too much. Suddenly, she needed the security marriage would offer. Needed him.

Firmly, he pushed his hips against her lower leg so she could feel the long outline of his fully-erect organ. "Please, Di. Can we?" he murmured breathlessly, coming back to her full lips to thrust his impatient tongue between them once more.

Completely under the spell of the moment, she returned his kiss greedily and nodded her head. It was a slight movement, but he felt it and responded with quick movements of his own. He sucked gently on one erect nipple, then the other, all the while whispering words of love against her stomach that she barely heard. One hand reached down the outside of her thigh, then swiftly back up the inside of her leg until his exploring fingers touched the warm mound only she had previously examined. He moved aside the lacy underpants, gasping in surprise at the moisture he found underneath. As if they had a mind of their own, his fingertips wound themselves in the long, black hair that covered the rise, curling and uncurling their wet tendrils until they found themselves dipping into the entrance of a damp tunnel.

"Take them off," he whispered urgently, his face flushed and his eyes bright. "I want to feel all of you."

Nervously, she pulled the white lace panties down her bare legs. She shivered, not with anticipation, but with fear that he would never fit up inside the tiny opening she had explored with her fingers.

While she watched, unable to move, wishing he was still wrapped around her, he unzipped the fly of his jeans, then pulled them down to reveal strong stomach muscles and a swollen penis which fell straight out to point directly at her stomach. Face flushed and blood pounding in her temples, she lifted her eyes quickly to his face. Time seemed to stop as they pressed their young bodies together, anxious to mold them into one.

His penetration was quick. She gulped in surprise at the pain— then the burning. Lost in amazement at his total possession of her, in the wonder of how her body so completely enveloped and grasped his swollen member, she clung to him, determined not to cry out. All her perceptions of what occurred between a man and a woman, all the romance stories she had pored over when she was alone in her room disappeared as the young man who owned her heart brought her through an intoxicating pool of sensations.

When she closed her eyes, it was like all the fireworks in the world were being lit under her lids. Her body, alternately hot and cold, shivered and palpitated, as Vito, intent on satisfying his own feelings of pleasure and lust, ignored her kitten-like cries and continued thrusting against her in rapid, short strokes. The feelings coursing through her body were shocking and shameful, but wonderful.

Suddenly, the throbbing was no longer painful. A new, even more thrilling sensation filled her loins and she responded to his movements, moaning and arching her back toward him, wordlessly submitting everything she had to offer. Her eyes closed. Her breath was ragged. Her legs wrapped around his in a vise no human could have undone and she allowed herself to surrender to the deep and complete ecstasy which ran through every inch of her body, teasingly arousing her skin, making her nipples stay erect. They touched the hair on his chest lightly and the sensation caused the hair on her arms to stand on end.

He moaned one last, loud, long time, then pressed his whole body against hers and shuddered. The intensity drained from her muscles and one by one they loosened, relaxing against his, the throbbing euphoria ebbing away. Yet, she did not want to let go and, with a muffled cry, pulled him closer to her, whispering his name over and over again, as if by doing so the moment would not be allowed to end.

Without moving, he wrapped the blanket over the lower half of his body and turned a bit on his side so he was not completely on top of her. She shivered, the February air sneaking in between them to return them to reality, yet not totally stealing the bliss written in the smile on her face and the subdued glimmer of her turquoise eyes. Her hair clung damp and black against her forehead, framing her porcelain face.

"I love you," he said softly, now nose-to-nose,
causing her to glow with remembered passion.

"I love you, too, Marcus," she answered, a purr in her voice.

"Vito," he said softly. "I'm Vito now. Remember?"

Diana smiled and reached up to stroke the angled planes of his face. "You'll always be Marcus Aurelius to me."

Chapter Five

Boston, March, 1973

Robbie stood at Gate 5, waiting patiently as Vito and Diana had a hurried, whispered conference on the other side of the waiting room. They would get married. He knew it. Nothing could make him happier. Vito was okay. A good guy. He'd make a great brother-in-law.

The drone of the planes' engines made most conversation impossible, yet everyone who streamed through the gate, past the pretty blond stewardess in the navy blue uniform, seemed to be talking.

"Hey, Vito!" Robbie called. "Get the lead out! You're going to miss your plane." He shifted from one leg to another as Vito absentmindedly waved in his direction, still concentrating on Diana. Finally, he kissed her one last time, lifted his duffel bag to his shoulder and strode towards Robbie. Diana was crying, dabbing at her red eyes with a bedraggled Kleenex like a silly fool. Robbie wouldn't cry. No way.

Extending his hand, he grasped Vito's and pulled him close. "Take care of yourself, buddy," he said. "Don't let the gooks get you."

Vito clutched Rob's shoulder, then punched him gently in the arm. "Hey, you little shit, you're almost as tall as me. When I get back, you *might* even be able to take me at arm-wrestling." Pulling away, his face became serious. "Listen, I want you to promise me you'll take care of your sister."

Robbie nodded and grimaced.

". . . and keep an eye on my GTO. Maybe give it a wax once in a while."

"On one condition," Robbie grinned, his heart beating fast.

"What's that?"

"You let me drive it when you come home. Deal?"

"Yeah, I guess so. Deal."

As Vito's tall frame disappeared through the doorway, Robbie's eyes moistened. With a quick swipe, he wiped the tears away, determined not to let his sister see.

Six months later, it was August, one of the hottest months in Boston's history. Graduation behind her, Diana had nothing more to do than wait for Marcus/Vito to come home. Shopping at Deluca's Market one sizzling afternoon, she heard Mr. Deluca talking with a customer at the meat counter.

"Some of them never come home," he was saying. "I remember the World War II, such a horrible war it was, and so many of our boys never came back. It's the same thing only it's not, know what I mean, Mrs. Bochetti?"

"But he was so young, poor Vito," Mrs. Bochetti answered.

Diana walked to the bread counter, pretending to inspect the Scala bread while she listened breathlessly.

"Poor Ricky and Estelle. What you have to go through when you lose a child! *Bah fungu!"* The old meat cutter slammed his knife down on his cutting board then guiltily turned toward where Diana had been standing, but she was already out the door and running down the street.

It seemed she hadn't even stopped to take a breath when she was suddenly in the dark, cool hallway of the apartment, but her heart was pounding and Mr. Deluca's words were echoing in her ears.

Robbie came out of his bedroom, a science fiction comic book in his hand and amazement on his face.

"You shouldn't' slam the door, you know," he began contritely. "Mama's sleeping." With an open mouth and raised eyebrows, he moved swiftly out of the way as she ran past him down the hallway.

"I don't care!" she screamed as she flew by her mother's bedroom and out onto the porch. "I don't care about her anymore!" Raising her face to the sky, she let out an animalistic wail that shocked the pigeons who habitually perched on the roofs above the little yard. They flew away with loud flapping noises, leaving scattered feathers and droppings behind.

In less than a moment, Robbie was beside her, holding her tight, while quaking, dry sobs wracked her body. Without a word, he gently stroked her head and patted her back, letting her weep until the sun went down and she was finally able to talk.

Though he had already supposed the tragedy which had befallen them, it was only after she was able to choke out her news that tears fell from his own eyes. Together they sat on the porch stairs, arms around each other and mourned the man they had both thought would be part of their little family forever.

After Robbie had finally gone to bed, she walked through the quiet apartment alone and exhausted.
Realizing she hadn't put her mother to bed for the first time in five years, she forced herself into the tiny bedroom, mechanically going to the bureau, and lifting out one of Rose's long cotton nightgowns.

With the gown pressed against her face she inhaled the fresh smell of her mother and lazy tears dripped down her cheeks. She stood still, her shoulders throbbing, tears wetting the neck of the gown, for many moments before rousing herself to continue with her duties.

Gently she lifted her mother off the chair, undressed her, washed her and slipped the nightgown over her head. Her tears still ran down her face as she took the silver-handled brush off her mother's bureau. Sitting on the windowsill, she turned Rose to her and began pulling the brush through her hair. Not a word was said.

Through the open window, the nighttime sounds of the city

floated like a balm. Diana found herself beginning to talk, matching the flow of her words to the strokes of the brush. In a monotone voice, she told her mother of her love for Vito, reliving every moment they spent together, even their times on the roof.

"I know you know what I mean. Mama. I used to hear the sounds coming from your room late at night when Papa was alive. You used to laugh. You used to beam when he'd come home from work, come up behind you and kiss you on the neck. You see. Mama, I know you. I understand. But, I can't . . ." She faltered. Stopping a moment to wipe a tear and to take a cleansing breath, she forced herself to continue. ". . . I can't give up the way you did. Robbie ... he misses you. He misses your stuffed artichokes, the datenut lambs you made for Easter, the way you cuddled him when he scraped his knee. If I gave up, too, Mama, what would he have left?"

As she talked, her grief subsided to a numbness, yet she longed for a comforting answer. A word. A hug.

Finally, she could stand it no longer.

Kneeling on the floor beside the woman's chair, she peered into the face, once full and alive, now sunken and dead.

"Oh, Mama! Why can't you hear me?"

Robbie stood, motionless, at his mother's bedroom door. Though his heart went out to his sister, he couldn't move. Couldn't comfort her. Wearing only a T-shirt and the bottoms of his cotton pajamas, he slipped through the screen door to the porch and took a deep breath before descending the stairs.

Within moments, he stood in front of the Vincentis' garage. He rolled the key in his hand, trying to stop the memories flooding into his mind. Inserting it into the lock with a quick turn, he opened the garage door. For a few brief moments, he simply stared at Vito's GTO gleaming in the single bulb's light. Then, almost mechanically, he took an old rag and the can of DuPont car polish off the shelf. The slow, circular polishing movements seemed to release something deep inside. He leaned against the cool steel of the car and let the tears flow, never realizing the name he uttered was not Vito's, but "Papa."

Chapter Six

Boston, Thanksgiving, 1976

"Them friggin' Irish potatoes! They wouldn't know how to play football if it was fuckin' written on the sky! Get 'em, Colucci! Run with that fuckin' ball!"

The cry came from the bench behind them. Diana rolled her eyes at Arnie sitting next to her, still in the suit and tie he had worn to work earlier that morning.

"This is going to be a fun one," he yelled above the crowd's clamor. "Bet you ten bucks we eat triumphant turkey today!"

"Go, Colucci!" The fat, bald man sitting behind them stood again, his cigar hanging precariously out of the side of his mouth, rooting Rob and the East Boston High football team on to victory over South Boston. The Thanksgiving game was typical of the long-standing rivalry between the Irish and Italian sections of Boston and was guaranteed to give the onlookers a little more than the normal football game excitement.

Rob had tamed his temper that year and brought his grades up high enough to win a space on the team—he had fallen behind after Vito's death, scraping by with C's, but Diana insisted on A's and B's, the grades she knew he was capable of, before she agreed to his trying out for the team. By the end of his first season, he was their prize quarterback. His years of racing the wind down the streets of East Boston had finally paid off. This was his season, his team, and his final, glorious senior year. Hard work had earned him the nickname "Cool Coined" and had even managed to put him in the running for a football scholarship at Boston College. Diana swelled with pride.

The skinny, wild-eyed kid, who had teased her unmercifully and lived only for his bicycle, had grown into a six-foot-tall seventeen-year-old with shoulders so wide he couldn't fit into the driver's seat of her 1968 Volkswagen. Just as well, she thought, since he still hadn't gotten over his addiction for driving as fast as legally possible. She had always regretted that the Vincent! family had given Marcus's GTO to Robbie —especially since he totaled it within only a few weeks. Her VW was the only thing she had to show for working in Scavullo's grocery store for the past four years —she intended to keep it in one piece.

"How are you going to pay for his college education?" Arnie asked, his nose red and running from the cold harbor wind which tore through East Boston Memorial Stadium.

"Don't know." She shook her head and stood as another "Cool Coined" cheer rocked the stadium's rafters. "He's going to have to get a better job. We can't both work in grocery stores for the rest of our lives. The money we make doesn't support us as it is, and Mama's not getting any better. The doctor keeps trying to get me to put her in a home."

"Why don't you?"

"Arnie, don't start lecturing me again. You know I can't do that." Brushing her long hair out of her eyes, she pulled the collar of her wool jacket up around her neck.

Amie Goldstein was the first to admit that, even without makeup, Diana Colucci was the prettiest of his clients. And the saddest. There were times he wanted to put his arms around her, to comfort her, but the young Italian woman wanted no pity. The only times he had seen her laugh Like a child or show any love since Marcus died was when she was with her brother. Occasionally, he would try to act the Dutch uncle and ask if she had found a romantic interest. But her answer was always a quick shake of her head and an immediate change of subject. Now, though her face was wind-burned and raw, her eyes glowed with pride and awe as she watched Rob drive his team to victory.

"You've got to start thinking about a nursing home, Di. You can't take care of her much longer," he persisted, and smiled at her stubbornly jutting chin.

"Run, Colucci, you muthafucka!" The man's cigar fell out of his mouth as Rob took off down the field, a blur of blue and yellow. Once again, there was pandemonium on the East Boston side of the stadium.

From where they sat, they could see some of the South Boston players were off the bench, yelling at the referee. Before another play could be made, the stands had emptied and the spectators were on the field. The red shirts and pompoms of the South Boston team mingled with the blue and yellow of East Boston, until the players were surrounded by angry spectators—ferociously beating on each other as well as on the members of both teams.

Diana saw Rob go down, then lost sight of him in the crowd. Scrambling to her feet, she realized that she and Amie were practically the only ones left in the bleachers. And the only reason she hadn't followed her friends and neighbors onto the field was because Arnie had a tight grip on her arm.

"Oh, shit! I knew this was going to be messy. Dammit, isn't there ever a year we can get through this game without a rumble?" Taking her elbow, he guided her toward the nearest exit.

"Let go of me!" She pulled away desperately, frantically searching for her brother. "1 can't leave without knowing if Robbie . . ."

"No way. You're not going out there on that field! Don't worry, your brother can take care of himself. He's a big boy."

As they neared the staircase which led out of the stadium, sirens filled the air and flashing blue lights appeared on both sides of the horseshoe ring of bleachers. Though the wails continued, no one on the field took notice and yells of "Goddamn guineas" and "Fucking Irish potatoes" could be heard even above the Boston Police loudspeakers.

"C'mon, we'll wait for Rob at home." She gave Arnie a dirty look, then let herself be propelled in the direction of his car.

Two hours and four cups of coffee later, the turkey was overcooked, and Diana worriedly paced the floor. When Rob finally stumbled into the Orleans Street apartment, his face was red and dirty, his right eye swollen, and dried blood covered both of his hands. Holding him up was a tiny redheaded girl wearing a South Boston cheerleader's uniform.

"We won!" Rob yelled as he and the girl came down the hall into the kitchen where Arnie and Diana sat. "And this," he said, holding out the girl's hand ceremoniously, "is my savior, Maryann Elizabeth Herlihy."

"You're drunk again." Diana slammed her cup down on the table and watched her brother weave into the middle of the floor. "Goddamn it, Rob, you're going to get thrown off the team if you keep this up!"

"Oh, dear sister, is this any way to treat a guest?" Stumbling, he dragged the woman he called Maryann with him. "Besides, loosen up. We won! First time in thirteen years! Can't you be happy?" He leaned forward, making smooching sounds with his lips.

To her right, Diana saw Arnie laughing behind his hand. She felt a smirk begin to creep across her face. Yes, even she had to admit Robbie was a clown.

"Nice to meet you," she said as she reached out her hand to the girl in the South Boston High cheerleader's uniform. "I hope you know what you're getting yourself into."

Though both factions would rather die than admit it, the Irish of South Boston share a lot in common with the Italians of East Boston. Both are the progeny of immigrants who came to the United States during the first half of the century to settle in tenement buildings alongside friends and family from the old country. Both nationalities have horrific tempers and are well-known for their barroom brawls. Both have strong family backgrounds and like to keep it that way. And both have stubborn streaks which sometimes get in the way of friendship or love.

The latter was the case with Rob and Maryann.

Only Rob's best friend, Tony DeMarco, would speak to him once the members of the football team found out he was going with a South Boston cheerleader. He let their comments go over his head until one of them called Maryann a "goddamn leprechaun"—then his temper took over.

One January afternoon Diana got a phone call from the police station to pick Rob up after he was arrested for literally throwing some unlucky fellow five or six feet through the air, all because of a comment about Maryann. Thankfully, no charges were pressed. Diana was less amused and more exasperated than she had been during his previous antics. After almost ten years of making excuses for him and bailing him out of potentially dangerous situations, she was beginning to lose her patience.

Maryann, on the other hand, endured her hardships silently. Her parents, Mary and Mike Herlihy, disapproved of their youngest daughter's relationship with a "goddamned wop," as Mike unceremoniously referred to Rob. For a long time, they even refused to meet him. However, the family unit was more important to them than their prejudices, and eventually they missed their daughter's presence at mealtimes and get-togethers so much that Mary called her daughter at the Colucci apartment to invite the young couple to Sunday dinner.

Gray-haired and only five-feet, six inches tall, Boston Police Officer Mike Herlihy intimidated Rob at first. He asked questions about school, football, and college until Rob's dark blue eyes smoldered and Maryann had to give him warning kicks under the table.

Though Maryann had sketched the Colucci family background for her parents, Rob specifically asked her not to say anything about his mother, and Mike Herlihy, nosy cop that he was, wanted to know why. Again and again, Mike asked questions about Rose and Tony. Again and again, Rob danced around the issue, asking for another helping of potatoes, complimenting Mary on her gravy, or busily buttering a thick slice of soda bread.

After supper the wily Irishman challenged his daughter's boyfriend to an arm wrestling contest on the kitchen table, which Herlihy easily won. He smiled winningly at the dark-haired boy who avoided his eyes.

"Never underestimate your opponents, my boy," Mike said, gleefully wagging a finger in Rob's face. "You never know what you're up against." Rob's abashed and awed expression did much to ease his way into the hearts of the older Herlihys.

And Mike never asked about Tony and Rose again.

During the next few months Maryann spent more and more time in East Boston. Her relationship with Rob would always be a point of contention with the Herlihy clan, a reason for her father to tease her, and a matter of discomfort. But the bouncy cheerleader with the chicken pox scars on her forehead and the best legs in South Boston High was so much in love with Rob that she wouldn't have cared if the Pope himself had attempted to curtail their relationship.

Of all the girls he had dated, Maryann was the only one he had allowed into the Colucci apartment, the only one who had established an intimacy with Rose and Diana, and the only one who was treated as a member of the family. It seemed to Diana that her brother had finally finished running away from life and she was happy to see him settling down at last.

Often Diana would come home from work to find Maryann in the kitchen preparing supper or sitting on the Herculon-covered couch in the living room watching television with Rob. It was comforting to have another woman around to talk to, and she found as much pleasure in the young woman's company as her brother did, never noticing the five-year age difference. Soon the women started sharing the cooking, and Maryann even took over some of the duties involved in caring for Rose without being asked.

Maryann encouraged Diana to come out of her shell, teaching her how to apply the right makeup to balance her olive-toned complexion while highlighting the warm turquoise of her eyes. With a little urging, she talked Diana into choosing clothes that complemented her tall, slim figure instead of hiding it under the shapeless cotton dresses and wool jumpers she had reverted to after Vito died. Little by little, she brought out the Diana from long ago.

And Diana was grateful for the reincarnation.

To Maryann, Diana was the quiet, reserved woman whom Rob adored, respected, and loved in a way he would no other. The boy who so fiercely grappled with life was almost reverent when he tall^ about his sister. Yet, should she walk into the room, he would argue with her about the slightest thing, then throw his arm around her slim shoulders, smile at her upturned face and say, "You know I was only kidding, Sis."

In those moments, Maryann felt the depth of the strong bond the Colucci siblings had, yet never became jealous or offended. Instead, her love for Rob and her respect for his sister grew and grew until the emotion made her chest pound. But the sweetest feeling of all was when she was included in those joint family hugs. It wasn't hard for Rob to see that his sister had changed since Maryann came into their lives, and he felt a deep sense of gratitude toward Maryann for helping Diana realize there was more to life than taking care of their mother and working in Scavullo's Grocery Store. Ever since he could remember, his sister had been more inclined to worry about him—would he be warm enough? was he well fed? had he done his homework?—than she would about whether her own hair was combed or if the clothes she had salvaged from Mrs. Marshia or Mrs. Talese fit her properly. It had been too long since his attractive twenty-two-year-old sister had gone on a date and he knew why. It wasn't that she was ugly; it was just that she didn't care. She had no interest in *any* men since Vito died.

Now, thanks to Maryann, Diana was comfortable with her glossy black shoulder-length hair, warm blue eyes, the lush mouth which opened to reveal straight, white teeth, and the elegant lines of her long, slim body. He had to take partial responsibility for that—she'd had plenty of exercise after years of running after him up and down the stairs and the streets of East Boston!

It didn't surprise Diana when, in May of 1977, Rob came to her to announce that he and Maryann would be married on his birthday that coming July. They were both graduating and, since neither one of them truly wanted to go to college, it seemed a logical decision. To them, anyway.

At first, she was dismayed and confused. "What about the football scholarship, Rob? You'll never get it again if you give it up now. You've got so much going for you."

"What do I have? I don't want to be a lawyer or a doctor. I just want a nice house and a family. I can't live without Maryann, Di, can't you understand that?"

"Of course I do." She placed her hand over her brother's as they sat at the kitchen table. Maryann busied herself at the stove, her full attention on Diana and Rob, though she said nothing. "I just hoped . . ."

"C'mon, Sis, you know you're the smart one in this family. I'm tired of working hard to get good grades. Never liked school anyway." Pulling his hand from Di's, he got up from the kitchen table and sauntered over to Maryann, looping his arm around her waist. "We're gonna make beautiful babies, huh, honey?" he crooned, kissing the squirming woman on the neck. "Graduation and a wedding within a month —how does that sound?"

"Rob! Pay attention to me!" She burst out of her chair, taking the young couple by surprise. "Maryann hasn't even finished high school . . . It's not fair to her or you to go into this marriage without a good job."

"And what about you? You going to stay at Scavullo's bagging someone else's fuckin' Cheerios for the rest of your life?" Rob took his hands away from Maryann and faced his sister, his flashing blue eyes as angry as hers.

"Well ... but . . ."

"Then what the hell are you still doing there? Shit, you're smarter than that."

"It's close to home. I've got Ma to think of. You have Maryann . . ."

Leaning on the table, hands spread apart, supporting his barrel chest, he lowered his head like a bull. She pulled back involuntarily, yet could still feel his hot breath on her face. For the first time in any confrontation with Rob she felt flustered and averted her eyes.

"Ma! What the fuck has she done for you lately? Don't you think it's slightly nuts that we should be still taking care of a woman who can't even shit and piss in a toilet? Christ, Di, you're going to go gray before you have a life of your own. At least I know enough to keep on living. You're dying here. Just like her!" He pointed angrily towards the bedroom.

She brushed past her brother's hulking form, defiance in the stiff squareness of her shoulders, her fists clenched.

"She's my mother, Rob. I can't turn my back on her." Turning the water on in the sink, she began to wash the three juice glasses they had used to drink the champagne Maryann had brought.

"Yeah? Well, what about you and me, Di? Don't we have a right to live? I'm goddamn sick and tired of this! Listen," he pleaded, pulling her by the arm and forcing her to look at him. Then he seemed to realize he was hurting her and held her against his chest, pushing her head gently against his shoulder. His voice softened. "I love you. Sis. I can't stand watching you throw your life away like this."

They held each other for a long time, oblivious to Maryann, until Rob finally pulled away to regard his sister seriously. His eyes were both questioning and apologetic. "I want you t&- start looking for another job. Get out of East Boston, okay?"

"Yeah, Rob, that's all well and good but what about . . . "

"We'll figure something out. We'll take care of Mom somehow, okay? Just start thinking about yourself."

"I don't want her to go to a nursing home."

Rob sighed. They'd had this discussion before. "It might have to happen, Di. It's a possibility. Let's just get ourselves out of this sewer. Deal?"

Wiping the back of her hand over her eyes, she exhaled. "Deal," she replied, a tired smile on her lips.

Chapter Seven

Boston, July, 1977

After graduation, the couple was quietly married with Maryann's parents, her brother and sisters, Diana, and Arnie the only people present. Rob found a job as a meat cutter at the First National in Revere and Maryann worked in a drugstore on Meridian Street, within walking distance of the apartment. Though the couple's combined salary was less than the rent for the apartment they shared with Diana, they decided to chip in until they could afford their own home.

Diana had given a sigh of relief when that decision was made. She wasn't sure she was ready to be alone, to face the prospects of making plans for her future'. Besides, she was comfortable with the noise and bustle Rob and Maryann brought to the apartment and found that, for the first time in years, she looked forward to coming home.

The laughter and pleasure she began to experience did little to influence her mother's lack of both. Rose had become completely incontinent, needing someone to watch over her twenty-four hours a day. Mrs. Scotti, who lived on the third floor, had been kind enough to watch her when they were all at work, but she was beginning to grumble. Rob made arrangements to be home on weekend nights so that Diana could do the grocery shopping and errands, but no one enjoyed cleaning up after Rose's messes. Even Diana was beginning to find her mother an unending, unsatisfying chore.

During one of their Coke-and-giggles sessions, Maryann's green eyes suddenly lost their sparkle and her normally curved lips pressed into a thin straight line.

"Diana, you've got to do something about your mother," she said, reaching across the table to put her hand on her sister-in-law's arm. "You can't handle her anymore and it really would be much more fair to her—and to you and Rob—to put her into a home where she can get proper care." Seeing Diana's mouth open to protest, she held up a finger. "Hear me out. You've taken care of Rose most of your life. You really lost your childhood as a result and now you're a grown woman who doesn't even know what it's like to go out for dinner with a man. How are you going to live like this? Like Rob says, you can't work for Mr. Scavullo for the rest of your life. Listen, I have an uncle who has a good friend with a shop on Charles Street. Mr. Monroe's looking for a retail assistant and I bet you'd fit right in. He pays well and you'd be able to get out of East Boston every day. C'mon, just try it."

Diana turned away, her eyes filling with tears, and looked out the back door to the tiny yard where the building's three tenants had planted grapevines. Glancing to the right, she could see Mama sitting in the rocking chair at her bedroom window looking down at the same yard. Even she had to admit her mother could see nothing. She didn't even know whether Rose could talk anymore—the woman hadn't uttered a word in the last three years. Her shoulders grew more and more stooped every day and her once strong, stubby fingers had grown white and thin from disuse.

There were some days that Rose involuntarily shivered as if a draft had suddenly passed through the room. Diana would lift the hand-crocheted afghan Rose had made long ago off the back of the chair and place it over her mother's bony shoulders, tucking the edges in around her lap, but the shivering didn't stop. It was often the only movement her mother made and one which she knew signaled Mama's intense discomfort. But there was nothing she could do. No way to stop it. It made her feel so . . . so impotent.

"She's my mother, Maryann. Could you send your mother to a home?"

Maryann's curls bobbed as she slid off the chair and walked over to her sister-in-law. Reaching up, she gently placed both hands on Diana's shoulders and turned her so that she looked directly at Rose.

"Look at her, Di. What do you see?"

"My mother . . ."

"No. Tell me what you see. Describe the woman sitting in that chair."

"Don't make me do this. You're only making me angry."

"Who are you angry at, Di? Me or the woman in the chair?"

"What are you, a shrink? No, leave me alone! I can't!" Pulling away, she reached for the screen door and flew through it, letting it slam behind her. On the porch, the summer heat enveloped her, bringing a line of sweat to her brow and above her lip. Gripped by a sudden pain through her shoulders which spread up the back of her neck, she gripped the wood railing and took several deep breaths.

The door behind her closed with a determined thud. Maryann stood beside her, unspeaking. Around them mosquitoes buzzed, pigeons crooned, and the drone of traffic and children playing in the late summer heat seemed very far away. Diana concentrated on counting the tomatoes on the vine in the yard beneath them.

"Arnie's been bugging me for the past four or five years to put Mom in a home, but I just can't do it," she finally said without turning around.

"Don't do this to yourself, Di. Don't do this to *us*. We can't take care of her anymore, hon. You've got to give in and begin to live a normal life."

Diana gripped the railing more tightly. "You know, when I was a little girl, there was nothing I loved more than to sit on my mother's lap and have her braid my hair. I felt so safe. So warm. So loved. She was the person I could run to, the one who would make everything better. When she . . . when she . . . went away ... I thought I would die. I didn't, though. I had things to do, people to take care of, just like she had. It felt good. So I did it. Now Rob's all grown up, he's going to have a family of his own, and Mama's still here. You know, sometimes it doesn't matter that she doesn't say anything or that she doesn't know I'm there. I can still go into her room late at night and talk to her. And even though she doesn't say an5^hing, she's there. Know what I mean?" Tears ran freely down her face though her voice remained strong. "How can I send her away? She would never have done that to me."

"It's not the same, Di." Maryann's eyes narrowed, her mouth a grim line. "You're a young, beautiful woman. I'm sure your Mom would have wanted to see you happy. She would want you to enjoy yourself, to live a full life—and she would probably hate herself for keeping you from it."

Pulling her shoulders up and back, Diana loosened her grip on the railing, her mind torn and confused. Shaking her head, she realized that Maryann, like Rob and Arnie, was right. Yet she could not rid herself of the guilt which plagued her constantly.

"If they ever did anything to her, if I ever found out she wasn't getting fed or if they let her stay dirty..."

"They wouldn't do that. My aunt is in Our Lady of Grace Nursing Home in Orient Heights, and they treat her like a queen. They ask the family what the patient's favorite meals are, and they make sure to cook a special dinner for them at least once a week. The rest of the time, they eat good, nutritious meals. And there are lots of other Italian women there. Probably some who speak your mother's language. And the doctors, Di, they're the best. Believe me."

She wiped one side of her face, then the other with a slim, shaking hand. "Really?"

"God, you know me. I wouldn't he about something like this."

With a quivering chin, Diana turned and took a deep, faltering breath, then allowed herself the luxury of sobbing against Maryann's shoulder.

Two weeks later. Rose Colucci was secured in Our Lady of Grace Rest Home, on a hill overlooking the Atlantic Ocean in the Orient Heights section of Winthrop, only a few miles away from the East Boston apartment where she had raised her children. Diana remembered it as the place where a huge statue of the Virgin Mary was lit up with thousands of blue lights during the Christmas season. When they were little. Papa brought them there to see the gigantic cross which could be seen for miles in any direction. They always knelt in front of the group of saints' statues in the outside courtyard and said a prayer for the rest of the Colucci family back in Italy. Maybe Mama would remember, she thought.

It took her another two weeks to get used to living alone in the apartment, having said goodbye and good luck to Rob and Maryann when they had found a house through one of Mike Herlihy's many

connections. Though she had a feeling that the house might have been the impetus behind
Maryann's conversation with her about moving Rose into a nursing home, that impression was a fleeting one for Diana was not long on blame, but proficient in understanding.

Arnie had come to dinner that first week, claiming to be proud of her for finally making the decision to carry on, and full of advice for what she should do with her life. When she could no longer stand his chatter, she rose from the table and gathered the dishes.

"I think you should definitely check out the secretarial programs at Fisher Junior College," he was saying. "Legal secretaries are making a mint these days and I have plenty of friends looking for someone capable and willing like you . . ."

"That's enough, Arnie." She rattled the dishes in the sink, causing him to stop short and take notice. "I've got a few dreams of my own."

"Oh?"

"No offense, but I really don't want to be stuck in an office at a desk."

"Well, that's okay. I was just suggesting . . ."

"I know and I appreciate it, but it's just dawned on me that I can finally do something / want to do and I think I'm going to try my wings. I can't afford to keep this apartment, pay all the heat and electricity bills, pay Mom's medical bills, my car insurance, and feed myself on less than $100 a week. I've got to get a better-paying job *now*. Not after college or a training program. Now." She stood against the stove, her arms behind her, her soft black hair falling loose and glossy to her shoulders. The night was warm and a sleeveless mini-dress was all she wore. With no shoes on her feet, no makeup on her face, and an expression of innocent anticipation, she looked as young and guileless as she had when Arnie first met her.

"God, I'm glad you're finally doing this." He rested one arm on the back of his chair, a surprised
smile on his face. "You've got guts, Gorgeous, I have to admit that. And you'll make it. I know you will." She sighed and grinned, pushing her hair back from her face. "We had dreams, you know. Marcus and I were going to conquer the world."

"You still can." His eyes softened. ^*You* still can."

Almost a month to the day after she made sure her mother was settled, Diana rode the train into the city for her interview with Gene Monroe, proprietor of All That Glitters on historic Charles Street.

When she told Mr. Scavullo of her decision to go for the interview, her old friend and employer had been kind and understanding. "I knew I wouldn't have you forever, *bella*. You too good for us. Too beautiful, too strong." He pointed to his brain. "Go. Go and make for yourself a good life. Get married. Have babies. Be happy."

Though she had no intention of having babies or getting married, she *did* want to be happy, to have no worries and to see what the world was like outside her little Italian neighborhood. There had been too little time to do anything besides buying the food, preparing it, taking care of her mother, and working these past few years.

She longed to be part of the little groups of women her age who took Saturdays off to rummage through Filene's basement or to have lunch in a crowded cafe on Tremont Street. She wanted to see the Christmas decorations on the Common, to sit beside the Swan Pond in the summer, to explore the back streets and small boutiques that clamored for space among the brownstones of Beacon Hill.

It's just a stepping-stone, she thought. Next, I'll see New York, then the rest of the East Coast. Maybe even Europe. Giggling at the thought, she forgot her nervousness about the interview and concentrated on watching the faces of her fellow train passengers, happy that she had as important an appointment as theirs.

As she walked through Boston Common she winced as her new heels cut into her ankles and began to wish she had worn old shoes. Every step took her closer to Charles Street. Every moment was one less she had to wait before finding out if she was good enough to work among the upper crust of Boston society. Was the dress she had chosen too short? Should she have pulled her hair up? Would her East Boston accent turn off her prospective employer? Did she have any right to think she could handle the job?

Preoccupied with thoughts of what she would say to the owner of All That Glitters, one of the wealthiest men this side of New York, she paid little attention to the other Bostonians sitting on park benches along the paths wandering through the Common. Though she noticed the admiring glances from businessmen as they hurried by, she refused to acknowledge them. Many times she thought of walking back to Park Street Station, taking the train to East Boston, and never leaving again. But each time she did, she knew she'd have to answer to Maryann, Rob, and Arnie. Besides, there was nothing there for her anymore. In spite of everything, Diana knew it was time to get on with her life. She only hoped she would have the strength to meet the challenge.

Early for her appointment, she leisurely walked to the swan boats in the Public Gardens. The pansies and petunias lining the walkways were in full bloom, giving life to the drab gray and brick buildings which surrounded the area and reminding Bostonians that winter does not last forever. She sat on a stone bench under an ancient oak tree and thought about her life, about where she was going and what she wanted to do. Her mind was racing and her hands trembled like cymbals.

Taking a deep breath, she rose and glanced down Newbury Street, feeling an unexpected pang of jealousy when she noticed the well-dressed women walking leisurely in and out of the fashionable boutiques lining the road leading away from the Gardens. The Ritz Carlton's multi-colored flags whipped in the wind as a long black limousine stopped underneath. A mink-clad woman exited and staked into the hotel. Another world, Diana thought. What the hell am I doing here?

Smoothing her new black linen dress, she pulled a mirror from her pocketbook, applied a little more lipstick and, with another deep breath, got up and walked on shaky legs across the Gardens to Charles Street.

Crossing at the light at the intersection of Beacon Street and Charles, she faced memories of the days when Marcus, Rob, and she took the train into town. They would walk down Charles Street to the Baskin-Robbins ice cream shop for what Marc called his "sugar fix."-

Lost in her daydreams, she was startled when an angry motorist beeped his horn. At the top of Beacon Hill, to her right, the State House dome, its gold roof gleaming, sat like a sentinel over the city its residents fondly called "Beantown." Each tiny street which led away from the gold dome was small enough to be considered a neighborhood, yet not quite as friendly as the ones she knew. Lined with brownstones sporting fancy wrought iron balustrades and balconies, the streets had been built and originally occupied by the oldest families in Boston, those that dated their ancestry back to the *Mayflower.*

For the most part, the buildings had been passed down through the generations and remained in the families. Inside were exquisite furnishings, uniformed maids and butlers, and exotic teas drunk from silver cups, Diana had heard. The newspapers often spoke of society balls and magnificent parties which only those of Yankee heritage could attend. Though this was the Boston with which the world was familiar, it was only a small part of the various communities which kept the city going, and was much resented by the immigrant families who paid the bulk of the city's taxes and represented the majority of the work force.

Understanding how it felt to be part of that work force didn't make Diana resent the magnates who ruled the corporations from their perches on Beacon Hill, but she admitted to feeling a bit awed by their power and influence. Perhaps "jealous" is the word she thought, ashamed to admit it.

Charles Street professed to be a neighborhood. Its small, unusual shops served the residents of the area as did Mr. Scavullo's Italian grocery store, but instead of selling capicolla and cured ham, they advertised bottles of Perrier, fresh fruits and vegetables, and twenty-two different kinds of yogurt. The smells from the restaurants which lined the street were just as wonderful as those which wafted from Sablone's and Santarpio's in East Boston, but Diana knew she couldn't afford to eat in any of them. Even if she could, she would probably come away still feeling hungry.

The Colonial-style lamps lining the once- cobblestoned street were originally lighted by gas, though they were now electric. They reminded her of a street from a Charles Dickens novel. She could easily imagine a gentleman in a long Edwardian coat and beaver top hat striding along the street holding his ladder and lamplighter in one hand, tipping his hat to the ladies with the other. Each light would be individually lit, giving the street a golden glow and illuminating the wares in shop windows.

Perhaps this one was once a cobbler shop; the next might have been a book store with shelves full of leather-bound volumes of Shakespeare and the Greek
classics which would be sold to proper Boston families, like the Cabots or the Lodges.

In the summer, black-hooded horse-drawn carriages would carry their wealthy clientele down the roadway to the Charles River for open-air symphonies and picnics, then back again to the quiet homes on the hill overlooking the Boston Common and Public Gardens. Diana hummed a Strauss waltz under her breath, ignoring the puzzled looks of passersby.

At Christmastime, women in ermine-trimmed capes, holding muffs to match, would scurry down the street. Their arms were full of gaily wrapped packages they would share with their families at home on Christmas morning beneath a huge fir tree graced with crystal and porcelain decorations from Europe, lit candles clipped to its branches. The fashionable ladies would throw holiday parties, each vying to be called the best hostess on "the Hill." Warmed cider, poured into sterling silver cups, would be laced with rum from the islands; fine foods would be shipped in from all over the world, to be served to the guests by butlers in white tails with black patent shoes sporting brass buckles.

She sighed. That was then, she reminded herself as she came to the shop where she would be interviewed. This is now. Though it was always much easier to live in daydreams, she shook herself and studied the window before her.

All That Glitters was a sizeable gift shop, located next to Marika's Antiques, the shop which any dealer worth his salt would tell you was *the* place to shop for antiques in Boston. Diana had heard that in the earlier part of the century Israel Sack, a Jewish immigrant who came through Ellis Island, had made his fortune as an antique ^dealer on this street, but no one had been able to match his talent for success since. The immigrant had gone from Charles Street to build an empire which continued to this day and which surpassed any other in the United States. Israel's sons continued to run the business in the same manner as their father. Because of the record-setting prices the company often paid for American antiques, Sack's influence was still felt on Charles Street by many of the dealers who operated shops there and who struggled to keep Boston the hub of the antiques world—though New York had long ago stolen their glory.

The windows of All That Glitters seemed to have been in place since the Revolution, the kind of wavy glass which made it difficult to see inside. Looking in the window gave Diana a wrinkled view of her face. She hurriedly patted her hair in place, bending this way and that to get a clear image of herself.

Silver coffee sets and crystal bowls with dainty silver spoons were meticulously arranged in the window facing the street. Gracefully arranged on white velvet-covered shelves, the pieces were placed as though someone might use them in their home that afternoon for a high tea with the Vanderbilts or Rockefellers. She sucked in her breath, her hand at her throat. Never had she seen anything so strikingly beautiful.

Neither prices nor maker's tags were displayed in the window. It was obvious that if a client didn't know what they were looking at or what it might be worth. Gene Monroe preferred they not find out. Perhaps it kept the business safe from vandalism and theft, she reasoned.

The bell on the door jingled melodiously. Afraid she would break something if she moved one way or the other, she remained standing in the doorway for a second until her eyes adjusted to the dim light. When she could see again, a tall, distinguished-looking gentleman with thinning blondish-gray hair stood in front of her, studying her face intently. Instantly, she was reminded of the English actor, Peter O'Toole.

Chapter Eight

"May I help you?" he asked quietly, his accent clipped and distinguished.

She wound her hands through the strap of her pocketbook. "I'm looking for Mr. Monroe. I have an appointment."

"I'm Gene Monroe." The man extended a limp, pale hand and motioned her to follow him. Over his shoulder, he added, "You must be Diana Colucci. I've been waiting for you. Would you like some tea? I was just about to have a cup."

Nodding mutely, she took the chance to scrutinize the man as he poured their tea into bone china cups. Clad in elegantly cut chinos, an open- necked, ivory colored silk shirt, and a beige cashmere sweater thrown haphazardly over his shoulders, Monroe appeared completely at ease though his movements were as curt and clipped as his speech. He poured the tea from a porcelain pot wrapped in a tea cozy and said nothing to relieve Diana's discomfort. His slightly lined forehead was wide and high, yet his face did not give the impression of being long, since his jawbone was just as wide as his forehead, setting off the rest of his features perfectly. In another setting, he would have been the epitome of a chairman of the board, for his eyes were quick and all-seeing, piercing yet veiled. Diana lowered hers and reached for the cup of tea, unsure of what else to do.

As though he wore a pair of half-glasses, Monroe surreptitiously watched her record every detail of his office with inquisitive eyes. His chair rolled silently backwards over a pale, thick carpet until it leaned against an oak bookcase jammed full of art and antiques books.

"So, you're little Maryann's sister-in-law, are you?" he finally said, leaning back and balancing his cup and saucer in his lap.

She nodded, feeling a bit overwhelmed by the opulence of the tiny office, which seemed of a different world than the shop out front. A rich, dark wood desk dominated one corner of the room. Bronze desk implements, which all seemed to feature a long-legged, slim fairy-type creature, lay on top of the desk. A green glass lamp cast a glow on the center of the desk's top and the long windows were covered with long, heavy red drapes which, though closed, did not bring the expected dark and dreary feeling to the room. Instead they gave her a feeling of warmth and richness, much like sitting in front of a fire on a snowy evening. In spite of herself, she relaxed.

"What makes you think you want to work in a shop, Diana? You don't mind if I call you Diana, do you?"

"No, of course not, Mr. Monroe."

"Gene, please. Mr. Monroe sounds so old. So stuffy. Please, continue."

"I enjoy working with people. Mr. Scavullo always said I was really good with customers. And I know how to handle the bookkeeping, the tax records, and advertising in local papers. Besides," she laughed quietly, "Maryann says I have to get out of East Boston."

"Do you always do what other people tell you to?"

Though the words were spoken quietly and reasonably, she bristled, remembering the many teachers with whom she had run-ins when Robbie was growing up and the bill collectors she had had to fend off. Why did they all have the same tone to their voices? "I do what my employers tell me to," she said. "And, yes, I *do* listen to good friends."

"There's a lot to learn in this business and I won't tolerate anyone who doesn't want to work. Don't think it's all standing behind the counter and smiling . . . . Where are you going?"

"I'm sorry, Mr. Monroe," she said, rising from her chair. "I'm no stranger to hard work and what you're saying to me is that I have strikes against me before I even begin this interview. That's not comfortable for me. I've always prided myself on finishing what I begin and, if I can't, I admit it from the very beginning."

No longer nervous, she held her shoulders straight and her pocketbook close to her body. How dare this man insult her during the first five minutes of their interview! Used to Italian warmth and passion, she had trouble dealing with his briskly cool attitude. "You've already decided I'm not going to make it, Mr. Monroe, so there's no point in continuing this conversation."

Reaching for the doorknob, she tried to quell the anger which had risen so suddenly. This was the type of behavior East Bostoners discussed in the safety of their own neighborhoods—the differences between the old Bostonians and the "new" immigrants were still as deep as a chasm and twice as hard to cross. No one she knew had managed to bridge the gap successfully. It was as though a wall existed between the two factions, and she wasn't in the mood to scramble over it.

"Wait a minute." Monroe uncrossed his long, thin legs and put his teacup back into its saucer.
Leaning forward, he scrutinized Diana's face once more. "It's been a long time since I've met someone with scruples. Let's start over again, shall we?"

Two hours and ten minutes later, Diana and Gene Monroe were on their third cup of tea. They had discussed her life and the direction she wanted it to take, and Monroe had described the type of business he ran and what he expected from his employees. They had come to the conclusion that perhaps they could work together.

She had surprised Monroe by insisting on a mutual evaluation after three months—her office practice course in high school had taught her that, evaluations were good for business as well as employees—and she was to be included in the company's health insurance plan immediately.

Gene Monroe, son of Taylor Livingston Monroe and Faith Tryon Monroe, direct descendant of the *Mayflower* Monroes, was extremely interested in the intense Mediterranean woman in front of him. She had style, though her pocketbook could not, as yet, support her tastes, and she was understated, quiet, and intelligent. All qualities he admired.

Shaking hands at the door, Monroe smiled for the first time that afternoon when he said, "You know the salary's not much right now, but prove yourself to me, Diana, and you never know what might happen."

Back in East Boston, she noticed, for the first time in her life, the ugly gray tone which pervaded the streets, the obnoxious smells which attacked her at every corner, and the bits of newspaper and garbage which rustled around her legs as she walked down Meridian Street.

Everything is so noisy and dirty here, she thought disconsolately. She sniffed when a mangy black-and-white dog lifted his leg on a fire hydrant in front of her and turned her head when a group of women dressed in black, arguing loudly and gesturing with fat, stubby fingers, brushed past her.

The apartment was quiet and dark. She threw her pocketbook on the kitchen table and walked to the back door, her footsteps echoing through the hall. Out of habit, she headed for the room overlooking the yard, as she had for the past ten years, but there was no one there. No Mama to talk to— even if she didn't talk back. No need to put water on the stove for tea or to start supper because there was no one but herself to feed.

Standing, arms folded across her chest, she leaned against the porch railing and looked down the line of brick buildings. The clotheslines were full of clean laundry, the women leaning over their porches to talk to their downstairs or upstairs neighbors, the windows of some buildings taped or boarded, the children's bicycles chained to stair railings.

She sighed, then smiled, the thought of her new job lighting her classic features. This was all temporary. Now there were hopes for a better future.

A door slammed, bringing her attention back to the present. She turned to see Robert carrying a laughing Maryann down the hallway to the kitchen.

"We have great news, Di!" he yelled as he dumped the tousled bundle into a kitchen chair. "Wait till you hear what we have to tell you."

"I have news, too." Closing the screen door behind her, she settled into the chair next to Maryann and gave her a wink.

"Okay. Toss a coin. See who tells first," Rob's tongue stuck out on the right side of his mouth, a childhood habit of concentration, as

he tossed the
coin into the air. "You call it," he said as it fell.

"Heads."

"It's tails!" Maryann squealed. "You tell her, honey."

"No, you tell her. It's as much your news as it is mine."

"Okay." The redhead turned her face to Diana. For the first time, Diana noticed Maryann looked as though she was lit from within. "We're having a baby, Di! You're going to be an aunt!"

"But . . . but . . . I'm not even used to being a sister-in-law yet."

"That's okay. Isn't it?" Maryann's face lost its sparkle momentarily, but quickly regained it when she saw the news begin to sink into Diana's brain, making the taller, darker woman's eyes fill with happy tears.

"Oh, God, Maryann, of course it's okay. I'm going to be an aunt." Her voice was quiet, almost reverent. "If only Mama and Papa were here."

Rob whirled from the refrigerator where he had been rescuing a bottle of Riunite they had put away for a special occasion. Bottle in hand, his eyes dark with anger, he turned on his sister. "What the hell do you mean by that? Why can't you give it up? They're gone. They're *both* gone and it's high time you learned it."

Maryann shrank into the chair and pulled her legs up to her chest. Diana's eyes narrowed. Feet apart, arms down at her sides, fists tightly clenched, she stared hard at her brother.

"Robert Anthony Coined, you'd better stop that right this instant," she hissed. "Just because you don't remember that much about Papa and you resented having to take care of Mama doesn't mean I have to stop loving them. You shut your mouth right now or I'll shut it for you."

"You and what army?"

Diana took two menacing steps toward him and her brother's face suddenly relaxed. "Here," he said, "you open this and we'll celebrate, okay? I'm sorry. I won't do it again. It's just that you've always been there, Di. No one else. And I really don't feel like I have any family other than you and Maryann."

Taking the bottle, she replied, "You really ought to learn to control your temper, Robert Anthony Coined. It's going to get you in trouble someday. And this drinking really has to stop. Especially if you're going to be a father."

Maryann, her small body still trembling with fear, forced herself between the two taller, darker people and took the bottle from Diana. "What's your news, Di?" she said in her best cheerful tone.

Forcing herself to stop staring at Robert, Diana replied, "I got the job."

Though they opened the champagne immediately, Diana reflected on the moment later when she w^ alone in her room and decided that, somehow, it all seemed anticlimactic.

Chapter Nine

Boston, November, 1980

The satin sheets rustled softly as Gene Monroe slid out of them and grabbed his paisley Polo robe from the bottom of the bed. The boy turned over, sighed, and went back to snoring softly. Gene held his breath a moment, not wanting to explain why he was getting up in the middle of the night. Satisfied that his lover was still asleep, he slid his arms into the robe and walked softly out of the room. Closing the twelve-foot mahogany door behind him quietly, he leaned against it briefly, his mind full of thoughts of the shop.

Scott Logan III, left alone in the king-sized Spanish four-poster bed, was the most recent in a long list of Harvard graduates Gene allowed himself the luxury of dating. When he, at thirty-six, had decided to openly admit his homosexuality, his Brahmin upbringing stepped in, forcing him to pick only the cream of the crop from the young lovers available to him. Thus far, except for one memorable exception, they were all Ivy League grads.

The exception had been a dark-eyed, full-lipped poet from Middlebury College in Vermont whose lack of a properly cut pair of pants caused Gene to buy the lad a complete wardrobe—a wardrobe which the ungrateful little snit promptly gave away after they ended the relationship.

Still, he was a lyrical and romantic poet with a knack for writing a ballad, a talent just about lost to writers of his generation. He had been allowed to spend a tempestuous summer in Monroe's summer home in Beverly Farms, Massachusetts. Locked away in the mansion, the poet had crafted some incredibly romantic verses and even more incredible sex. Gene felt devastated when the creature announced he "must move on, must expand my creativity."

Never again, the tall, stately gentleman from Beacon Hill promised himself. Never again would he fell in love. Yet here was another young lover threatening to steal the very breath from his body.

Taking another puff from his Gauloise, he stared out the balcony window overlooking Louisburg Square and his high-walled garden. During the summer, the garden was lush with euonymus, jackmanii, and hanging baskets, and was so beautiful that a writer had included photos of it in a book entitled *"Hidden Gardens of Beacon Hill"* Now, the November wind whipped the tall maples lining the paths in and around Mount Vernon Street.

He breathed heavily and tapped his index finger against his upper lip. Behind him the moon cast shadows on his collection of Galle glass, displayed on the mantle of one of five working fireplaces in the house. The mysterious smoky glass, the only group of items in the building less than one hundred and fifty years old, was publicly known as his whimsy. It was a wise investment, he thought, believing the value of the Art Nouveau art glass would rise to extraordinary proportions before the end of the twentieth century.

Though born to one of the wealthiest families in Boston, Monroe was not above a bit of horse-trading, as his grandfather used to call it, and when it came to investing in art or antiques to make money, he was one of the few in the world who had been able to choose wisely during the turbulent Sixties and Seventies.

The drawing room leading to the balcony, decorated as it had been since Monroe's grandfather bought the building in 1870, served as home to several pieces of furniture which had been declared priceless by the last insurance appraisal. Each piece was a family heirloom, treasured for its sentimental value, though he appreciated period furniture immensely.

The room's walls, a rich teak, reached from the wall-to-wall Herez carpet to the top of the twenty- foot ceilings. Card tables scattered throughout the room opened to reveal Oriental ivory chess pieces or English satinwood boxes holding cards monogrammed with the family initial. Portraits of members of the Monroe family, strategically placed along the room's four walls, were lit by tiny bulbs designed to be almost invisible. The lighting lent a naughty glint to Aunty Harriet's eye and gave Grandmother Grace an angelic halo, he often thought with a wry smile.

He contemplated his family now, his back to the Boston skyline, and sighed once more. Young Logan was becoming too much for him. The twenty- four-year-old child demanded all of his time, failing to understand that Gene had a business—a business about which he cared a great deal. Yet, the young medical student's body was delicious, fulfilling Monroe's every craving and leaving him totally satisfied. It was dangerous, he knew, and he didn't quite know what to do about the predicament he had gotten himself into.

Logan had been talking lately of becoming Monroe's partner in All That Glitters. "The shop interests me, Gene," he would murmur as he sensually stroked Gene's spine. "You really should let me help you."

"You're an intern, darling," he would answer. "There's nothing more important than that. What do you want with a measly little gift shop?"

"It's not measly and it's not little. It's a wonderful, dreamy place, and I want to be there with you to help you run it."

In truth, he neither needed nor wanted help with his shop. Though his aunts and cousins often scoffed at the thought of a Monroe being a shopkeeper, he found that being the owner of All That Glitters not only gave him the opportunity to satisfy his cravings for the beautiful and unique objects in the world; it also served as defense against the endless invitations to attend boring charity balls or to head some uninteresting college committee. If he wanted to attend a ball, he made sure it was a social occasion, not a business opportunity for someone looking for a handout.

Once his day on Charles Street ended, nothing prevented him from having dinner with his latest lover or spending the weekend at his mansion in Beverly or on the yacht moored in Provincetown. Twice a season he could take a week-long vacation in whatever part of the world he wanted to explore next, though there were few places left unvisited, and, now that he had Diana Colucci to run the shop, he could take off for auctions or art gallery openings in New York whenever he felt like it. Perhaps he would finally be able to explore the possibility of developing the line of antiques he had always yearned to bring into the shop.

Diana. He nodded, a satisfied smile curling his thin lips. He had expected a sweaty, dark-eyed, plump-hipped Italian woman, but what he had hired was a tall, quiet beauty with hair such a glossy shade of black that he half expected to see his reflection in it. And she had spunk. Class and spunk.

First impressions were always correct, he had decided early on, and his first impression when he interviewed her three years ago was that she would blend in perfectly with businesspeople and those who occupied the most affluent section of Boston. He was right. She had worked out very well. Very well indeed.

By increasing her salary piecemeal, introducing her to other shop owners who specialized in women's clothing, and dropping little hints, such as "Darling, your hair would really look much better if it were chin length," he urged his assistant to develop into the- elegant woman he instinctively knew was hidden under her East Boston accent. It hadn't been difficult. Her taste was impeccable; she carried herself straight, proudly and sensually; and she had an innate sense of what was right for her. When she bought a suit of mid-grade design, she wore it as if it were a Chanel. When she moved around the shop, she gave off an air of self-confidence. Her sweet, patient manner was the perfect foil for her incredible memory, and her way with a column of figures was a talent that would make the accountants at Arthur Anderson do a double take.

He shared his season's tickets to the ballet, opera, and symphony with his associate, consciously feeding her thirst for culture. Watching her face during her first ballet, he was convinced he had tapped a mine of enthusiasm for the gentle arts which he had grown up with and had become accustomed to. Her wide blue eyes were open, the lids blinking only when nature demanded it. Her mind was like a sponge, taking in all the notes of the symphony, the movements of the dancers and the colors of their costumes—recording them so she could play back the scenes whenever she wished. It appeared she was mesmerized, never realizing there were people in the audience just as bewitched by her as she was by what was happening on stage.

Little by little, he introduced her to his world, encouraging her to attend art shows, auctions, and show openings and wishing, for the first time in his life, that he had had children. His parental instincts became so strong with the independent, yet delicate, female that he even took it upon himself to meet her family. Surprised that her brother was as handsome as she. Gene reminded himself firmly that an attraction was not in order and promptly forgot the initial stirring he had felt in his loins when Robbie first shook his hand. His curiosity about Diana's life was now complete. He knew where she lived, what her childhood had been like, why she adored her brother and his family so much, and why she longed for more from her life.

He pulled on his Gauloise once more. She deserved more, he thought, as he had so often before. Much more.

With all her new sophistication and knowledge, he knew she was not aware of her appeal to the opposite sex. Though he had introduced her to his most affluent younger customers, she consistently turned a cold shoulder to their advances or, worse, ignored a gentleman's attentions completely.

Perhaps the reason for her coolness had, in part, to do with her feeling that the men of Beacon Hill were out of her league. He tried to convince her that was not the case, but she always walked away, a slight smile on her face, her mind obviously Occupied by thoughts of the past. The subject would change to one with which she felt safe— more and more frequently, that subject would be one associated with the arts.

Christof and Anthony, her brother's children, were only toddlers, yet they were the males Diana most preferred to be with and Monroe doubted if his stunning associate even noticed her lack of Saturday night dates.

In many ways, he could understand how her childhood had been, even though he never shared his reasons for that understanding. At the tender age of seven, he had lost the vivacious blonde socialite who had been his mother. She died in childbirth, her tiny daughter following a mere two days later.

Though his father had never been exceptionally affectionate, he was even less so after his beloved Faith died. His many businesses demanded his time, taking him further and further away from his son. Gene was placed with nannies at first and, as he got older, put into boarding schools. They were the best schools, of course, for Thomas Weldon Monroe would not let his son lack for a proper upbringing. But they were never in Boston, never where it would have been easy for him to visit Gene on a regular basis.

Thomas's sisters. Gene's aunts, made sure the special occasions were attended to—when he was a child, there were birthday parties complete with ponies and professional clowns, and, later, society galas when he, like so many others in Boston, was introduced to the people who, hopefully, would shape his future. None of it replaced being loved by a family.

He attended Harvard and Oxford, the colleges chosen for him, took their business and law courses as suggested by his aunts, and got the grades expected of him by his father—though he longed to study the arts. With the grace for which he would later be well known, he convinced his family to let him minor in the arts and became the star of his sculpture class, enamored by the grace of the Grecian statues he encountered in the museums of Europe and with the soft, muted colors of the French Impressionists. Little by little his other grades dropped, while his marks in the arts and antiquities classes soared. Yet he learned all the social graces and studied the correct languages, developing a perfect French accent, and acted as properly as was expected.

When his father made a comment about Gene's low level of interest in what he called "important" subjects, the boy immediately paid more attention, bringing his average up to compete with the highest in his class. He was not a teenager who sought attention. He had realized early in life that if he went along with the crowd, no one would notice his eccentricities or personal habits. Ultimately, his whimsical behavior was what endeared him to Europeans for almost ten years after graduation—they would have allowed him to stay if he had not been summoned back to Boston by his father.

When Gene turned thirty, Thomas Weldon Monroe took his son into the family banking business and attempted to teach the boy what he knew. It was too late by then. Gene had given up on ever feeling any love for his family and was beginning to turn to others, all notably male, for his affections. He had vicious arguments with his father about his sexuality, which surprised both of them because they considered themselves civilized people.

After one famous bout, Thomas quietly left for a European business trip and died there, at 62, of a massive heart attack.

Gene went to the funeral with none of the heart- wrenching anguish he had felt when his mother died, but with a sense of relief that he would finally be able to live his life the way he wanted. And with a tremendous guilt that he felt so free.

Against family protests, he sold the line of banks his father had worked so hard to keep running through the Depression, investing the money in additional real estate on Beacon Hill. The business of renting or selling the properties was turned over to his accountant, for he neither needed nor wanted the money. But he knew instinctively, as his father and grandfather before him, how to make it. Despite himself, he strengthened the family fortune, parlaying his father's money into a strong multimillion dollar base.

After wandering around the world for a couple of years, spending as much of the family money as he dared, he found himself bored and lonely. It was then that his love of porcelains, glass, and art took over. After listening to tales of Israel Sack and the other antique dealers who had populated Charles Street during the early part of the century, he decided he wanted a shop where he could meet the people of Boston on a regular basis. And he was happy simply to retire, at age 39, to the Beacon Hill home he had known as a child.

Though All That Glitters was born to stave off his boredom, it turned into much more than that. He discovered he loved the retail business, the constant flow of customers, and travelling to different countries to restock his shelves. It fed an artistic vein he had never been able to fulfill any other way. His European trips served his wandering nature and allowed him the luxury of bringing home "trinkets" for the Beacon Hill apartment. When he tired of a painting or sculpture, he would put it back on the market, always making a profit, which was invested in more real estate or sureties. His accountant loved the stability of it all. His fortune continued to grow into hundreds of millions of solid American dollars.

Antiques became his passion, and he often used them as accents in the shop though he never had the heart to put a price tag on them. It was much easier for him to part with new, unusual *objets d'art* than with an old, rare piece he might never see again. Now, at 51, the shop was Gene's whole life, and he could well understand why it held the same addictive qualities for Diana.

Of all her attributes, it was her astute salesmanship he admired most. During the time she had been with him, his sales had almost doubled and the number of customers who walked through his door on a regular basis had tripled. Since he had done nothing different in the arrangement of his stock or bought any items which could be considered unusual or different from those he normally carried, he realized the reason for the sudden change was purely and simply Diana Colucci.

Instinctively, she selected the right piece for the right person, convincing the customer, through a quiet conversation, a soft smile, or a well-placed, tasteful joke, that All That Glitters could meet their gift needs better than any other shop in Boston. Her attention to detail kept the shelves and displays immaculate. Her talent for decorating was unleashed when a new shipment came in. Her determination to do everything correctly caused her to study marketing ideas and retail manuals until she knew exactly how to get a piece in a more saleable position, as well as how to move something which had no chance of selling.

The Beacon Hill matrons felt they could trust the woman whose attentive, serious manner made them feel important. The way she met their eyes in conversation and remembered the names of their children and grandchildren proved she cared. Though the women knew she did not defer to them, she did not threaten them by trying to become like them. In fact, the only thing about herself that she valiantly fought to change was her strong East Boston accent. It wasn't hard —her voice never had taken on the slovenly tones, harsh syllables, and tough expressions of her fellow "Easties." Instead, its soft, insistent lilt seemed more European and proper Bostonians never appeared to mind that her "r's" were more rounded than theirs.

The new residents of the Hill, the shop owners and townhouse dwellers with forced and false Brahmin accents, counted on her to instruct them in the fine art of setting a table, the correct wine glasses to use, and the effect that silver and Limoges, rather than crystal and Belleek, could have on a buffet. She accomplished all of this without her customers realizing they had received a lesson in etiquette or that Diana had learned those lessons by watching her boss and by reading piles of books on the subject. The Corbys and Delcotts of Beacon Hill became permanent customers, referring their *nouveau riche* friends to All That Glitters, thus striking a well of new clientele Monroe had been unable to tap.

Night after night she left the shop and headed for Tremont Street where she raided the shelves at the Boston Public Library. She would tell him later of reading everything that was ever written about the items in All That Glitters' inventory, scouring the interior design books to learn how to decorate a home or set a table, even going so far as to read gourmet cookbooks and magazines in order to learn how to combine foods with complementary wines. Sometimes he would find her in his office, one of his antiques reference books on her knee, holding a piece of Belleek or Waterford in her hands under the light, her thick black brows knitted tightly together, her eyes rapidly moving from the book to the piece she held in her hands and back again.

The door behind him opened, interrupting Monroe's thoughts. He turned to see the silhouetted outline of his naked lover.

"Are you coming back to bed?" Logan asked quietly, as if speaking louder than a whisper would disturb the hushed atmosphere in the apartment.

"Let me finish my cigarette," he answered.

Taking the last few puffs quickly, he thought of the boy in his bed and his erection stiffened. Though the paisley robe bulged indiscreetly when he climbed back between the sheets, his last thought before pulling Logan's warm body close to his was of what he should give Diana Colucci for Christmas.

Chapter Ten

Boston, December, 1980

"You can't possibly be serious!" Diana sat on the same chair she had occupied when Gene interviewed her three years earlier, a ticket to Paris in her hands. "I can't go to Europe for Christmas. I just can't."

"Why not?" Her employer stood above her, the smile he had been wearing since handing her the Christmas present beginning to fade.

"Well, because . . . because Chris and Tony expect me to be there Christmas morning. I'm always with them and this year's going to be so special. I've bought them both their first train . . . "

"That's already taken care of. I spoke to Rob yesterday." Gene's face relaxed as he took his place behind the partner's desk. "And he told me to make sure you go with me, because if you don't he'll never forgive you. He also told me to tell you that you're invited to an early Christmas at his house next week, the 20th. It's close enough to the actual holiday that the children won't even notice the difference, and we can take off for the Continent the next morning."

Stupefied, she shook her head, her mind boggled by what the airplane ticket in her shaking hands represented. "I've never been on a plane," she said.

"There's always a first time. So pack your bags, my dear. We're off for the trip of your life."

"Who's going to mind the shop?"

"Miles will," he said, ushering her out and shutting the door in her astonished face.

Still in shock, she stood, her nose pressed to the oak panels of the door for a moment before whirling into the center of the room, the ticket tightly held against her breasts. She hardly noticed how close she came to knocking over the Waterford crèche which balanced precariously on a clear Lu- cite stand in the center of the room. Or that her outstretched arms came dangerously near the Royal Doulton Madonna arrangement she designed and decorated nearly two weeks ago. When she finally stopped spinning, she watched the snow falling against the shop window, its brilliance creating haloes around the street lamps. She let loose a luxuriously long and delighted sigh.

The white lights trimming the many-paned shop windows twinkled and complemented the fresh boughs attached to the outside trim. In both street facing windows, they had arranged winter scenes of Olde New England so well done that the *Boston Globe* had just featured them in a center spread. Perfect public relations, she had thought.

She shook her head. I won't be spending Christmas in New England this year, she thought jubilantly. Europe! Paris, Rome, Milan, Vienna!

Studying the itinerary tucked inside the gold-em- bossed Christmas card Gene had handed her, his words echoed in her mind: "You're everything a shop owner would want in an employee, Diana. Don't blush! It's true. You're here long before you should be, and you leave long after the shop has closed. You keep the books, order the merchandise, handle the customers with ease, and you care enough to educate yourself about the extra things you can do for them. For me. If it wasn't for you, my dear Diana, All That Glitters would still be just another gift shop run by an incredibly bored Bostonian. You've given this shop new life, new direction, and you've made my life a whole lot simpler. I trust you far more than any other clerk I've ever had —that's why I made you manager a year ago — and you just keep getting better. I'd leave the shop with you anytime and you, of all people, know that I don't leave All That Glitters unless I absolutely have to. If you had a shop down the street. I'd be *very* worried about my business."

With that, her boss had kissed her on the forehead and handed her the envelope, adding, "I want you to accompany me on my annual buying trip through Europe. This time I'm not going to factories and specialty shops. You, my dear, are responsible for my finally fulfilling a dream to make All That Glitters one of the best antique shops on the East Coast. No more dealing with merchandising salesmen and catalogs. We're going on a treasure hunt!

"Now, I've already booked the hotels and made appointments to see the dealers and auctioneers I know on the Continent. All you need to do is brush up on what you know about antiques and I'll do the rest. You *do* want to learn more, don't you?"

Though he arched an eyebrow at his employee, he didn't wait for her eager nod, knowing full well what the answer to his question would be. "You need to take the next step in your career, darling, and this is it. The flight leaves the 21st and we come home in mid-January. Christmas in Paris, New Year's in Vienna, and recuperation on the Riviera before we head for a buying spree in London. Don't look so shocked! Most women your age would be home packing their bags by now." Leaning back in his chair, he reached for some correspondence he had been in the process of answering. "Merry Christmas, Diana Colucci. Now, get out on the floor. There's still plenty of work to do."

The shop's doorbell brought her back to reality and she hurried behind the counter to tuck the tickets into her pocketbook before turning to her customer with a smile.

"Good afternoon, Mrs. Eaton."

The days passed painfully slowly, yet it seemed only moments ago that Gene had handed her the ticket, Diana thought, sitting in a luxuriously cushioned seat in the first-class section of Pan Am's Flight 486 to Orly Airport. A glass of white wine in her hand, her head spun from the events of the last two weeks.

She wore a winter white jersey skirt Maryann had discovered at the bottom of a heap on one of Filene's tables and a new white boiled wool jacket which matched the skirt perfectly. It was the same style she had seen on the well-dressed women who frequented the shop. Though the jacket was expensive, $200 more than she wanted to pay, it was a quality piece of clothing and she knew the investment would give her many days of wear in the years to come.

That morning she had pulled her hair back from her face, securing it with a large bone-colored clip and adding a pair of pearl earrings. The businesslike effect was exactly the image she wanted to project. However, she had taken her sister-in-law's advice to wear something comfortable for the long plane ride. As a result, she had the freedom to pull the jersey skirt over her legs when she drew them up underneath her.

Christmas had been spent, as planned, with Rob, Maryann, and the children. Although it was only the 20th of December, the children, Chris at three years and Tony at thirteen months, had not noticed. Their delighted squeals when they saw the brightly-colored packages Diana brought could be heard all the way down the street.

For a brief moment, she had been concerned that Rob and Maryann would find her presents too elaborate and would be offended. He still worked behind the meat counter at the grocery store, sometimes seven days a week, trying to support his little family in the best way he knew how; Maryann took in other people's children to supplement their income and enable her to stay with the boys.

After the presents were unwrapped, Diana realized she needn't have worried. They loved their gifts, but agreed that the best part of the Christmas celebration was that they were together. "It wouldn't have been Christmas without you, Di," her brother had said affectionately.

Later, when the wrapping paper was knee deep, Maryann, her hair disheveled and a look on her face reflected the bewilderment every mother feels on Christmas afternoon, suggested they start thinking about dinner.

"Rob, why don't you clean up, and Di, you take care of the kids while I check the turkey and start the veggies." She disappeared into the kitchen, looking almost relieved that she could escape the bedlam.

Scooping the children up, Diana settled in an armchair. For two hours she occupied them with stories and games. The warmth of the little bodies against hers brought a lump to her throat and memories of their births came unbidden to her mind as she dropped little kisses on their sweet- smelling necks, making each giggle.

She remembered waiting in the hospital for hours before Rob came out to announce each baby's arrival—both boys had taken their precious time being born, a fact Maryann constantly lamented. Later, Rob and Diana had stood, their arms wrapped around each other's waists, staring in the nursery window, making noises and sounds like "silly fools," as Maryann had affectionately termed them.

When she was younger, Diana had been convinced Rob was the only person for whom she would have given her life, but staring in the window of the nursery when Chris was born, she realized that everything had changed. And she had felt even more strongly when Tony was born, her father's namesake. It was a sign that Rob had come to accept his parents. A huge step in his life.

Now she had three men to love—one fully grown, two little ones—and she did so completely, with all of her heart.

When Rob finally finished restacking the now- opened presents, assembled the train set, the Fisher Price fire truck, and the wooden schoolhouse the children had received from Diana, and retrieved each little piece of paper and ribbon, he turned to find his sister asleep in the chair. Christopher under one arm, his chubby fist nestled against his cheek, and Anthony in her lap, his curly blond head against her breasts, she appeared to be smiling though her eyes were closed and her dark head slumped to the side. He smiled as he gently tucked one of Maryann's homemade afghans around the angelic group, then strode into the kitchen to take his wife in his arms for a loving bear hug.

"How about a Christmas romp?" he whispered against the soft curls surrounding Maryann's face.

"But Diana's right in the other room . . . "

"Sound asleep. Both boys, too," he said, his voice smoky with passion.

With the vegetables boiling madly on the stove behind them, he took Maryann slowly and fervently on top of the kitchen table, leaving her breathless. As he zipped his pants, she wiped the hair out of her eyes and grinned at him capriciously. "Is that just an appetizer or do I get the main course later?"

He leaned over her, kissing her forehead, the tip of her nose, both cheeks and, finally, her mouth. "You get whatever you want and more later. Maybe even dessert . . ."

They both giggled, remembering a night not too long ago when a whipped cream fight had ended up in their most passionate lovemaking session ever.

Suddenly, he was serious. "I love you, Mrs. Colucci."

"And I love you, too—you big brute."

"Watch that stuff. I'm starting to get hard again."

"Don't you dare—the dinner will burn."

Rob picked her up off the table, her legs wrapped around his waist and kissed her once more. "Okay, back to work, wench!"

As Maryann stirred the potatoes and turnips, he went to the kitchen door and peeked around the trim. "Honey, you've got to come see this," he said softly.

Spoon in her hand, she slid under his arm and together they stood watching the kids sleeping with Diana. "Couldn't ask for a better aunt," he whispered.

"I'm so glad she's finally getting away."

"One of her dreams."

Maryann smiled up at him. "Now we've all fulfilled our dreams."

"Oh? And what was yours?"

She grinned again. "To get laid on the kitchen table."

That evening the adults visited Rose in the nursing home, but not before Rob made a round of Black Russians for the three of them. Maryann had looked at Diana over the top of her glass and shrugged, as if to say "What did you expect?" Wisely, Diana pursed her lips shut, determined not to nag him about his drinking with Christmas just around the corner. Nothing should ruin this time of year.

In their mother's room, Diana led the way into conversation by chattering about her job, the upcoming trip, and what the boys had thought of their Christmas presents, while Rob and Maryann sat stiffly on the iron-and-naugahyde chairs the home provided for visitors.

"Mom, we brought you some presents." Watching her mother's face closely as she had for more than a decade, she had to admit there was no hint of recognition beyond the slow blinking of the old Italian woman's eyelids. Gone was the luster Rose's hair once had. Her eyes, though constantly vacant, seemed even emptier than before, and she wore a plain blue cotton housedress which hung from her bony chest.

The noises told them when they laid her on the bed at night, her knees immediately went up to her chest and she tucked her head down against them, curling into the fetal position. Feeling further away than ever from her mother, Diana sighed heavily.

"C'mon." Rob finally got up and lifted his sister by the elbow. "She doesn't hear you and you're just making yourself miserable. Let's go home." Reluctantly, she gathered her belongings. With one last glance at her mother, she allowed him to escort her out of the room.

As always, Maryann kept up a steady stream of conversation as they drove to the empty East Boston apartment. This time, however, Diana didn't feel it was necessary for her sister-in-law to try to lift her spirits. Guilty though it made her feel, she found it easier and easier to forget her mother each time she left the nursing home.

"Steak *au poivre* or chicken, miss?"

Diana started and put her daydream aside. "Oh ... I'm sorry. I have a choice?"

The stewardess nodded, "Steak or lemon chicken?"

"Chicken, please."

"And your companion?"

"I'm not sure. You'll have to wait until he returns."

Though she had no idea how long she had been lost in thought, she did know that Gene had been gone well over half an hour. Perhaps he was having a drink in one of the bars on board. Maybe he had met someone he knew. Maybe he was using the flight time to get to know the blonde tennis player he had eyed covertly while they waited to board the plane. Her boss tried diligently to keep his sex life private, but she had known for a long time of his affairs and respected his privilege of keeping that part of his life separate from business. She claimed the same privacy, though she had kept her love life a secret far better than Gene.

Well aware that Monroe had been trying to match her up with his male customers for the past couple of years, Diana also knew he thought she was being extremely cold when she consistently turned the men down. What he *didn't* know was that she refused dates simply because she was terrified of being caught in a conversation where she couldn't keep up. And what if they found out where she lived? How could she have someone pick her up at the apartment on Orleans Street?

However, she was not without dates, as she knew Monroe suspected —she dated boys from East Boston; some had grown up in the same neighborhood with her or had been classmates. None had affected her the way Vito had; in fact, her dates always seemed to want more than she was willing to give. Sex was fine. She needed and wanted that type of affection, but if her partner asked to spend more than one night a week with her, they never saw Diana Colucci on an intimate level again.

None of her dates ever realized her job meant more to her than her relationships. She chalked that up to the fact that Italian males never believed a woman could care about anything besides kids, kitchens, and coffee klatches.

To that ancient ideal, she thumbed her nose and as long as her sexual needs were met, she remained kind, charming, and compassionate. If they requested anything more, her face turned to stone, as if a shade had been dropped over her features and her first instinct was to pull away. Love, to Diana, equaled pain.

Gene settled himself into the seat beside her. Resplendent in a tailored gray silk suit which made him look every inch the distinguished banker his father had been, his blonde hair neatly combed to the side, a small gold ring on his right index finger and his Rolex on the other wrist, Monroe attracted the attention of both sexes. He reeked of money and status, carried himself with dignity, and exuded the confidence which had been part of his manner since his teenage years.

"Sorry. I saw a couple who used to rent our villa in St. Barth's. Just had to stop and say hello. Did they serve dinner yet?"

She shook her head, sending a sheaf of shiny black hair swinging over her cheeks. "I didn't order for you. You'd better tell them what you want."

While he went forward to speak to the attendant, she straightened out her skirt and put the flight magazine back into the pocket in the seat in front of her.

"Done," he announced, settling into the seat. "Now, my dear, we really do need to have a talk before we land. I'd like you to know where we're going and who we'll be seeing." He coughed politely behind his hand and leaned back.

"Meredith Shaw Villechaux, my cousin twice-removed, is putting us up in her villa in Fontainebleau. We'll stay there through Christmas. She always has a wonderful Christmas Eve masquerade ball, and on Christmas Day the place is full of musicians, jugglers, actors and such. 'Festive' is the word for cousin Meredith. You'll enjoy her. People often say she reminds them of Elizabeth Taylor; however, I feel Meredith has a little more class than an actress. Don't tell Liz I said that!" He wagged a finger playfully.

Trying very hard to control the butterflies in her stomach, Diana forced herself to sit and listen to her boss, though fairly bursting with questions. This couldn't possibly be happening to her! It was too much like a fairy tale!

"She married some count ages ago and has been spending his money—rather well, I imagine—ever since. Don't be surprised when you see her. She's not what you'd expect, coming from a family like mine. A large mouth, that woman has, but her heart is twice as large.

"From Meredith's we go to Vienna for the New Year's Ball Duchess Maria holds every year." He stopped for a moment, apparently in thought, then turned to her, concern on his face. "You *did* bring formal clothing, I hope."

Nodding, she felt suddenly aware the clothes she had been so excited about two weeks ago would seem like thrift shop rejects to the class of people Gene was describing. Having visited Arnie two days after getting the tickets from Monroe, she cajoled him into releasing some of the money she had been saving for the past three years and with over three thousand dollars in her hand, she had gone on the wildest shopping spree she ever imagined.

Later, when Maryann and she were sitting in a booth at Friendly's Restaurant on Tremont Street, legs stretched out in front of them, totally exhausted, she vaguely remembered buying two wonderfully sexy long gowns, three short formal dresses, two new suits suitable for business appointments, the jersey Skirt and boiled wool jacket she wore now, and, at Maryann's suggestion, a peignoir set in midnight blue chiffon. Boxes of shoes stood stacked beside them on the floor and in her pocketbook was her most cherished buy—a set of diamond studs which sparkled irresistibly when the saleswoman held them up against Diana's cheeks. In a quick two sentences, she told her boss of her purchases, watching his face in the hope he would give her a sign that what she brought was proper and acceptable.

Nodding solemnly, Monroe continued. "You'll need to be well rested after the parties because we have a full schedule of shop-hopping, auctions, and appointments to buy collections from some of my old friends on the Continent. You'll get an education, darling, be sure of that."

Happily, she nodded. There was nothing she wanted more than for Monroe to teach her all he knew. Gazing out the window at the passing blue and white sky, she sighed, thinking she had never been quite so optimistic about her future.

Chapter Eleven

Paris, Christmas, 1980

Diana's nose remained pressed against the window of the Citroen from the moment they left Orly Airport until the car wound its way through Paris and headed toward the Loire region and Chateauroux, Meredith's mansion. The elegant, pale- faced women who walked quickly along Paris's main streets fascinated her. The stone-fronted buildings appeared to have been in place so long they might have risen right out of the brick sidewalks. Her heart pounded as they circled the Arc de Triomphe, and she leaned her head back as far as it would go to see the top of the Eiffel Tower. Several times, she breathed a long, spellbound sigh or clasped her hands together over her open mouth. She knew she probably seemed like Dorothy in the Land of Oz, but she didn't care. She had waited a lifetime to see Europe—there was no need to act indifferent now that she was here.

"But, Monsieur, Paris at rush hour?" the chauffeur had protested.

"Mademoiselle has never been to the city." Gene patted the Frenchman's shoulder and nodded knowingly. "We have plenty of time to reach the estate before dear cousin Meredith starts throwing one of her famous fits."

The chauffeur obligingly drove past the world-famous monuments with the nonchalant attitude of one who had lived with the magnificent structures every day. Gene could have acted the same way since his first trip to Paris had been when he was just a boy. Diana was grateful he didn't. Instead, he regaled her with stories of how the city had changed, as well as telling her its long and romantically rich history. He told her of spending his college vacations exploring the streets of Paris and of scouring the museums and Parisian flea markets in search of the ultimate art or antique treasure.

"This is where I really learned how one could get addicted to antiques," he said as they passed yet another museum. "I made a lot of mistakes, picked up pieces of porcelain that were not really porcelain, bronzes that were only second-rate iron statues. After a while, I learned to study the dealers' expressions, knowing that only a rare few could keep a straight face, an honest face. You must be aware of what's going on in other peoples' minds in the antique business. It's almost a sixth sense. A study in psychology, if you will. By reading all the books, you learn the different styles, the eras, the ways to tell whether something has been repaired, but when it comes to dealing with people, it must be instinct. Instinct. So important."

He paused, as if giving the words a chance to settle in her mind. "Antique dealers spend all their time chasing treasures, making contacts with people who may turn around and sell their wares to someone else. It's a constant chase. A tiring chase. But, ah . . . that's what makes us all come back." He lit a cigarette before turning to contemplate the look on her face. "What do you think, Diana? Is it still something you want to do?"

"More than ever," she breathed.

"It's a lot of work. Sometimes a very frustrating job."

"That's all right. I still want to learn as much as you can teach me."

Turning from her boss, she looked once more out the window at the gray and brown streets of Paris. If I blink, she thought, it will all disappear and I'll be back on Orleans Street feeding Mama her supper. Casting a sidelong glance at Monroe, who sat casually wedged in the other corner of the seat, she thought of the incredible gamble he was taking on her ability to help him make the changes in his shop. With her hands clasped tightly around her -leather purse, she sent up a silent prayer that she would be able to meet his expectations.

Going south, the road became less traveled; the noisy bustle of the city was left further and further behind. Gene settled back and watched with unmitigated pleasure as Diana's eyes danced like a child seeing her first Christmas tree as the Citroen passed one castle after another.

"That one, with the octagonal tower, is where Catherine de Medici kept her potions and poisons." He pointed to their left. "Further down the road you'll see Chaumont and Chenoneaux, two castles which were gifts from Henry II to his women. Chenoneaux went to Diane de Poitiers, his favorite. Beautiful, isn't it? I'ye always thought it was such a graceful place. Chaumont, on the other hand, is gray and grim and was given to his wife, Catherine de Medici. When he died, Catherine forced Diane to exchange homes. She was a witch, that one."

He kept up his travel monologue throughout the trip, interrupted by constant questions from Diana, who seemed afraid she would miss something.

"Is Chateauroux as beautiful as the other castles we've seen?" Opening her window a bit, she shut it quickly when the cool winter air pushed its way inside. She imagined the air would smell different in the countryside, and she was right, though it was not heavy with blossoms as it must be during spring.

"You'll see," her employer said, folding his gray Hermes leather gloves in his lap.

Looking at him, she could hardly believe a gentleman of his stature held her in such high regard, but, she had to admit, her heart warmed with their friendship. She was grateful for the relationship they had built. His patience with her, his willingness to pass on the knowledge which had taken him years to accumulate, his trust and faith in her business judgment had helped her to grow. Now she felt on the verge of gaining an even deeper insight into a world which normally would have been far beyond her means.

The road changed suddenly from pavement to a light green gravel, accentuated by long lawns reaching out on both sides of the road in elegantly curved designs. A discreet sign indicated a change in speed was necessary. The Citroen rolled slowly along, giving them a chance to study the small groups of peacocks which appeared on the right side of the car as they preened and spread their colorful fans. Overhead a falcon soared, its wide wings floating effortlessly above the poplar trees bordering the road. His call pierced the air, sending shivers up her spine.

Though the season was wrong for flowers, in her imagination they bloomed profusely, lining the road with lush purple and pink blossoms right up to the front door of the chateau which they could now see in the distance.

"Is it . . . ?"

"Yes, my dear, it's Chateauroux, otherwise known as my dear cousin's *summer* home. 112 rooms, eight towers, a ballroom which has held 500 easily, 85 fireplaces, and no central heating. Just to get the place warm for the Christmas festivities costs Meredith a pretty penny, even for *her* large pocketbook."

Gene adjusted the scarf around his throat in anticipation of the chill he always felt when entering the bedroom Meredith reserved for him. He often wondered whether his cousin found a perverse pleasure in subjecting her guests to the dampness of the stone-walled rooms. Perhaps that was the reason she seldom ordered one of her staff to light a fire until the guests were ensconced in their suites. Knowing Meredith, it was just another way to flex her power. Shaking his shoulders, he dismissed the thought and focused on Diana's captivating face as she beheld his cousin's castle.

The stately white building, slightly Moorish in design, still retained its French flavor. Above the second and third tiers, gracefully arched windows looked out upon white and beige towers. Sculptured gardens sported gazebos and areas purely devoted to raising the prized English roses cherished by Merry's Japanese gardener, Mr. Yamamoto. Rich turquoise-colored tiles etched with gold and silver designs lined the arched entryway where the Citroen stopped, and inside the entry, long chains secured bronze lanterns that seemed as old as the castle.

They had not had time to get out of the car when, from behind the massive carved oak doors, came a contingent of black-and-white-suited maids and butlers,

"Mr. Monroe, how nice to have you back." A tall, balding man in black tails, white tie and vest, took Gene's briefcase and smiled warmly. "And this must be Miss Colucci," he commented in a distinctly British accent as he took Diana's bag. "The Countess has been expecting you. She's waiting in the library. Allow me to show you to your rooms before I take you to her."

Diana resisted the temptation to tilt her head back and look straight up at the hallway ceilings, painted with magnificent frescoes. The curve of each wall was delineated by hand-painted blue and white tiles, each depicting a different countryside scene, *I could spend the next two weeks just exploring this wonderful place,* she thought, *and still not see it all.*

Swallowing hard, she fought a sudden onslaught of homesickness and wished she could call Maryann right away to check on the boys. If things had been different, it would have been Mama who would have received the call. But the past would never change, and all she could do now was to look to the future. She smiled. The future, at least, appeared to be bright.

Following the butler's dark figure, her eyes took a moment to adjust to the muted reds and browns of the large lobby. On each wall were portraits of the Count's family. Gene told her, and though she had not seen examples other than in books, she knew intuitively that some of the paintings were done by 17th and 18th century artists.

The pink and gray marble floors echoed the staccato sound of her heels and the flat slap of Gene's shoes as they followed the butler up a wide, ornately decorated staircase. At the top, the man took an abrupt right, continuing down a long hall. Their footsteps became noiseless. The floor was covered with Orientals piled on top of each other, seemingly as thick as mattresses.

"Fernwood," Gene called, "don't tell me we're going down to the other end of the mansion. Merry knows how I hate the cold, and that end of the hall never seems to warm up."

"No, sir. Your regular room is ready," Fernwood answered without turning his head. "We've had a fire in the grate since early morning. I'm sure you'll be quite toasty."

Monroe winked in Diana's direction as he lit another Gauloise. "Never know about these English butlers in French mansions. Doesn't quite make sense, does it? Of course, butlers always should be English, shouldn't they?" he teased *sotto voce.* Though Fernwood didn't react, she was certain he had heard and she had the feeling Gene had teased him in this manner before.

"I'll show you your room, miss," Fernwood intoned, once he was satisfied Gene was comfortable and wanting for nothing. The sumptuously decorated suite, done in rich shades of purple with heavily carved mahogany bedroom pieces, came complete with roaring fire, as Fernwood had promised. Her boss winked at her one more time as he closed the heavy door.

And now for mine, she thought. Fernwood opened a door and led her inside, quickly walking over to the window to pull open the floor-length peach and white brocade curtains. The weak December sun was allowed one last chance to shine into the room, throwing a glint of gold around the edges of the furniture, making them appear soft and ethereal like an ancient photograph.

"Would you like a brandy or, perhaps, a cup of tea brought to you?" he asked as he opened her suitcase.

"No, thank you, Fernwood," she replied. All the books she had read never mentioned how to act with butlers. Should she tip him?

He nodded. "The maid will be in to help you unpack once you are settled. In the meantime, feel free to take a few moments to freshen up and just ring me when you're ready." He indicated she should pull on a gold rope which hung from the ceiling next to one of the bed's posters. She muffled a giggle. The only time she had ever seen such a device was in a "Three Stooges" movie she had watched with the boys one rainy Saturday afternoon. Her immediate thought was that if the butler kept pulling on the rope, it would bring something crashing down on his head. Ducking her chin, she made a pretense of getting something from her suitcase while the butler let himself out.

When the door closed, she turned to examine her room, a mischievous grin still playing about her lips. She was suddenly struck by how good it felt to smile again, how long she had felt serious, as if the problems of the world rested on her shoulders, and how much she heeded this vacation. For a moment, she stared out the window at the lengthening shadows in the garden beneath her balcony, watched the doves swoop in and around the towers above, and felt extremely lucky to be alive and well. And visiting France.

Sitting on the plush peach-colored down comforter covering the four-poster bed, she let her shoes slip off and took a moment to take in her surroundings. On a Louis XIV dressing table in the corner sat a bouquet of calla lilies in a gold Tiffany vase. The pure white of their blossoms matched the white and gold scrollwork covering every inch of the dressing table. Normally, the room, with its marble walls and red mahogany ceilings, would have been dark and dismal, but a feminine touch had brightened all the bleak corners without losing a bit of the pomp and circumstance.

The peach theme was repeated in a dressing screen standing in the far corner. Walking closer to it, she noticed it was a hand-painted pastel of women at the seashore, reminiscent of one she had seen sold at a Phillips auction in New York. Her curiosity made her get down on her hands and knees to search for a signature.

"I hope the maid cleaned under there." A low, sensuous voice, though quiet, startled her. Bringing her head up abruptly, she knocked the screen to the side. The woman chuckled softly and sashayed. into the room, closing the tall oak door behind her.

"I'm sorry," she continued, "I just couldn't wait to meet the only woman my cousin has ever brought home."

Gene had been right. The woman standing in front of Diana resembled a doyenne in every way. She was extremely plump and dressed from head to foot in what appeared to be layers of chiffon scarves. Why hadn't she knocked?

"Get up, cherie. Come," the Countess beckoned, patting a peach embroidered loveseat in front of one of the long windows. "Tell me all about you and Gene."

Smoothing her skirt, Diana simultaneously wiped the perspiration off both palms. "Gene's my boss. I think you have the wrong idea," she began, knowing her voice was stilted and anxious. "We're here for a business trip and ... it was my Christmas present because . . . well, I work for Mr. Monroe. I run the shop on Charles Street."

"Oh, *merde alors!*" Meredith slapped a plump thigh with her black lace fan. "I thought I was in for some juicy gossip." She sighed heavily. Every piece of chiffon appeared to breathe with her. "Guess Gene hasn't changed after all, eh?"

Diana smiled in spite of the Countess's apparent disappointment and shook her head. "I'm only here for business. And I'm glad we got that straightened out right away."

"Well, in that case . . ." Meredith reached out a bejeweled hand, a smile twinkling in her eyes and on her lips, "we'll have to make sure you meet someone truly wonderful. You know, all my friends call me a Jewish mother because I just adore matchmaking and you're so lovely it's going to be incredibly easy . . ."

Still talking a thousand words a minute, she ushered Diana down the hall to the library where Gene waited, a cognac in his hand and a meerschaum dangling from his mouth.

"Ah, she's gotten you already, I see." He walked towards them and kissed his cousin affectionately on both cheeks. Winking at Diana over Meredith's shoulder, he said, "Has she grilled you about my comings and goings yet?"

"Gene!" Slapping him playfully, Meredith swept into the center of the room. "How could you say such a thing?"

"Now come. Merry. Don't you think I know you by now? If you're not *finding* gossip, you're *making* some."

She plunked down on an overstuffed chair and folded one leg over the other with great difficulty. With a teasing look, she smiled at Diana. "What else could be more fun? God knows my life is horribly dull these days. So, Gene, tell me where you're off to when you leave us. We only have a few hours before the other guests start to arrive. I want to know *everything.*"

While Diana sat and listened, the two cousins spoke of people whose names seemed vaguely familiar. When the conversation became too family- centered for her to keep up, she daydreamed, looking around the room at the walls full of ancient leather-bound books. By the time the cognac had warmed her, she had unconsciously sunk her toes into the rug in front of her chair, and was almost drowsing.

"Diana, darling," Meredith's voice roused her. "Let me see what you plan to wear to the party. Perhaps I have some jewelry you could borrow. Lord knows, I never get to wear all of it myself. Besides, it's such fun to share, don't you think?" A swish of chiffon and Chanel No. 5, and Meredith motioned for her to follow.

Three hours later, in a Cinderella-like transformation, Diana was dressed in a hot pink, strapless silk gown Meredith had plucked from a closet bigger than most living rooms. The gown accentuated her full bosom and ivory skin while mysteriously coaxing her blue eyes to their fullest and deepest shade. Meredith felt sure some of the younger woman's sparkle was due to the excitement Diana felt in seeing herself transformed into the striking female before her in the cheval mirror. There had been days when she felt like that, too. Long ago. Too damn long ago. Now that thrill had to be stolen or gotten vicariously.

"Here, cherie," she crooned, sliding a pair of dangling diamond earrings against Diana's neck. "Put these on. They'll look even more dramatic once your hair is up. You don't need anything against your neck. It's perfect. The gown must be off your shoulders, your neck is so long and lovely. How many women try to have the looks you have naturally? God knows, I've had plenty of neck lifts and tummy tucks and I *still* don't even come close to svelte." She sighed, her large breasts heaving in rhythm, and turned to leave. "You're on your own now, my sweet. I'll see you downstairs at the ball. Must run and try to do some magic on myself. Never seems I can do as much for this old body as I can for others. Ciao!"

Closing the door, she took one long, last look at the raven-haired beauty and sighed. Those days were long ago, but how nice it would be to have someone new, someone really special, to show off to all the snobs who would soon fill the ballroom. With a thousand old memories bringing life to her limbs, she heard the door lock click and began humming a waltz as she headed down the hall to her own room.

Diana held the earrings in her hand. "Can you ever get a word in edgewise?" she asked the maid who continued bustling around her ankles, pulling the dress's skirt out here or smoothing a wrinkle there.

The maid smiled and shook her head as if not understanding a word Diana said. Without speaking, the woman finished doing her job, then ushered her into the hall where Gene leaned against the wall, smoking a cigarette and seemingly lost in thought. Looking up, he nodded approvingly.

"I'm going to have my work cut out for me," he murmured as he patted the hand she slipped through the crook in his arm. "It's a good thing you're just my employee and not my daughter or I'd feel inclined to defend your honor."

She smiled and patted her stomach, trying to calm the butterflies. "I'm a big girl," she answered with a confidence she didn't feel. "I'm sure I can take care of myself."

Together they walked noiselessly down the hallway and began the long descent down the twenty-foot-wide marble staircase. From the ballroom she heard the orchestra playing a Strauss waltz. She gripped his arm tightly when they came to the doorway of the room, already abuzz with guests.

"I don't know what to do," she whispered, her limbs suddenly frozen, refusing to move. I'm in over my head, she thought. These people are millionaires . . . billionaires . . . royalty and stars. God, get me out of here.

"Don't worry. They're just people, too." Gene ushered her past the refined group of party-goers clustered around the ballroom's entrance, nodding and smiling as he walked confidently into the hall. "You look wonderful. Just act like you go to these soirees every week. And smile, darling. You're having a good time. Don't ever let anyone think differently. That's the first trick you'll learn from these phonies."

Lifting his head, he spoke briefly to some of the couples they passed, then cast a sidelong glance at her. "You're doing just fine, Diana. Now just remember what I said, because I won't be next to you all night."

The orchestra stopped momentarily, then, without missing more than a few beats, struck up another waltz. She reached for a glass of champagne offered on a silver tray by a waiter dressed in tails. I'm going to be drunk, she thought, then I'll *really* make a fool of myself. Sipping the drink, a few bubbles escaped into her nose. She sneezed as a white-haired gentleman presented himself before her.

"May I have this dance, mademoiselle? It is all right. Gene, is it not?" he asked, bowing from the waist.

Nodding encouragingly. Gene stepped back, taking his glass as well as hers. "Another cousin," he said, as the white-haired man swept her away. "Albert Cameron Morgan, meet Diana Colucci."

With an encouraging smile, he watched for a few moments as they whirled around the floor, then disappeared into the burgeoning crowd.

She had little to worry about—Albert Cameron Morgan wasn't interested in carrying on a conversation. He seemed more concerned about who would see him on the dance floor and she suspected that he had chosen her just because she was young and fairly attractive. One, two, three. One, two, three. Those days in the kitchen with the long-handled broom were finally paying off. Surprisingly, he danced well. So smoothly, in fact, that she barely needed to count anymore. The music swirled around her as the women's dresses swished with their movement. She held her head high and her shoulders back. Morgan smiled up at her for she seemed to have grown several inches and was now taller than he. As she smiled back, she realized she was having a good time. Better than that, a grand time!

The next couple of hours passed in what seemed like a golden haze. Every time she caught a glimpse of herself in the mirrored wall, gliding by on one handsome man's arm after another, she could hardly believe her own reflection. She was introduced to aristocracy from all corners of Europe, even meeting a couple who, as Meredith whispered in her ear, were displaced Russian royalty. Faces previously seen only in international society columns floated by, sometimes acknowledging her presence with a regal smile or nod. Entranced, she took it all in, listening on the fringe of conversations about oil holdings, the latest film at Cannes, and last week's record-breaking sale at Sotheby's. More than once, she wished she had a tape recorder so she wouldn't have to rely on memory when reliving the evening for Maryann and Robert.

From his place leaning against an open balcony door, his usual cigarette in his hand, Gene watched his employee. He felt like he had done the society world a great favor by introducing her to the crowd gathered in Meredith's ballroom. It was good for a group like this to meet real people. Freshly exciting people. Women who were not only beautiful but intelligent. He grinned, taking another puff. And they didn't know who she was. It was driving them crazy.

Dukes and duchesses, wealthy oil magnates, and screen stars—all confessed their curiosity about Diana Colucci. Gene had underestimated her, though he was not amazed she was able to hold her own with people so easily bored with the wealth and whirlwind atmosphere of their own lives. Yet why should I be surprised, he mused. She can hold her own against Boston's matrons, the toughest critics in the universe. Europeans are easy after the Brahmin crowd.

With a sense of satisfaction, he nonchalantly nodded at a couple he vaguely remembered from the Riviera last year, then turned his attention back to Diana. A burgeoning pride filled his chest as he watched her talking to the Hardwicks—oil, weren't they?—and wondered if this was the way he would have felt had he had a daughter of his own.

Meredith, too, had seen Diana's transformation and knew she was responsible for part of it. The right clothes and jewelry always gave a woman extra confidence. But her thoughts focused on how to capitalize on the beauty's charms. Gene should be ashamed of himself if he hadn't thought the same way. What an addition to a business! Brains and beauty and, from what she could see, Diana also had an untapped sense of taste and elegance. Yes, he would do well to mine that talent. She must tell him so.

Once she was able to disengage Carla Giovanni— the poorest and most irritating of the well-known Giovanni shipping family-from bending her ear about the latest tragedy in her life. Merry headed over to her cousin. He stood by one of the balconies watching the swirling crowd pass him by.

"My darling Gene," she purred, sidling up to him, pressing her ample body against his angular frame, "The one talent you never had was dancing. You really should try it occasionally."

He shook his head. "It's much more fun watching from the sidelines. You wouldn't believe what I see. It's better than any theater or opera. Really, Merry, you ought to charge admission for ringside seats. Look over there—Countess Juanita is trying to hide her lover from her husband while the Count spends his dance time looking down as many bosoms as possible and . . ."

She chuckled and waved her feathered fan in front of her face. "That's not what I wanted to talk about, dear. I think you've found yourself a real treasure." She nodded toward Diana, who stood talking to a dark-haired gentleman. "What are you going to do with her? You can't keep her in stuffy old Boston . . ."

Gene laughed softly, then took a puff on his Gauloise. "Meredith, you underestimate me. Don't you think I've already begun training her? I must say, though, I never thought she would blend in quite so easily."

"Where did she come from. Gene? What's her background?" She steered her cousin to one of the eight strategically-located bars while he described Diana's tragic childhood. Listening silently, her eyes ever active, watching her guests, occasionally nodding and smiling, she never let her attention waver from her cousin.

"Such a romantic story," she said when he finished and reached for his champagne glass. "But we mustn't spread it around, dear cousin. If one of these pompous dukes falls for her, it would be much better if he knew nothing until afterwards."

Gene spun to face his cousin. "You can't try to run this woman's life. She's a person, not one of your play toys. And she's my employee. Besides, she won't allow it."

"Oh, come now. Do you think I would try to do that?"

"Most definitely. You've always gotten great pleasure out of manipulating people."

"Well, dearest cousin, I just hope you realize what a treasure you have there and that *you* use her to her fullest. Business tools are not just machines, you know. Some of the best assets are people. And I think you'd better pay attention to the one out there."

Chapter Twelve

Diana leaned her forehead on the South American's shoulder. He was the most attentive of the men who had danced with her this evening—and the most handsome—and she found herself liking the way he made her feel. His ample shoulder seemed the perfect place for a respite from the endless dancing. New shoes were definitely not meant to be broken in waltzing on marble floors.

The man was just a little taller than she, his coloring almost a mirror of her own, except that Luis Quintana's eyes were a deep brown and his skin more olive. He carried himself with a dignity befitting royalty, yet she instinctively realized his posture had more to do with how he felt about himself than with breeding. Dressed in a form-fitting white tux, the jacket of which was casually open, it was easy to see he kept himself in shape. The jacket's shoulders hugged him snugly while the cummerbund encircled a slim waist and flat, tight hips topped legs which moved quite smoothly to anything the orchestra could play. Forcing a smile to her Ups, she tried to quell her growing awareness of his body, the first signal that warned she might not make it through the evening alone. Closing her eyes, she tried not to imagine what he'd be like in bed.

In spite of the din made by three or four hundred people milling around the ballroom, she had discovered that the heavy-lidded, magnetic man was from Colombia, that his business took him all over the world, and that he knew a good many of the people who were guests at the mansion. He, too, had been asked to stay the weekend, and he seemed quite pleased she had the room directly below his. She instantly regretted telling him.

As he spoke, Luis's eyes were constantly in motion, taking in every little incident in the ballroom. His associates, as Quintana referred to them, stood on the side of the room, watching their boss and making themselves available whenever a drink needed freshening or a chair needed to be produced between dances.

The couple discovered a mutual appreciation of Chopin when the orchestra played one of his earlier concertos and there were other things—many other things—they shared in common. As they began discovering each other, Luis leaned his head toward Diana, giving her his full attention. His eyes held hers in an amiable and open fashion, a frank gaze that stirred her deeply and fully. It was a feeling she had not experienced in quite a while ... a stimulating, roller-coaster sensation she had no intention of stopping.

"It's very hot in here," the Colombian said softly, looking deeply into her eyes as if attempting to relay his innermost thoughts. "Why don't we find a balcony and cool off for a couple of moments?" With a crook of his finger, he summoned two fresh glasses of - champagne, then dismissed his colleague and led her to an open balcony door.

Once in the fresh December air, she shivered.

"Are you cold?" He pulled his jacket open to envelop both of them. The movement reminded her of another time. Another man. She pulled *away*. *"Do* you want to go back inside?"

"No ... no. It's just the shock of the fresh air after the warmth in the ballroom. It's refreshing, actually." She leaned toward him, crossing her arms beneath her chest, longing to wind those arms around his waist and stretch her fingers up under the jacket to feel the muscles she knew must be just beneath the starched white shirt.

Taking a deep breath, she tilted her head to the sky. The stars floated against a brilliant jet-black background, the same stars which had once formed a canopy over the apartment house in East Boston.

"Beautiful, aren't they?" he whispered against her neck.

She nodded and continued to stare overhead, wishing her stomach would quit rolling and hoping he wouldn't sense her nervousness.

"When I was a little boy," he said in a hushed, almost reverent tone, "we used to herd the sheep from the mountains and I, being the youngest, inevitably had to stay overnight with the herd while the others went for Supplies. My brothers thought they were making a joke on me, but I was never afraid. I knew as long as the stars were out, I could find my way home. And I knew they were the same stars that were over my mother's head at home. Just thinking of her, I would feel safe. She told me stories about the people who lived in the land above the clouds, wonderful fairy tales that made me unafraid of the nighttime.

"But when the night was cloudy, then I was truly afraid because I could not see the stars. My brothers would take advantage of it, making me cry by leaving me alone, until my mother finally assured me the stars were still there behind the clouds. Somehow that little piece of information has always stuck with me. Every time I look at a night sky, I see my mother's face."

Diana lowered her head and stole a look at the handsome South American. He seemed unaware that she was still beside him. She felt almost as though she intruded on a secret place as she watched him. A dozen assorted emotions flitted across his dark face.

"The stars, they kind of make everything all right. Do they not?" She saw her upturned face register in his eyes. Illuminated by the light from the ballroom, his pupils enlarged to take over the whole chocolate brown orb. Abruptly, he turned away, pulling his coat from behind her.

"Is your mother ... is she still alive?" she asked, wanting to recapture the moment.

His face stiffened. Turning his head, he coughed. "She died when I was twelve. The guerrillas came into camp one day, when all the men were gone, and burned the huts. My mother was in one of those huts, nursing my new baby brother."

At a loss for words, she wanted to comfort the dark-haired man, but she was afraid he would not accept her hug.

"We should go back in," Luis said gruffly, his back still to her. "It is cold."

Puzzled, she followed him back into the ballroom. The mystery he had just managed to evoke made her pay even more attention to him than before. She was curious. She wanted to know his whole life story. Growing up in another country, traveling around the world. His life had been so different from hers. Yet . . . yet ... his sense of family seemed so familiar. Maybe different nationalities Weren't so different after all.

Though they danced the rest of the evening held tightly in each other's arms, Luis Quintana immediately reverted to the charming, attentive, yet distant man he had been before their trip to the balcony. It appeared that the furtive glance into the past was as far as he would let her into his thoughts.

Perhaps it was just as well, she thought, mounting the stairs to her room later that night. It was his deep secretiveness she respected more than anything else. And Lord knows, the Colucci family had *its* share of secrets! In time, perhaps they could share them.

Gene Penchance Monroe climbed between the purple satin sheets covering his bed, his mind full of thoughts of the future and how Diana Colucci would fit into it. He was alone, yet not sorry he didn't have someone to share the bed. He had too much on his mind to act excited about any of the insipid twenty-year-old boys who flitted around the ballroom's edges. Most were Italian, French, or Spanish. Poor boys who found an entry into the party in the hopes of finding a benefactor. Not this man, he mused. I have better things to do with my time than to babysit a whining child.

Cuddling beneath the thick comforter, he reached for the light and turned it off, his brows knitted together in deep concentration. Merry's comments had begun a train of thought which led him to the conclusion that Diana was probably the best acquisition he had were made. Merry was right. For the first time in his life, he thought of bringing in a business partner, and it was slightly disconcerting that he should be considering a woman. Yet, his powerful business acumen told him he wouldn't be making a mistake.

Though bothered by the appearance of the dark-haired man whom neither he nor Meredith knew, he trusted Diana. Their partnership would last a long, long time, if she decided to accept his offer. Besides, by next week they would be with him in Vienna and the South American would definitely be somewhere else. There was little to worry about. And if need be, he'd make a query about the man. The Monroe name had enough power to enable him to dig up the dirt on just about anybody in Europe. Why should the Latino be any different?

Before lighting another Gauloise, he sent a short prayer to his mother, the way he had almost every evening since her death, asking her to keep watch over the woman he had come to consider as dearly as a daughter.

It excited him that he was finally going to have a willing student, someone who shared his thoughts, interests, and aspirations, to carry on his business—maybe even do a better job than he had done-someone to help him realize his dream of building an antiques business to rival Israel Sack. With a wry smile; Gene realized it was the closest he would come to having a child. An heir.

Once retired to their bedroom. Countess Meredith Aubry Villechaux took a long look at her husband, the thin, rather tepid-looking Count Henri Salazar Villechaux.

When she was younger, Merry delighted in slipping out of the mansion for a rendezvous with her latest beau. No one blamed her for wanting more excitement than that offered by the insipid Henri. But she had neither the inclination nor the strength for moonlight trysts anymore. Besides, it was easier to stay at the mansion and play one of the games she invented through the years. Lately, she had begun thinking that women's bodies were far more exciting than men's. A whole new world of sex had opened up, one which offered more of the creature comforts and affection she sought, but did not find, during the years when she screwed every man in sight.

It was amazing what boredom and laziness did for sexual relationships. Ten years ago, she would have been spending the evening in any room other than her own, perhaps even traveling to two or three rooms before the evening was over. All the men who waited for her then were young and handsome. But there weren't any young and handsome men waiting in the wings for her these days. And Henri had made it clear long ago that it was his turn. Ah well, it was his money, after all. And he wasn't such a bad sort. Kept out of her way, let her go wherever she pleased, could even carry on an intelligent conversation. He was the only one who shared her bedroom suite now. And, she admitted, she needed the games they played behind closed doors to deal with her reality.

The maid turned down the bedcovers with an efficient swing of her arms. Turning, she removed the hairpin holding her cap and a tumble of chestnut- colored curls fell to below her shoulders. Henri's eyes went from the maid to his wife. He gave an almost imperceptible nod.

With a tiny outstretched hand, the maid took the ruby and gold rings which Merry handed to her and tucked them in a jewel case on the dressing table, then assisted her mistress in removing the heavy gold necklace which nestled in the layers of fat around the plump neck.

Her husband nodded as the maid stepped behind Meredith and slid her dress zipper down with a slow, languorous motion.

"What did you think of him? Do you know him?" Merry turned her body until her breasts brushed against the smaller woman's cheek. The maid deftly slipped the dress over Meredith's waist and let it fall to the floor.

"No, I don't," answered Henri, pulling down the zipper of his trousers. "Never saw him before, cherie."

As the tiny maid took one of Merry's large breasts in her mouth and began to suck voraciously on the long, erect nipple. Merry quivered. Henri took his small, gray penis into his hand and stroked it gently.

"We need to find out . . . oooh ... a little more about him."

Getting up from the chair, Henri let his pants drop to the floor. He walked to the bed where his wife and maid were actively writhing on its brocade cover.

"Later, cherie. We can find out anything you want. Later."

Luis Quintana stood in front of his balcony door, his back to the room.

"Find out why Salazar has not returned the loan, Karl. I did not come here to take no for an answer."

Behind Luis, Karl Wenzel, his associate, nodded and slipped silently from the room. Quintana's foot tapped impatiently against the carpeted floor. His mind whirled with figures, appointments, bits of conversations he had had during the evening.

Count Beckerhoff needed a shipment by Monday. Carla wanted to know if he would join her in March for her annual Grecian gala. And the dark- haired beauty who had inspired him to talk about his family . . . who was she?

Closing his eyes, he imagined the Andes mountain air closing around him. He saw the small hut where he grew up, heard the goats bleating, smelled the simple supper his mother cooked on the fire outside. Not for a long, long time had he remembered his childhood.

He shook his head vehemently. He did not desire such memories. If he allowed himself to continue, the nightmare would begin once again.

He heard the door to his room close quietly. Without turning, he said, "Well?"

"He understands," Karl replied. "You will be paid before we leave."

Though Gene, Luis, and Meredith had no way of knowing it, Diana lay wide awake in her room down the hall. Several lit candles made soft and eerily beautiful designs on the wall. She watched them lazily, trying to squelch the adrenaline still coursing through her veins.

As Henri joined his wife and maid on the bed, Diana thought of the differences between the streets of East Boston and the streets of Paris. She thought of how she had grown up feeling her neighborhood was the center of the world. How wrong she had been!

When Gene put out his tenth Gauloise, Diana mused about how her future had suddenly become brighter.

When Luis reached behind him to close the balcony door, she

was thinking of the options which had been abruptly presented before her.

When Henri got out of bed and lit three cigarettes—one for himself and two for his partners- she planned the languages she would learn in order to make it easier to understand the world of antiques.

When Gene finally drifted off to a Nembutal-induced sleep, she began to realize how much she needed to learn and wondered how soon she could start.

When Luis dismissed his associate and began rebuttoning the pearl enclosures of his tuxedo shirt, she remembered Arnie's words of encouragement that she could do anything she wanted.

When the maid quietly left the Count and Countess's room, their sleeping forms barely visible under the layers of brocade bedspread she had thrown over them, Diana was making a mental list of the steps she needed to take in order to open a shop of her own.

And when everyone in the mansion had finally settled down for the night, she was still wide awake, every nerve in her body twitching with the excitement of knowing that she was on the threshold of a new world.

Toward daybreak, she thought more and more of Luis Quintana. Looking toward the ceiling, she wondered if he thought of her. Of course not, she reasoned. Why would an international businessman be interested in a young Italian shop clerk?

Exhausted, the feelings she hadn't wanted to acknowledge were finally fighting their way through. Basically, she figured she had no right to expect any kind of relationship from a man like the Colombian. So, why torture herself? She knew better than to believe she would ever be part of his world. Why should she play the game of dreaming it might happen? No one had gotten this far under her skin for many years. She was angry she had let it happen.

With an almost ferocious determination, she shut her eyes and let her exhaustion take over, just as the sun's rays began to shine in her window.

Chapter Thirteen

Vienna, New Year's, 1980

Diana surveyed the large packing crate one more time before the men closed its top. Its contents represented a total of more than forty hours of work done by her and her boss, and she wanted to make sure that not one of their treasures would be in danger of breaking during transit.

Gene had left her in charge of packaging the pieces to make the trip to Beacon Hill, assuring her he was totally confident she'd have no problem handling the assignment, while he visited friends who were in the process of selling their collection of eighteenth century German paintings. "I'll be back in time to get ready for the New Year's party at Duchess Maria's mansion," he had said on his way out the door.

It had been almost a week since they had traveled from Merry's chateau, through the towns between Paris and Vienna, stopping at so many that the trip was now a blur for Diana. Gene's delight in being the first to show her around Europe had surprised both of them. By the time they reached the borders of France, they had become so comfortable in each other's presence and such good traveling companions, that Diana was certain she wouldn't have wanted to see Europe with anyone else. He made sure she saw all the important tourist attractions as they drove across the Continent and his knowledge of the small towns was so complete that he also showed her what life was like "off the rosy highway," as he called the main thoroughfares. She delighted in his observations, listening with interest to his many stories, and recording every little detail in her memory so that she could dip back into them some cold, rainy Boston day. Remembering Europe would be a pastime she could enjoy well into her old age.

They bought three small Van Gogh oils in Geneva, spending over four hundred eighty thousand American dollars, then packaged them the next day to travel by special delivery to the Charles Street shop. Gene called Miles to warn him the paintings were coming and Diana could tell by his patient expression that the boy hadn't understood what changes were being made in All That Glitters.

"Just accept the package, Miles," he finally said, glancing at her in exasperation. "I'll explain all the rest when we get home. And, Miles, before I forget: put an ad in the *Globe* that says we'll be closed for renovations and new stock arrivals the week of February 15. And call the Arnold Agency; tell them we're adding antiques to the inventory and that they should put together a press release which says we're in Europe right now buying some fabulous stock. Tell them to hold it until they can read it to me over the phone. I'll call them later." He paused. "Yes, we're doing the store over." Another longer pause. "I'm not telling you anymore. Miles, because if I do the whole town will know what's going on by the time I get home." He laughed quietly. "Yes, I know all too well about your gossiping. I must go now. There'll be other packages arriving after this one. Just pile them all in the storeroom until we get back. And Miles? Remember to put on the alarm service every night, will you?"

Hanging up the phone, he turned with a pleased smile. "We've got him totally confused. He kept saying 'but . . . but ... I don't know anything about antiques.' All That Glitters will be the talk of the town now."

"Then why did you tell him not to say anything? If he calls Arnold and Company to get the press release done, someone there will leak the news . . ."

"That's just the point," he said smugly. "If you want to launch a new business in Beantown, all you have to do is try to keep it a secret. People get so curious, that you end up with free publicity because everyone is trying to find out what's going on. Everyone who's anyone in Boston knows about my antique collection. Now they're going to know that I'm finally going to share my knowledge with the rest of them, and they'll be killing each other trying to be first in the door to see what we've brought home." With his arms crossed over his chest and his feet propped on an overstuffed hassock, he looked as pleased as a cat who had just lapped a gallon of cream.

Diana reflected, in quiet moments, how different the antique business was from the gift shop business. There were no order forms to fill out, no factories to call, no automatic shipments of new stock in ninety days. In the antiques world, each piece had to be discovered separately, like a treasure hunt. Sometimes collections could be bought. Gene had explained, but those were few and far between. Most dealers spent the major portion of their days on the road, hunting for particular gems which would please their customers or for that special artifact which would net them a windfall—again, he reminded her, that didn't happen very often. But when it did, it made all the work and the hours spent traveling worthwhile.

"The antique business is like no other," he said one 163

as they drove along a winding country road in Germany, where freshly-fallen snow layered tree branches in diamond-like splendor. At any moment, she expected to see a blond knight on horseback appear through the tall, dark forest stretching out on each side of them. "I guess most dealers are gypsies at heart. You have to be in order to keep fresh stock in the shop. And to keep on top of what's happening. Perhaps that's what I like about it so much."

"Then why did you open a gift shop instead of an antique shop?"

"It was easier at the time. I had already done a lot of traveling. It was time for me to stay home. But I kept up with the auctions, made connections throughout the world when I bought my own collection. That's important, Diana. Don't forget your connections. And never, *never* bum your bridges. It's hard sometimes to keep a smile on your face when people grab a piece you've had your eye on or steal the clients who've been coming to you for years. But you should always learn by your mistakes and remember that you might need that person someday. Maybe they'll have something you'll want or you'll have something you can sell to them. They're like a small family, antique dealers, and the people who are your competitors will also be the people from whom you'll buy and to whom you'll sell."

A treasure hunt, indeed. The more she learned, the more surprising it became.

She sighed and adjusted two of the smaller bundles at the top of the crate, pressing more packing paper over and around them before closing the lid.

"There," she said, slapping the slats on the side of the crate, "it's done."

The tall, blond men in blue work suits had been standing by patiently waiting for her to finish readjusting the packing job they had done, and now looked at her with vague smiles.

"Okay, you can take it now." She motioned toward the door.

Again, they looked at her without expression. She pantomimed the action of picking up the crate and carrying it through the door. This time the men smiled broadly, spoke to each other in the clipped, guttural tones of the Austrian language, and ushered the crate out the door.

Leaning against the doorjamb, she watched them gingerly balance the heavy crate over the top of the hall staircase banister, holding her breath until they were no longer in sight.

"Next time," she said, closing the door, "I'll know how to speak the language."

Within moments, she was dressed and out the door. Vienna awaited her! The old Austrian city's architecture was a curious blend of old and new—from ancient, many-tiered and saint-bedecked churches to the simple Modernistic style of those buildings designed to house the country's many art collections. Forming an almost complete circle around the city, the Ringstrasse was the street where most of the magnificent Old World buildings of Vienna had been constructed. Diana headed straight for the National Art Gallery, which she found with the help of a city street map the front desk provided.

The brisk walk brought her back in time. Spires on top of the stone and mortar buildings surrounding her soared to the heavens, their pointed and jagged edges appearing more grotesque than godly. Every other building was festooned with statues of famous people and saints which loomed precariously on rooftops and in naves on the sides of each. Her imagination conjured up Strauss's waltzes to linger in the air around her. The Vienna Boys' Choir echoed in her head and the clattering hooves of the Lippizaner stallions cut through the cold streets.

Vienna was Old World Europe. Old customs, old religion, old manners and graces. She breathed in its ambience, listening to the silence of the snow falling against the faces of the stone statues and noticed the rosy, round cheeks of the Austrians as they scurried past her, wrapped, as she was, in layers of clothes with scarves around their necks and feces.

She left the Gallery several hours later, feeling lightheaded and ravenous. On the way back to the hotel, she passed a bakery whose windows were full of braided breads, fruit-filled turnovers, and luscious three-layered chocolate cakes. The smells permeated the tiny side street. Succumbing to a mouth-watering desire, she picked out a mocha torte, nodded to the white-haired woman who handed it to her, then tried to figure out how much she owed. Again, she found herself wishing she knew their language. Finally, the woman took a couple of pieces of change from Diana's outstretched hand, shook her head and muttered to another, younger, woman behind the counter.

Taking a deep breath, she inhaled the smell of the torte as she wandered back out onto the street. The air was nippier now than it had been earlier and the afternoon light was gone, replaced by the early dusk of winter. She glanced skyward, the torte halfway to her mouth. A blanket of stars made a brilliant showing in the clear black sky. No snow tonight, she thought briefly, and stood in the cold Austrian street for a moment, thinking of Vito Vincenti and the nights they had spent on the rooftops in East Boston, looking up at the same stars, sharing their dreams. She sighed. He would have been so happy to know she was finally traveling to the countries she had dreamed about as a child.

"If you're up there, Marcus/Vito," she whispered. "Just remember I love you." In the northern part of the sky, a star twinkled brightly and fell southward. She smiled, feeling as if she had been answered by her long-ago friend.

Monroe opened the door, holding a handkerchief over his mouth, trying desperately to stop the coughing spasm he had been enduring for almost ten minutes. The sight of Diana, her cheeks rosy from the brisk Vienna wind, her eyes bright and sparkling and a wide smile on her face, relieved the worry he had felt when returning to the suite to find her gone.

"Where've you been?" he finally managed. "I was worried."

"Out exploring. And wait until I tell you what I discovered at the museum . . ."

"Diana, you really should have left a note or . . ."

"I'm sorry. I thought I'd be back before you were." She pulled off her leather gloves and walked over to the phone. "You know, you've really been doing too much. Don't you think you ought to rest a while before we go out tonight?"

Nodding, he winced as another spasm caught him off guard.

"You look terrible. Haven't you been sleeping? You look like you've been in a fight . . . black eyes and everything." She picked up the phone. "I'm getting you some tea. Now just sit down for a while and let's see if we can't get you feeling better. You have plenty of time to take a nap before tonight. Besides, no one will even notice if we're late, will they?"

"It's only a cold," he protested, thinking only of crawling into bed. Why now? It was this weather. The dampness. Yes, that was it.

"Well, then you should give in to it for a while. Right?"

Scurrying around the room, she picked up the packages he had left on the floor near the door and placed them on his desk. With an imperious gesture, she ushered him into bed, then plumped the pillows.

Though he tried not to show his pleasure, a sigh escaped his lips.

"Florence Nightingale," he murmured as another coughing spell began.

While she worked, she told him of the ancient books she had found in the Gallery, filled with illuminated pages created by the monks so many years ago, and of how fascinated she was with the art form. He nodded in the appropriate places and smiled weakly, interested in what she said but concentrating on trying to catch his breath. The spasms made him weaker and uncaring about anything but getting rid of the damn cough. By the time the tea finally arrived, his hacking was even getting to her. In fact, she seemed ready to go down to the kitchen to get the brew herself. Thankfully, the cook had sent a whole pot along with a sampling of the hotel's pastries.

"Here, now drink this," she said, handing him a cup, "then lie down for a while. I'll find some cough syrup and you can take some when you get up."

"Diana, I really don't need you to take care of me . . ."

"Who's going to do it if I don't?"

He smiled. She had a point. Gratefully, he laid his head down on the fat pillows she piled up behind him and closed his eyes.

"Are you sure you're all right. Gene?" Adjusting the small diamond earrings she had bought in Boston, she cast a sidelong glance at her boss. "I don't really have to go. We've already been to one ball. It doesn't bother me if we stay here."

"You look too gorgeous to stay home." He knotted his tie, then pulled on the tails of his tux jacket. "Besides, I promised the Vanderkellers and the Whitmans that we'd meet them there."

Moments later she breathed in the cigar and cigarette smoke of more than three hundred guests who were, as she was, dressed in their finest clothes and maintaining an air of dignified excitement. She coughed. Funny, how an ugly habit like smoking could bring her crashing back to earth.

The mansion had seemed small and unassuming from the outside, but as soon as Diana stepped through the large double brass doors which separated it from the street, she found herself awed by its magnificence. The main ballroom, the size of a football field, sported ten crystal chandeliers suspended almost fifty feet in the air. Two tiers of seats surrounded the room, one encircling the ballroom floor and the other on the mezzanine, directly above, seemingly used for spectators rather than dancers. Fanciful bronze balustrades, decorated with finely- carved swirling roses entwined around the throats of grotesque dragons, accentuated the seating area. Around the perimeter of the room busts of half- dressed women, designed to serve as columns, stood stately against the walls. Ionic arches trimmed the ceiling and large brass roses followed its shape and were repeated around its edges. Bouquets of real pink roses cascaded from the doorways and balconies and were massed in large vases throughout the outer lobby, emitting a scent that reminded Diana of Mrs. Capocetti's treasured rose garden.

"It's beautiful," she breathed, though her words were lost in the cacophony of the crowd.

Each woman who walked in the ballroom door was handed a long-stemmed rose. Diana put her nose to hers and covertly watched the glamorous crowd surrounding her. Across the entryway to the ballroom stood doormen, dressed in waistcoats, knee britches, and ruffled shirts, standing stiffly at attention and nodding solemnly to those couples who chose to enter the ballroom to take their chance on
the crowded dance floor.

"I can't believe this," she said to Gene.

He nodded hello to an older couple dressed in black and white who nodded back and passed by. Then he coughed quietly into a long silk handkerchief he had begun keeping in his hand at all times. "Why not?" he asked.

"I never thought places like this really existed. 1 thought they were all part of the fairytales we used to read when I was a kid. This is 1981! People are starving all over the world, there are new flights to space every time you turn around, and wars in . . . Well . . . just about everywhere. How can these people just dance the night away? It's like something out of one of the romance novels 1 used to read."

"Come now, Diana. It's New Year's Eve. You're not supposed to be intellectualizing. Sometimes you're too down to earth, my dear. You really should learn to relax and enjoy yourself."

She made a face at him, though she knew he was right and

concentrated instead on trying to remember every detail. But she couldn't help trying to estimate what the blond woman in the corner paid for the marvelous red silk gown she wore or what the diamond necklace around her neck would buy. She couldn't help imagining that the bald, fat man to her right was a penniless Duke and that the red-haired older woman he was with was his long-suffering wife. Diana continued playing the game while Gene disappeared into the crowd in search of champagne. She was thoroughly engrossed in her imaginings when a male hand appeared out of nowhere to surround her elbow.

Turning, she reached out, expecting Gene to hand her a glass of champagne. Instead, her hand was grasped in Luis Quintana's.

"You have been expecting me perhaps?" he asked quietly, a smile pulling up one corner of his mouth.

His skin was as warmly brown and burnished as she remembered it. She stifled an impulse to touch his cheek. Did his eyes get sexier or had they been that black when they first met? Why were her knees refusing to stay stiff, to hold her up? Luis continued to smile questioningly at her, and she realized with a start that he was waiting for an answer.

"No ... uh ... no, I was expecting ... I was reaching for a glass of champagne."

"Oh, do you want one? I will get one for you." He turned to leave.

"No, no, that's okay. Gene just went to get some." The South American's face became serious. "I am terribly sorry. I have imposed. I did not realize . . ." "Gene's my boss," she explained quickly. "Maybe you know him? Gene Penchance Monroe, III?" Luis's eyes brightened as he shook his full head of black hair. "No, I do not. But it is good to hear that you are not here with a husband. You are not married, are you?"

It was Diana's turn to shake her head. She clasped her hands tighter around the rose. "Are you?"

He smiled, a languid, dreamy movement like the swish of a panther's tail. "I have not yet found someone who would have me." He smiled, his unblinking eyes boring into hers. "Is it not amazing that I should find you in this crowd?"

"Find me? Were you looking for me?" Diana stopped, flustered. "Of course you weren't looking for me. It's just a coincidence . . . "

"Actually, I must be honest. It is not. I was indeed looking for the blue-eyed woman who danced so well with me at Count Villechaux's Christmas ball. You are the best and most beautiful partner I have ever had. Shall we try again?" He lifted a cocked arm to her and gestured to the already-crowded dance floor.

"I can't. Really. I should wait for Gene . . . he's getting the champagne."

"Very well, then. We shall wait. But only if you promise to tell me where you will be next. In fact, I want to know everything about where you have been and what your life is like and . . .."

"Here, Di." Gene stood at her elbow, holding a glass of sparkling liquid toward her. He nodded with a puzzled look toward Luis.

She introduced the two men, amused to watch their rooster-like antics as they sized each other up, clearly defining their space. It was immediately apparent that Gene found Luis attractive, but the South American, like a well-trained fox, had already sniffed Gene and found him an opponent. The die was cast. Obviously the two were not about to become lifelong friends.

"Shall we dance now, Diana?" Luis held his elbow out again, his eyes never leaving Gene's face, a challenge in his stance that even she could not ignore.

"You don't mind, do you. Gene?" Though she never felt the need to ask her employer for permission, he seemed offended by Luis's proprietary arm on Diana's. She wanted to make sure the gentle man she worked for would not be upset by being left alone.

"Go along, darling. Enjoy yourself. I'll be fine. After all, I know just about everyone here." The dignified, blond Bostonian made an expansive gesture with one elegant hand, coughing slightly as Diana and Luis walked onto the crowded ballroom floor.

As Luis swung her into his arms and waltzed her into the middle of the undulating crowd, Diana immediately became aware of the fact that her nose was a little larger than normal, her fingernails not perfectly long, her hair not styled to perfection like the other women around her. Feeling paled by their sophistication and glamour, she felt certain they would be able to discern that her dress came from Filene's Basement and was not a designer original. Reminded of the East Boston High School dance she had attended with Marcus, she was, for a moment, suspended in time, dressed in a homemade velvet mini-dress, Marcus at her elbow, his face red with the exertion of trying to master the "jerk." Her eyes misted over, and she wondered what the people who had made fun of them that night would think of her now.

The memories drifted out of her mind as soon as Luis brought her into his arms. No longer was she worried about everyone else The only person who mattered was the one who was physically closest. And his presence was overpowering. His breath was on her cheek, his chest against hers. Taking a deep breath, she held herself upright and concentrated on the music and the sounds of the other dancers. But her mind kept wandering back to the man whose hard shoulders moved underneath her hands, whose palm rested against hers, whose pores she could practically count, whose body heat seared through her dress, arousing the bare skin underneath. She had never been warned about not allowing her primal needs to overpower her intellect; in fact, it seemed only natural to press her body closer to his, to feel his warmth and to revel in the affection he offered.

The orchestra played the waltz from "Swan Lake," one of her favorites. The first time she had seen the ballet a few years ago, she had fallen in love with the dancers, the music, the story, the sets. In fact, everything had been perfect, except for the guy who had brought her.

She hummed the music softly, a childhood habit of covering her nervousness. Luis tilted his head down to hers, his eyes crinkling with a smile. She stopped.

"Oh, do not stop. You have a lovely voice," he said.

She smiled back, directly into his captivating eyes. Within seconds, she hummed once more.

"Who is she?" A small, nervous man appeared at Gene's elbow. His ferret-like face framed a miniscule mouth overly-filled with large teeth. His hawk like nose was full of reddish pockmarks, the result, as Freddy was so fond of saying, of a deadly bout with measles. Gene had always suspected the truth to be the worst case of acne known to humankind.

"How did you know she was with me, Frederick?" Monroe pulled his cigarette to his mouth and watched the dancers on the ballroom floor, his eyes never turning to meet the smaller man's,

"I know exactly who she is. Merry doesn't waste any time."

"Then why did you ask me?"

The little man tittered, then lowered his lids coquettishly. "Wanted to see what you would say, of course." Frederick's high-pitched voice ended in a squeal.

Gene had known the precious gems dealer for the last twenty years, but had never quite been able to squelch the reaction he had toward him —he often recoiled from the man as sharply as he would if someone had scraped a fingernail across a blackboard. Yet, a relationship with Frederick Boccaccio was necessary if one wanted the real news about the European art and antique scene. Freddy knew everything about everybody, which is one reason why Merry and he got along so well.

A long time ago. Gene made the mistake of letting too much champagne go to his head and responded to Frederick's advances. The little man had never let him forget about the faux pas. He knew he held something akin to blackmail over Gene's head and did not fail to snatch every opportunity to use it.

"Who's the man with her?" Gene asked.

"South American. He's new in the country, though I've seen him a couple of times on the Mediterranean. Last name begins with a Q. Some hard-to-pronounce Latin name. Anyway, Gene, why do *you* want to know?" He batted his eyelashes again. Monroe turned his head, trying to hold back his disgust.

"Just curious. Find out for me, will you, Freddie, old boy?"

"What'll it get me?"

Gene chuckled softly, then pulled on his cigarette. Let the little worm wonder, he thought. With a mysterious smile, he pulled away from Frederick's clutches and disappeared into the crowd.

Chapter Fourteen

With a sensual deftness that made Diana's legs threaten to buckle, Luis slid her black crepe dress up past her hips, letting his fingers trail against her outer thighs. His touch was as soft as a child's. She sighed, her eyes glued to his face, her skin seeming to breathe flames. Each of her senses was heightened and she wanted to use them all.

Her nostrils flared with the deep, musky smell of him, her fingertips tingled with the touch of the curled black hairs on his arm. She listened for his breathing and the words he huskily whispered into her palms, against her thighs, under her hair. She wanted to understand what he was saying, to have his lips pressed against hers so that she could inhale his words, so that she could run her tongue against his lower lip and inside the wet cavern of his mouth.

But all she could do was to lie back and let him ravage every pore of her, every muscle in her body, every nerve ending unceasingly alive, crying out for more.

They were in his room at the Kahlenberg Hotel. The ball was long-forgotten. Gene Monroe and his friends temporarily ghosts from Diana's past. All she could focus on, all that her mind would accept, was that the dark South American who was making her body feel as if it had spent the last twenty-five years waiting for his touch was beside her, around her, atop her, and she wanted nothing else.

The hotel overlooked Vienna and the Danube, or so she heard. They had been whisked there in a stately black Mercedes limousine. She had been ushered into the lobby by a red-coated valet, and within seconds they were in his sumptuously appointed suite on the top floor. She knew they were on the edge of the woods, that the balcony would give her an incredible view of the city, but she had seen nothing but Luis's eyes.

She slid her fingers down to meet his, reveling in the inch-by-inch movement of his stroke. "Luis," she whispered. "I've never been so close to someone so soon."

"We're not children," he whispered back, his face barely visible in the darkness though his eyes glowed with a tiger-like brilliance. "We know what we want. At least I do. I want you, my dark Italian beauty. And your eyes have told me you feel the same. Why deny it?" His hands slid upwards to caress her warm, slim back, his fingers spreading until they stretched from shoulder to shoulder. She shivered, arching herself towards him.

"I've never . . ." She felt his fingers slip around her belly and over the mounds of her breasts. "I've never . . . fallen into bed with someone ... I didn't know."

"But, *cara,* we know each other. We've shared secrets we've never shared with anyone else. I know you love the stars as much as I. And I know why." His fingers found her nipple and pulled at it insistently. She pulled at her lower lip with her teeth, feeling as though she were drowning in his words, his faint Spanish accent, his velvety voice. "I know you want and need this pleasure as a cat needs milk," he continued. "What more do I need to know? What more do *we* need? You are part of me. I am *all* of you." He nuzzled her neck and she felt a warm, tingling sensation where he was rubbing his palm against the hardness of her erect nipple.

Diana's senses swam, her vision blurred, and all seemed unreal as his thumb and forefinger captured her areola, tracing it and pulling at it until it felt as if it were connected to the most sensitive parts of her body and they were all alive at once. She moaned as he sought her lips with his, surrounding her mouth as the stars surround the moon, completely and brilliantly. She moaned again, feeling all her senses avoiding her normally astute reasoning, acting as traitors, leaving her inviolate and open to attack. Everything was muffled, her body felt as though it were floating through a cloud. She moved slowly, like someone drugged, in a pleasant dreamlike state, with no control over any of her muscles.

Strong and persistent, Luis found his way, leaving her no defense, allowing her no route to escape, though she didn't even want to try. With his tongue he aroused the most sensitive areas of her neck and throat, his fingers simultaneously working on the erotic regions below the soft mound of her belly. Her legs moved in syncopated rhythm, ridding themselves of the black crepe dress which had fallen around them. Her body told him, in a language completely its own, that he was master and that it would obey his every command.

Never, in all the times Diana had made love, had she felt so powerless. Usually it was she who made the moves, she who was the animal, taking what she so desperately needed and giving the lover no sympathy. Sex had been a necessary evil, something she needed—had to have. It was the affection she did not otherwise get. Now she was getting both and something new besides.

When his mouth encompassed her nipple, now ripe and full enough to be plucked from its breast like a piece of fruit, she silently acknowledged she had been won and acquiesced without regrets. Yet, in the midst of the red haze of their lovemaking, Diana wondered why such a passion should cause a faint flutter of fear to develop in the land between her legs and why those legs clenched so tightly when he finally entered with an organ so swollen it seemed vulgar.

Murmuring like a creature in distress, she surrendered her individuality to him as the hunted surrenders to the hunter. And found it incredibly, exciting. Forbidden. Titillating.

Her orgasm came almost immediately.

Moments later, she lay back against the silk sheets, satiated and sensual, while he inserted a jazz cassette into a large, intimidating-looking stereo system in the corner of the room. Lazily he lit a cigarette and passed it to her. She shook her head, too drowsy to accept, unable to reach her hand out to steady his so she could take a drag. She blinked when the smoke drifted her way. Tears rose in her eyes, and her nose was offended by the strange smell. Though she wished he wouldn't smoke, she had no energy to ask him to stop. His cigarettes smelled like no American ones she knew. Probably a Colombian brand, she reasoned sleepily.

Luis inhaled the fragrance of the flaring embers, breathing in the white plume of smoke as though it were the scent of a woman's body. With a close-lipped smile, he reached across the pillow to fondle the jutting peaks of Diana's breasts. She felt her breath quicken and turned towards him.

"Do not go," he whispered against her throat as he aligned his body with hers. His hand drifted down the curve of her hip and settled between her legs. He moved it oh-so-gently. "Stay with me for the night."

The dark-haired woman lay against the satin sheets, one hand flung over the edge of the bed, one leg folded over the sheet. The light from the full moon cast seductive shadows where her breasts rose and fell above the sheets. Luis let his eyes roam over every inch of her that was exposed, then he lifted the sheet with his foot so he could look at the rest.

Diana slept on, apparently oblivious to the fact that she was being watched. He smiled and licked his lips. Before his organ could rise of its own accord, he reached for it, gently stroking it, teasing it. Then he sighed. No, there was work to do.

He quietly slipped into his pants. Before he even had the door to the hallway fully open, Karl stood at attention before him.

"Did Marco do as we told him?" Luis whispered, letting the door close behind him with a muted click.

Karl nodded and handed over a fat envelope.

Quickly flipping through the bills, Luis felt the familiar thrill he always had when handling money. "It is all here?"

Karl nodded again.

"And did you . . ."

Another nod and Karl pulled a blunt-nosed revolver from his pocket.

"Good." Luis opened the door again and stepped inside.

Diana had turned in her sleep. The valley of her spine was now completely exposed. Luis licked his middle finger before drawing it down her back. With a little shiver, she turned over, smiled at him sleepily, and lifted her arms in silent invitation.

The Mediterranean, February, 1981

"Pull!" The round gray disk shot out into the blueness of the sky and sea. Squinting, Diana lifted the borrowed shotgun to her shoulder, sighted the disk, and squeezed the trigger gently. She was rewarded when the gray circle disappeared into the winter sun, splintering into hundreds of pieces.

"That was marvelous!" Luis's voice came from the deck behind her. "You are an incredibly quick learner. Soon you'll be able to challenge Karl to a duel." He laughed into the wind, his dark hair tossed by the Mediterranean Sea's mischievous air currents. Karl, Luis's constant companion and most trusted assistant, was a blond German whose actions were as stealthy as a vampire's. His slow, sly smile gave Diana a chill. She had no interest in challenging him to a duel, or even to a conversation for that matter.

"No," she yelled back, "I could never shoot another living being." Putting the rifle down, she smiled at her teacher, a small Italian man with whom she often talked of Sicily, then turned to walk toward Luis.

She walked slowly, luxuriating in the feel of her linen slacks against her legs and of the silk shirt Luis had had especially made for her by a designer in Marseilles. The sea rolled beneath the yacht's bow. She held onto a side railing for a moment. Though the sun was at its peak, the cool sea air threatened to whip its way under the heavy Greek fisherman's sweater she had thrown on over the shirt. She pulled it tightly around her.

For over a month she had accompanied Luis and his Colombian crew through Greece and the ports on the Mediterranean, meeting people whose names she could barely pronounce, let alone remember. They had danced on the veranda of an all-white villa which overlooked the Parthenon. They had shopped in the open markets in Morocco, where Luis bought her intricately-woven gold bracelets with azure stones. In Alexandria, he surprised her with a complete wardrobe made exclusively for her out of the finest silks. She swore she had gained at least five pounds, but it didn't seem to matter. No matter what she wore or how she looked, he made love to her with an unceasing fervor and she
had never been quite so completely satisfied.

He was spoiling her, she knew, but she learned to live with his generosity, even to enjoy it. She had objected at first when he kept offering gifts, but when his black-fringed lids lowered, making him look like a little boy whose mother had forgotten Christmas, she had to give in. He was so proud to be able to buy her treasures, he had told her. Please would she let him continue to find pleasure that way?

When Luis had first proposed she stay in Europe longer than originally planned, she had looked at him tentatively. She wondered if he made the offer simply to be polite or whether he really wanted her to travel with him, wanted to teach her all he knew about Southern France, the Riviera, Madagascar, and Egypt, as he had whispered in her ear one night after many hours of making love.

"I'll have to talk to Gene," she had said, trying not to let a tremor of uneasiness creep into her voice. How could she continue building a relationship with a man like Luis? He was worldly, wealthy, handsome. She, a poor shop clerk from Boston, supposed to be spending this "vacation" working with her boss. But Luis insisted and, finally, she did speak to Gene.

"You will not have to worry about money," Luis said. "I will take care of everything and . . . hush, *mi cara* ... we shall enjoy it, shall we not? The Senor will understand. I am sure he will urge you to stay with me, as a matter of fact." He grinned broadly, his eyes crinkling in the sexy way which always made her return the smile and understand the meaning behind it: the promise of making love at every possible opportunity. He was insatiable. And, now, so was she.

It had not been easy to break the news to the man who was responsible for her being in Europe in the first place. She remained awake all night, pacing back and forth in her hotel room, trying to put together words that would not offend her employer. Yet, no matter how many times she argued with herself, Luis was right. She would never again have this chance and she imagined Gene would be the first to understand.

Gene's eyes had clouded. He turned 40 face the lace-curtained window and fell silent. With his back toward her, he said, "I'd never stop you from having an opportunity to explore. Go. Take as much time as you need. I'll stay in Europe, too. It'll give me more time to put together stock for the shop. Of course. I'll have to call Miles and tell him we won't be back when we had originally planned . . ."

Her heart twisted in her chest and she took a few steps toward the slim man at the window before realizing he was turning around anyway. With a smile, Gene reached a hand out and patted her shoulder, exerting just enough pressure to tell her she had come far enough.

He may understand, she thought, but he still wasn't ready for a hug.

"Don't worry about me, darling. I'll be able to take care of myself." His eyes flickered to the side. "Just please take care. You don't know this man . . . things are not always the way they look."

"But, I . . ."

"You're an innocent. You know nothing of what goes on in the rest of the world. Just take care. Please?"

She nodded, a lump in her throat, and reached out a hand. Thor held onto each other's hands for a moment before Gene pulled away. "You just have to promise me one thing," he said, lighting a cigarette.

"Anything, Gene."

"If anything happens, contact me immediately. Protect yourself." His eyes clouded and he pursed his lips thoughtfully. "Learn all you can. Try to continue the education we've begun so that this time won't be entirely wasted. I know Quintana collects art. Go to the auctions or sales with him, make mental notes, remember faces and, most importantly, study the art you see. Study *everything*. Make good use of this time, Diana. It's something you probably won't get again. We're going to be pretty busy when we go home." A serious smile stretched his mouth to one side and he stifled a cough. Diana nodded once more as she solemnly made the promise. Then the moment was over and Monroe turned away.

She left him packing his bag for a trip to Rome. Both had chatted gaily about who and what they expected to see. She embraced him fondly at the hotel's entrance as they waited for their drivers. "See you in Rome on February 20."

Gene had held her away by her elbows, fatherly concern on his face. "You know where I'll be if you need to get in touch with me. You *did* pack the itinerary, didn't you?"

She nodded, unable to speak, and throwing her carry-on bag over her shoulder, walked out the door.

Diana had kept her promise as she followed Luis through the south of Europe. At least once a week, they attended an auction or sale. Though she seldom understood the language, she made notes on certain artists and studied the faces of those who held their bidding card up on a consistent basis. But she knew she should have been doing more. She should have spent less time watching the dark eyes of the Colombian who stood beside her.

Quintana's taste wasn't what Gene had intimated it would be. He tended to collect nudes and slightly pornographic pieces he called "erotica." Not her taste at all. Occasionally, their conversations would drift into a discussion of art and she would try to teach him the little she knew. But he wasn't interested in learning. He bought antiques and art strictly to decorate, with very little knowledge of what he was buying. And, as far as she was concerned, not with very good taste. Yes, the pieces he purchased were quite expensive, sometimes exorbitantly so, but tasteful they were not.

Feeling a small pang of guilt, she strode toward the man whose bed she had shared since the beginning of the trip. Brushing her hair back, she slipped a smile into place. Perhaps he could learn, she thought. And connoisseurship wasn't everything. His generosity more than made up for what he lacked in knowledge.

In the yacht's lobby-like lower cabin, she paused momentarily so her eyes could adjust to the change in light. The smell of carnations permeated her nostrils as the flowers themselves slowly came into focus. Throughout the cabin were vases full of carnations in every color and description. Luis stood in the middle of the bouquets, a close-mouthed grin on his face, his arms crossed against his chest. His legs, bronze and muscled, stretched airily from his silk shorts. Diana shivered in her wool sweater and socks, wondering how he could be dressed for summer when it was the middle of February.

"Happy Valentine's Day," he said, one hand wiping a few errant strands of black hair from her cheek, his eyes never leaving her astonished face.

"Are these all . . . no, they couldn't be ... are they from your gardens in Colombia?"

Luis nodded, taking her hand. "So many questions. Just enjoy.

Are they not beautiful? A perfect Colombian import." He ran his fingers over the pink blossoms in the vase nearest him. "The only problem is keeping them fresh during shipment."

"God, Luis. It's just so overwhelming."

"Like you, *mi cara.*" He slid behind her as she bent her face into a yellow bouquet.

"You're spoiling me rotten!" Turning, she flung her arms around his neck, rewarding him with a bit of unrestrained affection which she usually reserved for the bedroom.

He nuzzled his face into her long hair. "If we were ashore, I would take you to the best restaurant in Rome, dressed in the finest silks and satins and diamonds, and show you off to all those . . . how do you say it? . . . drooling olive-skinned boys."

She laughed and pulled away so she could see his face, her arms still looped about his neck. "How am I going to be able to go home after all this?" "Home? Do not go home."

"I have to."

"Do you?"

She stopped, a curtain of hair falling over her eyes as she turned to stare out over the azure Mediterranean. "My family is there, Luis. I could never leave them. And I certainly can't allow you to pay my expenses indefinitely. I have a job. Responsibilities." "We could see them on vacations, bring them to Europe. You said your sister-in-law would love to know what the Continent is like. And I have plenty of work to keep you occupied forever. You can manage the carnation business and I will concentrate on the rest of the exports. Or, if you like, you buy antiques and art and decorate my houses."

She shook her head, not wanting to risk bringing anger to his dark features. They had begun having this conversation weeks ago, and her answers were always the same. He was persuasive, especially when the lights were out and they were in bed, entwined with each other. Then Luis was in control and Diana the controlled. But she tried to let him know her ties to home were stronger than the ones she felt to him, although she was beginning to doubt they were. It frustrated him to believe he couldn't have his way.

He looked past her moodily; then, recovering quickly, hugged her close once again. "I have another surprise for you."

"You've already done too much!" Sensing the tension in his muscles, Diana recapitulated. "But I'm dying to know what it is . . ."

"Since family is *muy importanto* . . ." He paused dramatically, and she had a momentary flash that he had somehow been able to get Robert, Maryann, and the kids on a plane and had had them flown to the yacht. ". . . I've been trying to find out where the Sicilian branch of the Colucci family lives. Karl found them last week and paid them a visit. And ... I think finally you will be able to meet your mother's family tomorrow."

Suddenly the carnation smell was cloying. Overwhelming. Diana desperately searched for a place to sit down, feeling all color disappear from her cheeks. An unbelieving gasp escaped her.

"Did I do wrong? Should I hot have?" Luis sat down beside her, ^most knocking over one of the flower-filled vases in the process. "I did not know you would react this way . . . "

"No . . . no . . . I just don't know what I did to deserve all this. How did you know I've always dreamed of meeting them? I didn't say anything. We never talked about it. All I said was that I knew they lived in Sicily, that I still got letters every once in a while."

"Do you think I do not know how you feel? Ah, *mi cara,* your emotions me written all over your face like a . . . like a road map. All I have to do is watch those beautiful eyes to tell what is going on in your mind. You cannot hide it, Diana." Taking her hand in his, he stroked it gently. "You have told me more just by listening to my stories than you would ever know. When I talk of my family, I can see the longing in your eyes, and I understand that need because it is one which I also have. If I cannot have my family, at least I can give you yours."

"Tomorrow?"

"We will lay anchor closer to Taormina in the morning. I have already told Karl to take you to the dock by speedboat and he'll have a car ready for you to take you to your family." He paused, seemingly unsure that she comprehended what he was saying. She nodded, turning her full attention to him and felt her color returning, the flutter of anticipation in her stomach. Her family. The family she had never seen!

"I can't believe this. I really can't believe all this." Then, she stopped abruptly. "You're not going with me, are you?"

Shaking his head, he sighed. "I have so much work to do, *cara.* We have been vacationing all this time and I have kept people waiting, have canceled appointments and meetings. You will be with your family, have your reunion, hug the grandmothers and the young babies, speak in Italian, and share stories. This is important for you. You need time alone. And I need to get back to work. Besides, Karl will take good care of you."

She slid her arm under Luis's thick, strong one and shivered as she looked in Karl's general direction. "He gives me the creeps," she murmured.

"Creeps?"

"Makes me nervous."

"Really? Karl would protect you to the death." Luis looked out to the deck where Karl stood against the rail, helping the shooting instructor clean the rifles. "You will get used to him. Besides, I am not letting you go into Sicily alone. You might not come back."

Lifting her head, she caught a glimmer of fear crossing Luis's chiseled features. A wave of affection stole through her for the man whose early childhood was so different from hers, yet so painfully similar. She held him, softly rubbing the curls at the back of his neck, inhaling the salt air which mingled with the scent of his soap.

"Luis, I love you," she murmured, as the slight rocking of the yacht made their bodies sway as they would while making love.

Luis stood back and watched the young American woman. Every time she walked into a room, his groin was seized with a spasm, a loss of power. At first, the feeling had thrilled him, but now it only served to remind him that he needed to get back into control.

He watched her stop to talk to the shooting instructor he had hired only last week and reminded himself to fire the man as soon as she stepped off the yacht. They shared the same heritage and that was dangerous. The man seemed interested in fathering her and that type of person could get into Luis's way. He didn't like *anyone* getting in his way, especially where women were concerned.

She talked, her face animated, a smile lifting her cheekbones and lighting her eyes. Her hands, pushed forward like she was swimming underwater, then they swept to the side in an expansive gesture. Those hands were constantly moving, emphasizing a point, underlining her words.

Last night he had held her hands down as she sat astride him, the areolas of her breasts above his face, her buttocks pressed tightly on each side of his already hardening cock. She was unable to talk, unable to continue what she had started to tell him simply because she couldn't move her hands. Finally, laughing, she fell on top of him, and he had pushed inside her once again, making her ride his engorged member as she might have a wild Arabian horse.

Luis closed his eyes, remembering the look of surprise and passion on her face, the moan which had unconsciously escaped her lips and the abandon with which she threw herself into the act of sex within seconds of his entering. Yes, he thought, there *was* a woman who could match his energy.

The realization caused a cold fist to grip his stomach. Everything had been perfect up till now, but she was beginning to ask questions he was having trouble answering. And he had almost answered her, had almost begun to trust her. Dangerous, he thought. Cannot trust anyone.

"Signore?" Karl interrupted his thoughts. Whirling to face him, Luis instantly wiped every trace of his daydream from his mind and body.

"Get Fernando in New York," Luis said, his voice deep, every muscle tensing in preparation for the work he had to accomplish in the next four days during Diana's absence. "Then I want the speedboat readied for tomorrow. You'll take Signorina Colucci to Sicily, make sure she's settled, then find Moretti. He owes me and it's about time we make him pay."

Standing in front of the chrome and glass Art Nouveau mirror, Diana stared at her reflection. Yet, it wasn't her oval face she saw. She stared into the mirror and through it, away from it, to other times and places, other situations. One finger absently stroked the silver hand mirror on the table, its curved handle resembling a rose branch. She traced the sensual lines, the delicate shape of the rose's rounded petals, the sharp point of the thorn. Beneath her bare feet a thick, deep carpet in shades of pink led up to the side of the bed, stopping only half an inch below the water-filled mattress.

The ceiling, designed by an Italian painter whose fame would never catch up with his ego, was an imitation of the great masters. She could barely stomach the bare-breasted woman and rosy-cheeked cherubs floating serenely across the twenty-foot ceiling. A horrible replica of Italian Renaissance, she thought.

Her eyes drifted to the bed and she contemplated lying on it, closing her eyes and letting her thoughts wash over her in a torrent, so she could pick out what made sense and discard the rest. But something stopped her. For the first and only time in her life, she could not reason, could not make logical sense of what was happening to her. Everything was going too fast. She felt too much, too strongly, for a m^ about whom she knew absolutely nothing. Her brain wasn't in gear. The logical, rational Diana had given way to a Diana solely motivated by sex, by love, by an emotion she had denied long ago.

This makes no sense, she thought. There's no reason why I should be floating on a yacht with a very rich, very handsome, very loving man. No reason to allow myself to get so carried away that I'm jeopardizing everything I've worked for the past three years.

But, then . . . She drew her fingers down the side of her linen pants, wiping the sweat from her palm, not looking at her constantly-chewed nails. Lifting her chest, she breathed deeply again as if her breath could somehow calm her. Every time she thought about being in bed with Luis, about being close to him, about his arm accidentally brushing hers or about twining her fingers in the hairs on his chest, her thoughts went haywire. Her body took over. And her body felt like a traitor.

She lowered her face into her hands and rubbed her temples deeply until she felt her skin turning red. Her family. Mama's sisters, my aunts and cousins. Perhaps being around relatives would help quell the fear that had been rising in her chest, the fear of not knowing what was going to happen next, the fear of letting down her guard, the fear of loving someone again. The fear of not being able to reason why she
was in love with someone she knew nothing about.

Maybe being away for a while would help.

He had tricked her last night, teasing her into talking without her hands and that trick had turned into a searing night of passion. Her hand involuntarily went to her chest. She unbuttoned the first two buttons on her shirt. Her rounded fingers were sensitive to the slight down of hair covering her chest, stretching down to the rise of her bosom. She traced the dip between her breasts, watching herself in the mirror as the third button slid out of its hole, then the fourth, revealing the lacy trimmings of her satin bra. Her breath quickened with the memory of Luis's moment of entry and she felt a warm wetness between her thighs. Deftly, she undid the front clasp of her bra and slid her fingers to the side to capture a nipple already hard with desire. She could not deny it, even the thought of his darkly muscled body aroused her.

Slowly, she walked to the bed behind her, undoing her pants zipper and letting the linen slide caressingly down her legs. She imagined Luis's black eyes in front of her face as she slid her other hand under the elastic waistband of her silk bikinis. Her fingertips reached the slippery folds of her vagina and she went quickly from arousal to orgasm, knowing that her need for sex would be what would get her into trouble someday. Dreamily, she wondered if she wanted to learn how to control that desire.

Chapter Fifteen

Sicily, February 18, 1981

Siracusa's dock was empty except for a few early morning fishermen. Disguised by a low rolling fog which obliterated sounds, the Ionian Sea left droplets of water on the bows of the small fishing boats, sailboats, and the few yachts moored at the dock. Through the mist, the sounds of a man singing a sad Italian love song could be heard., He grunted and sang, then grunted again. Though Diana couldn't see him, it was obvious he was working on his boat as his grunts and song matched the muted sounds of a creaking bow rubbing rhythmically against the old wooden dock.

Everything was gray. Nowhere were the brightly- colored signs she had become accustomed to seeing during the past four days. Also absent was the fisherman who had agreed to her impetuous request to return to the yacht before the sun broke through the morning haze.

She slid her foot in and out of her shoe, absently listening and watching for the little man in the New York Yankees baseball cap. Luis would be surprised, she thought. Her skin tingled when her mind randomly brought forward imagined scenes of her homecoming. She curled her toes and pulled her shoe closer as the images became more intense. Why am I always thinking of sex when I think of that man, she wondered, amused. Shoving her foot back into her shoe, she walked to the end of the dock. Where the hell was that fisherman?

The visit to her aunt's had been one of the noisiest reunions she could, have ever imagined. From the moment she stepped out of the taxi in tiny, sun- warmed Taormina, she had been pursued by relative after relative—aunts and friends of aunts; fat, toothless uncles who simply grinned at her or knowingly nudged the comrade who sat next to them; cousins who spoke quickly and eagerly in their eagerness to monopolize some of her time.

All of them wanted to know about America. All of them wanted to share stories of her mother and tell her news of the rest of her relatives, most of whom she had never seen. She listened eagerly, her straw sun hat on the ground between her feet, chin resting on her hand, elbow on her knee—every muscle in her body at attention as her volatile, verbal family built her family's history for her.

They told her stories of Rose's childhood, of how she would run down the town's curving mountain roads to catch her younger brothers and sisters for supper, of her lifelong romance with Tony,

and of their marriage, their young dreams, their hopes for a new life in America. All of them sobbed unabashedly when Diana, in halting Sicilian barely remembered from her childhood, explained how her father died and what happened to Rose afterward. They held her, in one immense group hug, when she, too, broke down, and they held her once again, later that night when the oil lamps had been lit. Someone
had found a concertina and played it while the young children invented crazy, happy dances for "la bella Americana." That time, her tears had been of joy.

She spent her days following the children through the tiny seacoast city's streets, breathing the mountain air, gazing at Mt. Etna, and exploring the tiny cottages where her mother's family lived. Her heart ached when she stood in front of the fifteenth century church of SS. Pietro e Paolo, simply because she knew it had been one of her mother's favorite places.

She stood with her shoulders back, her chin thrust forward, feeling her mother there at her side. It was like Rose had never really left the little island, but had simply gone to another place to rest. It had been one of the moving moments in Diana's life, and she hadn't wanted to leave the little church even when the children tugged at her hands and skirt. Smiling, she let them lead her down another rocky path and toward the quiet bustle of the little town.

The city was busy with tourists, for it was the winter season and Taormina's climate was especially delightful. She took advantage of the children's innocence and bribed them to take her to the ruined castle she had seen on the spur of Monte Tauro, knowing full well they had all been warned not to go that far from home. They walked beside her in silence as she circled outside the castle, turning from one direction to the other, making sure she did not miss a detail of the spectacular view of Etna and the sea, making sure all was indelibly impressed on her memory so that she could repeat it to Robert when she got home. How stupid of her not to have brought a camera, to be relying on a memory already full of stories and anecdotes which needed to be repeated. Yet, she reflected, her face tilted toward the winter sun, I wouldn't be here at all if it wasn't for Luis and his generosity. She knew Robert would understand.

Almost three months' worth of balls, trips through castles, meeting famous people, falling in love with Luis, and meeting her family, proved too much for her to bear. Standing on the precipice overlooking the island her mother and father had spent a childhood getting to know, she was overcome with a sense of peace. Yet the incredibly strong tug of homesickness she had been denying since Christmas surfaced and she knew she must go home soon.

"What's the matter, *bella?*" Aunt Cecile asked when Diana, hatless and windblown, walked into the house, much later that afternoon. The little woman barely reached Diana's shoulders, yet her mothering instinct reached deep inside to pull up an emotion she thought she had forgotten —the need to be mothered. For the first time in over ten years, she felt she had someone to lean on, someone who would take care of her, someone she didn't have to worry about taking care of or pleasing. It would be very easy to stay, she thought, as she nestled her face into her aunt's ample shoulder.

Sitting on a stool at the woman's feet, her long legs tucked close to her chest, she again talked about family, but this time of Robert, Maryann, Chris, and Tony. She told Aunt Cecile, whose dark brown eyes were lined with creases long and deep and filled with understanding, about her childhood, about being lonely, about raising Robert, and about loving him more than life itself. Her aunt listened intently throughout the story of Vito and her high school years. How she found Gene Monroe. How much she loved her job. She understood when Diana faltered a moment before talking about Luis, yet her smile grew wide, sending the wrinkles up to squeeze her eyes, almost making them disappear, when she realized her niece was in love.

Patting Diana on the shoulder, Aunt Cecile told her exactly what Mama would have. "Go to him! Tell him how you feel. You're young . . . have beautiful babies, and be happy."

Only because she couldn't get a fisherman to take her out to the yacht the previous day, Diana stayed in Siracusa and finally had the chance to take her boss's advice. As in Vienna, she found a museum. The Museo Nationale, located near the archaeological area where she had wandered past stone sarcophagi and imposing Roman buildings built before Christ was born, held one of the most interesting archaeological collections in Italy.

With Gene's words echoing through her mind, she dared to touch-pieces of pottery brought to the island in the third millennium B.C. and wandered through the exhibit of fossil bones of a dwarf elephant. She made mental notes on the pottery she might need to remember and looked with fascination and a little repulsion at the prehistoric bones, knowing she'd never have any use for *them*. Spending over five hours in the museum, she gathered pamphlets and books written in Italian and that evening lay on her stomach in her small hotel bed, poring over the information she had accumulated, deciphering it and committing what she could to memory. The pamphlets and information kept her mind from being preoccupied with Luis, a feat which was getting more and more difficult to accomplish.

The next morning, she awakened, still fully dressed, the pamphlets and books beneath her. Her first thought was of Luis.

Just when she was ready to give up and go back to the hotel, the fisherman in the Yankees cap strolled jauntily down the pier. She let him help her into a small motorboat hidden between two larger fishing craft and wondered uneasily if the boat would make it into the choppier waters where the *Vallidoria* lay anchored.

With her small suitcase bouncing against her knees, she tried to listen as the sailor yelled snatches of conversation into the air whipping around her ears. His efforts were lost, but he kept trying, and she felt obliged to nod and smile though she couldn't hear a word he said.

Pulling her sweater closer around her, she shifted her legs so that the suitcase blocked most of the cold morning sea wind. *By the time I get to the* Vallidoria, she thought. *I'm going to look like someone who's been through a hurricane. Hopefully, Luis won't be up yet and I can sneak to my cabin to do some repairs before I see him.* She smiled.

Half an hour later, they pulled up alongside Luis's boat. As the fisherman cut the motor and idled close to a rope ladder on the starboard side, her attention was drawn to the upper deck. The sun glinted in her eyes as she lifted her head to see who leaned over the rail, something long and silver in his hands. The sun was behind him, causing the figure to be perfectly silhouetted. It also made it perfectly impossible for her to see. She reached for her hat, carefully laid on the bottom of the boat so that it wouldn't blow away, and stood up, placing it on her head.

Karl straightened, his right hand swiftly lowering something to the deck.

"Ah, *now* I can see!" she said. "Karl, can you help me up?"

"You're back early." His German accent was cold and clipped, his hand a little too tight on her arm. "I was planning on picking you up tomorrow."

"Yeah, I know, but I kind of . . ." The dark look flitting across his face stopped her in mid-sentence. "What's the matter?"

"You should really let someone know when you change your mind like that." He stepped back from her, putting as much distance as possible between them.

Diana mentally shook her head. The man was an absolute iceberg. No matter what she did, he acted as if she had committed a crime of some sort. "I'm sure Luis will be happy to see me," she said, picking up her suitcase and heading below.

"Signorina!" The fisherman came up behind her. She had almost forgotten about him. "We done?"

Pulling the last of the lire from her bag, she handed it to the little man, her eyes never leaving Karl's face. He seemed determined to aggravate her. Well, fine. So be it. If that's what he wanted to do, she wouldn't let him get to her. He was the only thing rotten about this trip, she mused. Too bad Luis thought him so valuable.

When the motorboat whizzed away, the two of them were left face to face on the deck. "Are you going to move so I can go downstairs?" she asked softly. Pursing her lips, she cocked her head and tightened her grip on the suitcase. The yacht listed slightly as the motorboat's wake hit its bow. She leaned with it. Karl did the same. For a moment, all she could hear was the slap, slap, slap of the waves.

She waited quietly, as she had many times in East Boston when groups of boys filled the sidewalk, daring women to try to go by. Most would cross to the other side of the street. Diana just waited, learning to fill her mind with other things. It was her street as much as theirs, she figured. Why shouldn't she have the right to walk by without being accosted? Her patience worked every time. Karl finally slid his body to the right, allowing her barely a foot to pass him.

"Thanks," she muttered. With another shake of her head, she squeezed by, purposely bumping his leg with the corner of her suitcase.

He was right behind her, his every step matching hers. "Let me get that for you." His cold voice whistled past her ear as he pushed in front of her to open her cabin door.

What the hell is wrong with him? she wondered, stepping over the threshold. "Wait a minute!" He was trying to close the door and she wasn't even into the room. "I'm just dropping the suitcase off. I want to see Luis."

"No, that's not possible right now . . ."

"Excuse me?"

"I said that's not possible." Karl's large, blond body blocked the doorway.

This was getting to be a little too much. "C'mon, Karl," she urged, though a warning flip of her stomach told her not to push her luck. "Get out of my way. Right now."

His steady gray eyes shifted to the right then back again, as if making an important decision. Insolently, he gazed straight into her face once more, then walked away muttering in German.

Watching his retreating back, she knew he was headed for Luis's suite at the other end of the yacht. She passed on the opportunity to brush her hair and rushed after him, the heels of her flats clicking briskly against the Mexican tile hallway floor.

He was at Luis's door, angrily knocking at it, when she caught up with him. "What the hell's going on?" she asked him through clenched teeth. "Why are you acting so weird? Do you have to announce me to Luis? I'm not exactly a stranger, you know."

Again, he assumed a face-off position, practically growling at her, lip curled, nose flaring. "Fine. I will leave now. You Americans always get your own way, anyway." He stepped back and waved a straightened forearm in front of the teak door which led to Luis's rooms. "Be my guest." With one final snarl in her direction, he turned on a heel and walked away.

Bewildered, she dared not move for a second. He re-entered the lobby then turned right, heading for the deck. Good. Now she could surprise Luis without assistance.

She twisted the long brass Louis XIV doorknob slowly and pushed with her shoulder on the heavy teak cabin door. Luis must have the radio going, she thought, hearing voices coming from within. He won't hear me then. Smiling, she slid the door open another inch.

From where she stood, wedged between the door and the hallway, she could see the unmistakable shape of Luis's foot hanging off his bed. That lazy bum, she thought, unbuttoning the first couple of buttons of her silk shirt. I'll wake him up. Throwing the door completely open, she called his name softly, seductively. In the darkened cabin, all noise stopped.

"Who's that?" whispered a feminine voice.

She walked further into the chamber, her eyes quickly adjusting to the dim light of the black and gold Oriental cave Luis called his bedroom. Her hand fell from her buttons as the scene on the black lacquer four-poster bed became clear to her.

Luis lay back against the white satin sheets, his dark-haired legs spread wide, his head nestled against several pillows. He looked straight at her with a surprised and drunken half-smile.

On his right, a woman with waist-length red hair bent over his stomach. In her hand, she held a glass straw, one end in her left nostril. The straw leaned against a large mirror Luis held on his chest, and in the middle of the mirror a large pile of sparkling white powder caught Diana's attention. The woman snorted noisily, then lifted a disinterested eye.

On his left, another woman with equally long black hair, was almost as busy as her partner. With her left hand, she slowly stroked Luis's erect penis. With her right, she massaged the red-haired woman's clitoris. All three of them were naked and so entwined with each other it was hard to tell which body part belonged to whom.

Diana's stomach contracted violently. Her knees buckled and threatened to give way. Her breathing stopped. She stood in stunned silence, the picture of the three of them coming into clearer and clearer focus, its edges razor sharp and irritating. The scene contracted and expanded, as if it were breathing.

"What are you doing here, Diana?" Luis lifted his head off the bed, pushing at one girl, then the other. "What in HELL ARE YOU DOING HERE?"

Now she knew why Karl had stopped her. Now she realized what the "it" was that Luis imported. How he made his money. Now she knew why he got constant phone calls from Colombia and why their trip had been interrupted several times when he had to "meet someone at the airport." The smell in the hotel room the first night they made love wasn't a cigarette, it was a joint. Lies. All he had told her were lies. Suddenly she didn't want to be here, didn't want to be around him. His filthy money. His girls. His habits. His boat. His "associates'^. . .

She turned and ran through the door, not bothering to close it, not heading for her room, but for the deck. She ran with the urgency of someone who wanted to get away from the Devil, yet she didn't know where to go. She felt filthy. Debased. Raped. How could I have . . . how could he . . . Why didn't I know? God knows, there was enough drug dealing going on in East Boston. The Sixties. I'm not innocent. I know what's going on. How could I have?

When she got to the deck, Karl was waiting for her, the silver-barreled rifle loosely cradled in his hands. His lips stretched in an aberration of a smile.

"Where do you think you're going?" he asked, casually leaning against the railing, blocking her path.

"Anywhere but here. Take me to Sicily, Karl. Get the boat and take me back. NOW!" Ignoring the rifle, she pushed his shoulder toward the small speed-boat which hung suspended over the stern. "Hurry up! I want to leave."

"I don't think you're going anywhere. Miss Colucci." He brought the rifle to an upright position and placed his right hand on the long silver barrel.

"You don't expect me to stay *here,* do you?" Her hat whipped off and flew over the railing. For a brief moment, she thought of chasing it, then realized how foolish the idea was and turned back to her nemesis. "You really don't think *he* wants me to stay, do you?"

"Of course I do." Luis came up quietly behind Diana. His feet were bare. A white terry robe, obviously tied in haste, fell to his knees. Around his nostrils was a slight crust of white dust. "You are not leaving. You cannot leave now."

"And why not? I hope you don't think I'm going to join the little orgy you have going on below."

"Oh, that." He laughed, a raspy sound as though losing his voice. "You were gone, Diana. I am a man. But I love you. You know you're more important than those women downstairs, *mi cara"*

"My being gone is a poor excuse. I was foolish to believe you could possibly care for me the way I do for you. And I was also blind to what you've been doing right in front of my nose all this time. Of course you're dealing cocaine and not carnations! God, how could I be so stupid! If you think I'm going to be part of something like this, you're nuts. How dare you? And what makes you think you're going to continue to get away with this? Cocaine! What else, Luis? Prostitution? Heroin? Stolen goods? Probably all of the above . . . No, Luis, I want nothing more to do with you or anyone *like* you. You sicken me! They should put people like you out of their misery—permanently." She turned to Karl again. "Get the boat, Karl. I want to go back to Sicily."

The German looked over her head at his boss.

"Diana, be reasonable." Putting his hand on her shoulder, Luis tried to pull her towards him. "You do not want to do that. Why are you going to give up everything you could have with me? Come now. Stop being a ridiculous little girl. Go back to your cabin. I'll get rid of . . . them . . . and we will have a talk."

"Get your frigging hands off me!" Her voice was quiet, determined,' and cold. Luis dropped his hands immediately. His dark features showed surprise, then hardened. "I want nothing to do with you, your boat, your money, your girls, your cocaine, your gifts.

Nothing! Do you hear me? I want nothing to do with you, so keep your hands off me and stay away from me."

For a moment everything was silent except for Luis's labored breathing. "Let her go then." He nodded to Karl and pulled the robe's belt tighter with a close-fisted gesture. "Get the boat, Karl."

"Are you sure . . ."

"Do not question me, Carlos!" Luis whirled and placed both hands on the railing, lifting his snarled head of hair to the wind. "Just do it! If she wants to go, let her go. Who am I to keep a woman when she wants to leave?"

"La mato?"

"Why?" Luis looked quickly at her, as though guilty about something. Impossible, she thought. Why would he feel guilty?

"!ella saber" Karl said.

Luis laughed. She thought he had never looked uglier. Recoiling from the sound, she remembered how just a few short days ago she had loved him, had missed him so much that she came back early to be with him. Now his white-encrusted nose, the black circles under his eyes, the way his dark, hairy legs hung like the haunches of an animal from beneath the robe, created a picture of a man who disgusted her completely. And scared her.

She wondered what Karl had said to him, but forgot it quickly as the large blond brought the boat around and begrudgingly helped her into it. Within moments, the *Vallidoria* was far behind her and her face was turned towards Sicily.

Luis leaned against the railing, his body supported by his outstretched arms and hands that clenched the steel bar so tightly he imagined it would crumble within his grasp and that he would be thrown out onto the ocean, out to where the boat carrying the only woman he had ever loved was speeding into the distance, out to where he could pull her back to the *Vallidoria* by that thick black mass of hair so he could show her exactly how he knew they were meant to be together and how she should stay with him and get used to what he did for a living and he would show her how he loved her, he would rip the buttons off her shirt to get to her soft, tanned breasts, he would leave little bite marks on her skin so when she was in the shower afterward they would tingle and she would remember who put them there.

He took a long, shaky breath. Another line. Plenty more downstairs. Besides, she was gone now. Karl would make sure of that, though he'd better not hurt her. He wouldn't hurt her. He knew that Luis would kill him. No, she couldn't be killed. No, that couldn't be done. She might come around. Yes, she might understand what she's missing. She'd never find someone else as good as Luis Varquez de la Maria Quintana. She'd be back. Then he'd show her, he'd show her how much he loved her and why she needed him. She *did* need him. He could tell by the way she responded to him when they made love. She had that animal in her, the same one that tormented him, the one he could never satisfy. She was looking for the same thing that he was. The only difference between them was that he knew she'd never find it. Yes, she'd never find it, unless she came back to him.

He looked one last time at the silent horizon, shading his eyes to see whether he could distinguish the speck against the ocean that was the speedboat. It was gone. Sniffing loudly, he swallowed the coppery taste of his own blood. He rubbed the back of his right hand against his sore, encrusted nose, grimaced when he inadvertently tore off a piece of skin, then turned and padded softly down the stairs to the lower deck.

Chapter Sixteen

Rome, February 20, 1981

Gene lit another cigarette and glanced across the crowded concourse, then at his Rolex. Only one hour to flight time and no sign of Diana.

"I knew it," he muttered, twisting the gold and ruby band which was beginning to swim on his right ring finger. "She's staying with that. . . that. . . Colombian." Too refined to call Luis what he really wanted to, he busied himself watching the tourists swarming into the airport to begin their holidays in sunny Italy. Personally, he couldn't wait to get out of the country. The trip had been nothing as expected, and his cough was getting worse. No matter how hard he tried, he couldn't get a full night's sleep anymore. And he refused to give up smoking. No matter what.

Only a few days ago, Freddie had called with a piece of information that haunted Gene—so much so that he hadn't had a moments peace since.

"Your handsome Colombian is an importer, dear heart." Freddie's ingratiating voice attempted to purr.

"Of what?" Gene had demanded.

"More than one thing. The little devil's pretty busy. Coffee. Carnations. And, last but certainly not least, cocaine. The three c's." Freddie was still cackling at his own joke when Gene hung up.

Diana, he had thought. I have to get to Diana. But it had proved impossible. Even his strongest connections in the Mediterranean could not locate Quintana. He was mercurial, ghostlike, they said. And some of them hadn't even known who he was. Finally, with departure time drawing nearer, Gene gave lip. He was waiting for her as impatiently as an expectant father.

Just as he was about to walk the long corridor to the plane, he glimpsed a woman across the concourse, struggling with two large suitcases. A woman with long black hair who towered above the tiny Italians around her.

"Diana! Diana, over here!" he called, standing up to wave.

She wore an exquisitely-tailored and sedate cream- colored silk suit, its jacket unbuttoned to within an inch of her breasts. The slim skirt hugged her hips and allowed her strong calves only minimal movement, yet she strode with the easy grace of a panther sure of where it was going and how it was going to get there. The suit was accented with square gold earrings and a matching necklace which were Greek, Gene was sure, even from this distance. The whole ensemble was something with which he was unfamiliar. He must have bought them for her, he thought. It surprised him that the

Colombian had shown some taste, at least in women's clothing.

Diana's ebony hair swung shoulder length, straight and shining, yet as she drew closer, he saw that the sheen of her hair did not match the luminosity of her eyes, as it usually did.

She looked different. Changed. Her walk was more determined, her shoulders straighter and stronger under the weight of the two obviously heavy suitcases she carried, though she appeared not to notice her burden as she grimly walked toward him. Gone was the lightness of her smile; the brilliance of her turquoise eyes was dulled. The buoyancy of her long-legged stride had quieted to an elegant glide.

Although heads turned to watch her, she gazed straight ahead, her lips stretched in a straight line across her face, her expression detached. She had the look of a woman who had seen it all and was extremely bored by what she knew to be her future. It was a look which baffled him completely, a look which didn't belong to the Diana Colucci he knew.

"I don't get a smile?" he said as she dropped the two suitcases beside his chair. He hugged her to him and felt a hardness in her, though she responded to his affection with a squeeze and a light kiss on his cheek. "You don't look like you've had a very good time since you left Vienna. What's wrong, darling?"

"Nothing," she replied in the same forthright manner he remembered. She smiled. "Absolutely nothing."

He let the matter drop and launched into a diatribe only interrupted by his persistent cough and her questions. They shared what had happened to each of them in the past month-and-a-half with Gene monopolizing the conversation as they walked toward the gate. Still chattering, they passed the uniformed stewards and stewardesses and settled into their seats.

By the time Rome was beneath them, she had visibly relaxed, her face had softened and her stiff smile had begun to stretch into laughter at his stories about Frederick and what he called "the Viennese gang" of antiquers. He told her of his acquisitions— especially the royal set of Sevres porcelain and a painting by the German expressionist, Egon Schiele ("I have a feeling about him, Di—his paintings go for a pretty hefty price now, but I think we need to keep an eye on him.")—and tried to rouse some excitement in her about his plans for redecorating the shop.

She nodded in all the right places, listened with interest to his stories, and responded with a genuine fervor for his new shop strategy. Yet he could sense a tangible change, a reserved maturation, which had apparently crept over her in the time they had spent apart. At first, he thought her aloofness was a product of her fatigue. Or perhaps the visit with her family had been an emotional one, arousing old pains which she had long tried to deny.

But, no. When she spoke of the Colucci and Giannetti families, it was with warmth and passion. She told him of her cousins, her aunts and uncles, of where they lived, and of Taormina itself.

And when he questioned her about the rest of her trip, she described the museums she had visited, the open-air markets of Morocco, the way she had felt upon first seeing the Parthenon in Greece. She told him of the clothes she had bought, of learning how to shoot, of the quality of light upon the Mediterranean at the end of the day. Everything that was important about her trip, she shared. Yet, something was missing, something empty about her voice, her actions and her eyes.

Toward the end of the flight, when they were about to land in London, Gene finally realized what was wrong and almost slapped his forehead in disbelief. Not once had she mentioned Luis Quintana. Now is the time, he thought. I have to tell her.

"Diana, I know you might be angry with me, but I feel I have to tell you this," he began slowly. Reluctantly. "I did a little investigating while I was in Italy and had Frederick check into Luis's background." He stopped and lifted his wineglass to his lips, watching out of the corner of his eye for her reaction.

"Isn't that the ocean?" she said, turning toward the window.

"Diana, pay attention to me. I want you to hear this."

"Or is it the English Channel?"

"Frederick found out what he does for a living, Diana."

"I've always wanted to see London." Still, she didn't turn toward him.

"Diana!"

When she swiveled her head and her eyes met his, he could tell she already knew.

"I don't want to talk about it," she said, firmly yet quietly. "I know what you're going to say and I don't want to hear it."

"But, Diana . . ."

"Please, I'd rather forget about it."

"Luis is a dealer, Di. An international cocaine dealer with contacts throughout Europe. He's dangerous. You don't want to get involved with him."

"I know."

"What happened with him? Why won't you tell me about it?"

"It's over. We don't need to discuss it." Her eyes grew cold, her face like marble. Her hands were folded in her lap yet he could see the whiteness of her knuckles. He covered her hands with one of his, amazed at how cold she was.

"You need to talk about it. Listen, darling, I know that you're hurting and I want to help. Sometimes it helps to talk . . ."

She smiled ruefully. "Not this time. Gene." And turned back to the window.

"That bastard. What in hell did he do to you?"

When he got no answer, he took his hand away from hers and took another sip of wine. For several moments he sat, eyes straight, a million scenarios flashing through his mind. Had Luis hit her? He'd kill the bastard. Had he forced her to try cocaine? No, she would never have gone along with that. Had she seen him put together a deal? A possibility. What had happened? Whatever it was must, have been terrible to have elicited such a reaction from the quiet woman who sat at his side.

Finally, respectful of the distance she had put between them, yet still unable to let go of the need somehow to touch her, he reached over and turned her chin toward him. When her eyes met his, his were moist and hers, dry.

"You're like the child I never had," he began. "I hurt for you. Your pain is my pain. I just want you to know that. And if you ever want to talk about it. I'm here. Just please don't close yourself off like this."

Nodding, her mouth opened as if she were about to speak, then she closed it, licked her lips, and bit the top one with her bottom teeth. He could tell she was fighting tears, that she had probably been doing so for days.

"Let's forget about it, okay?" she said in a voice which sounded like a child's. "I just don't want to think about it anymore. It's over. I want to just . . . just . . . forget about it."

"You loved him, didn't you?"

She nodded and turned away once more. This time, he didn't bother her.

She stared unseeingly through the airplane's window, not noticing the bright sun glinting on the rain- filled clouds below them, not recognizing the peaks of English buildings when they began breaking through those clouds, not seeing anything but that which ran through her mind unbidden.

Her stomach muscles grew taut as she considered the days she spent with her family. She had done little crying. Actually, there had been no tears at all. Her throat had felt dry, as though she had wandered for months in the Sahara without any kind of fluid. Swallowing became difficult, almost impossible, and eating was out of the question. Ten pounds had slipped off her body as easily as if they were washed off in the bath.

When Karl brought the suitcases of clothes and jewelry which Luis had presented to her at various times during their "trip," as she had begun to chill it, she wanted to refuse them, but no one in the family was as tall as she and she had not been able to borrow clothes. She had little mon^ left to purchase a whole new wardrobe. And no choice but to accept those clothes, those gifts, she had once loved without reservation, though she now despised the man who had given them to her.

When she wore the silk blouses and pants or hung the gold necklaces around her neck, she felt weighted down with an unimaginable depression. She wanted to toss them one by one into the sea, to stand beside the castle and see the feather-light blouses float down past the cliffs into the slate-blue ocean beyond, to toss the jewelry and watch it sink quickly to the bottom. The only thing stopping her was her inbred lack of wastefulness, built from years of trying to run her household on a tight budget. Diana Colucci didn't know how to throw *anything* away, and it almost killed her not to have that freedom.

She listened for hours to her aunt's consoling words, allowed the older woman to cuddle her and murmur words of endearment into her hair; yet the words never seemed to penetrate to that deepest part of her, the part in so much pain she couldn't even begin to define it. They had all tried—every aunt, uncle, and cousin—to reach her in their own simple ways. But they couldn't. She had closed herself off. No more did she want to hurt. No longer did she trust or believe someone would love her as she had loved them. Totally and completely. There was no such thing as happily ever after, she decided. Cinderella was a lie. Sleeping Beauty, a farce. Snow White, a fable.

For the first twenty-four hours, the scene with Luis replayed itself in her brain over and over again. By the second day, Aunt Cecile was able to get her to talk about him. Their conversation lasted well into the evening. Aunt Cecile paced the tiny room, swearing in Sicilian, vowing revenge, promising to get one of their relatives to take care of Luis, to make sure he never walked like a man again. But Diana shook her head and laid her hand on her aunt's warm, pudgy arm, to make her promise not to do anything of the kind.

After that, she promised herself never to discuss the Colombian again. And that it would be a long time before she would give of herself so freely to another human being.

When the time came to leave her family, she kissed each one of them on both cheeks, held them tightly to her breast, and whispered promises of keeping in touch, of visiting often, of having the younger ones stay with her when they came to America to attend college. Then she got on the boat, faced Rome, and never looked back.

All the way to the airport she thought of her future, of Robert, Maryann, and the kids, and she began to make plans for herself. If Gene would still have her, she would work twice as hard as before to learn everything there was to know about the items she bought for the shop. She would fill her days and nights with the antique world that she loved, and she would never look back on those moments when a dark-haired, dark-eyed man had inhabited her life. And never again would she cry.

Chapter Seventeen

London, February 21, 1981

A light mist dusted her skin as she stepped from the cab Gene had hired to take them to an old friend's shop on King's Row. Their flight to New York wouldn't take off until the next morning, so he had called Peter Rivington from Rome to see whether they might stay with him.

"I wouldn't think of staying anywhere but Peter's when I'm in London," Gene commented, offering her shelter under the large black umbrella he had produced out of nowhere. "He knows all the gossip about Sotheby's, what's coming up on the block, and who consigned it. Who knows, we might be able to get an auction in while we're here."

They stood in front of a shop with multi-paned windows which looked as if it had come straight out of a Dickens novel. On the long windowsills, rows of tall, red, trumpet-like flowers added a dash of color to the dreary fogginess of the street. She wanted to be inside, to touch and smell them.

Gene took her elbow with a flourish, leading her to the door where he folded the umbrella and ushered her inside. She went straight to the flowers, touching one lightly with her finger.

"They're amaryllis," came an English voice from behind her.

"So beautiful," she replied without turning around. "Terence, I thought you'd be off to an auction or some kind of society tea this wet afternoon." Gene shook the umbrella and placed it in a corner. She watched the two men warmly shake hands. Gene had to look up at the sandy-haired Englishman whose back was to her. The man wore a tan cashmere sweater; a wise move, she thought with a shiver. After Italy's warmth, London's weather seemed even more damp and bone-chilling than she had expected it would.

"Where's your uncle?" Gene continued, looking past Terence toward the back of the crowded store. "He knew we were coming. He hasn't gone off on one of his chases, has he? Lord, he'll be gone for days . . ." Terence reassured Gene his uncle had not done one of his famous disappearing acts, and the men chuckled as they walked toward the back of the shop, leaving her alone and unintroduced, to explore what seemed to be an endless supply of antiques. Every square inch of the long, thin shop was full of porcelain statuettes she recognized as Dresden, immense pieces of dark oak furniture, blue and white Canton chargers and three-foot-tall Imari vases, piecrust Chippendale tables and Oriental carpets, piled one on top of the other on top of another. Desk sets by the dozens filled the top of a marquetry partners' desk. Art Deco chrome figurines depicting the graceful lines of ballerinas and greyhounds competed for space with heavy bronze busts of English literary figures. On the walls oils, watercolors, prints, lithographs, and tapestries hung, their frames almost touching. The ceilings were adorned with what seemed to be hundreds of hanging light fixtures, none of which appeared connected to electricity. The shop's light was dim; the smell, musty, as if the doors had never been opened any longer than necessary to allow a customer in.

She wandered past the amaryllis and beyond the window, venturing deeper into the shop in search of warmth. She went slowly, afraid her pocketbook would knock over a valuable knickknack or two. \^en she noticed that even the seats of the several wingback chairs throughout the shop were filled with oddities, she smiled. This Peter Rivington surely did believe in making use of his selling space.

Picking up a small book of poetry bound in dusty brown leather, she leafed through it gently, folding the pages back one by one. Reverently, she ran her fingers over the words printed in old English script.

"There are poems about the amaryllis in there." Turning quickly, she came face to face with Terence. His pale blue eyes were partially hidden behind gold- rimmed spectacles set at an odd angle on his thin nose and one side of his mouth was pulled upwards in a questioning smile. "Did you know that 'amaryllis' is another word for 'shepherd?'"

She shook her head and smiled back at the bookish young man.

"It's also Greek for 'fresh or new.' That's why my uncle likes to have them blooming in the window in the winter." He gestured with long, thin fingers back to the multi-paned glass and the red lily-like flowers occupying its sill. "Makes him feel as winter might not last forever after all. They *are* lovely, don't you agree?" Following his eyes to the flowers, she nodded again. Before she had a chance to speak, he was walking toward the window.

"Alas! what boots it with uncessant care
    To tend the homely, slighted, shepherd's trade.
    And strictly meditate the thankless Muse?
    Were it not better done, as others use.
    To sport with Amaryllis in the shade.
    Or with the tangles of Neaera's hair.
Fame is the spur that the clear spirit doth raise
(That last infirmity of noble mind)
    To scorn delights, and live laborious days;
    But the fair guerdon when we hope to find.
    And think to burst out with sudden blaze.
    Comes the blind Fury with th' abhorred shears
    And slits the thin-spun life."

His voice rang through the crowded shop, not muffled by the

many objects which lined its walls and filled its floors. The rich timbre of his words reached through her sorrow to remind her how many times she had found solace within the words on a book's printed pages or inside the lyrics of a poem by Emily Dickinson or Wallace Stevens. She held her breath in awe and waited a moment, letting the words rest like motes of dust upon her ears.

"Who wrote that?" she whispered.

"The greatest English writer who ever lived." Terence snipped a leaf off one of the plants efficiently. "Milton," he continued, turning to her with a smile. "Ever read him?"

"No ... I mean, I heard . . . he's awfully difficult, isn't he?"

"Isn't everything that's worth reading?"

Embarrassed, she turned to replace the small book where she had found it.

"No." He moved past her quietly, his footsteps almost soundless on the Oriental rug. She started, thinking she might have tipped something over and not heard it fall. He picked up the book she had just put down, reached for her hand and placed the book in her palm. "It's yours. Everyone should have the opportunity to read Milton."

"But you can't. . .You don't even know my name!"

"Well, what is it?"

"What's what?"

"Your name?"

"Oh. Diana. Diana Colucci." She closed her fingers around the soft leather binding and looked up into his smiling eyes.

With a deep bow like a knight of old England would make to a lady, he announced, "Terence John Pellican, at your service, mademoiselle. And now that we are duly acquainted, I hereby present you with Milton." He looked so like a gangly Ichabod Crane that she couldn't stop a giggle.

"Diana's a wonderful name, you know," he continued as if not hearing her laugh. "It means 'bright one.' There was a Roman goddess by that name as well. You just came from Rome, didn't you?" He turned and blew the dust from a set of bronze bookends without looking at her or waiting for her answer. "The most important of all the temples on the Aventine is Diana's. She's also the protector of the lower classes, the slaves. Are you that type of person?"

"Boy, for an Englishman you talk awfully fast." "Are we supposed to be slow?" He stopped. She had to arch her neck back to see his face. Though his words were sharp, his features were amused. "You Yanks don't have the market on speed, you know. In fact, I think the Italians might have that. You're not Italian, are you?" His eyes rested on her hair, then roamed her face to her eyes. "Can't be. You have blue eyes."

"Oh, but I am. Sicilian." She was beginning to enjoy their conversation almost as much as she enjoyed the shop itself.

"Sicilian! The worst kind!"

"I beg your pardon!"

"They have to be the fastest of all the Italians, even worse than those bloody Romans. If they can't speak quickly, they keep up with their hands. And driving! My word, they think it's necessary to speed everywhere. It's in their blood, I believe."

She laughed at his awkward imitation of an Italian speaking, his hands flying through the air. Smiling, he slid them back into his sweater's pockets. "Would you like some tea?"

"But of course," she teased, already liking Peter Rivington's nephew. "This is England, isn't it? And it *is* past four o'clock."

Five hours later, she was settled into an overstuffed arm chair in Peter Rivington's apartment above the shop, feeling warm and content, her after-dinner tea nestled in her hands.

Gene sat cross-legged in the chair opposite her, listening intently as Peter shared more of his fascinating stories about London's antiques world, Paris's flea markets, and the many treasures which had come into his hands through the years. Terence bustled about in the tiny kitchen, preparing a plate of English butter cookies for dessert and bringing in yet another pot of boiling water.

Peter was an invalid, confined to an ancient oak- and-wicker wheelchair in which he scuttled around dangerously fast within the small apartment. At 83 years old, he said, "I'm not ready to give up the business yet! Just let those young antiquers try to unseat me. They've already seen what it's like to try to outbid me at auction. And none of them knows the business anymore. In it for a fast pound or two, they are!"

She tucked her legs underneath her, leaning a bit closer to the fire burning brightly in the grate beside her, quite satisfied to sit and listen to the gossip the three men shared, keeping her eyes and ears open for any bits of information she could store for later use. Occasionally, one of them would ask her a question or she would catch Terence peering at her quizzically as if wondering what she was doing in Gene's company, but other than that, she had been left alone to loll in the chair and enjoy the warm safety she felt in their company.

The apartment was as crowded with antiques as the shop below, though there were fewer items to move from the chairs so that they could sit down. She learned that

3 had been in business since his early teens and, that Terence joined him at the tender age of fourteen, not bothering to finish school so he could help his ailing uncle. Little had they realized Peter would continue to be a strong figure in London's antique business and that Terence would stay on indefinitely.

His lack of education was not apparent in Terence's demeanor. In fact, she had a sneaking suspicion that he had been schooled much better at home and in his uncle's business than he would have been at any university. His mind was sharp and unyielding, his historical knowledge of the items his uncle sold was complete, and his literary tidbits continually surprised her. He made her smile when he bandied words with Gene, often topping her boss, a feat-she had never been able to accomplish and never expected she would. She wondered why he had not married or had children, but realized it was probably because he was so devoted to his uncle, as well as to the world of antiques in which he had been raised.

"It's an addiction," he said when she asked him why he had become so involved. "To have beautiful things within your grasp at any hour of the day, to be able to buy and sell like a stockbroker, to learn the history of the world through the objects it produced. What better life could there be?"

By the next morning when it was time to return to the airport, Diana felt as though she had made a new friend and shook Terence's hand warmly before getting into the cab beside Gene.

"Why not drop me a line when you finish Milton?" Terence suggested as the fog around them slowly whirled and lifted.

"I'll do that," she promised, giving him a little wave before closing the cab door. The last thing she saw as the vehicle moved down King's Row was a blurry image of the amaryllis in the window.

Chapter Eighteen

Boston, February 23, 1981

"There's one over there," Maryann pointed in the direction of an empty space by a large cement pole. Behind her, the boys were itchy, wanting out of the jail called a car. "I shouldn't have told them we were going to see Di," she mused, a smile on her face, as Robert pulled into the parking space and shut off the car.

She had to force her grin. Since their argument back at the house, a dark cloud appeared to be hanging over Rob's head. Well, she didn't care. There was no need for him to be smoking pot with the kids around. Sure, she knew it relaxed him. Knew it was probably safer than drinking. Hell, he was even a nicer person when he had a few tokes. But, damn it, not around the kids!

"Oh, well, you'll learn not to make promises before they're teenagers. I'm sure," he replied, a vacant look in his eyes.

Maryann didn't answer, wondering whether Rob was deep iii thought or still a little high. Probably both. God, if he could only learn to deal with life. Roll with the punches.

He had been quiet throughout the half-hour drive to Logan Airport, looking straight ahead, both hands gripping the wheel of the ancient Volkswagen Diana had given them just after they got married. He maneuvered the vehicle expertly through Boston's traffic, ignoring his sons' battle cries. Both were belted into car seats and were as gloomy as the gray winter rain which had been falling for the past three days.

It was an early thaw, an unseasonably warm February, producing floods in low-lying regions and seeming to make the winter snow dirtier than it had already become. The weather made Robert's mood worse and, for the first time in their married life, Maryann felt unsure of what to say to him.

Busying herself undoing Chris from his car seat as Robert took care of Tony, she decided to venture one more try at conversation. "Which gate did she say she was coming in?"

"She didn't."

She sighed and shook her head. For someone who was assumed to be the stronger of the species, he was making a poor showing. She supposed, however, that at times like these, the women were always the ones to be leaned upon. Funny, he didn't show any signs of leaning, just retreated further and further into himself, away from her and the kids. Would it get worse as they got older or would she someday be able to get through to him like she used to?

She hurried after him, her four-year-old son on her hip, balanced precariously. Her heels clacked against the cement blocks of the parking lot. Robert's hulking form passed through the automatic doors and headed for the Pan Am information desk, leaving her to fumble for herself. With a flash of Irish indignation, she swore under her breath and promised herself he would pay for this—one way or the other—someday. Not now, though. As much as she knew he hated to admit it, he was hurting. And she never had any patience with people who kicked others when they were down. She certainly wasn't about to start doing something like that now.

"Is Di-Di coming on the plane?" Chris asked, a little too loudly and right into her left ear.

"Yes, sweetheart, Auntie Di is coming on one of those big planes. See?" She pointed to a TWA flight which had just landed as her younger son clapped chubby hands in glee.

"Plane! See, Daddy? Plane!" Tony chortled.

Robert stopped. He turned to Maryann and Chris, an apology in his eyes. "That's a big one, Chris. Maybe someday we'll go on one, too." Standing in the middle of rushing travelers, he waited for his family to catch up with him.

Maryann smiled at him tentatively, shifting Chris to her other hip and reaching a hand up to stroke Rob's bearded cheek. "It's going to be okay, honey, don't worry." He nodded and put his free arm around her shoulder as they walked to Gate 10.

"That must be them now," he said. A line of people was filing through a door beneath a sign which simply said "10/CUSTOMS." Robert's head swung back and forth as he pushed through the crowd surging toward them.

"Can you see her?" she asked, cursing her height as she did every time she couldn't see over the heads of even the shortest human beings. She shifted Chris again and smiled at Tony's face peeking at her over Robert's shoulder. The toddler had a red lollipop in his hand which he was earnestly trying to stick into his father's ear.

"Yup, she's coming." He lifted a hand and waved, trying to stretch a smile across his mouth. He was failing miserably.

God, Robbie, she thought, let her at least get off the plane before you tell her. And don't let her see you're stoned.

"Di-Di!" Chris shouted at the sign of his aunt's familiar dark head.

"DiDiDiDiDi," Tony echoed, bouncing up and down in his father's arms.

Within seconds, Diana was in front of them, her arms outstretched to take both boys, smothering their faces with kisses and comments about how big they had grown. Maryann and Robert stood to the side, watching her greet their children and waiting patiently for their chance to welcome her home. As she glanced upward at her husband's face, she was amazed to find him looking at least twenty years older than he had only moments ago.

"And you guys!" Diana finally turned to them, her face beaming, arms still full of both nephews who had their little hands around her neck. "I've missed you so much and I have scads to tell you. Gene?"

Gene? Where did he go?"

"Right behind you." The elegant blond man poked a finger at Chris's nose and played a momentary game of peek-a-boo with Tony before coming around to join the adults. "Weather's just like it was when we left London. How are you, Rob?" He reached out a hand, then dropped it to his side when he realized Rob was busy staring at his sister. "And Maryann? You've held down the fort with this handful of a family of yours, I see." They hugged warmly. Gene bending deep to encompass Maryann in his one free arm. "This airport is still one of the craziest in the world, don't you think, Di?" They turned to see Diana looking, bewildered, at her younger brother, almost as though she were reading his mind.

"What's wrong?" Diana asked.

"Mama died two days ago." Robert replied without hesitation, in a rush as though he had been holding his breath and the words just happened to come out when he exhaled.

"Robert!" Maryann grabbed her husband's arm, then quickly turned to catch the two toddlers slithering out of Diana's arms. "Couldn't you have waited a moment or two?"

Diana's color instantly drained. Her knees began to buckle visibly. Quickly grabbing her by the elbows. Gene ushered her to one of the orange plastic bucket seats that were now empty. He eased her into it, then sat down next to her, urging her to bend her head onto her lap. "You'll faint otherwise," he said in a conversational tone as if this happened to him every day of the week. Lifting his head, he met Maryann's eyes and Robert's stone-cold gaze. "When?"

"Two days ago." Rob took a seat next to Diana, both hands palm up in his lap. "In her sleep. No pain whatsoever. They found her that way when they went in to get her for breakfast."

"Why didn't you call me?" Diana's voice was muffled. Though she tried to lift her head. Gene's hand stayed on the back of her neck and she didn't have the apparent strength to move it.

"Didn't know where you were."

"Arnie?"

"Took care of all the arrangements. Funeral's today. It's only us. There's no one else to be there, so they held it over until you got here. We can go there on the way home. And Arnie wants to see us before the end of the week."

"Yes, we'll go there on the way home." Her voice was dead, but when she lifted her head, the color had come back into her cheeks.

Maryann knelt beside her on the floor, releasing the children to roam throughout the waiting area. "Are you all right, honey?" Pushing Diana's hair off her cheek, she was surprised at the heat and moistness she felt there. "Can I get you some water?"

Diana nodded and gave her a meek smile. "Was a shock," she said with a nervous little laugh, looking from Gene to Robert and back again. "Never got that close to fainting before."

"I'm sorry, Di. I guess I should have waited a couple of

minutes," Rob said, looking at his hands, large and useless, against his jeans. "I just didn't know how to tell you and I've been holding it in for the past couple of days. You know, I just didn't . . ." Without warning, his large blue eyes filled with tears which rolled haphazardly down his face. He brought both hands up to wipe them away, as if they embarrassed him. "I feel so bad. I just feel so useless."

"Don't." Gene reached over to pat the large shoulder which had once gone onto a football field sans pads. "We all feel like that when someone dies."

"How would you know?" Rob's eyes warned Gene that he was stepping into family territory and that he didn't belong there.

"I lost my father when I was just about your age. There's no words that can describe how guilty you feel, even if you weren't responsible. Or how alone." "Sorry," Robert muttered as he passed his hand once again over his wet cheek. "I guess I just never expected ... I sort of thought she'd come back someday . . ." "We knew a long time ago, Robbie," Diana said softly, reaching to comfort her brother as she had millions of times during their lives and her face softened. "I know. But I always thought. . ."

Over his head, Diana met Maryann's eyes. A silent conversation passed between them, and Maryann nodded. "Let's get out of here," she said softly. "We can talk in the car."

Walking through the crowded terminal, Maryann felt a pang of resentment that her husband was better able to talk to his sister than he was to her, but shook the feeling, discarding it as inappropriate. She herded her children back into her arms and acted as shepherdess for the flock of adults which she had to urge onto their feet and out the long corridor which led to the parking lot.

"Would you mind if we went alone?" Diana asked Gene as they stood outside in the drizzling rain. The automatic door opened every time they shifted their weight. "I think I just need to be with my family right now."

"Of course I don't mind, darling." He leaned over to kiss her lightly on her cheek, then took both of her hands in his. "Promise me you'll call as soon as you get home. And don't worry about making it to work until you feel you can. Promise?"

She nodded, then stood and watched his neatly-clad figure disappear into a waiting Yellow Cab. On the other side of the street, Maryann waited, her hair starting to curl in every direction.

"I've got the goddamn frizzies again," she said as they walked companionably to the car. "Happens every time it rains. Without fail."

Diana smiled, though her mind was elsewhere. She was marveling at the fact that she didn't feel like crying. An odd sort of calm had pervaded her senses, making her feel like her feet weren't even touching the ground. It wasn't happiness. Not by a long shot. But it wasn't the pressing grief she expected to feel. It was almost. . .

no, it couldn't be. . . yes, I need to be honest with myself, she thought. It was almost a sense of relief.

There was only one other car in the funeral home's parking lot besides theirs. It was vaguely familiar, though she couldn't place it until they entered the building and she heard Arnie's voice. Subdued and constant, it seemed to be coming from the room to her left, the one which had a sign outside the door designating it, at least for the time being, as Rose Colucci's resting place.

The smell of gladioli, chrysanthemums, and roses floated through the stale air. The heat was stifling. She wondered briefly if they kept the rooms warm just to keep the flowers alive.

Suddenly, the smells and sounds transported her back to 1967. She was twelve. Rob was nine. It wasn't their mother lying in front of them in a polished mahogany coffin. In fact, the coffin wasn't even open: the room was full of burly men who appeared uncomfortable in ties which made their necks bulge and crying, dark-haired women who patted her and her brother on their heads like they were pet canines. The pain of just being in the same room, among adults whom she had only seen once or twice, had been almost too much for her to bear.

She held onto Rob's hand so tightly that he kicked her in the ankle, but she hadn't minded. Her father was in that coffin and she wanted to wail. The stab of pain made her bite her lip, but the howl remained inside.

"Diana? Rob? Maryann? I just wanted to tell you how sorry I am." Arnie stood in front of them, as he had over a decade ago, his glasses slightly askew, his hands stretched out to each of them. He went slowly from one to the other, ending with Diana, folding her against his bony chest and patting her hair awkwardly. She wanted to cry, but couldn't summon the tears as she had so many years ago.

"Thanks, Arnie," she said softly as she walked past him toward the center of the room.

For what seemed hours, she stood in front of her mother's coffin, not recognizing the woman who lay in it. She wasn't seeing the tiny form against the satin pillows, but another woman who leaned from the second floor window to lustily call her children to supper. She saw the dark-haired woman whose eyes lit up every time her husband came through the door, swinging his aluminum lunch pail, both children in tow —Diana, hanging off his belt; Rob, lifted high on his shoulders. She smelled the rich, spicy aroma of *braciole* and meatballs instead of the cloying florist's smell which invaded the room. She heard the sounds of the streets rather than the muted organ strains which floated ethereally through the funeral home.

"Mama, I went home for you. Back to Sicily. They all miss you and they told me wonderful stories about you and Papa. Aunt Cecile sends her love. She told me to give you a big hug. And your nieces and nephews. Mama. You wouldn't recognize them. There are so many and each one is innocent. Innocent and beautiful.

"Sicily is beautiful. Mama. I never realized how beautiful it would be. I saw where you lived and the school you went to. I met your friends and all the people who lived in the village. Even stood on the hillside that looked down into the sea. You know, Mama, the one where Papa proposed to you." She took a deep breath, finding herself wordless. "But it's time for you to go home now. Go now. We love you. Mama. We've always loved you."

She was vaguely aware that she was alone, that the others had left the room to give her the privacy she needed. She took a couple of steps closer, knelt on the red velvet padded knee-rest in front of her mother, and just stared. Rose still wore her wedding band, though it floated down by the tip of her finger, ready to fall off. Diana tried to slip it back, but it fell into her palm. It was warm.

Tentatively, she took the ring into her hand and noticed, for the first time, the inscription on the inside of the band. It simply said "Amore." It was almost as though her mother was finally speaking to her. She tried to slip the ring on her ring finger, but her mother's hands were much smaller than hers and it would not go past the first knuckle. With a hesitant gesture, she slid the gold band on her pinky and it went calmly, though snugly.

Lifting her eyes once more, she looked upon her mother's face and smiled. "Thank you, Mama," she S2ud quietly and rose to leave.

She found Maryann, Robert, Arnie, and the boys huddled in a small room at the end of a long hallway carpeted in dark blues and greens. The walls were papered with that nubby kind of paper that resembles cut velvet. She let her fingers trail along the wall, her equilibrium faltering a little as she drew nearer to the soothing sound of voices.

They were sitting there quietly. Patiently. Obviously waiting for her. She closed the door behind her, immediately struck by a sense of claustrophobia. Opening the door again, she took the only seat in the room.

"Are you okay?" Maryann asked, a concerned look on her face, her hand on Diana's forearm. Tony sat on his mother's lap, busily studying, with crossed eyes, a pencil he held in his chubby fingers. Chris, sprawled on the floor between his father's legs, drew a happy face with a pen stamped with the name of the funeral home.

Diana nodded. She smiled weakly at Arnie then looked at Rob who avoided her glance, lifting his eyes in Arnie's direction instead. In the back of her mind ran a hope that the boys wouldn't remember this day, that she would be able to forget it, too.

"I have something to tell you," Arnie began, "but I wanted to wait until you were all here before I said anything." He cleared his throat nervously and folded his hands on the table in front of him. For a moment, he played with his college ring, a bulbous gold and black emblem with a ruby set in the middle.

"When your father died, as you know, I took over handling the bills for his estate. You guys lived on a certain amount of money every month. Not much, I realize, but it got you through and paid the bills that needed to be paid." He coughed again, then placed his hands back in the same position. "Tony was concerned about taking care of his family. He believed in insurance and savings accounts, investments that would grow with time. He was a squirrel, that man." He laughed affectionately.

"He left enough to take care of a family of five. I guess he and your mother had, at one point, discussed having more kids. Well, with that kind of money, I knew it would take care of you for a while and that if you had all of it you would —no offense, Diana— spend it all. So, I took the liberty of investing some of the insurance money your father left for you kids, because I didn't know how things would go with your mother. He left me in charge, you know, and it was a good thing, after what happened to your mother. He knew her pretty well, I guess. Her strengths and weaknesses." The lawyer coughed and took another breath.

"Anyway, I continued paying the life insurance policy on her which your father took out when he worked at Bethlehem Steel. Good thing I did. When your mother went into the nursing home last year, the investments helped pay her medical bills." He raised his eyes to Diana who was listening in awe.

"But / paid her bills," she said.

"Some of them. Not all. I had the home send me the balance. See, I knew exactly what you could afford and I . . . well, 1 really didn't want you to extend yourself too far."

"What's the point, Arnie?" It was Robert's turn to interrupt,

"The point is that the investments 1 made for you really worked out much better than 1 thought they would. When your mother died, the nursing home bills were paid, the funeral is all taken care of—by the way, you guys have to get together and choose a stone and where you want her buried —and there was some left over. There also is the insurance money."

"How much?" Robert asked, sitting on the edge of his chair. Diana shot him a warning look. He grimaced, folded his arms across his chest, and leaned back.

"Well, there's $50,000 of insurance money, $23,575 of investments, after funeral expenses, of course. A total of $73,575." Arnie sat back, his eyes volleying from Diana to Robert, then to Maryann, who sat silently, her mouth open with amazement.

"Seventy-three thousand dollars." Diana's voice was reverent. She had never thought her mother would have left them anything. In fact, for a moment on the way to the funeral home, she had considered asking Gene for the money to bury Rose. But, no, it hadn't been their mother. It had been Papa. Papa and Arnie. She felt warm, as if she had gotten a hug from the grave. Goose pimples broke out on the fleshy part of her arms.

"Now there's the matter of how it will be split," Arnie continued, his business voice taking over, a crispness to it Diana had only witnessed when she talked to him in his office, when it was necessary for him to be professional. "Di, you're the oldest. Your father wanted it to go straight to you."

She began shaking her head even before he finished speaking. "No, that's not the way I want it. Anything that's coming to us is coming to both of us. To Robert and to me. You make sure that's the way it's done, Arnie."

"I thought you'd say that, so I took the liberty of making up some papers, an agreement of sorts, which stipulates the way the money will be split. Fifty-fifty, I assume?"

She nodded again.

"This is just a formality, you know. Just something for the insurance company. And the checks will be ready as soon as you like."

Robert's grim look had disappeared. He shared a smile with his wife, then picked up the pen. "Where do I sign?"

Though turned off a bit by his anxious approach, Diana smiled, too, then looked down at her nephews. "Wait a minute," she said.' "What about the boys? Shouldn't we put something aside for them?"

"I think that's up to their parents, don't you?" Arnie raised his eyebrows, causing his glasses to teeter even further to the right than normal.

"Don't worry, Di. We'll take care of the kids. Put something away for college or buy some U.S. savings bonds." Robert's hand was still on the pen, his fingers inching their way to the blue-bound document on the desk between them.

Diana knew exactly what was going through his mind. Gone were the worries about money, the agony over meeting the mortgage payment every month, the trials and tribulations with the VW. He envisioned new furniture, a new sports car, a mortgage-free future. Looking at Maryann, she knew those thoughts also coursed through her sister-in-law's mind.

"Okay, let's do it. Let's get out of this hole once and for all."

Chapter Nineteen

Boston, April 5, 1981

In the hazy spring afternoon sun, Gene Penchance Monroe's Beacon Hill apartment took on a light akin to what skiers called "Alpen glow"—that golden resonance which lasts only moments at the end of a cold winter day, a treasure which floats mystically over the top of the mountains painting them a warm, almost tender, color like that of the most precious metals. Gene loved this time of day, this time of *year,* and was satisfied at having picked this very weekend as the debut for his new shop.

All That Glitters now featured items from the glorious past of countries all over the world. He was sure it would be what would make his shop one of the best known of all the antiques shops which had come and gone in America's oldest towns. In the past hundred years, no one had been able to open an antique shop in Boston of this caliber. It had exceeded all of his expectations.

Yes, the Sack family had done a good job—had made a nice name for themselves, in fact—but they had not received their due rewards until moving their business to New York. Gene was sure he could not only do better than they had in Boston, but could also out stock their New York shop. He had as much knowledge as they did, as many worldly connections and as perfect a shop location, as well as something more—the finesse, the physical Yankee heritage, and a financial mind second only to that of a top stockbroker. It would take all his charm, and probably every penny left to him by the narrow-faced Brahmins whose portraits hung on his apartment walls, but he would do it. This business was what he was born to do.

People would always love beautiful things. That was his brass ring. Gene would *always* give his clientele the most sublime *objets d'art* he could find. Even if he had to travel to every corner of the world to obtain them. In fact, that's just what he planned to do. The European trip had netted a few gems, but there were many others as yet unearthed. As he had reminded Diana many times in the past month, he'd only just begun.

The gala he planned to celebrate the new opening had been fodder for the Boston gossip columnists for the past month. Rose Kennedy had sent back a positive RSVP, the reporters noted, and she didn't go out these days unless a Cardinal invited her. All the Beacon Hill loyalists would be there, including Mayor Kevin White and Governor Michael Dukakis. Collectors of all genres had been invited, from the New York Mellons to Bill Cosby, collector of art and fine furniture; the Pendletons of Montgomery, Alabama, and Barbra Streisand, afficionado of all things Art Nouveau. The directors of the Winterthur Museum, Boston's Museum of Fine Arts, the Guggenheim, and the curator of the US. Department of State's Fine Arts Committee had all answered their invitations promptly and positively. For those who mattered, it was an imperative gathering. And almost all of them had said yes—probably out of curiosity—but nevertheless, they said yes.

None of them would get a private showing. No one knew what kind of objects Gene had chosen to stock his shop. Yet everybody knew and respected his taste in fine antiques, his knowledge of period furniture and porcelains, and his ability to make a deal. Few would make the mistake of *not* showing up, he felt sure, for there was one thing all antique collectors had in common: the pleasure of the hunt.

Standing by the window overlooking the small courtyard, he sighed. He had succeeded in getting at least partially dressed, even had the silk tie, which would encircle the high collar of his formal shirt, slung loosely around his neck. But he hadn't buttoned the black opal buttons on that shirt, hadn't tucked its tails into his highly-creased-and-shiny tux pants, and hadn't hung up the phone he had held in his hands for the past ten minutes.

As if he didn't know how it had gotten there, he looked at the black receiver, then put it quickly into its holder on the Chippendale piecrust table at his side. The table tilted precariously. Dazed, he caught and righted it, then turned away from the window.

So much for having a special guest this evening, he thought despondently. I should have known better than to leave a handsome young man like Scott Logan unaccompanied for almost three months. Should have brought him with me. Maybe the trip would have been better if I had someone to talk to when Diana had gone off with that Colombian. Maybe, maybe, maybe. Things wouldn't change now. He knew that. But, still, what would have happened if. .
.

He had been calling Logan every hour or two since returning from Europe almost a month and a half ago. Either the answering machine was on or there was simply no answer at the intern's Jamaica Plains apartment. He had left countless messages, At first, they were curious: "Where are you, Scottie? I'm back and I have lots of presents for you. Give me a call when you get home." Then, he had gotten a bit more insistent: "Scott, I've been calling for five days. You've got to be home at one point or another. I'd appreciate a call. Please." And, after two weeks, angry: "Listen, Logan, this answering machine you're using has been paid for with *my* money. That apartment you're renting was paid for —a year in advance—by yours truly. You'd think you would at least feel guilty about that and give me the decency of a phone call!"

But, this past week, he'd simply left meek messages. He was too tired to do otherwise. "Scott? I'm reopening the shop next week and would love to have you at the opening. Please, Scott? You said you were interested in All That Glitters and the party's going to be something Boston hasn't seen the likes of in years. Please call me back. In case you've lost the number, it's 227-5386."

Sighing once again, his shoulders bowed inward toward his chest. Everything hurt, from the top of his silvery-blonde head right down to the heels of his patent-leather-clad feet. He felt old, much older than his 64 years. And he was beginning to look it, too. No more disguising the wrinkles crowding around his eyes. No amount of sun could keep his tanned face from looking sallow and no vitamin could put the saucy spring back into his step which had been there only one short year ago.

He coughed into a closed fist and felt the bones in his chest throb. For a moment he stood there, in that golden glow which had invaded his apartment, and waited for the pain to subside. "I have to get some help," he finally conceded, walking to the bathroom. "Just not smart anymore," he said to the image in the mirror as he wrapped one end of his black silk tie around the other. "Must have emphysema or something." He wheezed as he pushed the opal buttons through the thrice-sewn holes in the white shirt.

Standing up Straight, he slid his arms into his jacket and practiced forcing a smile onto his lips. He caught his reflection in the mirror. The smile was worse than a grimace. Shaking his head, he strode out of the bathroom, grabbing a package of Gauloises off the Louis XIV marble-top table next to the door. Looking once more over the apartment and satisfied he had everything he needed, he opened the front door and slid silently into the chandelier-lit hallway.

All That Glitters had literally been transformed by the time Diana and Gene returned from Europe. She could hardly believe this was the same plaster-filled place she walked into that first day back. Gene had started the refurbishing while still in Europe, ordering Miles to have the workers clean out the two apartments above the shop—one had been used for storage, the other had been empty for almost two years. Then the walls between the rooms were taken down and the plaster stripped off so that the bare, ancient brick was exposed. Staircases were replaced and widened so the three floors would be connected and inventory could be easily brought from one tier to the other. Some walls were replaced with white plasterboard, the kind which made it easy to hang works of art. New windows were put in, replacing the tiny ones which barely let in a ray of sunshine. Track lighting was installed after the electricians had updated the whole electrical system, the floors were sanded and polished, and, finally, movers were hired to carry the larger pieces of furniture to their new "homes" on the second and third floors. All That Glitters was now the largest antique shop on Charles Street.

Formally clad, instantly recognizable dignitaries, designers, and debutantes mingled about on the second floor where Diana stood, Waterford champagne glasses gracing their tastefully bejeweled hands. Below her, on the first floor. Gene greeted his guests after the butler announced them, and above her, on the third floor. Miles was in charge of watching the action.

Because Gene had known it would take more than three of them to attend to all the guests and possible sales, Maryann and Robert also floated around, more to keep the clientele occupied than to actually handle any business. Neither of them knew much about antiques, Diana mused, as she watched Robert caught in the middle of a noisy reunion between one of the younger Rockefeller women and an old friend from Radcliffe. Since successfully investing Mama's money in a better house, car, and other luxuries, both were relaxed and well-dressed, fitting in with the coolly-elegant crowd swirling around them.

Her eye wandered around the room critically. She could hardly believe they had accomplished everything they set out to do a few short months ago. Just this afternoon, she had been running about in jeans and an old sweatshirt — was that only two hours ago?—trying to arrange last-minute items in appropriate spaces, making sure the tables were placed where they would not be bumped and knocked over, assuring herself the lighting was right and that everything in the three-story shop was tagged with the item's inventory numbers. She had finished putting the master list on their new computer only moments before rushing out the door to get dressed.

"No prices," she had said to Gene. "The only way we're going to make sales is if we can talk to the customers. Might stop some of them from coming in again." He had guffawed, not because he thought she was wrong but because *she* had now begun to tell *him* how to run the business. And she had been right! •

"Mrs. Logan, how nice to see you." Reaching to shake the octogenarian's hand, Diana moved closer. The Beacon Hill matron was one of her favorite customers, and it was obvious she seemed a little overwhelmed by the crowds.

"Diana! How lovely you look! Scarlet is a wonderful color for you. You should wear it all the time. Are those earrings rubies? My, my. They must weigh down your lobes." She reached a trembling hand to touch the antique ruby earrings Diana had bought at a recent Skinner estate auction. Diana tilted her head so Mrs. Logan wouldn't have to reach too high and smiled down at her.

"Would you like a fresh drink?" she asked.

"That would be lovely." Mrs. Logan followed her to the corner where a maid in a black and white uniform made her way through the crowd offering champagne glasses from a sterling silver platter. "Never expected to see half my neighbors here. Gene has quite outdone himself. And, you know, I think I might just have to have the Queen Anne tilt-top over there. I believe it would fit nicely in the little alcove in my upstairs hallway. I'm always looking for a place to put my gloves and purse, you know." Her last comment was in *sotto voce,* though her falsetto rose above the heads of the other customers milling around them. "Could you please hold it for me, dear?"

"Of course," Diana answered, looking over the woman's head at the new group working their way up the stairs from the first floor.

Even the stairways had been utilized. They had spent two days arranging the paintings bought in Europe and purchased at Sotheby's most recent art auctions. Each one was hung exactly right and given the space it deserved as well as the necessary lighting. Each was given a tag which gave the name of the work and its artist, the year it was done, the artist's background, and any other tidbits she was able to dig up about the period.

She spent many evenings at the Boston Public Library and made several appointments with different curators at the Museum of Fine Arts in order to get all the necessary information. At this point, she had so many facts and figures in her head, she wasn't quite sure which information belonged to which painting. But when a piece of art was in front of her, when she was able to study the lines and the colors, her feel for it brought all the details magically together, and her enthusiasm overrode all confusion.

"Excuse me, Mrs. Logan." She slipped away from the old woman, a rustle of the off-the-shoulder scarlet taffeta dress the only noise she made as she crossed the ancient Hamadan carpet.

"Maryann, could you please take care of Mrs. Logan?" Diana touched her sister-in-law's arm and gestured toward the slightly confused woman. "She wants me to hold the Queen Anne over there against the wall."

"The Queen Anne?"

"The table. She'll show you. You might want to keep her talking for a while, too. She seems a bit alone."

Maryann, her reddish curls bobbing and her long black jersey skirt swirling around her ankles, walked toward Mrs. Logan. Satisfied that the woman would be taken care of, Diana concentrated on watching the other guests.

Gene and she had decided weeks ago that they would not offer their guests any food for the simple reason that if their clients had more than a glass of champagne to occupy their hands, there was a greater chance something could be dropped on the carpets or splashed on the furniture. Instead, they invited a select few to join them for dinner in a specially reserved room at the Ritz Carlton and had arranged for a group of horse-drawn carriages to meet them at the front door of the Charles Street shop at 8 p.m. Three hours was quite enough for an open house, just enough to whet everyone's appetite. There would be plenty of time for their guests to visit the shop when there weren't so many people around.

"Try not to push too much business," Gene warned his staff when they were sitting down midst the jumbled pieces of the shop*less than a week ago. "1 want to make this a celebration, not a sale-abra- tion. We're an antiques shop, not a used car dealership."

"Excuse me, Diana." Sandy McLelland of the Virginia McLellands stood in front of her. In her late twenties, Sandy was dressed simply in a light blue, knee-length linen dress Diana recognized as Balenciaga. Her trademark string of flawless pearls hung around her neck. She played with the beads as she talked. "I want you to meet my husband and my mother-in-law, Chester and Irene McLelland. Chester, Mother, this is Diana Col — "

"Well, I can't tell you how nice it is to meet you. Miss Cole," Chester's chunky, almost bald mother replied, pumping enthusiastically on Diana's hand. "I certainly have heard a lot about Boston and its brick buildings and tiny streets, but I never expected to actually be in one of those old townhouses like we are right this minute. Why, I can almost see Paul Revere and hear the bell a-ringing to call the Yankees to war against the Brits. This town has so much character, doesn't it, Chester?"

Mrs. McLelland barely waited for her son's brief nod or to take a breath before continuing, her plump fingers now wrapped around the upper part of Diana's bare arm. "And, you know. I've always heard about these Boston parties, but, well, with the horses and all, we don't often get away from Virginia and the parties in Washington—D.C., that is —are so numerous that we just have no need."

She tittered and steered Diana toward the other end of the room where a full, twenty-paned window, which matched the one on the first floor, was surrounded by wingback chairs of all periods and descriptions. Diana had supervised the arrangement herself, realizing some of the customers might like to rest and gaze out over the traffic on Charles Street. "Sandy and Chester so love it up here that they thought I should come with them, but 1 told them, I did, Sandy, I said, and Chet, you just need to make sure that you get me a nice big room overlooking those Public Gardens. So, they did. They did! They got me into the Ritz Carlton and ... I say, aren't you having a dinner there this evening?"

Diana nodded, wondering when the woman was going to run out of breath.

"Wouldn't it be nice if we could all get together? You're such a nice, lovely woman. I bet you have all kinds of business to attend to after leaving the shop, don't you?" She winked, an almost lascivious act, and plunked Diana down into one of the wingbacks while she settled her ample form in the one opposite.

"You know, 1 think I'm just going to have to take two of these back home with me. Do you deliver, honey? Miss Cole? Diana?"

She was unable to answer, having suddenly become aware of a dark-haired man standing behind Mrs. McLelland's chair. The man stared directly into her eyes with a roguish grin, then lifted his champagne glass in salute and turned his back to them.

"My de-ah, are you all right? Why, you've gone absolutely lily white! Chet? Sandy? Look at Miss Cole. She's white as a ghost. Here, de-ah, take some of this."

A glass was forced between her lips. Someone bent her head and poured a sip of the cold champagne down her throat. No, it couldn't be, she reasoned, taking a deep breath and putting a hand out to stop Mrs. McLelland from forcing another mouthful on her. Luis wouldn't dare come to the opening! She must be seeing things.

Throughout the past month, she had thought often of the Colombian, preferring to tag him with that term rather than to use his name—anything to distance herself from what had happened. But her thoughts were confined to nighttime hours, when all was quiet in the Orleans Street apartment and no one could see the pain he still wrought in her soul. She dreamed of him and often woke with her hand between her legs, satisfying herself the way he had.

"I just saw something . . ." she said, rising out of the chair and straightening her dress. ". . . surprised me. Excuse me, please, Mrs. McLelland." She reached down to pat the woman on her shoulder. "Perhaps I'll see you later this evening and . . ." Fighting to retain some of her composure, she took another deep breath. ". . . let's talk about the chairs later. I'll make sure we don't promise them to anyone else."

Managing a wan smile, she moved to the left. He had waited behind a group that was enthusiastically debating the differences between New Orleans jazz and Mississippi blues. Taking another couple of steps to the right, she got a glimpse of the back of his head. He appeared to be alone, one hand in the pocket of his black tux, the other lifting his champagne glass to his lips. She moved another foot and was able to see the side of his face.

Yes, that was Luis's nose, those were his full lips gently touching the rim of the glass and his long lashes brushing his cheeks as he looked down at the Oriental rug. Satisfied, she strode over to him, nodding to those she brushed by, touching a few she knew on their arms or shoulders, murmuring hellos.

"What are you doing here?" She forced a smile over her clenched teeth and spoke in a hissing whisper.

"I wanted to enjoy the party. To wish you luck." The bastard smiled directly into her eyes. She had forgotten his soft Spanish accent and the arrogant way he used his eyes to tear every shred of material off her body. Desperately she tried to stop her traitorous senses from responding to his sexual challenge and pulled her arms across her chest. Her mind was saying "make him leave"; her body craved the release only he had been able to give her.

"And to see you again," he added in a low, intimate tone. He was teasing her—she could tell by the way his left eye closed a little and the left side of his mouth lifted in a tight, sexy smile.

"I told you I never wanted to see you again." "Was I supposed to believe you? Ah, *cara.* You are so beautiful when you are angry." He reached for her, caressing her arm lightly with two fingertips. She brushed them away with the back of her hand.

"Stop it. I want you to leave. You don't belong here. I don't want you here. Get the hell out of this shop, right now!" Her voice rose a little. She glanced nervously to the side, hoping none of the guests had heard her. Smiling, she nodded to the McLellands who sat in a little group by the window, apparently fascinated by her conversation with Luis. She turned her body a little so they wouldn't be able to see her face. "Get out of here," she whispered. "I don't want you in my life. I don't even want you in Boston!" Luis clucked his tongue and moved closer. She could smell the pungent odor of his cologne, could feel the heat of his body and almost see the ripples of his leg muscles through his well-fitted trousers.

"You know you do not mean what you are saying. We had a little fight. Now it is time to make up, *mi cara*"

"No, it's not." A slightly cold man's hand gripped her shoulder. For a moment, she thought it was she who had spoken, but then realized it had been Gene. His head was tilted downward, his eyes narrowed as they looked straight into Luis's face. "You weren't invited to this party, Mr. Quintana. I suggest you do as the lady says. Don't make me get the gendarmes in here to remove you. It could be quite embarrassing."

Never removing his eyes from her face, Luis handed his champagne glass to Gene and gave both of them a little bow. "No one embarrasses Luis de la Maria Quintana," he hissed and slid between them, slowly wending his way through the crowd, then down the stairs.

Gene, his hand still on Diana's shoulder, nodded to several people and managed a smile. "Are you all right?" he asked quietly.

"I'll be fine." She watched the McLellands moving en masse toward her.

"We've decided on all four of the chairs. Miss Cole," Mrs. McLelland drawled.

Gene raised an eyebrow at Diana. Miss Cole? he seemed to say. "Can you hold them for us?"

Diana nodded, about to say "Of course" when the Virginia McLellands surrounded her like bees around honey and took her over to the window to tell them about the chairs.

Robert snapped his silver cigarette lighter once more. No use. No fluid. "Shit," he muttered. "One lousy cigarette is all I want. Can't keep standing up there, watching all these tight-asses, without a cigarette."

"Here." A - gold lighter flickered in front of Robert's nose. The end of his Winston flared.

"Thanks. Thought I was going to pass out in there. Stifling, isn't it?" He looked at the well- dressed, swarthy man who was putting the lighter back into his pocket.

"Hmm . . ." The man looked anxiously up and down the street. There were no parking spaces anywhere on Charles Street, but that, as Robert knew, was not unusual. It was one of the reasons he had suggested to Maryann that they take a cab.

"Waiting for a ride?"

"Yes, I guess my car had to go around the block." The man looked directly at Robert and his eyes flickered briefly.

"Colombia, South America."

"Colombia, huh? Is that close to Brazil?"

"We share a border, but Colombia is further north."

"Oh." Conversation lapsed for a few moments and Luis took to staring down the street again. Robert lifted his head back and up, lazily blowing smoke circles into the springtime sky.

"Hey, how about us going for a drink?" Robert offered, stubbing his cigarette out on the sidewalk beneath his foot. "I could go for a beer, how 'bout you?"

Luis hesitated for a brief second, then looked at Robert thoughtfully. "Yes. Yes, I think that would be a good idea."

"There's a place up the street that has a big screen TV. Like basketball?"

Luis lifted an eyebrow and nodded again.

"Let's go, then." Robert straightened his shoulders and loosened the tie which had been threatening to strangle him all night. "Betcha Maryann doesn't even notice I'm gone."

They laughed as they headed down Charles Street toward the Sevens Bar and Grill.

The Ritz Carlton's staff had outdone themselves, Diana thought. She tapped her fingers against one of the muted pastel tablecloths layered on top of each of the large round tables occupying the room and savored the quiet moment she had been allowed. When she walked in, it was the signal to start placing glasses of water in front of each plate. As she got their guests seated, the waiters and waitresses began bringing out tropical fruit cups. A hearts of palm salad was next, followed by the chef's specialty, a lightly broiled Boston cod, accented by fresh asparagus. For those who had room, Diana and Gene decided on a Yankee pudding for dessert—thinking it might be in keeping with the "antiqueness" of the occasion. Surprisingly, she heard murmurs from all sides, especially from those who grew up in Boston, that the pudding brought back childhood memories of grandparents and wood-burning stoves.

Then it was time for a little socializing while coffee was being served. To her right. Rose Kennedy bent her aristocratic head forward to hear something Gene had said. Diana was amazed at the ease with which Gene had moved from one crowd to another, making sure everyone was made to feel important. Yet, I shouldn't be, she mused. It was like that in Europe, too.

Across the room sat the Mayor, turning from one constituent to the other, his slim form easily commanding the table. He presided over a heated discussion about the best restaurant in Boston. La Streisand had just left in a whirl of permed auburn hair and clanking bracelets. Maryann's fascinated eyes followed the actress until she and her entourage
were well out of sight.

As Diana roamed the room, thanking those she knew for coming and introducing herself to those she didn't, she found herself presented by the McLellands as "Ms. Cole" on several occasions.

She reminded herself to correct their faux pas sometime when the old woman could stop talking for a moment. Funny, she kind of liked the name. At least no one seemed to have a problem pronouncing it as they did "Colucci."

Thankfully, no one had seen or overheard the minor skirmish she and Gene had had with Luis. At least they had not mentioned it, nor did she feel anyone looking at her strangely. She allowed her shoulders to relax. It was the only thing which marred an otherwise perfect evening, yet the frustration she felt once Luis left had occupied her mind and body ever since. Even now, she could feel Gene turn to look at her every once in a while. Though she was grateful he was the only one in the room who knew, she wished he'd just forget about it the way she was trying to.

Lifting a finger to her mouth, she absentmindedly chewed on her nail. For a few seconds, she wasn't even aware of what she was doing; then, with a start, she dropped her hand to her lap and looked around guiltily. Damn, she thought. How in hell am I going to stop how I feel about that man when I can't even stop chewing my nails?

Determined to stop ruminating, she turned to Bunny Lawrence, heiress to the Kankakee Sugar fortune, and began a discussion about American pewter. Bunny's favorite collectible. The woman had already sunk nearly half a million dollars into English and American pewter pieces, filling both her Long Island and Marblehead homes with tankards, platters, mugs, plates, and the like. Diana knew she'd soon be on the lookout for more and listened closely so that she and Gene could fill in the gaps in the Lawrence collection.

"Goddamn, those Celtics are good!" Rob held his fifth glass of beer in one hand and a cigarette in the other.

Luis glanced at the younger man, then took another sip of cognac. Was it possible that Diana's younger brother was as simple-minded as he seemed? Typical American. Loud, obnoxious, and totally oblivious to the world beyond Boston. How different from his sister.

Across the smoke-filled barroom, Karl sat at a small table, tapping his fingers impatiently and occasionally glancing at his watch. Luis shot him a dark, warning look. Karl immediately folded his arms across his chest. He did not understand, Luis thought.

"Are the Celtics your favorite team?" Luis leaned toward Robert as if he were truly interested in the answer to his question.

"Aw, man, they're the greatest," Rob slurred, the ashes of his cigarette falling onto his pants leg.

Repulsed, Luis got off the stool and pulled at his suit jacket.

"Where you going, man?" Rob asked, swaying as he spoke.

"To the bathroom," Luis replied. "For a pick-me- up, as you Americans call it." He smiled meaningfully, though he was sure Robert did not understand why.

"Love those pick-me-ups," Rob said. "I'll come, too."

Over the top of his companion's head, Luis nodded to Karl and tipped his index finger to his nose. The three of them filed into the tiny bathroom, Karl reeling away from Rob as Luis introduced them.

"So, where's the pick-me-up?" Rob looked around the bathroom, waving his bottle of beer like a scepter, "You got a couple joints or somethin'? Bet it's good stuff, huh? You must get really good grass down in Colombia."

"Better than marijuana." Karl took a silver vial from his pocket. "Much better."

East Boston's streets were quiet as Diana slowly walked home. The best time of the day, she figured. Four a.m. Too late for most party goers; too early for workers.

. She had refused a ride from Maryann, who spent the evening wandering around the dining room looking for her husband. Robert finally walked in half an hour before the guests started to depart, looking like he had just been through a college football game.' His tie was undone, his blue eyes glassy, his smile a bit too wide. Though Diana was curious, especially when she could see that the couple was arguing, she was too preoccupied with guests to find out what was going on. When it came time to leave, she figured Robert and Maryann didn't need her in the car to argue—and she hadn't wanted to hear them anyway.

The "T" cars from Arlington Street to Maverick Station had been empty, except for a few rather harmless drunks and an occasional security guard. Even so, she kept her keys in her fist with a few poking through her fingers, just in case she needed to defend herself—a trick she had learned years ago in high school.

Her feet hurt by the time she reached Orleans Street and she longed to take off the scarlet high heels which matched her dress, but knew if she did, she'd probably cut her foot. Broken glass was scattered over the sidewalk, the result of kids tossing their soda bottles against the brick tenement walls. Bits of newspaper and candy wrappers lay idle in the early morning quiet against the edges of curbs. There were no sounds of cars, no rabble of kids playing in the streets, just the eerie breathing sound a city makes at night and, occasionally, the muffled roar of an airplane leaving from Logan.

She looked upward, past the roofs of the buildings lining the narrow street. The sky was a streaked vista of blue, yellow, and pink, the stars winking out like extinguished light bulbs, the moon a hollow crescent fading quickly. Thank God for the sky, she thought wearily. At least there's *something* pretty in this neighborhood.

As she slid her key into the front door's lock, she heard the faint whir of an automobile's motor. A long, black limousine backed slowly into view. The rear passenger window slid down with a whine. She turned the key again, hoping it would catch and open the door so she could slip inside. She didn't want to be caught alone at this hour.

"Diana." Luis's commanding voice shattered the stillness. "I would like to speak to you. I have been waiting a very long time to speak to you." He got out of the car, still in his tux though the tie was askew and his hair was mussed.

She found herself looking for the telltale ring of white around his nose, and in doing so, could see that his eyes were exceptionally dark, the pupils large. She turned the key again, her heart beating madly against her chest bone, and was relieved when the door opened.

"Please, Diana. Just one moment. Please."

"I don't have anything to say to you, Mr. Quintana."

"Mr. Quintana?" He was closer now. His hand on her elbow, pulling her back out to the sidewalk. "I can remember when you would whisper names much
less formal than that one."

His breath stunk of stale liquor, yet she found she had trouble quelling the stirrings below the line of her bikini underwear. "Not anymore," she answered, trying to appear calm. "Now let go of me. I told you when we were at the shop that I didn't want you here. That goes double for my home. Forget you know where it is!"

"I am distressed." He patted his hand over the place where his heart should be. "No one has ever treated Luis Quintana the way you have."

"There's always a first." She took the chance to slip inside and slammed the door before he had the opportunity to stop her.

"Diana!" He pounded on the heavy maple door. Ignoring the pounding, she moved up the stairs toward her apartment. "Diana!" The voice was less strident. She thought she heard him swear, then, only seconds later, the sound of a powerful motor and spinning tires.

With shaking hands, she put the key into her apartment door, opened it, then closed the door behind her. Not realizing why, she walked into her bedroom and stood quietly behind the curtains. The limousine circled around the block again and idled in front of her building. It stayed there for several long moments, then slid silently down the street like a black ghost, with only a flicker of headlights to remind her it had been there at all.

She let her keys clatter to her bureau, the sound echoing in the empty room. With little thought for where they landed, she stripped off the taffeta dress, strapless white lace bra and matching bikinis, and slid between the sheets. Turning on her bedside light, she spread the books she was currently reading across her lap. Milton's *Paradise Lost,* Hemingway's short stories, Steinbeck's *The Grapes of Wrath,* or a dry, intellectual tome on the art of the Italian Renaissance. She chose the Milton, simply because it was the lightest in physical weight, and opened it. But she couldn't concentrate.

Looking out at the sky again, she noted the colors had turned a bit brighter, illuminating the sign on the bubble gum factory across the street.

She yawned. Maybe it was time to move.

Chapter Twenty

Saugus, Massachusetts, September 10, 1981

Maryann dramatically wiped at the disappearing white suds she had splashed all over her jeans. Her formal, "lady-of-the-ball" stance contrasted comically with the ancient Bruins sweatshirt and torn jeans she wore. "Melts in nicely with the peanut butter and jam, don't you think, m'dear?" She did a twirl and curtsey for Diana, who was wiping the dishes.

"Attractive," Diana answered, nodding her head. "Now, come on, quit fooling around and answer me. I really want them to go." Placing another blue and white stoneware plate on the shelf above her, she reached for a dripping cup in the drainer. As she swirled her dishcloth around it, she watched Maryann's face. It was possible, just possible, that Maryann might give in. But she couldn't push too much more. Her sister-in-law's indecision could easily turn to aggravation, and Diana knew how mercurial Maryann's moods were—subject to change at any given moment.

Late afternoon sunlight filtered in through the cheery orange' and yellow flowered priscillas, falling on the immaculate counters surrounding the room. Blue and white porcelain canisters stood in a perfectly straight line like tin Civil War soldiers. Every modern appliance known to the American public was hung, hidden, or handily placed on those counters. Maryann didn't have time for what she called "the old fashioned shit."

As she walked from the sink to the cupboards, the Mexican tile floor felt cool beneath Diana's bare feet, like smooth babies' bottoms. Under the oak harvest table, a group of Tonka trucks served as a temporary home for some G.I. Joe dolls, which hung in various positions from the cabs, some even lying under the tires as if caught there inadvertently by enemy fire. The boys had just reluctantly given up on the game of pretending to drive the trucks to whatever cities Maryann or Diana would call out and left their mother and aunt in relative peace for the first time today. All that the two women could see from the window above the sink was one head the color of taffy and the other as black as Diana's, both nodding excitedly.

"They're not old enough," Maryann protested, quieter this time, her arms to their elbows in suds. "Really, Diana, I don't think . . ."

"Oh, come on. How old do you have to be for Disney World? Is there an age limit here?"

"That's not it. They're not old enough . . . you know they've never been away overnight."

She had been wrong to hope Maryann would take her offer. Maybe there was more to it. Maybe Maryann was simply afraid to be alone with Rob. She knew how difficult Rob could be when he got into his black moods and Maryann had intimated more than once that he'd been drinking too much. Perhaps relieving them of the kids would provide the bridge they needed to save their floundering marriage. Part of her reasoning was selfish—Maryann had become more than just a sister-in-law—she was Diana's link with reality, a home base, a family. She often seemed like the only family Diana h^, and without Maryann there would be no Chris, no Tony, none of the special glue that kept her together. She needed that safety net.

Maryann looked out the window. "The kids are getting along really well today; don't you think?" "There *is* something else, isn't there?" Diana drew herself slowly out of her seat, almost afraid to go to Maryann, to turn her around, to face her eye-to-eye.

"Chris is coming out of his shy stage, you know. Maybe he'll be my doctor after all."

"Maryann! Talk to me . . ."

"Tony, on the other hand, he's just like his father. Stubborn. Yet, he's loving. Yes, he loves Chris just as much as your brother loves you." Suddenly Maryann's shoulders shook and she clutched the edge of the sink.

"What is it? Talk to me." Diana hugged her from behind, leaning her cheek against Maryann's hair. "It's Rob, isn't it? Is he drinking again? Has he done something to you and the kids?" Oh, please tell me he hasn't hit you, she thought.

"I'm sure he doesn't mean it," Maryann managed between dry sobs. "He's not usually a cruel man. It's just . . . it's just . . ." She pulled her small frame erect and shrugged Diana off. "Take them. Take the kids to Disney World. It'll be good for them."

Four days was long enough, Diana thought, lifting her weary legs up on the bed and adjusting herself so she could see through the door to where the boys slept. They were lonesome for their mother, especially at night, so Diana tried to make bedtime as busy as possible, reading to them and letting them leave the television on until they fell asleep. Tonight, Chris refused to take off his Mickey Mouse ears. They were now cock-eyed, smashed against the pillow, probably would be irreversibly squished by the next morning. Tony had run out of energy early in the day, though she had rented a carriage for him. He was still young enough to need to cuddle a stuffed animal under his chubby arm while sleeping. Tonight's choice was a plush Donald Duck almost as big as he was.

Every day at the park had been a new experience, and almost as tiring as the one before. Blearily, Diana checked her watch, amazed to discover it was only 7:30 p.m. "Good thing I don't have to do this every day," she mused, turning down the television set and picking up the phone. She had already checked in with Rob and Maryann and, to her great relief, both sounded happy and relaxed. Maybe they'd had a chance to talk, to work things out.

Gene had been on her mind for the past two days. Though he had told her not to call, warning her in his raspy voice to go and have a good time and not to spend one second thinking of the shop, she called All That Glitters anyway and spoke to Miles yesterday. He told her of the many phone calls she received from Luis and the bouquets of carnations scattered all over the shop, also thanks to Luis. It irritated her that that was all Miles could think about.

"What about Gene?" she finally interrupted and Miles settled down long enough to report that he hadn't heard from their boss for at least a couple of days.

It didn't make sense, she thought, as the operator connected her to the Boston number. Gene didn't have the strength to go anywhere. His cough had gotten much worse since the opening. He rapidly lost weight and took to his bed, paying attention to what the doctor told him. It was totally unlike him to give in to his illness, which made her more acutely aware of just how ill he had become.

Meredith answered the phone. "It would be all right if he wasn't so damned stubborn," she retorted after making sure Gene was not awake to hear. "I hired a masseuse and she'll be coming in on a regular basis once you get back. And the nurse you hired quit yesterday because he started giving her a hard time. Does he do this with you, cherie?"

"Not usually," Diana answered, using the remote to switch off the television set. "Has he been taking his medicine?"

"He says he has. The doctor came yesterday to check on him. He was here for a long time, but Gene wouldn't tell me what he said. I heard them arguing about the hospital, but you know my cousin . . . when he wants to tell you, he'll tell you. Otherwise, don't ask."

They talked for a few more moments about the shop and how quiet it was in Boston at this time of year. Diana would have talked to Gene personally, but since he was sleeping quietly, for what Merry reported was the first time that day, she didn't want to disturb him. Besides, Merry needed the break. She imagined the Countess settling into one of Gene's leather library chairs with a good, juicy mystery. Merry had confessed a weakness for P.D. James during one of their discussions, which had surprised her. Merry seemed more a social butterfly than a bookworm, but Diana had known the Countess long enough now to realize that she was full of surprises—you could count on nothing to be characteristic.

Yet, coming straight from Paris to Boston as soon as she heard of Gene's illness *was* characteristically Merry, he told Diana. "Her heart is as big as her mammary glands," he had added, a wry smile on his face.

"Has the housekeeper fed my fish?" Diana asked, finding a pause in their conversation.

"I did, cherie. Sorry, but I just *had* to take a peek at your little place, since it's just downstairs. Gene said you wouldn't mind. I love what you've done with the fireplace. I never thought of setting a collection of candlesticks in there. And the bedroom—all white and lace. Just what I would have expected. I hope you don't mind me looking around."

Diana giggled. "I hope it was clean. I don't remember having time to even pick up a broom since I moved in." That had been less than three months ago.

The main reason for moving was that Luis simply would not leave her alone. It was getting to the point where she didn't even want to go home anymore. The large apartment echoed with her loneliness. The streets of East Boston seemed dirtier and poorer every time she walked toward the brick tenement, toward the promise of a can of cold ravioli for supper, and no human conversation for the rest of the evening. To have to spend her days among beautiful things, then brave the evenings in a damp, dark apartment where she couldn't even get an ivy to grow against the kitchen window depressed her. To contend with knocks on the door after midnight and phone calls throughout the wee hours of the morning became too much to handle. Luis succeeded in making her home life miserable.

Gene became less able to take care of himself and the shop, and she had grown less and less capable of turning away Luis and his bouquets of flowers. When he forced her to take advantage of the empty apartment below his, Diana was secretly relieved. She paid no rent since he owned the building and insisted that if she gave him as much as a penny, he'd evict her. But the best part was not having to wake up in the middle of the night to Luis pounding on the door or to hear his voice on her answering machine when she got home after work. No more flowers, no more phone calls or visits. No more Luis. She had left no forwarding address and her new phone number was unlisted. For the first time in months, she could walk a street without looking behind her for a black limousine.

Thrilled to have a place of her own, Diana furnished the high-ceilinged apartment with auction finds like Victorian ladies' prints, odd-sized mirrors grouped on her bathroom walls, and Audubon prints of farm birds for her kitchen. Despite the time and money she lavished on decorating her five rooms, she spent most of her time with Gene on the upper two floors of the building.

She registered with the phone company as Diana Cole—just in case Luis had contacts there who could get her new unlisted number—and the name had started taking hold with her customers too. "No offense, Diana," Gene had said, "but it *is* an easier name to remember."

Moving to Beacon Hill gave her a totally different lifestyle to match her new name. She bought her groceries at the small stores on Charles Street, went out for dinner two or three times a week with Gene and Miles after work—until Gene became too ill to leave his apartment, flew to New York for auctions once a week, and later, when Gene finally conceded to his illness, spent her free evenings reading to him.

Once in a while Gene gave her his ballet or symphony tickets and, though she attended alone unless he found her a "date," she found a certain solace in the luxury those events afforded her. With every week, her mood lifted and she found herself becoming quite comfortable with her new position in society.

She eagerly took in everything being around Gene offered. Especially his love of fine literature. On his bedside stand were copies of classic French plays by Moliere which she read to become familiar with the language and small leather-bound copies of Spanish poetry, which she read strictly for love of the form. She practiced her accents on him and he'd correct her if he was able, but, more often, would simply be lulled into sleep by her soft voice. While he slept, she continued reading, sharpening her knowledge of French, Spanish, and German, a habit she had begun after their return from Europe.

She had even fallen into the routine of ending her day with a run on the Common. Though the newspapers warned against the dangers of women jogging alone, Diana found it a great way to relieve stress, to free her mind of inconsequential matters, and to get the exercise she missed by sitting all day at the shop. Besides, it was energizing. Surprisingly, she got her best ideas when running and had taken to bringing a small tape recorder with her so she could dictate quick notes without missing a step.

Gene became thinner and thinner, often agonizing over that fact when he stood in front of a mirror. Yet he wouldn't quit smoking and she soon grew tired of nagging him. Little did he know she intercepted his weekly supply of Gauloise at the tobacco store and had the cigarettes re-rolled, replaced with a low-tar brand. It had taken some cajoling and a bit of extra money to the tobacconist, but at least she had the comfort of knowing Gene was not putting extra nicotine into his already-diseased lungs.

Though the doctor visited on a regular basis. Gene never shared the diagnosis or prognosis of his illness with anyone, including her. Occasionally, she would find him sitting in the wing chair in his bedroom after the doctor left, just staring pensively out the window, looking a bit like her mother had. Pretending not to notice his mood, she would throw open the windows and straighten his bed, chattering aimlessly about one thing or another, sharing stories from the shop he rarely found the strength to visit anymore. They never spoke of his illness, but she made herself a promise, sitting on the queen-sized bed in the hotel at Disney World, that she would force him to tell her about it when she got home tomorrow. Or else she'd go to the doctor's and find out for herself.

When she entered Gene's apartment late the next evening, she heard two quiet voices coming from the master bedroom. Leaving her suitcase on the marble hallway floor, she stripped off her gloves, dropped them on the table against the wall, and headed for the sound. All the lights in the apartment were off, except for some small fairy lamps which softly lit dim corners and provided the light needed to get to the bedroom door.

She knocked softly and heard Gene's raspy, "Come in." Pushing open the door, she saw Meredith sitting in a boudoir chair to the right of the bed, a book open in her lap.

"Ahhh. 1 go away for a couple of days and someone's there immediately to fill my shoes," Diana teased, a casual wave of her hand indicating she was talking of the book Merry held. "Have" you two been behaving? No arguing, I hope."

The cousins looked at each other, Gene from his spot in the middle of the king-sized bed where he lay propped up by pillows, and Merry from her chair. "We were just reminiscing," Merry replied, motioning that Diana should sit in the chair on Gene's left. "Haven't had time to talk about the old days like this in years, have we, Gene?" She reached her plump, bejeweled hand to pat Gene's thin, veined one. The curved lines of her face were softened by her affection for him. She wore little makeup, the lack of it making her look younger rather than older. Diana knew there was no way Merry would walk about the grounds at the villa this way and that her relaxed manner served as proof she accepted Diana as family.

"Can you imagine the two of us growing up together?" Merry asked, raising an eyebrow.

Diana smiled. "You two must have gotten into a lot of trouble."

Coughing, Gene clenched at his chest with one bony hand. "She was the troublemaker. I just watched."

"Likely story, cherie.'' Merry majestically rose and bent over, giving Gene a peck on the forehead and smoothing the gray satin comforter which covered him. "It's time for my beauty sleep." She winked at Diana. "You two have a lot to discuss, and I know Gene's beginning to get tired. Don't argue with me, young man. I'm still boss until Diana unpacks her suitcase. Try to just talk about the important things, d'accord, cherie?" She nodded toward Diana. "He needs his beauty sleep, too."

Gene picked up a pillow, playfully pretending to throw it at his cousin before she ducked out the door.

"Looks like you had a good visit. It's probably been much more pleasurable than having me around, huh?" Diana rose to straighten out the room, taking Kleenex boxes off the bedside stand and emptying glasses of water which had obviously been there all day. Meredith had plenty of maids. She wasn't used to picking up.

"Sit." Though the command was given in a tired voice. Gene waved his hand at her peremptorily. "We need to talk."

She took her seat, concerned about his abruptness. Was he angry that she had taken a short vacation? He had said it was okay, had urged her to do it. Yet, should she have stayed home? Did something happen at the shop while she was gone? Something which Miles hadn't told her?

Gene looked at the ceiling, staring beyond the finials of the finely-carved bed posters, apparently collecting his thoughts. She felt frozen to the chair, like a child admonished by her teacher. She was anxious for him to speak, to tell her what was wrong.

"I rewrote my will while you were gone," he began. With an obvious effort, he hitched himself up further onto the pillows and fought for another breath. "Scott no longer gets a dime."

"Well, he shouldn't." She couldn't help being relieved that nothing was wrong beyond a change in some legal documents. "He hasn't even bothered to call to see if you're all right."

"Yes, but he knows. Others have told him."

"Oh?"

"And still . . .." He drifted again, staring at the ceiling, as if haunted by memories he could not purge. "That's not the point. The point is that I wanted you to know I have added your name to the codicil."

"Gene!"

"I'm too ill to argue. Please don't make me try."

"But, Gene . . ."

"It's my decision and it's final. I just . . . wanted to let . . . you know."

"Gene, I don't want anything from you. You have given me a job, a trip to Europe, a . . ."

"And you've been the only one . . . who's been here for me, besides Merry, ... in the past couple of months.'' Gene took another raspy breath, his anger seemingly making him stronger than he had been a moment ago. "Do you know what all of Boston is saying? They're saying I have AIDS." He laughed, then began a coughing fit which split the bedroom's still air with the intensity of a buzz saw.

She ran to the bathroom, retrieved one of the glasses, and quickly filled it with water. He was still coughing when she got back to the bed and lifted the glass to his lips. Thankfully, his own hands were quivering so badly, she didn't need to cover up that hers were as well. AIDS. It had been a nightmare she had dismissed. Or at least *tried* to dismiss.

Finally, the fit subsided and he lay back against the pillows once again. "AIDS," he muttered. "That's why no one will come to see me."

The possibility of Gene having the dreaded disease had passed through her mind more than once in the past couple of months, but she had forced it out of her thoughts.

, "You're the only one who's been here, Diana."

She nodded, not knowing how to reply or even whether he expected her to. For several moments they sat in the quiet apartment in companionable silence. It seemed the city had stopped breathing, the cars had stopped running, that even the refrigerator in the kitchen had taken a momentary break.

"It's *not* AIDS, you know." His face was almost as gray as the sheets beneath him. "But it might as well be."

Monroe's head rose, his eyes sharp and clear, as if he knew her unspoken question and was warning her not to ask it. "Diana, read to me. I want to hear some Yeats. Read me *The Wild Swans at Coole.*"

She hesitated, knowing that Yeats's more mature poems were

full of the poet's concerns with immortality, full of thoughts of death. If she had to read poetry like that, she'd surely break down. He wouldn't want that. No. She couldn't give in. She bit her lip. Hard. And wondered how much time he had left. God, she hated Scottie for what he had done to this gentleman.

"Please?" he asked faintly.

Her arms felt heavy and numb as she fumbled through the pile of books on the bedside table. Finding the leather-bound volume, Diana opened to the first page, took a deep, shaky breath, and began:

"The trees are in their autumn beauty.
The woodland paths are dry,
Under the October twilight the water
Mirrors a still sky;
Upon the brimming water among the stones
Are nine-and-fifty swans."

Boston, November 15, 1981

When it was over, when Gene's funeral flowers were strewn on his grave and all the notables and soon-to-be-notables had returned to their homes in quietly chauffeur-driven long black automobiles, Diana felt comfortable in the knowledge that, though Gene never came right out and told her he was dying, they had had plenty of time to say good-bye.

Though everyone still insisted he had had AIDS, she knew they were wrong, having visited his doctor long ago. Lung cancer had proved to be Gene Monroe's final downfall.

At the funeral, she made sure to comment quietly to the worst gossips that Gene's cancer had been caused by his lifelong smoking habit, that his lungs had been so black his doctor had joked about Gene's secret life as a miner, and that Gene had continued to smoke right up until the moment of his death. "Can you imagine some thought he had AIDS?" she said, a purposefully shocked expression on her face. "How totally stupid of those people." And she walked away.

She stifled a smile each time someone tried to hide their chagrin. Gene had always loved drama and intrigue. Knowing that he was the center of attention even after his death would have given him a chuckle. And he had always loved having the last laugh. It gave her a sense of satisfaction to be able to give him that final gift.

She had spent every evening at his side after their talk that night in September, postponing her runs in the Common until after he fell asleep. She read Dickinson and Dickens to him or, on his better days, played a long game of chess which stretched, in spurts, through naptimes and mealtimes until someone finally won. They talked incessantly about world politics, especially about Britain's new

163

female prime minister, in office for only two years and making waves in Britain's political climate. Gene supposedly had known her when she was a member of parliament. They talked about antiques, their childhoods, and people they had known. They laughed about the actor who played the Lone Ranger fighting to keep his mask and the resulting spate of comics' routines focusing on the incident. They discussed Sotheby's October sale of the Honeyman collection of scientific books and manuscripts which brought almost half a million pounds and had the antiques world abuzz. And talked of other trends in the business as though Gene were still actively involved in that world, as though he would return to it one day. On other days, their talk was simpler. Sometimes they'd spend the whole day questioning and answering each other in one-word abbreviated sentences— "Breakfast?" "Yes." "Read?" "Not now." On those days, she described the weather for him, what the traffic was like on Charles Street, how sales were at the shop. Anything that might lead to something deeper, something memorable.

She kept a journal of comments he made and her daily conversations with Maryann revolved almost completely around what he had said or done. As a result, she found herself losing touch with Rob, Maryann, and the boys. It's okay, she often told herself. They understand.

Sometimes Gene wanted to hear her talk about her dreams, her hopes, claiming to find her love for life infinitely fascinating. He would lie in bed, urging her to continue or asking her questions and sometimes asking her to repeat certain stories later on—stories about her nephews and their latest antics were his favorites. She had to be careful not to get him laughing or his spine-ripping cough would start up again, leaving him even weaker than before.

Little could be done about rebuilding the shop's inventory during that period. She simply wasn't at All That Glitters enough to keep sales up and couldn't afford to leave Gene long enough to make even lightning trips to attend New York or London auctions.

Having no other choice, Diana relied on Miles to re-stock the shop's three floors with the items she had been putting in storage for the past six months. Could she have known this was going to happen? Was that, why she always bought more than they needed? Or had she been trying to fill a void in herself somehow by buying everything in sight? Whatever the case, the warehouse full of antiques had come in handy.

It didn't frustrate her to curtail the activities she had come to love so deeply. In fact, the moments spent with Gene talking about the antique business were far more illuminating than any book she could read about different aspects of collecting or restoration. She often wished she had put some of the information he had shared with her on tape. His opinions were old-Boston-preservation in tone, his thoughts about everything historical or antique. His feelings were strong against breaking up famous collections—believing they should not be parceled out to the general public. "Probably my banker father in me," he had said. "I don't have any problems with the new trend of corporations buying art collections. At least the pieces are kept in a cohesive unit that way. Just don't break them up. It takes too many years to put a really fine collection together."

They had learned a lot from each other, growing closer than some people did with members of their own family.

Now she sat in the empty apartment where Gene Penchance Monroe's family looked down from the walls at her, as if questioning what she was going to do next. It was a peaceful feeling, not a threatening one, almost like an invisible hug. She felt as though she had their support, that they had been watching the whole time Gene was sick and had approved of his choice of an heir.

His money, stocks and bonds, many buildings, the shop, and all of his personal belongings, except for some family photographs Merry wanted, were hers now. She didn't know what to do with all of it. The huge responsibility overwhelmed her. She didn't even know all that his estate entailed. In fact, she didn't even want to *think* about it for a long while. She simply couldn't cope with it all.

She sat in the library—her library, she realized with a start—for the rest of the afternoon, still in the simple black linen slit-skirted Bill Blass suit she had worn to the funeral, letting the dust in the closed-up room settle around her, and waiting for evening to steal into the apartment once more.

Chapter Twenty-one

London, July, 1982

Diana lifted the Russian samovar to the light, turning it a little to the left, then a little to the right, running her fingers over its jewel-encrusted body. It was heavier and larger than others she had seen. They must have made tea for a very large crowd with this one, she thought. She examined it more closely, her shoulders beginning to ache from holding it up for so long. The ruby near the bottom rim was a bit loose and the silver around it appeared to be newly-soldered. Probably a replacement gem. She wondered if it had the same age the other jewels did and reached into her pocket for her magnifying glass to get a better look.

The samovar, at least one hundred and fifty years old, according to Sotheby's catalog listing, belonged in the Rothmark Collection since the Grand Duke himself commissioned its creation in 1823. It had gone through the family from great-grandfather down to its latest owner, and seller, Vincent Rothmark IV. Now Sotheby's was attempting to sell not only the samovar, but the rest of Rothmark's collection as well. Rumor had it that Vincent had blown his inheritance and that selling the collection was his way of recouping in order to buy another Arabian race horse.

Unlike what might be expected of someone with his noble heritage, Vincent Rothmark IV was a rogue, notorious for everything—from bed-hopping to lewd and lascivious poetry, which he recited in the most austere public places. In spite of all his character flaws, Rothmark was extremely handsome, as she had found out.

I must like dark men, she reasoned, pushing her fingers gently against the jewels again, rolling the samovar in her hands, deep in concentration about both the antique and the man who had owned it. Vincent's Turkish background was reflected in his smoky good looks. Diana half-expected him to wear a long, flowing white robe like Lawrence of Arabia. Perhaps he did. When he was home. Relaxed. She smiled as her mind conjured up an image of him greeting her at the door of his boudoir, his robe open, his smile inviting her to come in. Shaking her head, she forced herself back to reality.

He liked her. She could tell by the way their eyes connected and held when Sarah Purnell, Sotheby's latest auction assistant, had introduced them. It was as though they had physically touched, as if they had caressed long and lovingly. He liked her, all right. And she liked him, too. Yet she felt guilty about it, turning away when he caught her letting her eyes rove over his body. All her Italian Catholic standards surfaced at times like that. Unfortunately, she was from a good-girls-get-married-bad-girls-leave kind of neighborhood. Everyone in East Boston knew the girls who liked sex and now she was one of them. She felt an almost tangible pressure to be good, pure, virginal. But, of course, she was not. It was not that easy. She simply could not live without outward showings of love, yet she had trouble expressing that need unless it was through impersonal sex.

Impersonal sex. How gauche. There was that stirring in her loins again.

Dismissing the thought that she might have a chance to. see Vincent later, she put the samovar back on the table and took a couple of steps backwards to look at it from a distance, to assess its value. Her retreat brought her directly, and clumsily, into contact with another auction goer. Ass to ass.

"Oh, I'm so sorry." The contents of Diana's pocketbook spilled on the floor as she whipped around to apologize. Seeing her possessions flying, she quickly bent to retrieve them without looking directly at the stranger.

A light-haired man in a cashmere sweater knelt next to her, his face blocked by the 18th century globe between them. She could smell the slight dampness of his sweater, that unmistakable mustiness which seemed to permeate all of the hotel rooms in London. He must have just come in from the misty Mayfair streets. "Let me help," he suggested as he retrieved Diana's umbrella, datebook, and her keys with long, nimble fingers.

Something about the voice, the Britishness of it or its upward hit, made her turn. "Terence Pellican," she said in soft wonderment. "How the hell *are* you?"

"Diana! I didn't know you were going to be in London. Why didn't you call? We could have had lunch. I haven't seen you in ages!" He helped her to her feet and stood next to her. Adjusting his glasses, he ran his hand through his hair in a sweeping front-to-back motion.

"Much has happened since I last saw you.!' Diana put the brush and lip-gloss she held in her hand back into her pocketbook, busying herself with straightening them rather than facing the prospect of telling Terence of Gene's death, all daydreaming of Vincent Rothmark IV was instantly forgotten, dismissed until further notice.

"I know." He touched her arm lightly. She looked up into pale bluish-green eyes framed in light brown lashes, eyes that were both pained and understanding. Of course he would know—Terence, of all people, would know. "Did you hear about my uncle?" he continued.

"No. What happened?"

"He's gone, too, Diana. Around the same time as Gene. But, unlike Gene, Uncle died penniless. The stock in Amaryllis was all he had left. I'm afraid we're going to have to auction off the contents to pay the bills. Frightfully embarrassing, if I say so myself."

"How horrible! I didn't hear. If I had, I would have ... Is there anything I can do?"

With a little laugh and another long swipe at his hair, he said, "Buy Amaryllis. Give this poor Londoner a job," he teased with a Sir Francis Drake-like bow.

"That's a great idea," she answered, though she hadn't thought about the prospect for even a few seconds. *She* wasn't joking and she knew, as she walked toward the auction hall with Terence, that Gene would have heartily approved of the way she was about to use her inheritance.

Diana checked her watch. Fifteen more minutes and it would be time to meet Terence for dinner to discuss the details of buying Amaryllis. She stood, staring out into the late London afternoon's gray skies, her naked back to the completely satiated man on the bed behind her. She could hear the light snoring which meant he was drowsing. Why did men always do that? The first thing she wanted to do was get out of bed and stretch, especially when there was no one in bed worth staying there for. That had been the case ever since she left Luis, even though she was embarrassed to admit it. She wouldn't have been able to name the men who shared her bed in the past couple of years even if someone put a gun to her head.

Pulling back the heavy tweed curtains, she shivered a bit and looked out over Kensington Gardens. Should have wrapped the flannel covers over me, she thought. The chill of the floor beneath her bare feet, the slight draft from the window caressing her breasts, made her tingle, aroused her nipples. They puckered and pointed straight up like blossoming tulips.

Though she heard a rustle behind her, she didn't move.

Vincent was well-versed in lovemaking, but she had no real need for a second round. That was for lovers. Casual sex was easier than surrendering herself to a relationship. She wanted the affection, the caresses, the warmth that came from physical contact with a man. But after that, there was nothing left to hold onto. Unless you were in love with your partner. And she hadn't found anyone to love since ... no, she wouldn't think about that bastard again.

After a rousing night of sex, after the intense warmth and the convulsive orgasm, she needed to feel the chill, the rudeness, of the cold air against her skin where the man had warmed her only moments before. It was almost as good, almost as necessary, as taking a long, hot shower once he had left, once she was again alone. It was a habit she had gotten into during the past two years. Easier that way. Less painful.

"Lovely Diana," Rothmark murmured. She heard the sheets rustle again and knew that he could see the curve of her thighs, the downy mist which settled between them and the high jut of her breasts, all outlined in the moonlight streaming through the window. She turned slightly, hesitatingly. Did she need another dose of warmth? She only had fifteen minutes.

"Come here, my darling. I need you." His voice was not half as tempting as the distinct rise in the bedcovers he had loosely tossed over his lower body. "Sweet Diana," he whispered again as she crawled in beside him, and as she fitted him with the condom she had taken to carrying in her purse after Gene's death. "Easy, my love. Easy."

Boston, August, 1982

Within a few weeks, Amaryllis of London was Diana's. There had been several hurried consultations with Arnie about the purchase, the bulk of which was done over the phone. The two of them were so busy these days that it was getting hard to meet in person. They used to have time for lunch at least once a week. Not now.

Arnie was thinking of running for Attorney General and his prospects looked good. Diana's prospects were equally good. She had even begun to learn how to spend the endless supply of money Gene left her. A fire-red Porsche 911 was kept safely locked in the garage below her building. She had looked at a few country estates north of London and had spoiled her nephews with expensive presents from all over the world.

Had Maryann accepted her offer of financial help, she would have been happy. But her sister-in- law was stubborn, so giving the kids presents was the easiest way to offer some sort of support. "If I have it, why can't I share it with you?" she had pleaded. "What fun is having money if I have to spend it alone?"

No longer did Diana have to worry about keeping a budget or how much of a profit she could make on a piece so she could cover her expenses. Yet, could she relax now? No way. She had the germ of an idea, just the beginning of a plan, and buying Amaryllis was the spark to set it dl in motion. Though it had taken time to get used to her new freedoms, she had spent the time wisely, investing in antiques sure to double in value within the next couple of years. And she had been watching. Waiting. Learning. Now was the time to make her move.

For the first time in her business career, the Boston newspapers had mentioned her in their society columns. She heard rumors that people were appreciative of what she was beginning to do with Gene's estate—which she finally found out totaled somewhere around $3 million in cash, stocks, and securities; over $6 million in real estate—the Beacon Hill house, several others in the area, a villa in St. Barth's, and a small home in the Arkansas mountains, of all places; and over $15 million invested in the All That Glitters building and the stock gracing its three floors and filling the South Boston warehouse. It was more than she ever dreamed of handling, and she had come to rely on Amie, as in days past, to help her manage the myriad complications attached to her fortune.

Though she had been nervous about stepping out of her East Boston background and into Boston's social limelight, it had not been as difficult a transition as she had imagined. Bostonians not only approved of Diana Cole, they heartily applauded her, supporting her as if she had actually been Monroe's, daughter. Now she knew how important it had been to be seen with him, and how much care he had taken to pave the way for her. Most everyone on Beacon Hill already knew her and those who didn't, wanted to.

When she bought the London shop, other antique dealers across the country started paying attention to what she bought at auctions. She almost laughed at the thought that the people *she* had once watched were now watching *her*. Takes money to make money, I guess, she mused. And to be recognized.

The years she had spent educating herself were finally starting to pay off. She understood enough French, Spanish, and German to attend sales in those countries and buy intelligently. She had even seriously considered making an excursion to South America, to tap into a new market, one which had not attracted others before. After that, perhaps Africa.

Japan had proved a miraculous coup—the perfect buying arena. The Japanese antique merchants already loved her, securing the best hotel suite whenever she visited, and even telling her where the best deals might be made—information traditionally reserved for male ears only. She spent over a month in Kyoto the year before, learning their customs and history in order to better understand their art and porcelains. "Hands-on training always proves the best instruction," Gene had once said. He was right. The Japanese admired someone who valued learning as much as she did. Each time she left the country, it was with a healthy respect for the people over whom she physically towered.

She could recognize antique items from most comers of the universe, and was able to date them and discern who made them as quickly as a museum expert. It was a skill she believed was absolutely necessary when you reached a certain level in the antique world. She had decided long ago not to tolerate any less than the best in herself and was just now realizing that, no matter how much she learned, there would always be more. Her appetite for gathering information had become insatiable.

Not surprisingly, she respected her antique world peers more than she respected doctors, lawyers, judges, or men like Donald Trump, who built empires with annual incomes once far beyond her wildest dreams. She supposed it was because antiquers were historians; they were, art experts; they were salespeople of the highest caliber; gamblers who used their knowledge in order to hedge their bets on what a piece might be worth; and they were, finally, people who enjoyed fine literature and music as much as the objects they sold to make their living. What more respectable profession could there be?

Often, just before she buckled her seat belt for a trans-oceanic flight or settled into a comfortable chair after a long day at work, she spent a quiet moment imagining what her parents might have said if they knew what she had become. Would they respect her as much as Diana did those antiquers around her? Would they see worth in a person who sold old items, items sometimes bought from estates, family items given to a stranger? Would they realize how much she had learned, how incredibly proud she felt to be out of the tenements and into a life with a satin lining stitched with the finest things the world had to offer? She *knew* Gene would. And she smiled to think that he knew exactly what he was doing when he turned his business over to her. Keeping the store's integrity was what had been most important to him. She had assumed that legacy with the easy grace of a newly- born dolphin learning to swim.

"What you're outlining is revolutionary, you know that, don't you?" Terence said as he poured them yet another cup of tea one foggy September afternoon. "No one's ever put together an antiques empire of this magnitude. You're talking millions of dollars."

"There's a first time for everything," she retorted. "And I made a promise that Gene's money would be used well."

He studied "her thoughtfully. "I never thought I'd see this happen, but if anyone can do it, you can." "With your help, Terence."

He nodded and smiled. She could tell he totally approved.

Chapter Twenty-two

Boston, September, 1984

The silver razor blade Rob held between his fingers quivered in anticipation. Before him, on a square-cut, beveled edge mirror, the pile of pinkish-white powder glimmered as though diamonds had been sifted through it. The blade squeaked across the glass. Rob recoiled, shivering, as he had in grammar school when the teacher's chalk screeched against the blackboard.

Across the table, Luis sat, his feet propped against a heavily-scrolled mahogany chair. They were alone. Karl was on an errand—to bring more of the white powder for his boss. Only half an hour ago, the pile before them had been twice its size.

Luis chuckled and sniffed loudly. "Such an amateur you are. Signor Colucci."

Rob's head lifted sharply. His eyes felt dry and he knew his lids fluttered as quickly as a hummingbird's wings. "But I learn quickly," he retorted, his words pushed past the lump in his throat. "Here, you want a line or not?"

"That is a child's size." Luis reached a brown hand across the table. His diamond pinky ring competed with the shimmering pile into which he dipped his personal razor. Splitting the pile in fourths, he whipped the sections into crookedly fat six-inch lines, then leaned back and smiled. "As you say, Signor Colucci, 'go for it.' "

The afternoon sunlight warmed the area around her desk and illuminated the dust motes settling on the Louis IV vanity to her right. Diana had spent the day rearranging the upper floors of the shop, making phone calls to prospective clients regarding the Monet collection she had just acquired, and successfully making appointments for several people interested in seeing the paintings. The day had been a long one and she was enjoying the menial task of opening the mail, her feet up on the partially-open drawer on the lower left of the desk.

When the phone rang, she had been thinking of Gene as she flipped through the Tribal Arts auction catalog. Still engrossed in the catalog, she answered the call, barely concentrating on Maryann's voice until she almost screamed, "Diana, have you heard a word I said? Your brother's in the hospital!" Shaking herself from her reverie, the Sotheby's catalog dropped off her lap to the floor. Her heels clunked nosily against the hardwood floor.

"What happened?"

"I don't know yet. It looked to me like it was a heart attack or something. He came home and wasn't even in the house five minutes when all of a sudden, he just couldn't breathe and he fell to the floor clutching at his chest, his eyes real wide and, God, Diana, I'm scared. Come right away, okay? We're at the Mass General emergency room. You've got to come right away. Please?"

Within moments, Diana dashed in the glass sliding doors at the Massachusetts General Hospital. She had run all the way from the shop and was out of breath, but there in half the time it would have taken to retrieve her car from the garage and join the slow-moving rush hour traffic on Storrow Drive.

It didn't take her long to spot Maryann's wild red hair or the two gangly boys who tore across the waiting room screaming, "Auntie Di, Auntie Di!" Then Tony yelled, "Daddy's got tubes up his nose and he looks really funny!"

"Oh, my God," she whispered, catching her sister-in-law's ^e and heading in that direction, both boys grappling around her knees. A cold fear captured the pit of her stomach. She felt a line of sweat breaking out on her brow. Grabbing Tony's hand, she took Chris by the shoulder and wove her way through the lobby. Why was this place always crowded? Didn't Boston ever have a day, just *one* day, when no one was hurt or sick?

"What is it?" she demanded as soon as they were within speaking distance. Instantly, she regretted her tone and the imperious way she had asked the question, but Maryann barely seemed to notice.

"Probably a heart attack. They've got him hooked up to all the machines now, taking an EKG and stuff. We'll know in a little while." Her small face was white, her usually-red lips a pale gray. She looked as though she might have a heart attack herself. "Diana, they're saying something about him being addicted to cocaine. That he *has* been for at least a couple of years. How could that be? Oh, God, when my father finds out, he'll have the whole Boston Police force watching me . . ."

Diana nodded. Though Mike Herlihy had learned to tolerate Rob, she knew Mike still made comments about Rob's lack of a "real" job every once in a while. Had even tried to convince him to go to the police academy. But Rob resisted. He wanted his own life, he said, and he had never wanted anything to do with law and justice.

For a moment, the calls on the hospital's intercom system filled the empty air between the sisters- in-law. Grateful for the interruption, Diana suddenly had a sinking feeling that threatened to pull her body down to the floor, and she knew she'd be no help to anyone if she passed out. She shook her head violently, as if the motion would clear her mind and help her to put her thoughts together to concentrate on what was happening.

"No. They must be wrong," she insisted, though something told her they were right and that she, in some strange way, had been responsible. Robert was only twenty-six. How could he have had a heart attack? Or be addicted to coke? No, this couldn't be possible.

The two women waited quietly for two hours in the Cardiac Care Unit, holding each other's hands as though the simple act of touching would help them pool their strength. Maryann called her older sister, Judith, to come and take the boys to her house. They were in the way of nurses and doctors scurrying by to attend to Robert and the other patients in the ward. And neither Diana nor Maryann was capable of taking care of them.

Diana felt she should say something to Maryann, soothe the younger woman, assure her that everything was going to be all right. She tried a couple of times, but fear sealed her lips. Fear that she might be wrong. Fear that nothing was going to be all right ever again. She sat beside Maryann, flipping through a magazine inattentively, not seeing the pictures. Maryann, on the other hand, was anything but still. She tapped her sneakered foot against the cold tile floor, drummed her small fingers against the plastic and wood arm of the chair, paced the little room until Diana thought she must be dizzy as hell, and peered into the glass-encased cardiac unit so many times the nurses were starting to appear irritated.

Finally, a woman in a white jacket came to the door of the waiting room. She looked from one anxious face to the other. "Mrs. Colucci?"

"Yes, that's me," Maryann answered in a thin, shaking voice. "Is he all right? Can we see him?"

"I'm Dr. Goodwin," the woman continued impersonally, without glancing at Maryann. She flipped the pages of the chart she held. "You can see your husband now. But only for five minutes. Follow me."

Maryann nodded to Diana and reached out for a quick embrace, then followed the doctor, holding her purse tightly against her stomach as if it would protect her from anything the doctor might have to tell her. Diana could hear their murmuring voices, could see Maryann's concerned expression as they talked, watched her nod and ask questions. They walked down the short hall and into a glass-walled area. When she stood, she could see Maryann walking falteringly, then quickly, to a bed in the corner of the room where a patient lay silent and still, connected to wires and bottles, a monitor blinking ferociously at his side.

Now that she was alone, her mind exploded with possibilities she hadn't wanted to face before. Robert. The thrill-seeker. The kid the rest of the neighborhood kids emulated because he was always the first—the first to get arrested for speeding, the first to play football without pads, the first to ride his bike off a barely-anchored board which sent him flying into the air like Evil Knievel. And after Marcus died, things only got worse. First, the GTO. Then, after Mama died, the Corvette. And the drinking. And the marijuana, which he thought she knew nothing about. One thing after another, almost as though he had a death wish.

Why should cocaine be any different? He had always wanted or needed a thrill. But why now? Why did he have to do it when there were two little children who counted on him, who depended on him for support and protection? What obsessive need made him reach out for something as false, as deceiving, as coke? The thought of Robbie being entranced by the same ugly addiction as Luis caused an acrid taste to rise in her mouth.

All indications through the past four or five years had been that he was happy. And why wouldn't he be? He had enough money to pay his bills with the inheritance. His home was beautiful and in a good neighborhood, just the opposite from the one in which he had grown up. His wife adored him without reservation. And his boys were healthy, intelligent, and well-behaved. What more could he possibly want? Diana would have given anything to have the family life Robert had. He knew that. Yet, it didn't appear to matter that *she* was envious of *him*. He still had to get attention, an extra thrill, explore yet another danger. Why, goddammit, why?

When Maryann exited the unit, her face frozen and ghostly, the doctor motioned to Diana that she could come in.

"Five minutes," Dr. Goodwin repeated with a stern look.

Diana found herself walking toward the figure in the bed as slowly as Maryann had. She wasn't sure she wanted to see Rob like this, unsure of how she'd react. As she got closer, she could see his face, almost as white as the pillow beneath it. Small plastic tubes extended from his nose upward into upside-down bottles of slowly-dripping liquid. Wires were attached to his chest, reaching out in different directions like an octopus. The monitor above his head beeped slowly, the sounds following the peaks and valleys of the green line on the screen.

She didn't know where to put her hands, whether he was awake, or even whether she should kiss him. For a moment, she stood motionless by the side of the bed, her arms rigidly at her sides, afraid to breathe.

His stiff black eyelids fluttered like an injured bird's wings as he opened them and stared blankly at her. The lines on his face made him look seventy. Beneath his eyes were dark, pronounced bags which hadn't been there before. The skin around his lips was loose, weak, as though the tubes of oxygen inserted into his mouth had stretched it. Tubes filled his nostrils as well, and his nose was chapped and raw. Why hadn't she noticed it before? How long had it been since she had actually seen him? A month? Two?

"Hi," he whispered weakly, almost apologetically.

Diana reached out to hold his groping fingers. "Hi, yourself. So, how are you doing?" The words were empty, meaningless. She wanted to say so much more, but was acutely aware of the beeping screen to the right of his head. The horrible hospital smell reminded her of the many days she spent sitting beside her mother's bed in the nursing home, holding an unresponsive hand and looking into unseeing eyes. She felt woozy and held tightly to the silver bar on the side of the bed. At least Robert was awake. At least he was talking to her.

"Guess I fucked up." He licked his lips, a film dulling his

normally bright eyes. A white crust had formed in the corners of his mouth, obviously the after effects of some kind of medicine. "Can I have some water?" He gave ho* a feeble smile and licked his lips again.

"Nurse?" Unwilling to let go of his hand, to loosen the firm grip she had on him, she lifted her voice once again, searching the hallways with her eyes for someone who could help them. Could *anyone* help them? Was it too late? "Nurse?"

A white-uniformed woman with short, curly gray hair poked her head around the door. "Yes?"

"He wants some water. Can he have a glass?" "Just a few sips," the nurse replied, bringing a small blue cup to Diana. "Don't let him gulp it." With a starched rustle and a forced smile, she was gone.

Diana brought the plastic cup to his lips, putting her hand under his head to help him reach it. He was heavy. Not the light boniness of Gene or Mama, but an immense, real weight.

"Thought I was finished taking care of you a long time ago," she teased, trying to pull her lips into a grin.

He leaned back against the pillows with a sigh and closed his eyes. "Guess not. Sis."

Without thinking, she bent over his pillow. "Why, Robert? Why cocaine?"

His eyelashes flew open. The siblings stared into each other's eyes. Rob had never been able to lie to her when she forced him to look at her like this. She knew he wouldn't now.

"It was there. I liked it," he whispered hoarsely. "Don't worry about me. I'll be all right. Ain't gonna happen again."

A few moments later, she left him snoring peacefully. Yet, she felt that a part of her stayed in there with him as she walked toward Maryann, who was sitting in the corner of the waiting room, looking totally bedraggled and defeated.

As she walked those few steps, her anger grew like a roaring waterfall, picking up bits and pieces of rock as it tore its way down the side of a mountain. She was rent with sympathy for Maryann, as well as frustration with her brother. When he got out of that damn hospital bed, he'd have to answer to her. She wouldn't allow him to destroy what was left of her family.

Patting Maryann on the arm, she slipped into the seat beside her and gave her what she hoped was a brave smile.

"When did this start?" she began. "Who . . . "

Maryann shivered and blew her nose into a wad of Kleenex. "You know how much he drinks . . . and . . . and ... he smokes too much. God, Di, I don't know when he started. I just know he's been acting weird. Spending more and more time away from the house. Comes home at dawn." She sniffed -again. "I thought he was cheating on me. God, I feel like such a shit . . . "

"Who?" Diana bent forward and stroked Maryann's damp hair away from her forehead.

"Who what?"

"Who sells it to him?"

"Who sells it to him?" Maryann's face was blank, as if she just realized he must have bought it and realized that was the reason the family had been broke for so long. "God knows. I don't know him anymore. Ever since your mother died, we've just . . . we've just ... we don't know each other anymore." Her shoulders shook again and she bobbed her head, fiercely fighting the noisy sobs escaping her throat.

This isn't the time to talk, Diana knew. She squeezed her sister-in-law's shoulder, making a mental note to bring up the subject some other time. They had to talk. There would be no turning away from it now.

For another half-hour they simply waited together, wordlessly, until the doctor came back and sat in the chair opposite them.

"I think we're out of the woods," she said. "Robert has had a slight heart attack, nothing major, and he should be fine this evening. The best thing for him now is just to get some rest and I suggest you two do the same. There'll be plenty of time to visit when he's out of the Unit."

Diana saw Maryann to a cab, gave her a kiss, and promised to call later. "He'll be fine," she reassured her sister-in-law with more confidence than she felt. "When we get him out of here, we'll take turns beating him up, okay?" Maryann nodded feebly, as though too exhausted to do more. The cab rolled away, leaving Diana alone on the sidewalk.

Slowly, she walked through the humid Indian summer air back to All That Glitters, running over the past year in her mind, putting together the pieces, reliving portions of conversations with Maryann or Robert, and trying to understand how all the events had led up to what she had just experienced in the hospital's cardiac unit.

Yes, Rob had been losing weight. She had put it down to maturity, no more baby fat, never suspecting there was another, more sinister, reason for the loss. And Maryann had often commented about not seeing much of her husband anymore. Diana had attributed *that* to Rob's need to succeed, to the overtime he was putting in at the grocery store in his bid to take over the manager's position. It was the same need she fed on a daily basis —only hers was more consuming. Rob had a family to keep him home more often.

Yet, the kids often called Diana late at night to talk to her when Rob wasn't there. And he hadn't been at the airport when Maryann came to meet them after their trip to Disney World. She remembered Maryann's face that day and realized now that she had been bravely covering for him. How good she was at fielding the children's questions about their father. And how easily the kids were satisfied. It must have been going on for a long time. They were all used to it. All except Diana.

How could she have been so goddamn blind? How could she

have missed all the signs? How could she not have noticed Robert's absence from family functions like the boys' birthday parties and the plays they were in at the daycare center? How could she have accepted the feeble excuses and been unaware of the loneliness Maryann and the children had been enduring?

Maryann had once mentioned the inheritance was going more quickly than she expected. Diana figured Rob had paid off the house so they wouldn't have to worry about a mortgage. Now she knew where the money had gone. Up his nose. Now she knew why Maryann was constantly joking about "going down for the third time," about not being able to afford "extras" like dessert when she had invited Diana over for dinner.

Goddammit! She had missed *all* the evidence. Every last bit!

Pulling open the door to the shop, Diana walked into its dark coolness as though pulling a two-hundred-pound weight behind her. Miles looked up briefly from his Station behind the front desk and watched in awe as she lowered herself painfully onto an Empire fainting couch.

"'What's wrong, Di?" Concern was etched on his rather simple, honest face. Though not an exceptionally intelligent person. Miles was dependable, loyal, and plodding in a way which endeared him to their customers.

"My brother's in the hospital," she muttered, her voice lost in the ring of the shop's telephone. Lost in thoughts of Robert, she ignored Miles's courteous voice as he answered the phone and didn't connect again with reality until he touched her softly on the elbow.

"It's him again," Miles said. "I told him you weren't here, but he says he knows you are and insists on speaking with you."

"Luis?"

"Yes."

"No. No way. I don't want to talk to him. Especially now. Tell him I'm not here."

Miles returned to the phone, spoke a few words into it, and lifted his eyebrows in her direction. With his hand over the receiver, he said, "He knows your brother is in the hospital and that you're here. He claims it's imperative that he speak with you immediately."

Diana narrowed her eyes, felt her brows making a deep furrow in her forehead, and thought about shaking her head again. But Miles was nervous, uncomfortable about dealing with the Colombian who had been calling on a daily basis since the shop re-opened well over two years ago. Time to give the poor boy a break and deal with Luis personally.

"Yes, Luis. What do you want?" She held the phone clenched in her fingers, wishing she had not chosen to have her nails polished so she could bite them, could pull at the cuticles until the pain in her fingers brought out the pain she felt in her heart.

"Diana, *mi cara*. I am so sorry to hear of your brother's illness. I wanted to let you know that I will be here, in Boston, if you need me. You know, of course, that Quintana Corporation has an office on

State Street now?"

She didn't. Nor did she care. "How did you know about my brother? I just came from the hospital."

"We are friends, Diana. Did you not know that? We have been friends for a long time."

Her mouth dropped open. Tilting her head back, she put her hand to her lips. Suddenly, she realized where Rob had gotten his cocaine.

"No, I didn't know that, Luis," she said through clenched teeth. "But I'll tell you one thing. I want you to stay away from him from now on, hear me? Don't you dare involve my family in your dirty business. Do you understand?"

The Colombian's soft laugh irritated her as much as if she had been forced to chew broken glass. "I am afraid it is too late, *mi cara*. Your brother likes the coca leaf a little more than he should." He clucked his tongue sarcastically. "It really is a shame, but you should have known better than to push away Luis de la Maria Quintana. No woman does that to me, Diana. Not even you."

The phone went dead. Her stomach filled with a cold, stagnant fear. She felt responsible for her brother being in the hospital. She, Luis, and cocaine. Without another word to Miles, she strode out of the shop and headed towards the Boston Common and Arnie Goldstein's Tremont Street office.

Her fury with Luis made her strides long, her thoughts frenzied, yet her mind was so clear that she felt capable of anything . . . even murder. Walking through the Common, over the hills and paths once trod by small herds of cows, she relived every moment spent with Luis, her thoughts blue- edged like the brightest and hottest of flames. She heard his sarcastic voice slicing through the late summer air above the cries of children splashing in the Common's fountains. She saw his dark beauty repeated in every male face she brushed angrily by. Her fingernails scraped against the palms of her hands as her arms rhythmically pumped against her sides and she tasted the drop of blood she had torn out of her bottom lip.

That frigging bastard wouldn't get away with this! She'd fight him! She'd do battle with him if it took every last ounce of her strength!

By the time she reached Tremont Street, the clothes on her back were drenched and her hair hung in wet strands against her face. She knew she looked horrible, could feel the questioning glances of office personnel as she boarded the elevator to Arnie's fifteenth floor office, but she no longer cared. Shivering against the sudden onslaught of air conditioning, she pulled her shoulders back and strode past Arnie's astonished secretary right into his office. He was on the phone, shocked to see her, but he knew her well enough to wave his secretary out the door and cut his conversation short.

"What's the matter, Di?" he asked, even before hanging up the phone. "God, you look horrible! What the hell's going on?"

Shaking her head, she took a couple of deep breaths, aware that, winded, she had lost the ability to talk.

He rounded his desk and came to sit beside her, reaching for her hands and placing them between his own. His office had just been redone and Diana had not yet had a chance to see it. She took a few seconds to glance around, noticing the photo of his kids, his favorite, still held a prominent place on his desk. It made her want to cry because it instantly reminded her of Chris and Tony. Her beautiful boys.

A plush blue carpet had been laid on the once- bare floor and Arnie's old oak desk had been replaced with a new mahogany one, a much larger, more impressive place for him to pile his paper- filled files. He had never been very neat. She smiled and turned to her old friend.

"Rob's in the hospital," she started, holding a finger up to silence him until she finished. "Heart attack. They say he's been using cocaine. I know he's not the easiest guy to get along with, Arnie, but he's my brother. The worst part is that bastard, Luis Quintana, is behind it. He's trying to get back at me."

"Whoa! Whoa! Get back at you for what? And who's Luis Quintana?"

Diana sighed. So this is what it had come to. For years, she had held the story of Luis Quintana inside, not ever believing it necessary to relive the nightmare, to admit the horrible mistake she had made. With Arnie watching her compassionately, she told him the tale of her trip to Europe, her affair with Quintana, and her discovery of his illegal business dealings. He sat quietly, nodding in places, reaching for a cigarette when Diana was nearing the end. He puffed and took off his glasses, rubbing the ridges on his nose where the rims had bitten.

"Jesus, Di, I never realized . . . "

"Neither did Rob. That's why he fell into the trap Luis set for him. That bastard." Out of her chair now, she paced the floor, committing to memory the titles of the books against the wall, stopping momentarily in front of the painting of the Old North Church which graced the only blank wall in the office. "What in hell am I going to do, Arnie? You've got to help me."

"Has he promised to leave Rob alone?"

"Sort of. I don't know how much to believe, though. The man is slime. Absolutely, positively . . . not the kind of person you could trust. Believe me."

"1 suppose I could start an investigation. Being in the limelight these days certainly has helped me to get new contacts. I could use some of them, get the ball rolling. But if he's as big as you say he is, it might take a while. And I can't promise anything, hon." He stroked his chin thoughtfully. "Are you prepared to go through with all of this? To testify, if need be? It could be dangerous. Very dangerous. Those Colombians have been known to bump people off quicker and more efficiently than the Mafia. You'd be taking one hell of a chance."

"What choice do I have? What else can I do?" "Well . . . " Arnie uncrossed his legs and settled back in the chair, slid his glasses back on his nose, and stared thoughtfully at Diana. "Does he want something from you?"

She stopped pacing and returned her lawyer's stare. "What do you mean?"

"He's obviously doing this to get back at you. Maybe the only way you're going to stop him is to make some kind of a deal with him."

"Arnie! I don't believe you just said that! What kind of a deal could I possibly make with an asshole like him? Go to bed with him? Be his white slave? Oh, no. I've worked too goddamn hard to give it all up for this . . . this . . . creep."

The room was deadly silent. All Diana could hear were the sounds of her own breathing and the pounding of her heart. She had never felt so angry or so out of control in her whole life. The bastard had her—by her invisible balls.

Arnie leaned forward, his elbows on his knees. "I'm not saying that. I just think that making some kind of a deal with him will buy you some time until I can get the ball rolling on my end. I'm going to do everything possible, but sometimes it takes a long time. Do you understand?"

"No. No, I don't. But I don't seem to understand much of anything anymore. Thanks, Arnie, but I don't want to play it that way. Maybe I should just get someone else's help. Maybe I should go to the cops." She started walking toward the door.

He was out of the chair in an instant and caught her just as she reached the doorknob. They stood nose to nose. She could smell his aftershave. The onions he had for lunch were pungent on his breath. "Don't do it," he said quietly. "It won't work. You'll only end up having more problems than you do now. You want to get yourself killed? Take your time and think about what you're doing, Diana. You're playing with fire and you're going to get burned very badly. Think about what I've said. Please."

She turned her head away, unable to look into the lawyer's eyes. "Yeah. Okay. I'll think about it. But I can promise you one thing. He's not going to get away with it. No frigging way he's getting away with this."

When the door stopped reverberating. Attorney General Arnold Goldstein walked over to his new desk and picked up the receiver of his new phone. "Sylvia. Get me David Potsdam at the Federal Bureau of Investigation."

He sat down behind the desk, both hands flat on its top, waiting for his secretary to beep him. When the sound finally came, he reached for the phone and spoke quickly into it. Within moments, he was assured that the investigator would find out everything there was to know about a certain Luis de la Maria Quintana and the Quintana Corporation, and that he'd get back to the Attorney General by that afternoon. It was all he could do, but at least it was a beginning.

Arnie leaned back in the chair, then twirled it to face the plate glass window which gave him a pigeon's view of Boston Common. He was just in time to see Diana's glossy black head as she crossed Tremont Street and headed back to her shop. He closed his eyes, transported back in time to remember the solemn promise he had made the girl's father a quarter of a century ago.

"Don't worry, Tony," he whispered, his words falling into the dead air in the office. "I haven't forgotten."

Chapter Twenty-three

Nahant, December, 1984

The steely winter sky tumbled slowly out toward the peninsula of Nahant as Diana turned the Porsche down the straightaway leading to that exclusive community. The day was cold, bitterly cold, and the wind whipped the car, almost throwing it against the low cement wall which separated one side of the road from the other. In the distance, she could barely see Boston's skyline, its block like buildings serving as shadowy reminders of the grim task she faced.

On her right Lynn Harbor rolled in a mass of deep grayish-green waves. One of the most active small harbors north of Boston, all the boats were safely docked or taken completely out of the water during weather like this. To her left was Nahant Beach, the strip of land stretching from the peninsula community to the mainland, connecting the two like a throat connects a head to its body.

While in high school, she had often ridden down to the beach with Marcus and Rob on a sultry summer night. They would stop at the Tides, the restaurant at the northern end of the strip, get a quart of fried clams and some Cokes, then walk the length of the beach to the children's playground on the Lynn end. If they had continued, they could have walked straight to Marblehead, but Nahant was the "in" place to be, the place where all the high school students spent their summer vacations. Marblehead was for retirees and wealthy sailors.

She gunned the Porsche on that last stretch of road, remembering Marcus doing the same with his GTO, and reveled in the strength of her car, as he had in his. The speedometer passed sixty, seventy, and was on its way to eighty when she finally realized she had to slow down for the upcoming intersection. Begrudgingly, she downshifted, feeling the familiar thrill begin to subside. It seemed the busier she got, the faster she drove. And she liked it. Finally, she had come to understand the feeling of power, the exhilaration of speed that both Marcus and Rob enjoyed. A fast car pulsing beneath her felt almost as exciting as the first time with a new man.

Reaching the familiar Tides Restaurant sign, she slowed to a crawl, wanting to delay reaching Luis de la Maria Quintana's mansion as long as she could. Though the decision to help Luis decorate his house had been hers, though she hoped it had been the right choice and that she could offer Rob some protection, she still hated every stinking minute of it.

"It is so wonderful you are going to do this for me," Luis had purred when she called him after thinking over Arnie's suggestion about making a deal. She had been shocked that the agreement—the bribe —to keep Luis from selling Rob more coke had been as simple as promising to decorate Luis's house.

"I am sure you will love the house," he said, "and, with your touch, it will be the most beautiful on the peninsula."

It *was* a gorgeous house, Diana had to admit. And she also reluctantly admitted enjoying purchasing the art and furnishings which now filled the twenty- room Victorian. The best part was that she had an unlimited budget. And, though she knew where the money came from, she was determined to spend as much of it as possible. In fact, she found herself trying to spend it all so he would have nothing left over with which to purchase more cocaine. But it seemed that when it came to money, Luis had an unlimited supply. No matter how much she paid for Quintana's art and antiques, he never complained. Instead, he urged her on as if her connection with his money was a substitute for another kind of connection. Or that she would get so hooked, so addicted, so unable to live without his money, that she would also be unable to live without him.

Because she knew in the back of her mind that he was doing his best to control her, the first time she went to his house, she had taken special care to choose something from her wardrobe which completely disguised the natural curves of her body. She didn't want Quintana to think she was trying to seduce him. And she was also terrified that if he tried anything, she would lose control. That couldn't happen. She couldn't let it, but he hadn't even been there. She had worried for nothing. Nor was he present during many of the other visits she had made to the house. Ultimately, she had been allowed to explore the estate alone, except for the obligatory henchman following her wordlessly from room to room like a sinister shadow.

The house sat on a bluff overlooking the very end of the peninsula, a short distance from the old Coast Guard base, which sat in abandoned ruin. A tall, imposing form with myriad turrets, gables, and windows, it reminded Diana of a haunted English mansion.

Today its dark gray exterior mirrored the angry color of the waves smashing against the rocks below. Four towers flew up from the roof at odd angles, as though the architect had changed his mind several times, but instead of removing the originals, simply added new ones. Each tower was encircled with windows gabled with Renaissance details and each of those windows looked out onto a breathtaking view of the Atlantic Ocean or toward Boston Harbor.

Originally the house had been surrounded with ancient pine trees which eclipsed the three-and-a-half- story structure. Diana remembered from her drives with Marcus and Rob that before Luis bought the house and removed the trees—"1 have to be able to see clearly in all directions," he had remarked—you could not see the building from the road. They had kidded each other that a witch lived there, that she was ageless and blind, but able to hear everything that happened within a hundred miles. Little did she realize how close the childish imagining would bring her.

A long, winding drive led up the bluff to the mansion's front entrance, one which proved to be a slippery danger in the wintertime. She dreaded negotiating it today, especially after the previous night's ice storm.

When she pulled up to the gate to announce her arrival to the twenty-four-hour-a-day guard, Diana could see that the drive had already been sanded. She breathed a sigh of relief. As soon as the sigh left her mouth, she could also see the reason why— Luis's stretch limousine sat in front of the house's main entrance. He must have just arrived because the chauffeur still stood beside the car, gesturing to someone inside the entry that he was about to move the car to the five-car garage behind the house.

"Shit!" she whispered, punching the steering wheel lightly. As she maneuvered the Porsche into a parking space near the limo, she realized she hadn't expected Luis, had gotten used to his not being around. Thankfully, this would be one of the last times she would have to visit. The deal they had made only included filling the house with antiques and art, redecorating some of the rooms, and making the house as much of a showcase of respectability as possible. And she was almost finished. As soon as the shipment of porcelains and silver came in from Europe, the house would be complete. She would never have to come here again. Only then would she feel confident that Luis would cut Rob off from the coke supply her brother craved. That is, if Luis kept his half of the deal. She often wondered whether he would. And also why she had allowed herself to be talked into participating in such a ruse.

All for Rob. Always for Rob. She shivered. When would he be able to take care of himself? Would he ever stop being so self-destructive? She shook her head, reminding herself of Maryann, Chris, and Tony, the other three lives at stake. Whatever she needed to do to keep her family safe was worth it. Anything.

The bitter ocean wind cut through her wool coat and whipped her hair above her head. Several moments passed before the door opened to let her into the marble hallway.

"Hello, Karl," she said. "I thought you'd seen me pull in."

The blond looked at her with cold, blue eyes and nodded curtly.

"I'm just here to see whether the Orientals were put in their proper rooms." Pulling off her gray leather gloves and slipping her arms out of her coat sleeves, she handed both to Karl and quickly checked to see if Luis was in the lobby. He wasn't. "Not speaking, eh?" she said to Karl, unable to resist needling him. When he gave her another blank look, she gave him back One just as frigid as his. Her days of being intimidated by him had long been over and he knew it.

From the library to the right of the hallway, she heard muffled voices. The double mahogany doors were shut, thank God, and she glided noiselessly by, heading for the upstairs suites, thankful she wouldn't have to face Luis right away.

Once out of the entry, the foyer's ceilings rose upward, opening up to the master staircase which led to the upper floors. With a sense of pride, she reached to straighten a fourteenth century Flemish tapestry she had personally hung on the teak wood staircase wall and smiled. The tapestry had been one of her prize finds at a German auction less than a month ago. Terence had attended the sale with her. They had both been unimpressed by the collection of antique beer steins, illustrated books, and Dresden porcelains. "A nice collection, but nothing out of the ordinary," Terence had commented. They were about to declare the sale a waste of time when the tapestry came up on the block. Diana's interest was piqued. With the knowledge that she had unlimited funds and a perfect spot for the tapestry, she battled some of the most prominent European dealers for the rare hanging, a scene of a fourteenth-century maiden offering a rose to her lute-playing courtier.

Later, Terence said she paid too much for it, but she hadn't cared. It wasn't her money and even if she had paid five times what the piece was worth, she would still make a profit by adding it to the inventory earmarked for the Quintana mansion. Besides, it fit perfectly in this twelve-foot section of wall. Now, softly lit by recessed lighting, the maid and her suitor seemed to come to life and the muted colors of the tapestry glowed warmly against the reddish-black paneling.

At the top of the wide marble staircase, a large cathedral window overlooked the rocky cliffs leading down to the Atlantic Ocean. The spectacular view always stopped her for a moment, enticing her to sit on the wide sill and watch the ever-changing movements of the ocean. But not today. She did not enjoy being in this house when Luis was around. His presence changed everything.

All the "help"—or his "associates," as he preferred calling them—were more alert, almost as though mistreating her would better prove their loyalty to Luis. She knew they thought her an intruder, an interloper and foreigner, but it wasn't only Diana they watched closely. More guards were posted around the exterior of the house when Luis was present; more staff people wandered the halls, all armed with menacing weapons of all kinds; more maids puttered in the already immaculate rooms; and the kitchen staff grew to include two hand-chosen French chefs, on call twenty-four hours a day to prepare whatever Signor Quintana or his guests desired. The mansion seemed smaller to Diana when the staff filled its hall§. A kind of military atmosphere prevailed and she never quite got used to it, always leaving with the jittery feeling that, at any moment, an out-and-out war might explode within the mansion.

She walked along the second floor hallway. On its walls hung various oil portraits of formidable heritage. Some were European, some American, but all the subjects had stern expressions on their aristocratic faces. She had hoped they would frighten Luis somehow, awaken his naturally superstitious tendencies, had even tried to find some which had histories of haunting their former homes. Anything to give him the shivers.

"Hello, Abigail Johnson," she said quietly to the white-bonneted Puritan spinster on her right. Absently she flicked a piece of dust off the gilt frame. "And how are you today, Mr. Prior?" The dark-browed minister on the opposite wall seemed more Satanic than holy. Moving more quickly, she passed the rest of the portraits.

Ah, the Turkish runner was in its proper place in the hall. A perfect fit; And the men had even remembered to cut the pad just a little bit smaller than the rug so it wouldn't show beneath it. It was a very valuable runner, a Holbein, one of the earliest- known of the Islamic carpet patterns and had originally been made for the floor of a mosque in the Turkish town of Konya. Shaking her head, she almost walked to the side of it. After paying well over $200,000 for the runner, she felt guilty putting her heels on its ancient threads. What the hell. It was Luis's. Why should she care? Defiantly, she veered and walked over the rug's far right corner—yet still kept her heels a hairbreadth off the carpet.

She had made an enemy when she purchased this rug. One of London's Arabic rug merchants had reportedly been waiting for the Holbein to come onto the market for many years. Diana amazed him and the other rug dealers by being willing to pay whatever was necessary to get the carpet. Amal Haziz had left Sotheby's muttering ancient curses against her under his breath, Terence told her later. Perhaps the curses would be transferred to the rug's new owner. What a wicked thought!

Sliding open a bedroom door, one of four on the second floor, she promised herself to check this room quickly. The largest of the bedrooms, this was the one Luis had chosen as his and she didn't want him to find her here. Knowing his taste tended towards gaudy, or, at the very least, gauche, she had been tempted to decorate it with architectural elements from a Parisian bordello that had recently been torn down. But she couldn't bring herself to buy the gilt figures of naked women and the horribly ornate furniture which had once filled the building. Even at Luis's expense.

Instead, she filled the room with red and gold Indian draperies, rare picture rugs depicting mythological beasts like two-headed dragons and winged lions. Large brass Russian samovars, and ancient
Burmese statues filled the corners of the room like solid ghosts. It was like entering one of the rooms at the Taj Mahal. She had been told Luis loved it. It figures, she thought; I hate it. After checking to see whether the new rugs were in place, she gave the room one last withering glance and turned to leave.

"I am so glad I caught you." Luis leaned against the doorway's frame, looking like a wealthy businessman in his finely-tailored gray suit and tie, rather than a drug dealer. "Do you have a moment to have a cup of tea?" He started walking toward her, his heavily-lidded eyes probing her as if she were one of his possessions.

"No, I don't." She checked her watch needlessly, not wanting to look at his face. "I have to get back to the office. In fact, I should be there right now. There's a shipment coming in from Europe. Your dishes and silverware, in fact. I should be there to receive the call." She was talking too quickly, too nervously. Tilting her shoulder, she attempted to walk past him, but his arm shot out in front of her.

"Just a few moments it would take," the Spanish voice purred in her ear. "Just stay for a few moments. I would like to discuss what you have done here. You would not deny me the opportunity to speak with my decorator, now would you?"

Diana sucked in some air and pushed his arm away. "Don't touch me, okay? We're not friends and I'm not doing this because I *want* to."

His eyes turned a callous pewter. "Business, Diana. That is all I want to discuss." Taking his arm away, he stared defiantly at her. All friendliness was gone.

"Okay. If that's all it's going to be. If you want anything more, I leave. Get it?."

With an apologetic grin, he threw his hands up in the air. "Got it," he replied.

His attitude change was too abrupt. She had already seen the unhidden cruelty and hatred in his eyes and knew that he needed very little coaxing to become violent. Only a few weeks earlier, she had been in the house when he was meeting in the library with Karl and had been witness to his temper. Furniture had been thrown across the room, one of the Degas paintings she had just hung on the library wall had been irreparably torn, the Handel lamp on one of the side tables had fallen to the floor, broken into a million pieces. Yet, he hadn't cared. "They can be replaced," he said, stomping past her like a large and angry rhinoceros.

With a sadness akin to what she had felt when Gene died, she had taken the Degas off the wall and inspected the rip. The masterpiece looked ruined and it brought tears to her eyes to think that such an unthinking, unfeeling ■ man could be allowed to own such a piece of art, and that she was the tool he used to accumulate such treasures. With little hope, she wrapped the painting and personally took it to an expert who worked for the Museum of Fine Arts, an expert who didn't know whether or not he could repair the damage.

"Come," Luis commanded, holding out his arm. "The cook has already started the tea. There is a fire in the library. It is warmer there. While we walk, you can tell me about the paintings and the furniture you have bought for me. Since I now own these treasures, I should know their history, should I not?"

For a moment, she felt he might have read her mind, or maybe felt contrite about the damage he'd caused. Was it possible? He seemed genuinely interested to know about the portraits lining the hallway. Though she had already described the items in his bedroom to him in a formal letter, he still had questions.

"Pictorial rugs are rare, are they not?" he said as they passed a portrait of a stern-faced Quaker known to her simply as "William."

She nodded, folding both arms behind her back. "Each one tells a story, like Native American rugs." "Perhaps you will tell me the story of mine." Luis smiled at her and she felt a momentary tug as she had when they first met. Turning away quickly, she gestured to the next painting, one of a woman in a high-necked ruffle.

"She's said to have been related to Mary, Queen of Scots."

"Mary, Queen of Scots. Who was she, Diana?" "You don't know Mary, Queen of Scots?" Diana laughed derisively, then stopped when seeing the wounded expression flit across his dark features. Even though she hated him, she couldn't purposely hurt him. Or anyone else. She chided herself for being so meek. "I'm sorry. I forgot that you didn't have the benefit of an American education."

He turned to look at another portrait, his back toward her. "Or *any* education, for that matter." His voice was serious. Almost sad.

Instead of commenting any further or bothering to illuminate him on Mary, Queen of Scots, she went on ahead. "This one," she said, pointing to a child who sat with a ball in her lap and a pug-faced dog next to her, "was done by Ammi Phillips. She's a well-known folk artist. Supposedly the little girl died shortly after her portrait was done."

"How *critique.*" He stood quietly at Diana's side, gazing at the painting. Once again, she felt a tug of sympathy. Catching herself, she walked on, only stopping when she reached the top of the staircase.

"Is there anything else you want to see before we go downstairs?" she asked as she waited for him to catch up with her.

"Have you finished the bedrooms at the other end of the hall, *mi cara?*"

She winced, wanting immediately to remind him she was not his "mi cara" and that she resented him taking the liberty to call her so intimate a name. But she decided against a rebuke. It was the first time in a long while that they had been able to talk without arguing. Safer to keep it that way. "Yes, I have. Each one is decorated in a different period. We can take a peek if you like."

"I like."

"The first one is done in Art Nouveau. I bought most of the pieces in Paris and Vienna because that's where the master furniture makers worked." She opened the door to a room a little smaller than Luis's. The eleven-foot-tall headboard almost touched the twelve-foot-high ceiling and was a swirling mahogany landscape of roses and hearts. A matching vanity sat to the bed's right, its mirror encased in an extravagant heart. Carved mahogany roses graced the knee of each leg. The only appropriate bedspread she could find was a golden silk tapestry from Vienna. Its scalloped hem followed the curves of the furniture, lying against the pale ivory rug on the floor.

"Art Nouveau. First part of the century, correct?"

When she nodded, Luis smiled as if he had been awarded a prize.

"I took the liberty of buying a Limoges bureau set for the vanity," she said. "All hand-painted and signed by the artist." She held up the mirror, a gold-trimmed beauty which repeated the pattern of the bedroom set. "It's perfect for this room, don't you think?"

"You have very good taste, Diana," Luis replied as he took the mirror from her hand and inspected it carefully. "It's beautiful, just like the woman who chose it."

Again, she refused to acknowledge the comment and turned to walk out of the room. "The other bedroom is done in High Victorian furnishings," she commented over her shoulder, trying to calm the butterflies racing madly through her stomach. The hair on her arms rose straight up as if she had walked through a chilly air current. Why am I still attracted to this man? this monster? she asked herself as she walked back into the hallway and toward the next room. How can I be so ridiculous? This man is an animal. A bastard. A dope dealer.

"High Victorian." Luis closed the door behind them. "Like the Queen of England?" He seemed determined to prove that he knew more than she thought he did, as if that would matter to her, as if it would make a difference. And he was being his most charming self, a self that Diana knew all too well, the self which had drawn her to him from the very beginning. She curbed the urge to tell him to shut up, to' remind him that he didn't need to be nice to her.

She led the way into the next room. Its> windows were draped with several layers of heavy red velvet brocade and each wall was covered with ornaments, prints, and what she liked to call "Victorian gee-gaws." She had decorated the room as authentically as it would have been during the period, utilizing every square inch of space. The bed she had chosen was just as tall as the one in the room next door, but this one was made of oak and was heavily carved with almost abstract flowers and vine§. Three matching bureaus lined the walls, a vanity sat in one corner next to the window, and commodes took up the space on each side of the bed. Beneath Diana's feet lay several Orientals. A large Hamadan graced the entrance to the room, a Heriz covered one corner, and runners were laid on both sides of the massive bed. As a result, not an inch of bare floor could be seen anywhere in the room.

"How depressing," he said. "Has the maid seen this yet?"

Diana laughed. "The Victorians liked to fill every 313 inch of space. They also liked their possessions."

"I see that. The upstairs maid is going to hate it." Walking slowly around the jam-packed room, he shook his head. "I am glad my room is not decorated this way," he said as he made his way back into the hallway. "And the last bedroom, the one next to mine. How is it decorated?"

"In Georgian furnishings and silver accents. Would you like to see it?"

"No, it is not necessary. The tea must be ready by now." He offered her his arm and this time, surprising herself, Diana took it. When he smiled down at her, she smiled back, thinking they might have finally come to a truce. Inwardly, she winced at her optimism, but perhaps Arnie was right. Perhaps she had given Luis the false sense of power he wanted. Maybe that was all right, she thought. Just as long as he didn't take advantage of it.

Luis watched the dark-haired woman in the chair opposite him. She was avoiding him, he knew. Staring absently into the flames of the fire, she refused to meet his eyes, refused even to tilt her head in his direction. That was fine. He could watch her profile from this angle and could enjoy her discomfort. Whenever he faced one of his competitors, he always made it a point to make them feel as comfortable as possible before making his quiet threats. It never failed to throw them off, to give him more power than he already had. And he loved that feeling.

But this woman. She had control over him, even when she wasn't aware of it. And that angered him more because she was a *woman*. He had never been beaten before. Never. And most assuredly not by a mere *woman*. At this very moment, he wanted to take that gleaming black head in his hands, to bend it back and force her to take his mouth upon hers. And if she didn't cooperate, he'd simply snap that long, lovely neck. Then he would be able to take whatever he wanted from her. Anytime.

"Your choice of furnishings for the master bedroom was marvelous," he said amiably, reaching for the silver teapot to pour more of the amber liquid into the Sevres cups.

"I'm glad you like it." Diana's voice was flat. It was painfully obvious she didn't want to talk to him. The thought made him all the more angry.

Straining to keep his temper in check, he said. "You have made this house a home, *mi cara.*"

When she didn't reply, Luis gripped the sides of his chair so hard the leather squeaked and almost ripped beneath his fingers. "Your brother . . . how is he?" he said, satisfied that she finally looked at him with beautifully angry turquoise eyes.

"He's fine. Listen, Luis, you promised . . ."

"So I did. And I have not broken that promise." Though I would like to, he added silently. I would like to have you panting and writhing beneath me right now, in front of the fire, on the invaluable Persian you have chosen for this floor. I would fuck you until you could not breathe while I told you all about the carpet. You think I do not know anything, but I do. I know everything there is to know about you, *mi cara.*

"I was just curious," he said. "I have not seen my friend in a while. Is it wrong to ask for friends?"

She got up, placing her teacup and saucer on the table carefully.

"If you're quite finished, I must go. I have things to do."

He waited for her to round the chair and head for the door before saying, "Well, no, not quite. I still have a few more things to say. Miss Cole. Or are they calling you Diana Colucci again? Which name do you use now, Diana? I want to make sure I have the right one . . ."

He heard her footsteps stop and the swish of her skirt as she turned to come back to face him. "How long have you known?" she asked.

"How could I not?" he replied. "Your name is constantly in the society pages of the newspaper. Do you think I do not read them? I have known about your other name for quite a while now." He rose out of the chair, enjoying the fact that he was taller than she and could look down on her upturned face. "I also know about your home on Beacon Hill and about the country house in London. I know about Amaryllis and about all of your plans."

"You couldn't . . ." She took two steps towards him. "What are you going to do, Luis? I've done everything you asked. I've decorated the house-kept my part of the bargain. Now you keep yours. You promised you would leave me and my family alone. You promised you'd stay away from Robbie. That you wouldn't sell him any more coke."

"So I did, Diana. So I did. And I will."

"Then, why are you telling me this?"

"I just thought you should know." She was close enough to kiss. And, finally, looked vulnerable enough to take. He put his cup and saucer down and grabbed her arm, pulling her roughly toward him. Bending his head, he smothered her mouth with his, ignoring the fact that she was kicking him and that her high heels were boring into his feet. The coke was making his pulse race, making his blood hot. He wanted her. Right here. Right now. Even more than he wanted his cocaine. He gripped her other arm and pulled her down to the rug. In the movement, his mouth slipped off hers, and she let loose with a high-pitched shriek.

"What good do you think that is going to do, you little bitch?" he hissed. "You are in *my home*. The only people who will hear you are *my people*. Why not just relax and enjoy it, *mi cara?* You always did before."

He was having a hard time holding her. She was stronger than he anticipated. Maneuvering his body so that he lay on top of her, he let go of her arms momentarily. Deftly, she rolled out from under him to stand above him, her heel poised so that if he moved, it would jab into his eye. The cunt, he thought bitterly.

He laughed, at first softly, then louder and louder until he was almost hysterical. When he finished, the look on her face was one of bewilderment.

"You have won. Miss Cole. But, as they say, only the battle. Not the war," he gasped. "Go. Get out of here. And do not ever come to this house again."

Diana ran for the door and slammed it behind her.

A long time passed before Luis got up off the floor to walk to the library safe and filled his nose with the pinkish-white powder he had left there. During those long moments on the floor, he fought emotions no one else had ever made him feel. Embarrassment. Defeat. The only thing that brought him any solace was that there had been no witnesses to his shame.

He took one more snort of his precious coca, then threw the gold straw across the room. "No more!" he shouted. "You are finished, Diana Cole!"

Chapter Twenty-four

Paris, March, 1985

Diana had never seen the streets of Paris so empty. It must be because the weather's been exceptionally cold, she thought. The French were simply refusing to come out of their warm apartments. She walked next to Terence silently, bringing her wool collar up around her mouth and pressing forward, their bodies at almost a ninety-degree angle against the wind whipping around their faces. Maybe the French had the right idea—maybe she should have stayed inside as well.

"How much further?" she yelled.

He popped his head up momentarily to check where they were. "It's just around the corner," he yelled back.

Thank God, she thought, and pressed on with him at her side.

They had had a long conversation that morning while sitting in a cafe near Montmartre. She had decided to put her business plan into motion and was excited that Terence had been as optimistic about it as she.

"We'll move the Charles Street shop to Newbury Street," she said, stirring her cafe au lait, then wrapping her hands around the fat cup to keep them warm. "That seems to be where the. galleries are heading these days. I've got too much space on Charles Street and won't be able to handle it all now that Miles is gone. Can't say that I blame him for moving to New York, but 1 wish he'd waited until I got a shop set up there."

"What about Amaryllis?" Terence looked worried, as though afraid he'd lose his position as manager once she started putting the wheels into motion.

"Didn't I tell you? All That Glitters will be reconstructed— everything will be connected to Amaryllis instead. Shouldn't take more than a couple of years to put it all into effect. First, there'll be Amaryllis of London, then I'll take All that Glitters' inventory to the new shop on Newbury Street that will be Amaryllis of Boston. Then, later. I'll open one in New York, maybe even Paris someday . . . "

Diana's plan was simple. Build an antiques empire that stretched from one continent to another, concentrating on the United States first, opening shops in New York and Beverly Hills, in addition to moving the Charles Street shop to the gallery area on Newbury Street. All would be different, yet under the same management. Later, branches would open in Paris and Rome—and who knows where else. A multi-million-dollar empire, to market her antiques the way other people marketed new items. It was unheard of and something for which she knew she would have little support in the antiques world. But she had thought about it for a long time and was sure it would work. With the right employees. And the right shop space. And the perfect, knock-'me- dead inventory ...

"What about me?" he asked, when she finally ran out of breath.

"I want you to come to Boston. The Newbury shop will be the base of operations and that's where I want you. You're the only one I trust to manage

She reached across the table, holding her breath when she saw waves of doubt passing over Pellican's thin face. "Will you come?" When he nodded and smiled, she sighed deeply with relief and toasted him with her cafe au lait.

"To Amaryllis International," she said as they clinked their cups.

Boston

"Is there any way we can nail this guy?" Arnie Goldstein sat behind his desk, a sheaf of computer reports in front of him. On top of a file folder sat half a dozen photos of Luis Quintana—all of which had been taken with zoom lenses by the best undercover investigators in the country.

"We want him. The Drug Enforcement guys want him. Even the President wants him," Agent Nicholson of the FBI reported with a determined grin. "Our only problem is we haven't been able to flush him out. He's so goddamn well-protected and has so many legitimate businesses stateside that we're finding it hard to really . . ."

"Is he paying taxes?"

The agent shook his head. "Still a Colombian resident. He goes back every month or so just to maintain that status."

Arnie loosened his tie and shuffled the papers once again. "There's got to be a way. How about getting someone to infiltrate the organization?" Quintana was responsible for most of the shipments coming in to the East Coast. Everybody knew it, but when his lackeys were- caught, they seemed more ready to die than to give up information.

"His people are so tightly connected to the cartel that anyone who's not Colombian is instantly suspect."

Goldstein ran his fingers through his thinning hair. "There's got to be a way," he muttered. "There's *got* to be a way,"

Paris

"Is this it?" Diana asked as she and Terence stopped in front of a stone-faced building in deep disrepair. Its window frames appeared unpainted for years, the door scarred and dented, and the stairs barely safe to walk on. She looked at Terence. doubtfully. "Can't be. Doesn't look like there's anyone here," she said before he had a chance to answer her question.

He pulled a piece of paper from his coat pocket, comparing the address on it to the tarnished brass numbers beside the building's front door. "This is it," he said, walking up the stairs, tapping each with the umbrella he constantly carried. "Be careful, it looks like these might not stay in one place. The mortar's all broken through.

195

See there?"

"God, Terence, I hope this isn't a wild goose chase."

"Never know until we go in, will we, love?"

The letter she had received a few weeks earlier described the estate as belonging to a poor relation of Napoleon Bonaparte. She had doubted its authenticity, but after checking with contacts in London and Paris, found that there was, indeed, a family which had not yet given up its belongings. Yet, no one knew where they were or even if they were still alive. After much consternation, she figured it was worth a trip to check it out.

The listing included with the letter was impressive. Armchairs made by J. Delaunay of Paris, most of which had been sold to President John Adams in 1784; a brocade-covered dressing chair, originally made for Marie Antoinette's *grand cabinet interieur* at Versailles; a set of late-eighteenth-century Sevres porcelain in its entirety; a pair of andirons attributed to Pierre Philippe Thomire; a long list of furniture made for Louis XVI; and many other items including looking glasses, porcelains, and silver desk sets. The total worth of the goods, by Diana's estimation, was well over three million American dollars. Mouthwatering, she immediately thought of filling the London shop with the collection. If, that is, it could be had for the right price.

One of the things about which she reminded Terence as they waited for someone to answer the door was that if her plan was to work, each shop had to have its own specialty. It meant getting rid of most of the stock filling the dusty, dark interior of Amaryllis of London. Terence had no objection. Most of the items had been there for years anyway, he said. If they hadn't sold by now, they certainly weren't going to sell simply because a new owner had taken over.

He rang the bell once more and smiled at her when they heard feeble footsteps from within, echoing like hoof beats down a long hallway. When the door finally opened, she was amazed to see a small, white-haired man wearing knee britches and lifting a monocle to his watery eye. Heavy, peasant-style shoes with thick cobbled soles seemed to have made the clopping noise heard only seconds before.

"Bonjour," he said in a gravelly voice, looking from Terence to Diana.

She reached out her hand. *"Je m'appelle Diana Cole et il s'appelle Terence Pellican."*

"Ah, Mademoiselle Cole. Monsieur Pellican. Come in. please. 1 have been waiting for you."

Two hours later, Diana and Terence left the disintegrating house, having discovered the truth to the old adage that looks are sometimes deceiving. Everything listed in the letter had remained in the house—some pieces covered with drop cloths, some not in the greatest condition—but it was all there and more. They purchased every last stick of furniture and accessories Monsieur Albert Bonaparte had to offer. Satisfied that she had helped an old man enjoy his retirement, she paid a fair price for the items, meeting the amount the man wrote shakily on her note pad, as if he didn't want to say the figure aloud. It was one of the simplest and best deals she had ever made.

"I feel like celebrating," she said to Terence as they walked back to their hotel. The Paris sun broke through the dark gray March clouds to shine momentarily on the Seine before disappearing once again. "Let's have a really fabulous dinner tonight and go to the opera. What do you say? 1 could use a break."

He nodded regally and followed her along the cobblestone street to their hotel. "It doesn't stop, does it, Di?" His voice came from behind her.

She paused and turned to him. "What doesn't stop?"

'The excitement, the pleasure of making a purchase like that one. In this business, it doesn't matter how many times you find something fabulous, each time it's bloody thrilling."

She laughed. The sound was caught and tossed behind her by the late winter wind. Yes, it *was* bloody exciting. She wouldn't have chosen any other profession. Linking arms, they chatted gaily all the way back to Le Grand Hotel.

Boston

Boston's night lights wavered iii front of Arnie's eyes as he looked out the office window. Another late night. Estelle would be worried, as usual, though he had called hours ago. One more phone call and he'd head home. Easier just to appear than to try to explain over the phone.

Tapping a pencil against the desk, he watched couples lean into the late winter wind as they strode along the Common's paths. Bound for a nice evening meal or the theater, he thought. His mouth watered and his stomach growled as he tried to remember the last time he had had a chance to gobble something other than a Big Mac. The phone continued to buzz in his ear. Two more rings and he'd hang up. Try again tomorrow.

Rob's growling baritone finally broke the ringing.

"Rob? Arnie. Listen, kid, I have to talk to you . . . Yeah, it's important. I'm concerned about the company you're keeping these days . . . Don't take offense . . . Yeah, Quintana. He's bad news, Robbie. Really. Not someone you want to get involved with . . . Yeah, I know you're a big boy . . . Yeah, I know I should mind my own business, but I promised your father."

Arnie held the phone away from his ear, wincing with surprise at the anger he had aroused. "Rob . . . Rob . . . hold it a minute ... I love you like a son. I just wanted to warn you—we're going after him. I don't want you caught in the crossfire."

Silence. Then the dial tone. Wearily, Arnie placed the phone back in its cradle.

Canterbury, England

Behind her, the fire roared in the grate like a small furnace. Diana reached once again for the white porcelain teapot. "More?" she asked Terence, who sat in an overstuffed leather wing chair opposite her. He shook his head, feeling rather sleepy. She insisted on keeping fires going in all twelve fireplaces, even if no one was in the room. Since he couldn't change his habit of wearing flannel underwear and at least two layers of wool shirts and sweaters, he always suffered when he visited what she called her "London country house."

"It's Canterbury, Di," he teased her. "Londoners don't really consider it the city."

"I know, but I do."

The estate, managed by a Canterbury family— Mum, Dad, and two teenaged children—when Diana wasn't there, sat in the shadow of Canterbury Cathedral, and was one of the few homes in the small town which had a fair amount of land around it. Former owners had filled the garden with sculptured yews and fruit trees. In the summer, there were roses everywhere, some strains over 150 years old. Terence remembered the first time Diana had seen the property: she went from bush to bush, holding her hair back with one hand so she could bend her head to inhale their fragrance. She had invited him to stay there then, but he declined, preferring the cluttered familiarity of the apartment he still occupied above Amaryllis.

Most of the furnishings had come with the mansion, including several fourteenth and fifteenth century English tapestries depicting real or mythological battles. They hung on the upper portions of the main hall's walls, originally used to keep in the heat, now just decoration. Some of them had started to decay after central heating was installed, so Diana had them taken down, cleaned, restored, and put back up, with the intention of rotating them once a year so that further deterioration could be avoided.

He looked around him sleepily. Italianate frescoes covered the thirty-foot ceilings, gold gilt and pastel angels reminiscent of Michelangelo and, somehow, out of place here. The walls were paneled in dark teak and the large, open fireplace flanked by carved columns of medieval figures. Throughout the rest of the house, Diana had hung a collection of English hunt paintings and, in her bedroom, beautiful examples of works by Gainsborough, Hogarth, and Turner.

The only modern convenience besides the central heating, which, in large part, did not work, was a heated indoor swimming pool. For that simple reason, Terence felt he could probably live here forever—despite the fact that Diana insisted on roasting him to death in all the other rooms.

"Terence, come back to the country house with me," Diana had said as their cab wound its way through the deepening twilight to cross Westminster Bridge, heading off toward the Houses of Parliament and Big Ben. "We can have Mildred cook us a meat- pie, then we'll play a game of chess. How about it? I really need a bit of relaxation after the past couple of days."

It hadn't been hard to resist. Paris, though a profitable visit, had been difficult. Too much to do and too little time to do it. And the bone-chilling cold made traveling about rather difficult. He was just as ready as she to take advantage of some home cooking.

The night after their purchase of the Napoleon family collection, Diana and Terence had dinner in a small bistro near the hotel. The waiter had just placed their main course on the table when a small, wizened man, holding a cigarette in an ivory holder, had tentatively approached them.

"Diana?" One eye closed, his tone was questioning. "Aren't you Gene Monroe's assistant, Diana?"

"Frederick!" She leaped out of her chair, giving the small man a hug as though he were an old friend, then asked him to join them. They spent the evening sharing reminiscences of Gene Monroe, stories of auctions on the Continent, and of mutual friends Diana had met years earlier. When their cappuccino reached the table, she got down to business.

"Still selling estate jewelry, Freddie?"

"Always." The dealer took a puff from the cigarette in its ivory holder and blew it into the air over her head. He reminded Terence of a fire-breathing dragon or a weasel, red-rimmed beady eyes dashing from one side to the other, his voice actually hissing rather than speaking. He realized he didn't like the man at all.

"What do you have?" she asked.

"Oh, a little of this. Little of that. You are looking for something special, perhaps?"

Nonchalantly, Diana sat back, lifting her napkin from her lap and putting it on the table. Then she looked for their waiter as though ready to leave. "Not really," she said. "Just curious what you had in inventory."

The weasel leaned forward, seeming to realize he had a possible sale within reach. He began rattling off the bulk of his inventory, his small eyes narrowing, as though trying to discern Diana's reactions. Terence wondered how she. could sit there so patiently, listening to a man so obviously corrupt.

She nodded calmly, smiling one of her enigmatic smiles, purposely acting disinterested, though he could tell she was not. Finally, she put both hands flat on the table. "I wouldn't mind doing a little business with you, Freddie, but I have to be honest."

"Of course. Always the best policy," Freddie replied, eyes glittering like a cat's who had just trapped a bird.

She leaned a little closer. "One fake and that's it. 1 don't deal with cons."

"Mademoiselle! You shame me!" Freddie pulled his napkin to

his lips with shaking fingers, but recovered quickly. "How can you accuse me of such a thing?"

"Gene and 1 talked about more than just your social activities, Freddie. He shared everything."

Freddie dropped his eyes, then looked back into Diana's face. "Gene was always one of my best customers. Not a wiser man when it came to rubies and emeralds. You have his acumen and more. You'll go far, my dear."

By the end of the evening, Diana had made an appointment with Freddie to visit her in Boston with some of his stock. Terence realized that by being totally upfront about her business dealings, she had probably nipped the possibility of being deceived before the weasel even thought about it.

She had also made one of the best antique jewelry contacts in the world. Another specialty to add to her growing list.

Nahant, Massachusetts

Luis hung up the phone with a disgruntled look. The Nahant house was empty except for Karl, who sat in the leather armchair on the other side of the library. A big shipment due to arrive momentarily from Miami occupied the rest of Luis's associates. Karl flipped the barrel on his Sig Sauer one more time. The clacking sound split the silence in the oak paneled room.

"She's still not home?" Karl asked without lifting his blond head.

With a nonchalant sweep of his hand, Luis grumbled and sat down at his desk. "Did you have Enrique follow her?"

"Yes, I already told you that. She left for London five days ago. Alone."

"Something is going on. Has he followed her?"

"He lost her in Paris. She was on foot with that English guy. The one she bought the shop from." Karl closed the barrel once more and laid the gun on the table next to him. "Why don't you just ignore her? She's nothing. Nobody. I can get you any woman you want . . ."

Instantaneously, Luis was in front of him, one hand around Karl's neck. "Do not tell me of other women," he said. "None will ever match Diana Colucci."

Canterbury

"Terence. Your move." Diana's voice brought him back to reality. He glanced at his watch, not surprised that both hands stretched straight up.

"I'm afraid I'm drowsing on you, sweets," he commented with a yawn. "Do you mind if we finish this tomorrow?"

"Never fails. You do this to me every time. I've almost got you in checkmate and you want to quit on me. No way, Pellican. Make your move."

They played for another hour. He watched her square-tipped fingers make move after decisive move, not trusting himself to lift his eyes to meet hers. He kept reminding himself that she was his boss. And his friend.

Finally, she captured his queen. "There! Checkmate!" she said triumphantly. "Now you can go to bed."

The fire was almost out. He rose from the chair, took the poker and stoked it a bit. "Di?" he said, his back still toward her.

"Mmmm?" The ivory chess pieces clinked against each other as she put them away.

"Do you date?"

The clinking stopped. He knew she was looking at him. He stoked the fire once more.

"Why do you ask that, Terence?"

"Just curious."

Another pause. "No, not really. I don't have time."

"What *do* you do in your spare time?"

She laughed and the delightful sound brought him around. The firelight put small circles of pink into her usually pale cheeks, reddened her lips, and put a gold tinge into her raven hair. He thought her more beautiful than any of the portraits Gainsborough had ever painted. Catching his breath, he wanted to go to her, to pull her to him and put his thin lips on her full ones.

"Terence Pellican, you really are a funny duck," she said. "First of all, I don't *have* any spare time. Secondly, what free moments I *do* have I spend with Rob and Maryann and the kids. Real exciting, huh?" Terence smiled in spite of himself. "You amaze me sometimes, Ms. Cole."

"Why?"

"It's almost like you're two different people. One is a businessperson of almost terrifying dimensions. The other is a woman who would rather read a book to a seven-year-old than attend a society function attended by world-famous people. What do they call those multi-personalities?"

"Crazy." She chuckled and rose from her chair. "Really, Terence, I think you need some sleep. Go to bed, you silly Englishman." Reaching for him, she squeezed his arm and kissed him lightly on the cheek before turning to leave.

He watched her leave, white jersey skirt slightly swaying, head up, shoulders back, long legs stretching forward like a cat's, and thought he had probably made the biggest mistake of his life by becoming her employee instead of her lover. And probably the best decision, as well. Catching himself about to fall into a well of self-pity, he straightened his glasses and extinguished the lights before heading in the direction of his own room.

Climbing into the flannel-sheeted bed beneath two down comforters she insisted upon using even during London's humid summer, Diana watched the fire's dying embers in the small, marble-tiled fireplace against the opposite wall. This house was wonderful, a true English treasure, but the damn stone walls kept it too cold. Always shivering, she wriggled, trying to find a warm spot in the bed, then reached for the slim volume of Whitman's *Leaves of Grass* on the bedside stand next to her.

Terence had certainly acted strangely tonight. Wasn't even into the chess game. He usually beat her badly. It had been a surprise to win. Even more surprising to be faced with such personal questions. Not like him. Not at all.

She lifted the book and opened to her marker. Within moments, she was engrossed in Whitman's lilting words, the simple images, and was ignoring the lonely sounds of the wind whistling through the chimney and the nagging echoes of Terence's words. Turning the page, she remembered the stories Mildred had told her about the knights buried within the mansion's four-feet-thick walls, but pushed the thought of her house being haunted out of her mind.

Yet, something kept creeping back into her subconscious and when she finally fell to sleep, it was to dream of dark, cloudy places, dimly-lit faces. She awakened several times in the night, expecting to see a ghostly visage at the foot of the four-poster.

Chapter Twenty-five

Boston, April, 1985

Diana shoved her keys into her pocket, checked the apartment once more, and hurried to the door. She hated being late and this was the new manager's first day. Usually she got to the shop early, straightened out incidental matters, then spent the day training new personnel or doing whatever else required her attention. But nothing had gone as expected this morning, and she felt almost nervous when faced with the prospect of apologizing for her tardiness to her new employee.

She had hired the statuesque Jamaican woman shortly before leaving for a buying spree in Paris. During the interview, the woman stated in a low, lilting voice that her name was Sarah—accent on the last syllable—Pennington, and that she had graduated from Oxford, specializing in Renaissance. Most impressive, Diana had thought, and intimidating. Nothing could get under her skin faster than someone with more education than she. It had always been a soft spot.

As they agreed on a salary, Diana speculated that Sarah would prove invaluable once the business started to grow. When All That Glitters became Amaryllis of Boston, there would be a need for someone with her talents. And persistence. Yes, she had been a good choice, Diana thought.

Just as she reached for the door, the telephone rang. She hesitated, wavering between answering it or letting the machine take a message, then decided on the latter, dropping her briefcase on the chair nearest the door.

Her brother sounded like he was in a distant country, one which didn't have adequate telephone service. "Have you seen Maryann, Di? Or the kids?"

"No, of course not, Robbie. It's only 8:30 in the morning. Where are you? How come you're not at work?" Checking her hair once more in the mirror above the phone, she tapped her fingers impatiently against the receiver.

"I'm sick. Not going to work. You sure you haven't seen them?" Rob's voice wavered.

"Of course not. Why aren't they there with you? Don't the kids have to go to school today?"

"She left. Maryann left. We ... ah ... we sorta had a fight last night. She took the kids. Hasn't been back since." His words grew strained, rushed. Diana's tapping fingernails stopped abruptly.

"What did you fight about, Rob? You're not doing coke again, are you?"

"Fuck you, Di! What the fuck! You don't ever stop, do you? Perfect little businesswoman. Wasn't around to see us when her boss was sick. Took all her time to take care of *him*. Never bothered with her family till after the guy was dead. Now she's Miss Millionaire, bouncing dl over the world, making deals and buying all kinds of old shit. Well, what about us? Huh, Di? You forget you got a family? You're a tightass, Di, just like Luis says. A fucking tightass."

Oh, shit. The rambling words, the quick subject changes, and his uneven temper meant only one thing. Cocaine. The moment Luis's name was mentioned, she realized her deal with the Colombian had been as empty as all the other promises he made. Damn it! Why can't the bastard leave my family out of this?

"Robbie, slow down. Tell me where you are and I'll come over."

"Don't want you here! Don't you dare come here! Just want Maryann." He began to cry. He was probably pushing the heel of his hand against his eyes the way he did when he was a child. She could hear him sniffling as though his nose was full of mucus. Her sickened stomach turned. Glancing at her watch, she decided to call Mr. Thomas at Weldon's, the shop next to hers, to have him open the door for Sarah. She'd have to take over until Diana got there. What a first day. Trial by fire. No time to think about whether or not she could handle it. There was no choice.

"I can't live without my kids, Di." Robbie had calmed down, but the tremor in his voice was more pronounced. He sounded not quite sure of where or who he was. "They mean everything to me."

"I know, hon. We'll get them back. Don't worry. You just tell me where you are." And I'll take care of getting you to stop using that crap as soon as I get my hands on you, she thought. But not now. Now I just need to get to you.

"Where the fuck do you *think* I am?" His moment of self-pity was over as quickly as a snap of the fingers. He sounded dark. Violent. She began to get frightened.

"Home?" she asked, as reasonably as she could.

"Yeah . . . home . . . fucking place is a mess. Those goddamn kids don't know what it means to pick up their toys." In the background, something shattered. Was he starting to throw things? It was an old habit. A sure sign of his frustration. Something else thudded against a hard surface. He grunted as though holding the phone while picking <u>things</u> off the floor. Breakable things. "Goddamn kids! Forget it! 1 don't want them back!" he screamed. "Fucking spick! *You* told him not to give me any more. Huh? It's your fault, Diana. It's *your* fault!"

Abruptly, the phone connection ended and the dial tone returned. Diana grabbed her pocketbook and slammed the door shut behind her, taking the stairs two at a time to the garage below.

She wove the ear through Boston's tiny side streets, leaning on the horn and yelling out the window at passersby who wouldn't get out of her way quickly enough. Each stoplight seemed interminable.

Each raindrop splashing against the Porsche's roof sounded like a thunderclap. Twice she thought she saw blue flashing lights in her rearview mirror. Both times she ignored them, sidling her way in and out of traffic, never knowing whether the cops wanted to stop her or whether they were on their way to some other crime.

Crime. She was guilty. Just as guilty as Luis.

Robbie. His nose full of deadening white powder. By now he'd be rampaging through the house, throwing "Star Wars" figures one way, toy trucks another. Oh, God.

She maneuvered the car down Route 99 in Everett, thankful that most of the traffic was heading the other way. Taking a few shortcuts, she soon found herself in Saugus, passing the New England Shopping Center. One more roundabout, she reminded herself, and tried to wipe the image of Robbie shaking like an addict out of her mind.

Her fingers clenched and unclenched. Their sweatiness made it almost impossible to hold the wheel.

Robbie wouldn't have, hit Maryann, would he? He wouldn't have scared the boys . . . but why else would they leave? What kind of panic had he caused? What had *Luis* caused?

She fought back the panicked feeling racing through every part of her body, tried to force herself to remain calm, tried to focus on the road, never knowing whether her vision was blurred because of tears or the rain which now fell heavier and harder against her windshield.

Finally, Rob's house came into view. She pulled into the driveway and threw open the car door. Sheets of icy rain relentlessly pummeled her face, soaking clear through her raincoat. Her legs felt like sodden masses, too heavy to move, too uncomfortable to slide gracefully against each other. The Valente heels were ruined, would have to be discarded.

"Robbie!" she screamed, trying to reach the small window at the top of the door. "Let me in!" She couldn't see through the window even when she stretched to her full five feet, seven inches. The best she could do was to slide her fingertips around the window's edge.

Maybe the back door.

She ran down the stairs and around the corner of the house, heels digging into puddles of mud, slowing her progress considerably.

"Rob! Robert Anthony Colucci, open this goddamn door right this minute!" With iron fists, she pounded against the window. A slap of thunder directly overhead rocked her, vibrating through her entire body. The rain came down harder, feeling like pinpricks against her skin. "Damn it, Rob! It's pouring out here. Let me in!"

His Corvette was parked in the driveway at an odd angle, its front right wheel on the grass he had so carefully trimmed the first summer they had owned the house. A pair of bright pink plastic flamingoes lay face down in the mud. Maryann had told her about those last week—laughing at Rob for buying them.

He had to be here. No way he'd leave his Vette to go walking in this downpour.

Through the back door window, she noticed several days' worth of dishes in the sink, the milk container still open on the kitchen table, toys strewn everywhere, and a broken bottle of pickles in a green puddle on the floor. Must have been knocked off the table when Rob started throwing things. God, what a mess. Maryann would never let her house get like this. She even had a fit when someone walked in with their shoes on, no matter how dry the ground outside.

Diana toyed with the idea of breaking the window. No. They'd only need to replace it. The cellar. The bulkhead door. She headed that way, balancing on her toes so her heels wouldn't slide into the wet, muddy grass. Bingo. It was open and so was the cellar door.

Slipping into the dark basement, she paused for a moment to listen. Silence. Absolute and complete quiet. Maybe he *did* leave. But how? Not in the car. Had Luis beat her here? She hoped not.

Her shoes squeaked with water. She pulled them off, holding them by their toes so their heels could be used as weapons if necessary. Little puddles of moisture squeezed out of her stockings onto the floor. She had the urge to strip off all her clothes and throw them immediately into Maryann's dryer. Shrugging out of the sodden raincoat, she laid it on the banister leading upstairs.

The kitchen door was closed and the stairway leading to it seemed like a sinister underground tunnel—no light, no welcoming warmth. Still no sounds from the house. Part of her didn't want to. go any further. Part of her wanted to flee. Another part of her was so curious about Robbie that she wanted to race up the stairs, through the door, to find him. No matter what. But the greatest, strongest, emotion was anger. A strong, totally destructive anger that made her mind vividly invent ways to ruin the man who had made all of this happen. Luís de la María Quintana. Damn it, she wished she'd never met him, had never fallen in love with him, had resisted the spell he had cast over her.

Her stocking feet pounded against the wooden stairs.

The house, deadly silent, reeked of rotten food. Diana clamped a hand over her mouth and picked her way around the remnants of a Lego blocks set scattered over the hallway floor. What had they fought about? Was Rob right? Could she have helped? Should she have been around more often? Had she let him down? If she'd been there, could she have stopped him from doing the drugs Luis offered? She held her breath, then released it shakily.

"Robert? Rob, are you here?" Out of force of habit, she closed an open closet door, listening to its lock click into place. She expected Rob to come out of the bathroom, a grin on his face, wearing an old T-shirt and a pair of ancient sweat pants with the East Boston High stripe down their side. She *wanted* him to. Wanted to fight with him, wanted to scream into his face that he was destroying the only family she had, the only brother she had, wanted to make up afterwards, tell him how much she loved him. Wanted to say she was sorry.

Her knees threatened to buckle. "Rob?"

Resisting the urge to clean the kitchen, she skirted the room and headed for the parlor. Through the picture window, the street was barely visible, encased in walls of gray rain. The sound of it hammering against the metal overhang outside above the front door echoed throughout the room. She stood for a moment, feeling her heart pound as hard as the downpour outside, suppressing a sudden urge to flee, to back out the same way she came in.

"Rob?" she called, quieter this time. Maybe he was upstairs, sleeping off his drug-induced state in the double bed he shared with Maryann. Upstairs. She turned to make the climb and noticed a shoe on the floor. An adult-sized shoe. A Nike sneaker that seemed to be connected to a foot.

"No," she whispered, her hand on the back of the couch to steady herself. She put one foot in front of the other. Mechanically. Unwillingly. "No." Her brother, her once beautifully young and innocent brother, lay face-up on the Chinese carpet Maryann bought only weeks before. Her pride and joy. Rob's face was almost the same color as its powder-blue background. One leg was bent at an angle away from his body, the other stretched straight out. His hair was messy, greasy, like he hadn't washed it in days. There was a line of dirt under his fingernails. And the needle stuck straight out of his arm like a stiletto.

Diana couldn't take her eyes off the belt fastened tightly around his forearm. The hand-tooled leather belt she had bought for Tony at Disney World. The leatherworker had designed it especially for him, tooling Tony's name in rolling script across its length while they watched, adorning it with a cowboy hat and a rearing Appaloosa at Tony's request.

He wore it constantly. Maryann had to punch extra holes in the leather when it grew too small for him. Now the belt was around his father's arm, a tourniquet, making it easy for Rob to pick a vein into which to plunge his needle.

She kept her eyes on the belt as she bent toward her brother, picking up his blue-nailed hand to check for the pulse she already knew she would not find.

She kept her eyes on the belt as she groped for the phone on the hallway wall and dialed the operator.

She kept her eyes on the belt as the ambulance raced through the relentless rain, bright red lights flashing. She watched the belt dangle off the white- sheeted stretcher, saw it almost catch in the stainless steel wheels. She held the edge of the leather, running her fingers over the T, the O, the N, and the Y as the ambulance sped down the highway. And she held the belt wrapped around her fist when they disengaged her hand from her brother's arm, informing her as kindly as they could that, no, they could not revive him, that he would never be alive again. That he couldn't hear her whispering, "I'm sorry. Oh

God, Robbie, I'm so sorry."

Chapter Twenty-six

Boston, May, 1985

Diana pulled the pillow over her head, ignoring the slivers of sunlight forcing their way through the blinds.

"Diana! Open the goddamn door!" Maryann's voice, insistent and angry, filtered through the comforter.

Three weeks had passed since Robert's funeral. Still she refused to get out of bed, go to work, feed herself, or perform any kind of task requiring her to talk to another human being. She quit, no longer wanted to be part of the world, wanted everyone to simply leave her alone, to let her grieve, wail, pound the walls. Alone.

Maryann had faithfully come to the apartment every day for two weeks. Every day her threats became louder, her pounding stronger. She *had* to come to the door; there was no other way of getting through—Diana had made sure of that. The phone had been disconnected and the lock had been changed so Maryann and the workers at All that Glitters could not come in unannounced, yet none of it stopped her persistent sister-in-law.

"Leave me alone," she grumbled, face down in the pillow. "Go away."

"Diana! I know you're in there! You can't hide forever. Get up and answer this goddamn door or I'm going to call the police to knock it down." Silence for a few seconds. "I mean it, Di. You owe it to me to answer this frigging door. He was *my* husband. You're not the only one who's hurting. What about the boys? He was *their* father. They don't know what to do without him and don't you think they're asking about you? Diana? Diana Colucci! Open the door! I'm going to call the police if you don't get out here by the time I count to ten. I've had it with you. This is ridiculous."

Heaving one leg over the edge of the bed, she squinted against the sunlight. Don't want to do this. Don't want to talk to Maryann or anyone else for that matter, but the woman is giving me a headache. Only way to get rid of her is to let her in. Besides, no need to have the carved mahogany door damaged by any overly zealous cops.

"Four . . . five . . ."

Dragging one slippered foot behind the other, she pushed her arms into the chenille robe lying on the end of her bed and made her way to the door.

"Eight . . . nine . . ."

"I'm coming," she called. Then, louder: "I'm coming. Don't have a heart attack."

Maryann brushed past her angrily, almost knocking her down.

"You look horrible."

"Thanks."

"It wasn't meant as a compliment." Pulling off her gloves, she surveyed the normally picture-perfect apartment. "This place is a pigsty. What have you been doing, staying in bed?"

Diana nodded, put a hand to her forehead, and sank into the couch.

"Thanks for your support this past couple of weeks. The kids and I sure appreciated it."

Maryann's voice was sarcastic, her bright green eyes cold.

"Sorry. I can't always be the strong one, Mare. I can't always take care of everyone else. You know, sometimes I'd like someone just to take care of me. Just once I'd like someone to help me out." Fidgeting, she pulled the robe over her feet, wishing Maryann would leave.

She didn't. She just ignored the last comment. "When are you going back to work?"

"Don't know."

"Sarah's been calling me every day, you know. I have no idea what to tell her about the shop. Terence is calling from England, Miles has called from New York, Merry has called from France. What do you want me to tell all these people? That you died, too?"

Diana shrugged. Please go away, she thought.

Maryann sank into the chair opposite her. "I've never seen you look so lousy."

"You don't look so great yourself."

"It hasn't exactly been a good year. Husbands don't die every day, you know. Besides, I never had much experience with dope." She laughed sardonically. "Dope. What an appropriate name. Dope for a dope." She laughed again, though there was no glee in her eyes. With a sweeping gesture of her hand, she straightened her unruly mass of auburn hair. "He never was real smart, your brother, but I sure didn't think he'd be stupid enough to kill himself. Guess it runs in the family. *You* just don't have the guts to do it with a needle."

"What do you mean? That's not fair, Maryann." Diana's head snapped up, her senses fully alert for the first time in days.

"You obviously don't care that the world is continuing to go on or that I might need someone to lean on, or even that maybe we could lean on each other. Or how about the two little boys who are asking me questions I can't handle. Questions like 'Where's Auntie Di?'" Finally losing her composure, Maryann's face crumpled. Large tears rolled down her cheeks as she sobbed uncontrollably. "I hate you, Di. I hate that you found him and that you met Luis and that he's still calling me for money and that Robert died and that you're hiding away while I have to deal with all of it alone. I hate you for being so goddamn perfect, for always doing the right thing at the right time. How could Robert ever keep up? He wasn't like you. He kept it all inside. He blamed himself for not being able to take care of *you.*"

Unable to speak, Diana's eyes filled up, as they had so many times during the past few weeks. It was amazing there were any tears left. She watched her sister-in-law cry for a few moments, then untangled her legs and took the few steps to reach the chair where Maryann sat, a fragile mass of misery.

Placing a hand on the smaller woman's shoulder, she said, "Don't. Don't cry, Mare. I'm not perfect." She snorted and shook her head. What a joke. "Me? Perfect? I'm so damn perfect I managed to get my own brother killed. So perfectly stupid that Luis hurt me in the worst way possible—just because I wouldn't do what he wanted. And he succeeded. And you know what the worst part is? 1 can't make him pay for it. He'll never be punished for what he's done. No, Mare, I couldn't be perfect if 1 tried. I'm not even close." She patted Maryann's shoulder once more, a heavy weight on her chest pulling her down. "Don't cry, hon. Please don't cry."

"Why shouldn't I? Are you going to make everything all better? Are you going to bring Robert back and make him ^lean and whole again? Are you going to get up with the kids in the middle of the night when they're screaming for their father?" Maryann's shoulders convulsed once more. Her moans filled the dusty room. "How -can you do this to me?"

Diana settled onto the chair, squeezing in beside Maryann, to wrap her arms around her. She held her tightly and rocked back and forth, as she had so many times with Robert and, many years later, with his sons. "Shhh . . .," she said, unable to think of anything else. "It's going to be all right."

Maryann sniffled. "No, it isn't. It'll never be all right ever again." Fishing through her coat pocket, she came up with a bedraggled tissue and wiped her nose. "You know, I always knew, deep down, that there was something missing inside Robert. Didn't know what it was—still don't—but thought I might be able to see it if I kept on trying. I loved him so much that I thought maybe ... just maybe ... I could help him find what he had lost."

"It's not your fault, hon," Diana replied, "and it's not something either you or I had any control over. If I've found out one thing being alone the past three weeks, that's it. We can't take the blame for any of this, as much as we'd like to, as much as it would make us feel better. I've known about Robert's insecurities ever since Dad died, but I've denied them because I didn't know how to help. I spent all those years trying to put him back together, trying to replace all the things Dad could have been to him and Mama . . . but I simply wasn't. It was just too painful for me. Keeping all three of us together was too big a job to handle without trying to figure everything else out. And no matter what I thought, I couldn't replace our parents for him. No one could. Maybe I tried because I understood what was happening when Mama went off into her own little world. Maybe I dealt with everything better than he did because I could remember good times, times before Dad died, when he and

Mama used to hug and kiss and laugh." Stopping to take a breath, she realized the words were going to continue, in a rush, unstoppable, like the flow of tears had been.

"That's what I remember, Maryann. Not the days when she sat in her room, looking out the window. That wasn't Mama. Mama laughed and cried and yelled. She gossiped with Mrs. Scarlotti. She went to the store every day to talk to everyone in her mixed-up Italian. She was the one who sat in the audience when I was in a school play, clapping and smiling, though she didn't understand a word of English. Robbie doesn't remember that. He was too little."

She didn't loosen her hold on Maryann. Finally being able to talk about her pain was a welcome release, even though she knew the suffering she felt now would probably last forever. But it couldn't get any worse. It couldn't possibly be any worse than it had been this past couple of weeks. "Robert, well ... he never forgave Mama for leaving him, for not taking care of us, for giving up. I understood that. Guess I tried to make up for it, but I never could. It was never enough. You know, deep inside, I think he hated himself. Blamed himself for Dad and Mama leaving. Then he got even worse after we lost Marcus ... He never really accepted death . . . was never able to *tell* anyone how much he hurt. And I couldn't help, because I really didn't understand myself." She paused, trembling. "I wanted to, though. God, I should've been able to help. I should've gotten him to AA or some kind of counseling. Especially when Luis started him on the cocaine. I should have seen the signs."

Maryann turned her tear-stained face to look at Diana. "I don't think he *wanted* any help. No matter how close we were to him, Robert was always alone."

The two women sat for a long moment, their arms wrapped around each other, each immersed in her own memories. Diana became aware of the itchiness of her unwashed robe, of the lank strands of hair around her face, of the film coating every one of her teeth. Finally, she felt the need to open the blinds, to let the spring sun in. To get on with her life. To go back to work. To find out what had been happening in the world.

"Maryann?"

"Hmmm . . ."

"What did you mean when you said Luis was bugging you for the money Rob owed him?"

"You killed him just as surely as if you had pushed the needle into his vein!" Diana stood, hands on her hips, feet apart, jaw set, staring ferociously at a particularly calm Luis de la Maria Quintana. He sat, hands folded like an altar boy's on his lap, one elegant leg draped over the other, a faint smile on his face.

"He chose his own death," he said softly, flicking an imaginary speck off the lapel of his finely-tailored jacket.

Quintana's office, in the penthouse suite of the newly-erected office building at One State Street, was two blocks from Arnie's office, a short walk from the Charles Street shop. Light gray tailored couches were scattered throughout the lobby, surrounded by glass-topped marble tables and exotic plants. Salmon-colored silk curtains hung at the wall-to-wall windows overlooking Boston Harbor. A discreet gold plaque on the office door announced that visitors were about to enter the Quintana Enterprises conglomerate, known internationally for importing Colombian products like carnations and coffee.

And cocaine, Diana added silently as she pushed past the startled receptionist.

"I'm not asking you anymore, Luis. I'm *telling* you. Stay away from Maryann. Forget about what Robert owed you, *if* he owed you anything at all. Or else . . ."

Luis's heavily-lidded eyes regarded her sardonically. "Or else what?"

She lifted her chin, looking slightly over his head, past his dark eyes, his sensuous lips, out toward the Boston skyline. "You'll have to answer to me."

"Oh?"

"Yes. You know what I know about you, Luis. You wouldn't want your reputation ruined, would you?"

He turned his high-backed, calfskin chair to the window, his back to Diana. "Are you threatening me?"

"I'm *promising* you."

"And how do you think you are going to do this, *mi cara?*"

She bristled at the affectionate term. "I have ways. You're not the only one with money now, Senor Quintana."

"Money's not the only thing I have, Ms. Cole." His voice was cold, the emphasis on her name distinct and pointed. The chair whirled around. She could see the fire in his eyes. "Do not ever threaten a Colombian, Diana. You do not know the power I have."

Leaning on his desk, she lowered her head like a ram and met his eyes with a blazing anger of her own. "You're not in your own country, Quintana. Don't underestimate the power of the United States government. Back off! Leave my family alone!" "On one condition . . ." He settled back into his chair and folded his hands back into his lap.

"I'm not prepared to meet *any* of your conditions."

"You have two nephews, do you not? Christopher and Anthony, I believe their names are . . ." Calmly, he picked at a nail, dropping his eyes as well as his voice.

She swallowed. Where the hell did this asshole get off bringing the kids into this? When was he going to quit? She nodded, then realizing he wasn't looking at her. "Luis, don't . . ."

"We might make a deal. A very profitable deal. Good for you and most beneficial for me. And your nephews would be safe for eternity. Such a fair price to pay, would you say?"

"Luis, I've had it with your deals! You've broken every single promise you've ever made to me!"

He held up one finger, his diamond ring sparkling in the late-afternoon sunlight streaming through the plate-glass window behind him. "Not everyone, *mi cara*. You are wrong. I promised you I would love you forever, did I not? And I shall, *mi cara*. That will never stop."

His words silenced her as nothing else ever would. She fought the urge to remember the first time he had said he loved her, remembering with trepidation the exact moment, at the height of her climax, that she had screamed she loved him, too. She shivered.

"No more deals, Luis."

"Okay. I will remember that. And so shall you, Diana." He flicked his fingers toward the door, a dismissing gesture. "Tell your sister-in-law I will expect to see the $12,000 her husband owed me within a couple of weeks or . . ."

"You can't do this!"

"No, Diana, you are wrong. I can do anything I wish. You are the one who cannot push Luis Quintana around." He rose from his chair and leaned threateningly toward her. "That is one lesson *you* must learn. Now, you may leave."

She hesitated, rapidly going over her options. "What if *I* pay you what Robert owes you? I'll give you a check right now." Reaching into her Gucci shoulder bag, she pulled out a slim checkbook.

"I do not want your money."

"What *do* you want? And what will *I* get for it?" Gritting her teeth, she wondered how it had all come to this. Why did he have the power to make her bend to his every wish? He had her family, the only thing she cared about in his grasp. She narrowed her eyes, determined to make him realize how much she hated him. And, instead, realized how much she hated herself for having fallen in love with him.

"You are shipping in containers of antiques from Europe and the Orient, are you not?"

She nodded mutely.

"You plan on opening new shops, moving your Charles Street shop to Newbury Street, putting together a conglomerate. Sort of what I have here." He got out of the chair and walked around the desk past her, deliberately brushing her body with his, leaving a whiff of his cologne to linger seductively. She steeled herself, straightened her shoulders, and gripped her checkbook with white fingers.

"How do you know all this?"

"I have my ways."

She could almost feel him smiling, though he was behind her. She didn't dare look in his direction. "What do you want?"

"Shipments from South America."

"I don't have anything coming from that area." "You will."

"I will?"

"You will make some trips down there, make contacts, bring back whatever you wish."

"Why?"

"Because 1 want you to. Because 1 need a new outlet to bring my product into the country. You will provide it for me."

"Oh, no. Not cocaine. No. I refuse."

"Do you love your nephews?"

Diana whirled around. "You wouldn't . . ."

"I would." Luis stood at the door, arms folded across his chest, his face in the Shadows.

"I can't."

"You do not have a choice. The shipments or your nephews."

"No, you're wrong, Luis. I *do* have a choice. And 1 choose not to be part of your world. And I'm giving you fair warning to stay away from the kids. Don't push me any further!" On the way out, she slammed the door behind her. And since the elevator was not open and waiting, she took the stairs two at a time, down all five flights, then practically ran to Tremont Street and Arnie's office.

"Goddamn it! How can you sit there so calmly and tell me you lost him again?" Arnie slammed the dashboard with the flat of his hand, startling the man beside him.

"He's too good. He's got all the bases covered," the Drug Enforcement agent reported in a flat tone.

Amie glanced at him. How come these guys all looked alike? Gray flannel suits, white shirts, dark ties, receding hairlines. None of them even had a mustache, a scar, a super-large nose. Maybe they were clones or something.

"Okay, so what's next?" Arnie asked, feeling helpless, yet wondering if Luis would actually follow through on his threats to harm Diana's nephews. Though he had told Diana less than an hour earlier that he would offer her all the protection he could, he was beginning to wonder how much was actually possible.

"We'll ghost him," the agent continued. "Make sure he knows we're on him constantly. Give the Colucci kids extra protection. An agent around the clock, maybe. And he'll get the message. These guys always manage to foul up sooner or later."

Arnie chuckled, though he wasn't amused. "Sooner or later," he echoed. "How much longer can we hold on?"

"As long as it takes," the officer replied in the same even tone the Attorney General had used.

Chapter Twenty-seven

New York, September, 1987

"Sarah! Miles! Help me move this table over there. It doesn't look right."

Diana pulled her blue satin gown up to her knees, careful not to wrinkle it, as the three of them jockeyed the ornately-decorated French Art Nouveau table into position. "Only half an hour more," she said to no one in particular, though both Sarah and Miles paid close attention. "Miles, did you call the Mayor?"

"Yes, Diana, I told you I did an hour ago." Behind his boss's back, he raised his eyebrows at Sarah and smiled. "And everything else is ready, too."

Giving the shop one last moment of scrutiny, Diana nodded. Nothing better go wrong. She was too exhausted to fix anything else. She had flown in from Boston that afternoon, spending the morning at Tony's school where he had the lead in a play given by Miss Parkinson's second grade class.

Since her confrontation with Maryann, she had spent more time with her nephews than she had before Robert's death. She took the three of them to Europe with her as often as she could, teaching the boys bits and pieces of French, Italian, and German, while treating Maryann to a new wardrobe and glimpses of the jet-setter's life. Maryann always preferred going home to the trip itself. "Guess I'm a housewife at heart," she would say. But the boys were always up for an adventure, and Diana did her best to give it to them.

Miles reached for a sterling silver tray on top of a brass-trimmed Art Deco hall table and gestured to one of the waitresses to fill it with hors d'oeuvres.

"And the Tylers? They called?" Diana slipped an emerald post in one ear. Her dress, designed especially for her by Balenciaga himself, rustled softly as she turned to find the other earring.

"Yes, Di. Everyone's called and confirmed." Miles raised his eyebrows once more at Sarah, who was straightening the Matisse on the far wall. She turned to Diana. The Jamaican woman was a stunning sight, dressed in a long, white crepe gown, its cowl thrown over her closely-cropped black head.

"All of New York is curious about you and this shop, don't you know? They heard about the soiree you threw for Amaryllis of Boston and are expecting the same treatment." Her words gently rolled over each other, separated only by the clipped preciseness of her British accent. "The Big Apple thinks it must be the shiniest, most expensive diamond in all the cities of the northeast United States."

"We won't disappoint them." Diana smiled.

She had designed each shop in the Amaryllis chain for a specific purpose, to accommodate a specific type of clientele. The quiet elegance which pervaded Amaryllis of Boston was more comfortable for its patrons than the musky, jumbled atmosphere of Amaryllis of London, where Continental furniture and porcelains fought for space beside paintings by Degas and Monet. The New York shop, designed to have the feel of a gallery, was filled with Manship sculptures and Jane Peterson oils, with high-style Art Deco and Art Nouveau furniture. When Amaryllis of Beverly Hills opened in less than six months, she planned to hang Indian baskets on its whitewashed walls and install Texas-style furniture to grace its cool, tile floors.

Even the music playing softly in each shop had been chosen to reflect their individuality. In Boston, the symphonic strains of Beethoven or Brahms rose over the sounds of traffic on fashionable Newbury Street. New York's patrons would enjoy soft jazz, while Beverly Hills clientele would be treated to the finest in country and western music; Edith Piaf's velvety, romantic voice greeted Londoners on a regular basis.

No other antique dealer designed themes for their shops or utilized the area's own defining characteristics when choosing stock. In her innovative way, Diana had proven, without a doubt, that antiques did not have to be sold under layers of dust or in unattractive, sterile settings. In fact, she spent as much time training her staff as she did choosing the wares, figuring it wise to do so and that, in the long run, it would be time well spent.

Yet, she still did most of the buying herself. The thrill of garnering new and beautiful objects was just not something she could give up, not something she was willing to share with anyone. Except Terence.

When the opening of the Amaryllis/Beverly Hills was imminent, Diana had flown in from London, meeting Terence at La Guardia. While in the taxi en route to Sotheby's, she changed from her tweeds into a beige silk jacket, and applied her makeup.

"I heard Sack is supposed to be there," she said, sliding her feet out of low traveling shoes and into a pair of sienna-colored Ferragamo heels. "He doesn't know you, so I want you to go to the back of the hall and watch the bidding action, okay?" When he nodded, she continued, "I want this Van Gogh, and with all the press it's gotten, it'll be the biggest coup of my career. God knows how much I'll have to pay." She rolled her eyes. "You watch Sack and his boys. Make sure they don't pick up on my bidding. I want to be the follower, not the leader, on this one. Understand? These guys are going to learn their lesson once and for all. I'm not going to let *anyone* outbid me anymore. Those days are over. If I'm going to get anywhere in this business. I'll have to start taking control."

Snapping her briefcase shut, she looked Terence in the eye, her face like that of a tigress ready to do battle for her cubs.

Diana was out of the cab and five steps in front of Terence within seconds after they pulled up in front of the world-famous auction house. He had to stretch his long legs to keep up with her and be able to hear what she was saying.

In a staccato voice, she reeled off the other items in the auction on which she had her eye—a sumptuous Tiffany boudoir lamp, a set of Belgian lace tablecloths rumored to have belonged to French royalty, a set of Georgian silver goblets, and various French porcelain serving dishes. Speaking more softly and slowly once they entered the hallway where other dealers were milling about, she said, "Terence, get yourself a catalog and act like you don't know me. That's the only way I'll get anything done." With a nod and a wink, she spun away, melting into the crowd.

Pellican watched his boss closely that day and often told the story to anyone who would listen— how Diana Cole, determined to get stock for the new shop, steamrolled her way over any other dealer who dared outbid her, easily winning the lamp, silver, and porcelains during the first couple of hours of the auction. She hadn't needed Terence's help, but he quietly kept watch, waiting while she put the necessary distance between Amaryllis and the competition.

The bidding for the small painting, one of Van Gogh's less conspicuous still lives, started at $800,000. Terence had to admit that the deep purple of the irises was magnificent; the flowers, sunlight beaming in gently from the upper right of the painting to illuminate their stems, were superbly executed—the master's touch. Because it had never before been on the market, every international dealer of importance had come.

But only one of them would take it home.

From his seat near the rear of the room, he saw Diana's hand fly into the air, challenging the first couple of bids. Then she simply lifted one long, slim finger to keep the auctioneer informed of her wish to remain in the bidding. Glancing at the other side of the room, Terence noticed her competition was one of the men from Israel Sack's firm. Diana had been right. She always was.

"Six million, five on Ms. Cole," the auctioneer droned. The Sack's bidding paddle rose again and the man glanced confidently across at Diana. She hesitated, ever so slightly, then turned to stare, long and hard, at Sack's bidder as if deciding whether to continue. Slowly, she lowered her hand into her lap, then turned her classic profile forward. A decisive move. The move of one who had declined to bid any further. Terence's cue.

"Seven million once. Twice."

Terence's paddle flew into the air.

"Eight million dollars to the new bidder in back. Thank you, sir." The crowd murmured in surprise and Sack's representative turned to figure out who had come into the bidding so late. Adjusting his glasses, Terence tried to keep a smug grin off his face. As with poker, he knew to be careful not to let the opposition know his feelings ... or his next move.

"Eight million in the back. I have eight million. Do I have nine?"

With an irritated growl. Sack's man lifted his paddle once again. Terence nodded, and the auctioneer recognized the bid with a flourish. The Sack paddle rose to counter, and Terence nodded again. Finally, the bid was up to twelve million. The Sack paddle was last in the air, causing the dealer to smile vainly, like one who had already won. Though the crowd turned to look at the back of the room, Terence let the bid rest.

One last time, the auctioneer called for bids. Once. Twice. Three times. Diana's slim white hand rose swiftly. From where Pellican stood, he saw her magnificent ebony head turn slowly to glare at her competition. As the auctioneer asked for final bids. Sack's man, shocked by her sudden re-entrance into the bidding, neglected to raise his own paddle.

The crowd clapped politely, acknowledging both the impressive price and the sophisticated manner in which Diana had captured it.

After the auction, picture hat back in place on her head, she graciously accepted the congratulations of the other dealers and collectors before exiting into New York's autumnal dusk.

"You did it, Di," Terence said affectionately, grabbing her hand and squeezing it.

For one split second, her sophistication vanished as she let loose with a war whoop, sending her hat flying through the air like an uncaged bird. Without missing a beat, she grinned sheepishly at him, then did an impromptu Mexican hat dance around the brim of her stylish black straw as it lay on the dirty city sidewalk. Then, she retrieved it and continued to walk, stately and dignified, to the waiting cab as if nothing out of the ordinary had happened.

In the cab, he turned to share his boss's elation only to find her face pale and her hands shaking. "Terence," she whispered. "That's the most money I've ever spent in my whole life."

News of the sale made Jill of New York's evening newspapers. Amaryllis of Boston's phone continued to ring for almost a week with requests for interviews from newspapers, magazines, and television talk show hosts. The buy put the final sheen on the Cole reputation; a business move par excellence, Diana's brilliance was no longer in question anywhere in the antiques world.

Her rapidly-expanding, multimillion dollar business had become too much for Arnie to handle. He had conceded this only months earlier, handing her business bookkeeping and contractual matters over to another member of his firm. Jennifer Weldon was a spunky, wise-cracking Harvard graduate who, in turn, hired a team of bookkeepers, tax experts, financial wizards and contractual attorneys to help her do the job Arnie once had done alone. Though it took her a while to deal with Diana's calls from wherever she happened to be, her lightning decisions to spend incredible sums of money, and her habit of rolling money from one account into another, Jennifer learned to cope.

"She expected to be dealing with dolts from Fortune 500 companies, Di," Goldstein had said, "not with a spitfire entrepreneur like you. Give her time."

Diana had, and Jennifer proved an invaluable asset. But Arnie was still the rock, part of the "family," who knew her better than anyone else. She often stopped into his office to check on him, his ever-growing bevy of sons and daughters, and especially to inquire about his work as Attorney General. Their bond went beyond legalities, beyond the investigation he continued to conduct into the life of Luis de la Maria Quintana.

Diana stopped mid-step and mid-daydream.

Luis. She half-expected to see him tonight. He made it a point of keeping himself visible, as if she could forget the deal they had made and the position he had her in. If Arnie could find some way to stop him, dig up some damaging evidence about him, some manner in which they could get him out of the country, she knew he would. But Luis had his international dealings so well protected that even Arnie couldn't break through.

She had continued to bring in the South American shipments, concentrating on how much she loved the Mayan vases and Chilean pottery, the Peruvian blankets and Brazilian jewelry, rather than speculating on how the cocaine was packed in and around her purchases. She never saw the shipment until after Luis had extracted his goods. And she didn't want to.

Turning to check the clock once more, she reflected that time was her enemy, yet also her ally. It was the only item she could buy for Arnie, the only thing on her side in her war against the Colombian.

"Showtime, everyone," she said brightly to the small group of servers milling around in the middle of the shop. She snatched a ramake off one of the silver trays. "I'm famished," she said, winking at Sarah as she stuffed the bacon-wrapped treat neatly into her mouth. "Haven't eaten anything since . . . hmmm ... I think it was last Tuesday."

"Not quite show time yet, Di." Miles rubbed an imaginary spot on the Tiffany stained glass window which hung in a specially-made alcove in the center of the room. "You really don't know New Yorkers. They're *never* on time like Bostonians. Another half-hour, maybe, before the first person shows up, and I'll guarantee you there'll still be people coming in when we're ready to go home. There. How does that look?" He tilted the jewel-colored window, a study of a peacock spreading its feathers. Sarah nodded. Diana was still looking out the window at the traffic on Fifth Avenue.

Nothing fascinated her more than the headlong rush of New Yorkers going one place or another, yet she never felt comfortable.

Everything went too quickly, nothing was savored or appreciated. And the streets were far too dirty and dangerous to make her feel safe.

Give me Paris any day, she thought. Or Boston.

Amaryllis of Boston was home for Diana and Terence. She found it comforting, familiar; Terence found it stimulating, a place that needed polishing, decorating, and rearranging on a regular basis. She'd leave Amaryllis of New York to Sarah and Miles. They seemed to enjoy it far more than she did.

Looking at them huddled in a corner, giggling like teenagers, she wondered if they had become more than just workmates. Earlier, when she was rushing around trying to tie up last-minute loose ends, she overheard them discussing a late-night, homemade Jamaican dinner at Sardi's. "I'll make some wild rice with my special apricot dressing and trussed-up chicken. You like spices, don't you?" Sarah had said. They reminded her of Terence and herself—building a good, solid friendship based on mutual respect and admiration. She smiled. Nothing she liked more than seeing happy employees.

"I'm going into my office for a minute," she called, turning from the window. "If you're right. Miles, I still have another fifteen minutes before people start coming in."

"Don't worry, Di. We're here, an5rway." He smiled at his co-worker.

The plushly-carpeted office was quiet, its walls soundproofed to keep out the New York bustle, its window draped with a heavy linen curtain designed to keep heat and coolness in, noise out. The top of her marquetry desk was empty except for a small crystal lamp and a French-style phone. On the wall above her desk hung a hand-carved sign that simply said PASSION. Her favorite word.

In the second it took for her call to go through, she checked her watch once more. "The boys still up?" she asked when Maryann answered.

"Of course. They've been hoping you'd call."

Chris was the first on the phone. "Howyadoin', Auntie Di? Is it rainin' there? Is here. Tony and I just got out of the tub and Mom's goin' to let us watch a video before we go to bed."

"She finally figured out how to make the work, huh?"

"Yeah . . . well, you know you're better at that stuff than Mom is. Actually, I showed her how to do it." His nine-year-old pride came through strongly. "Can't tell her I said that, though," he whispered conspiratorially.

"Don't worry, your secret's safe with me. So, are we going fishing tomorrow?"

"Yup. Even dug some worms up today." "Terrific. Well, sweetheart. I'll see you tomorrow. Have a good night's sleep and let me talk to Tony, okay?"

At seven, Tony was the quieter of the two. A shy, small, blond boy, he was often lost in his brother's shadow, two steps behind the much faster, much darker sibling. If someone who didn't know them saw Diana with her nephews, they always assumed Chris was her son and Tony, just a small friend. They didn't look enough alike to be brothers.

"Auntie Di?"

"Hi, Babe."

"Chris says I can't stay up and watch the movie." "What does Mom say?"

"Um ... I haven't asked her yet."

"Well, don't you think she's the boss, not Chris?"

"Yeah, I guess so."

"You were really good in the play today. I especially liked the part where you huffed and puffed and blew the house down."

His small giggle brought a grin to Diana's face. "Did you really?"

"Of course! You were the best one and I'm really proud of you."

"I love you. Auntie Di."

"I love you, too, sweetheart. Now, go watch your movie and tell Chris I said not to be a bully, okay? And, honey, don't hang up! Put Mommy on."

She heard Maryann scolding the two boys before she reached the phone. "I don't know what you do to them, but they always act nicer to each other when they're finished talking to you."

"Just magic, I guess."

"Coming home tomorrow?"

"Yeah, I promised I'd take them fishing, then I'm off to London again. Terence is going with me to Sotheby's, then I'm going to fly over to Paris to see Merry for a few days. Heard she's got pneumonia."

"Pneumonia? I hope she's okay. Give her my love. And, Di? I think you really ought to watch how much time you spend with Terence."

"Why?"

"The guy's madly in love with you."

Taken aback, Diana snorted. "No way."

"I've seen the way he looks at you," Maryann's voice was teasing, yet serious. "Better watch out. He doesn't know how wild and wooly you are." "I'm not . . ."

"C'mon, you're talking to *me,* Di. Not one of your clients. I know how many nights this month you spent with that . . . that stockbroker guy— what's his name?"

"Oh, David. Actually, I'm going to tell him we can't see each other anymore." The man was handsome, wealthy, and kind, but he'd been pushing to spend more time with her, and she just wasn't ready for a relationship. All she wanted was an occasional date and someone who would show her some affection. As soon as a man started wanting something more, she felt like a trapped wild animal, and her first urge was to bolt.

"Well, if you don't want Terry, push him in my direction. I think he's kind of cute and I *love* that British accent. David, you can keep. Too rich for *my* blood."

"Maryann!"

On the Boston side of the phone, her sister-in- law chortled.

"You're a nut," Diana said, shaking her head. "Listen, 1 have to go. I'll talk to you tomorrow."

"Have fun, sweetie. Make sure you sell lots of stuff and find out some juicy gossip to tell me."

"If they come."

"They'll come. Who wouldn't to a party given by Diana Cole, queen of the antiques world?" Maryann was still giggling when Diana hung up. She wondered for a moment whether her sister-in-law might have had a few too many glasses of wine, then dismissed the thought. It was good to hear her laugh again.

Boston, September, 1987

"So, then what?" Maryann sat, her legs tucked up under her, crunching an apple, eyes on Diana. Every time Diana came home from a trip or a party, Maryann could barely wait to hear all about it. Somehow she got a vicarious pleasure from Diana's stories, even though she harbored no jealousy. She felt no need to have a life other than the one she shared with her boys—and she guarded that life with the ferocity of a mother lion.

"Then Liza says: T think I really like the Tiffany window, too. Whaddya say, Harry? Think it'll fit?' And, Harry, her interior designer, this little man with beady eyes and thousands of gold chains around his neck, says: 'It's lovely, dearie, but the Malibu house isn't exactly around the corner.'" Diana mimicked the man humorously, her hands fluttering like large butterflies.

"Did you tell him you have a special computerized packaging service and you can deliver anywhere in the world?"

"Of course. Give me a bite." Diana grabbed the apple from her, chomped a piece, then handed it back.

It was mid-afternoon and quiet in the tiny Saugus kitchen. The boys, satisfied after their morning at the brook —each brought home two small catfish —were outside trying to maneuver the new bikes Diana had bought for them that weekend. Both women were clad in old Levis, sweatshirts, and sneakers. Diana's dark hair was caught up into a ponytail. She wore no makeup. Yet, Maryann thought, she looks better than the models on the cover of magazines like *Cosmopolitan.*

"So, go on. Tell me about Luis again."

"Do I have to?" Diana stretched her legs and propped them on the edge of one of the other kitchen chairs. "He's such a jerk. You know I don't like talking about him."

"But I need to know what's going on, Di! You can't keep me in the dark about that . . . that . . . asshole."

"Okay. He came in about 9:30 and had two women with him, one on each arm. They were loaded, full to the eyeballs with coke. I could tell right away. Sarah was so upset she wanted to call the NYPD, but I told her to calm down, that I'd take care of it. Well, wouldn't you know ... he walks right up to Gloria Vanderbilt and starts telling her how much he hated her book. She was shocked and I was more embarrassed than I've ever been in my whole life. I took him aside, both women still connected to his arms, and asked him very nicely to leave: but he just smiled at me, with that damn white ring around his nose, like he owned the place. I wish Arnie had been there. He would've finally gotten some evidence to use against the bastard. But, of course not —and the

Colombian gets away with it again. For the zillionth time in almost ten years. Really gives you the feeling our government's inept. Or that *everyone's* on the Quintana payroll."

She got up from the table and walked quickly to the sink, ran herself a glass of water, then leaned against the counter drinking it. "I can't stand it anymore, Mare. I really can't. He's responsible for ruining people's lives. Yet, he's making money hand over fist, feeding kids' addictions. It just doesn't make sense. God, it makes me sick."

Maryann tossed her apple core into the basket without moving from the chair. She nodded, thinking she shouldn't have brought up the subject. Diana looked as though she was in tremendous pain. And she should be —she had so much to lose! Night after night Maryann stared at the ceiling, feeling guilty for getting Diana so deeply involved. She felt trapped by Robert's mistakes and, though she'd never tell Diana, there were times she hated him more than she ever thought she'd hate anyone in her entire life.

"I know, but be patient," she said. "Arnie will find something soon and we'll be able to see the bastard go to jail. He'll pay for Robert's death. Goddamn bastard! We're just going to have to wait. Patience, love."

The kitchen was silent. They could hear the boys arguing outside. Chris's voice, as always, was stronger, more insistent than his little brother's. Both women rigidly held their bodies against the kitchen chairs in which they sat. Luis was still too volcanic a subject for either of them to discuss for more than a few moments at a time, Maryann thought ruefully. Would there come a day when this nightmare could finally be put to rest?

"We'd better get them before they kill each other," she finally said, pulling her legs out from underneath her and making a move for the door.

"Sit. I'll do it." Diana's hand was already on the doorknob. "I need something to take my mind off Mr. Quintana, anyway."

As she walked to the other side of the house where she could hear Tony crying and Chris's taunting voice, thoughts of the previous night flew through her mind. Luis with his women. Luis's rude voice insisting she redecorate his house. Luis telling Miles he wanted to purchase three of the Matisse paintings she had worked so hard to procure for the shop's opening. Luis finally leaving, making sure to whisper: "I still love you, *mi cara*. And I will have you in my bed once again," in her ear. She shivered, though it wasn't cold. There would never be another man she would hate more.

"Hey! Hey, Chris, leave your brother alone!" She pulled the two boys apart, astonished that Tony's face was dirty and tear-streaked. "What have you been doing to him?" Holding her older nephew by the arm, she tilted his face up to hers with one finger, looking warningly into his eyes.

"He keeps crying about Daddy. I'm sick of hearing it." Chris's look was defiant but scared, a nine- year-old who was the spitting image of his father, with one major difference: he held *nothing* inside.

Tony whimpered, scuffing the toe of his sneaker into the dust. "He says Daddy's never coming back. He is, though, isn't he. Auntie Di? Did he really leave us forever?"

"Oh, guys . . . come here." She hugged them to her. Chris's arms slid around her waist; Tony's hugged her hips. Pulling them to the front stairs, she sat down, one nephew on each side. "Now, listen to me carefully, okay? Chris is right, Tony.
Daddy's not coming back. When people die, they go away forever. But that doesn't mean he isn't watching over you all the time. I know your Daddy, and he loved you so much that he'll always be with you. Right in here." She patted the chest of Tony's mud-splattered shirt. "People never go away if you keep them in your heart, right?" Another sob escaped, but he nodded seriously, as though he was finally understanding.

"And, *you,* my man." Looking at Chris, she hugged the older boy tighter. "You have to remember you only have one brother and that you're the older one. He's only seven, Chris. You've got to be a little more protective and a lot less destructive. Do you know what that means?"

"Yeah, I gotta stop beating him up. But tell him to listen to me. Auntie Di." Chris's voice was bored, defiant. Diana realized there were a lot of things he probably didn't understand, too, and that it was safer that his anger be directed at his brother rather than at her or his mother.

"I know you guys miss your father. You'd be crazy if you didn't. But now there's just the four of us and we're a family. We have to make sure we take *care* of each other and that we love each other more than we do anyone else. Right?"

Both boys nodded solemnly.

"And loving each other means you treat each other nicely, share your toys, and don't beat each other up. Understand?" They nodded again, glancing at each other sheepishly. "So do I have your promise that you're going to start being nicer to each other?"

"Yeah, I guess so." Chris looked tentatively at his younger brother.

Tony sniffled one last time and wiped a dirty hand across his nose. "Auntie Di?"

"Yes?"

"Does this mean I have to give Chris my G. I. Joe?"

Hugging him quickly to her so he wouldn't see her barely-suppressed grin, Diana said, "Of course not. But you might have to give *me* one."

"Aw, you're spoofin' me."

Another quick squeeze and she rose. "So, you guys learn how to ride these bikes yet, or what?" When the three of them trooped back into Maryann's spotless kitchen, they were teasing each other as if nothing had happened. And Diana was determined that Maryann would never find out otherwise.

Chapter Twenty-eight

Beverly Hills, May, 1988

"So, what do you think? Big enough? Secluded enough?"

Diana nodded. "Best thing we've seen in the past few days." She walked over to the parlor's wall-to-wall windows which looked out onto a kidney-shaped swimming pool. Below the house, steep cliffs shifted her view down to the palm-lined street. If she looked straight ahead, she could see the Pacific Ocean, but her attention was riveted on the muscular blond real estate agent standing patiently behind her. A Beach Boy, she thought. A true California surfin' fool.

Todd Leon was young. Too young to be so wealthy, though she had a good idea how he had been so successful. A white, toothy smile, trim body, and quick wit were only a few of the charms Leon had revealed in the past few days. She felt her groin ache for his one talent she was sure would outshine all the others. Ashamed of herself, she turned from the window and walked over the pink marble floor toward the space-age kitchen, complete with a controlled-climate wine closet. Todd followed her.

"What kind of offer do you want to make, Ms. Cole?" he asked with a smile, his eyes patient yet flirtatious, as if he was unsure whether their business was over.

"What's the price again?"

"Two and a half."

"Million."

"Correct."

"Offer them two. It's not worth a penny more." She started to walk past him, then stopped. Looking straight into his eyes, she said, "Do you suppose I could see the master bedroom again?"

An hour later, she drove up Route 1, toward San Francisco. The Mercedes convertible's top was down, a Beach Boys tape in the car's cassette player, the music at full blast. She had a smile on her face and no underwear on her rear end.

He had taken her quickly, which came as a welcome surprise. A kiss, a touch, her blouse was off, her bra unsnapped, her lace bikini underwear slipped to her knees. Then she was under him on the pale pink bedroom carpet.

"Stay still," he whispered. "Relax." A light whisk of his tongue and her right nipple was erect, begging for more. "Beautiful breasts. So round, so perfect." He brought himself up to his elbows, appraising them as one might a fine painting. She arched herself toward him. "Relax, sweetheart. There's plenty of time." Voice like kitten's fur, a touch like the feather from a bird's wing, and her other nipple was fully aroused. For long moments, he held his head above her rising and falling breasts, simply breathing on them until she was sure she would burst.

"Please . . ."

"Slowly," he urged, drawing his tongue around her areola. "Let me savor you."

She brought her arms up, aching to hold him, to feel the warm skin beneath his shirt, to pull the belt out of his pants, to ease down the zipper and slide her hand inside. He pushed her arms back down, pinning her elbows gently to the floor with his hands.

"Let me do all the work. You just enjoy."

Inch by excruciating inch, Todd Leon devoured her body, sometimes stopping to breathe, to make her push her hips against him, to moan softly with desire. When his head nestled between her legs, she thought her heart would explode, thought briefly how embarrassing it would be if she died right there, her body to be found by the Beverly Hills Police. When his tongue found the most sensitive area on her body, she cried out as one orgasm after another pummeled through her veins, leaving her breathless. When he left, still fully clothed, pushing his hair back with a teenage-like grin, he had never entered her, yet she knew that in that brief half-hour she had had enough passion to last her all year.

"Two million?" he said, hand on the doorknob. She nodded, reaching for the silk Bill Blass shirtdress she had bought the day before on Rodeo Drive.

"I'll call you tomorrow," he said. "I'm sure they'll accept. It's been on the market almost a year."

"I'll be in San Francisco. Better catch me before 7 a.m. The auction starts at 9."

"I know. Oh, by the way, can I have these?" He held her lace bikinis in his hand.

Shaking her head, Diana laughed. "You Californians are something else."

Before he left, he buried his face in the bikinis and gave her a lascivious wink.

Boston

"So, did you buy it?" Maryann bustled about the kitchen, cleaning imaginary crumbs off the stove, then grabbed the broom.

"Will you sit down a second? God, woman, you're like a whirlwind. Do you ever rest? Yes, I bought it."

"What's it like?"

"Big. Beautiful. Nice pool. Typical California house. The kids'll love it."

"And the opening of the new shop? That went okay?"

"Yup," Diana replied, slathering more peanut butter on her

English muffin. "Everyone came. The Rodeo Drive crowd loves lavish openings. They're much easier than the New Yorkers. Everybody wants to party. Everyone seems to have more money, too, and they all want to buy bigger and better antiques than the next person. Clint Eastwood came and Steve Martin and the Jimmy Stewarts — she's such a nice woman. Even Willie Nelson showed up."

"Willie Nelson? In Beverly Hills? I thought that wasn't his style."

"Maybe it's the Southwestern pottery that brought him in. He bought four dough bowls, some fabulous Anasazi vases, and a ton of Navajo jewelry. I'm going to have to go back to Santa Fe again soon for more stock."

"Why don't you hire someone else to shop for that stuff?"

"Because I like to do it. It's fun. Besides, it's my money. I don't want anyone else spending it."

Maryann finally put the broom down and brought her coffee cup to the table. There were circles under her eyes and her hair looked like it hadn't been washed in a couple of days. "So, who was he?" she asked with a grin on her face.

"I'll tell you all about it if you tell me what's wrong," Diana countered.

"Just had a bad week, that's all. Now, spill. What does he look like? Are you going to see him again?"

"Mare! You're more interested in *my* love life than in your own. C'mon, Rob's been dead for over two years. Don't you think it's time you stopped being a voyeur and started dating again?"

"I'm not a voyeur, just a listener. There's a difference, you know."

"Yeah, the difference is you get off hearing about my love affairs."

"Well, they're more interesting than hearing about whose G.I. Joe is the biggest and strongest." She lowered her voice and brought her arms akimbo, imitating her oldest son. "Besides, you get out more often than I do."

"Is that the problem? Have you been hanging around the house since I left? Why don't you call Terence? I told you he'd go out with you, but you just have to take the first step."

"Well . . ."

"That's it! Go take a shower, lady, and call a babysitter for the kids. I've got tickets to the ballet I wasn't going to use. We'll have a girl's night out. Dinner at the Bayside, the ballet, and late drinks someplace interesting—I don't know where yet. Come on. Get a move on. I'll make sure the boys get in and start their homework. Come on! Get out of the chair, you old hag!"

Maryann shook her head, protesting all the way to the bathroom. She started laughing when Diana turned the shower on and handed her a facecloth. "Okay, I give, but you really have to stop doing this."

"And you have to stop being so nosy about my love life."

"There a guy in Beverly Hills! You hot shit! A movie star? A director?"

"A real-estate agent."

"A real-estate agent?"

"Yeah."

Diana smiled, closing the shower curtain on her sister-in-law.

From behind the curtain, Maryann yelled, "You know, you really should start thinking about relationships instead of affairs, Di."

"Why? And take away all your fun?" As she closed the door and started down the stairs, she wondered how the hell she was going to get ballet tickets on such late notice.

Chapter Twenty-nine

Nahant, December, 1990

Luis stood at the tall library window watching the snowfall. After all the years he had spent travelling around the world, after all the million-dollar business deals he had made, after all the tumultuous relationships he had formed and destroyed since leaving Colombia, the natural miracle of white flakes falling from the sky still fascinated <u>him</u> as much as it had the first time he had seen it. He pressed his fingertips to the cold windowpane like a child, resisting the urge to put the tip of his nose to the window as well.

Beyond the expanse of lawn which stretched forward from the library windows, the storm seemed to be getting worse. He couldn't see the massive gate leading into his property and the constantly moving searchlights did little to penetrate the white blanket. At times like these, he felt safe, warm, like he did long ago when his mother was still alive.

What would she have thought of Diana Colucci, he wondered, pulling his hand away from the icy window. Would she have been able to take the young woman and mold her into the Spanish wife he wanted Diana to be? No, probably not. The American woman would have been too strong, too wily, too intelligent, even for his poor mother. No woman should be allowed to be so powerful, he thought, pulling his face away from the window. No woman had ever been strong enough to test him the way she had. His moment of solace over, he began to concentrate on the familiar throb between his eyes—while he tried to push thoughts of Colombia out of his mind.

Yes, things might have been different if Mama was still alive. Perhaps he would not have followed his friend, Paco, to Medellin during his fifteenth summer. Perhaps he would be a shepherd now instead of a businessman. His product would have been wool or alpaca instead of the precious coca. If Mama had not died. If she had not been raped and burnt. If she was still at the little hut they called their home. If she had been able to raise her children as she had planned.

The thought brought his eyes to the ever-present pile of shimmering powder on his desktop. Lazily, he swung his long, gold razor through the mound, drawing the pile into abstract designs, cutting it in half, quarters, eighths, then sweeping it all together again.

In less than an hour, he would be meeting with Karl to discuss the latest shipments. As in any other business, the finances had to be kept straight. But he would be able to handle it. Coca made him quicker, smarter. He settled into the chair and put the gold straw to his nose. One long snort and the tingling, burning sensation reached into the space between his eyebrows, freezing them. Another line and he would want someone to talk to, someone who would hear his ideas about the future, his plans, his schemes. He pressed the buzzer on his desk to summon Karl.

For years, he had relied on Karl for many things: protection, information, and, most importanto, to juggle appointments. Lately, Karl had proven to have a much better feel for the finances of the organization than Luis. Once the German had started handling the carnation- and coffee-importing businesses, they had begun to double in profit. Now he was beginning to work with Luis on the cocaine accounts. Luis was not sure whether it was Karl's mathematical skills or his cold-blooded ruthlessness, but whatever it was, business was good. Very good. Perhaps they had succeeded because Luis made sure Karl did not touch the coca. If one of them was straight, both of them could work at maximum capacity.

He laughed quietly. "More for me," he said aloud. His words fell as softly as the snow outside. "So much more for me," he said again. Louder, this time. He pressed the buzzer again, jerking his finger erratically, knowing that the harsh sound would set things moving in the hallway outside. "Karl? Where the hell are you, you German bastard? Get in here!"

Luis pulled the razor through the pile again, carved out a few more finger-thick lines. Turning his chair, he stared out the window once more into the swirling, white blankness. Snow, he thought. That is what the Americans call cocaine. Cool and white. Stinging little particles. None of them alike.

He chuckled mirthlessly as he pulled the mirror to him and lifted the straw to his nose once again.

Boston

Shoving the last of the cheese and tomato sandwich into his mouth, Arnie walked to the phone, one eye still on the television set. The New England Patriots were beating the Jets unmercifully. Shit, he thought, one day out of the year I get to relax, no one home, great game on, and the G.D. telephone has to ring.

"Hello," he said, trying to swallow the dry mouthful.

"Agent Nicholson here, sir. We've made contact with the subject."

Arnie pulled his eyes away from the television and focused on the agent's voice. "You've got the tap in?"

"Yes, sir."

"How?"

Not a word. Okay, Arnie thought, guess I'm not supposed to know what happens in the background. "So what's going on?" he continued, impatient with the man's silence.

"The subject telephoned a certain Diana Cole only a few moments ago, sir. We taped said conversation and I thought you might like to hear it."

"Over the phone?"

"No, sir. I was going to bring it to your home."

"Can it wait?" From the corner of his eye, Arnie saw the ball sail over the touchdown zone. Whose goal? Christ, Luis had been harassing Diana for years. Just because this hot shot agent's got the wires finally hooked, he wants to share everything. Arnie watched the TV without actually seeing it.

Bet I could tell you exactly what the asshole said, Mr. Hot Shot Agent, he thought. Bet I could repeat the conversation word for word. "So, can it wait?" he repeated. "He's been saying the same thing for years and he'll keep on saying the same damn thing and he'll keep on threatening her until someone puts a bullet between those blasted black eyes."

"Uh ... I guess so, sir. Shall I come over later this evening?"

Arnie smiled, imagining Nicholson to be as vapid and Insignificant as the others he had met. Did they purposely hire people who were non-memorable? "Yeah, about 8 p.m."

As the Attorney General hung up the phone, New England scored again. "Shit!" he muttered, sliding into his leather recliner. "When am I ever going to learn I should tape these damn games!"

Though he settled into the rhythm of the game, Arnie's thoughts were on Diana, His stomach burned relentlessly despite the roll of Turns he kept clutched in his right band. He found himself wondering where Estelle was and when she'd be home. His wife, the only one who understood, would certainly be able to help him through the latest crisis. Maybe even calm his stomach down with one of her special concoctions.

By the time the Patriots launched their last pass, it was 9:45 p.m. and Arnie had lost all interest in the game.

Nahant

Karl closed the door behind him and hesitated for a moment. From behind his desk, Luis waved him into the room. Usually Quintana didn't like other people around when he was on the phone, but this time he continued speaking rapid-fire Spanish as he paced with the cordless phone. Finally, the conversation was over. For a moment, he stood immobile, his eyes downcast, the phone still in his hand, before addressing Karl.

"Garcia and Gomez were stopped at the border," Luis reported. "That means no shipment this month. Some of the guards went to the government." With a growl, he banged his fist on his desk, sending the mirror and its pile of powder into the air. He watched silently as it fell to the floor, idly thinking how he'd like to see the pile of cocaine fall again, only this time in slow motion. But the thought was quickly replaced by another. And another. Until each thought skipped over the next so rapidly that none of them appeared complete.

"We still have the shipment Hernandez brought in," Karl was saying. "We can cut it down a bit more and make up for the profit we will lose on this one."

"That is not why I am angry," Luis replied. "This seems to be happening more and more often. All my profit is going to pay the bastards at the customs offices and *polizio"* Luis bent over and picked the mirror shards off the floor. Licking his finger, he wiped the residue of white powder off the broken bits, not seeming to notice when the powder became mixed with blood. He sucked his finger, the acrid, coppery taste mixing with the cocaine's bitter sting.

"Nothing has been right since . . ." Without finishing the sentence, he dropped the shard in the basket and walked toward the window. "She is bad luck. The worst."

"Who?" Taking a step forward, Karl bent to pick up the rest of the- mirror.

"Diana Maria Colucci. She will wreck my life yet."

"But she's not responsible for Garcia . . . "

"Do not argue with me!" The Colombian screamed as he whirled around. "The stars were wrong. She should be here with me. Instead . . ." He leaned on his desk, struggling to control the tic developing in the corner of his right eye. "We must bring her down. The bitch must pay for what she has done to me."

He watched a sneer creep over Karl's face as the man bowed and walked backwards out the door.

Boston

"What do you mean, there was more than one call? Why didn't you call me again? Why didn't you come over when the second call came in?" Arnie angrily pushed the agent aside and grabbed the glass of whiskey and Coke he had left on the table. The amber liquid burned a little as it went down his throat. He waited impatiently for the liquor to calm the anger welling inside him.

"Play it!" he ordered, though Nicholson and his partner were already setting up the tape machine. Arnie circled them like a preying hawk as they plugged the machine into a wall outlet and began rewinding the tape. Muttering to himself, he wondered why he had allowed things to go this far. Yes, he wanted Quintana. Yes, he had to be brought to justice. But the man was a maniac, responsible for hundreds—probably thousands—of deaths. Only last week, five agents had been killed off the Florida coast when they tried to stop one of Quintana's shipments. Did they find out who was responsible for those deaths? No! But Arnie would bet his whole career that Quintana was behind it. All of it. The man was brilliant, he reluctantly had to admit. But so was Hitler. And neither of them was a likable man. Arnie wouldn't want either involved with anyone he cared about. He squeezed his fingers around the glass.

Diana. She had no idea what was going on. No protection

beyond the careful shadowing of Drug Enforcement agents. And they were not allowed close enough to protect her adequately. If they were, Quintana's men might pick up their scent. Couldn't have that, now, could we?

"Play it." Nicholson nodded to Arnie. Glass still in hand, the Attorney General slumped into a nearby chair.

Nahant

Karl came into the library once more. "I believe we can do it if we place the coca in with her antiques."

"How many shipments will it take before she's caught?" Luis smiled. Perhaps everything would turn out his way after all.

"There's one in the spring, then another in late summer. I'll have to make sure we get someone into her organization before that. If the *polizio* are watching her, they'll never see the other shipments we're bringing in." Karl placed his fingers in a teepee in front of his nose and looked at his boss over the top of his hands. "Those dogs are so stupid, they'll watch her and watch her until they catch her. In the meantime, we'll be able to get business back to normal."

Luis cut himself another line. "Good," he said. *"Muy bueno."*

He felt Karl watching him closely and lifted his eyes to meet the German's. Karl turned away, shuffling some papers.

"You do not approve, my friend?" he asked, wiping the last smudge of cocaine into his mouth and rubbing it against his gums. The numbing effect took place right away.

Karl shrugged.

"Come now, tell me what you are thinking." Luis leaned back, stretching his arms above his head.

"There are things we should be paying attention to other than this damn woman," Karl snarled.

Luis slapped both hands against the desk. "You do as I tell you!"

"But to be intimidated by a woman, to let her control you . . ."

"She is *not* controlling me! She is a flea on my back, a nothing!"

Karl shrugged again. Luis felt the heat rise behind his eyes and tried to force himself to remain calm, but what he really wanted to do was strangle the cool look off the German's face.

"Go!" Luis screamed. "And do not question me again!"

Karl met his eyes once more, then rose and walked out the library door, closing it softly behind him.

Boston

The tape clicked off with a finality that caused Arnie to jump. He sat for a moment, the empty glass dangling from his fingertips, his other hand gently massaging his wide brow.

235

"What next?" he asked tiredly.

Nicholson glanced at his partner. It seemed he was trying to maintain his calm, but was having a hard time doing so. "I think this is perfect," he said.

"What?" Arnie came out of his chair to stand immediately in front of Nicholson. "This madman decides to turn the cops on Diana, decides to blackmail her by putting coke on her antiques shipments, then just sits back and waits for her to get caught and you think it's perfect? What are you? Just as nuts as Quintana?"

"Listen to me for a minute," Nicholson urged, spreading both hands out to his sides in a gesture of peace. "If the Customs Department and the Boston Police don't know what's going on, then none of Quintana's men can cover for him, right?" Amie nodded, unconvinced. What did the B.P.D. have to do with this?"

"Give me a minute, sir." The agent walked back to the tape and unplugged it. The act seemed designed to give him a few seconds to collect his thoughts. "Quintana's man has already placed the tip which means he just wants the cops to start keeping an eye on Ms. Cole. Almost like a feinting maneuver in football, know what I mean?"

Amie nodded, anxious for the agent to get to the point.

"If the cops are watching Amaryllis's shipments, Quintana's own shipments won't be watched as closely. So, while the B.P.D. and the customs guys are busy, Quintana gets more coke into the country. Get it? By diverting attention to Ms. Cole, he's buying time for himself."

"And getting revenge, too." Arnie wrung his hands. "No, I can't allow this to happen, I know what you're getting at and I don't want Diana used as bait."

"But we can give her protection and Quintana will never know what's happening. He'll walk right into the trap. A reverse set-up. God knows what will happen otherwise. I have a feeling he's planning the biggest drop this country's ever seen. Using Diana Cole to trap him is our only chance. And he'll never spot it because he has no idea what's going on. And neither does she." He paused dramatically and his sigh smelled metallic, like Coca-Cola. "It's the only way, Mr. Goldstein."

For a moment, the room was silent except for the muted tick of the grandfather clock in the hallway.

"I don't like it," Arnie said slowly. "It's too goddamn dangerous."

"She'll have complete protection. I promise. Night and day. There'll be no way the Colombians can get to her."

"Can you guarantee that?"

"Nothing's ever completely guaranteed, sir, except that we're born and we die. This is the only way." "I still don't like-it."

"But do you agree?"

Arnie sighed deeply. "Do I have a choice?" He looked from one officer to the other, then unconsciously let his eyes flicker to the photo of Diana and Rob over his fireplace. They smiled out of the frame, arms thrown around each other, dark faces so alike they could have been twins. "Do *any* of us really have any choices?" he muttered.

Chapter Thirty

Boston, August, 1991

It had been a tough week, the hottest week he could remember. And, somehow, this last bust made him feel worse than usual.

Through his rearview mirror. Detective Steve Deluca covertly watched his prisoner, the legendary Diana Cole, climb into the back seat of his squad car. She wasn't going to try to escape or cause any trouble. In fact, throughout the booking procedure at the Charles Street Station, she had gazed into the distance, as though by doing so she could totally remove herself from the situation. No, an escape attempt wasn't what was gnawing at him. There was something else about her, something that reminded him of someone he knew long ago, yet he wasn't able to place it.

The feeling continued to nag him as he inched along the length of Newbury Street in the stop- and-go rush hour traffic. It'd take forever to get to the Massachusetts Correctional Institute this way, especially on a hot August Friday afternoon. On days like this, Bostonians seemed to leave at precisely the same moment, heading out of town for New Hampshire or the Cape. He tapped two fingers against the hub of the steering wheel, playing the drum solo from the classic rock 'n' roll song, "Wipeout," a habit he had been unable to shake since high school.

At forty-one, Deluca felt complimented that people thought he still looked to be in his mid-twenties. He figured the off-hours spent at a gym near his three-room apartment on Revere Beach were worthwhile. Not only did he keep in shape, he also unconsciously gave himself an excuse not to socialize with any of the guys from the Precinct. It wasn't that he didn't like them. It was just too difficult making new friends after losing Pete Sheldon, his first partner, to an addict's gun. Steve just couldn't get close anymore. To anyone.

He glanced in the mirror again and found himself smoothing down the unruly curls which flopped randomly across his forehead. For the first time in a long time, his unkempt appearance bothered him.

So, who are you, Diana Cole? he thought. Who do you remind me of?

She was a cool one, all right, though she had let her guard down when she talked to her sister-in- law. Though he had tried not to listen in on the conversation, he had noticed the concern in her eyes and her obvious affection for the woman she had called Maryann. The warmth she felt had softened the classical planes of her face so that she was no longer the sophisticated, wealthy store owner they had come to arrest, but a typical Italian female, much like his own sisters. Yet, his sisters would have been louder, more emotional than

Diana Cole. The differences between them reminded him only too clearly of his own humble upbringing in East Boston, living over his father's grocery store.

Again, his eyes were drawn to the woman in the back seat, and he marveled at her calmness. Staring out the window at the Charles River, Diana Cole sat as elegantly poised as if she were going to the opera or the symphony. Deluca had no problem imagining her in a satin ball gown, glass of champagne in hand, regally drifting through a crowd of proper Bostonians, charming every last one as though they were her lowly subjects. Yet something told him there was more beneath the woman's placid surface. Something passionate. And sadness, tremendous sadness. Though her face was immobile, Steve felt her sorrow and pain as acutely as if she had been wailing in grief. The feeling shocked him.

He exhaled loudly and grimaced, finally concentrating on the traffic ahead of him.

Entering the Massachusetts Correctional Institute in Framingham, Diana moved stiffly, her hands held together in front of her by the handcuffs Cottrell had insisted on putting on. The sun reflected off the car's hood, blinding her momentarily. She lowered her head, accidentally leaning against Deluca before Cottrell tugged her unceremoniously into the Institute's pale green lobby. Deluca reached out, their eyes met, but he never touched her. Though his grimy appearance repulsed her, there was something about him ...

It took a few moments for her eyes to adjust, but when they did, she wished they hadn't. The Institute's bleak interior was enhanced by a stench of ammonia so strong she lost her breath.

On her right a large, obviously drunk, gray-haired woman sat in a chair which leaned at a precarious angle against the wall. She was surrounded by various plastic bags and her tattered black wool coat brushed against Diana's leg. Diana shrank from the woman's filth, noting that a fly crawled up the side of the woman's face.

This can't possibly be happening, she thought with a sense of the surreal. I can't bear to spend more than five minutes in this place. God, Terence, get to Arnie immediately. Please don't leave me here.

Out of the corner of her eye, she saw Officer Deluca glance sympathetically in her direction. Their eyes met and, finding a strange comfort in his presence, Diana lifted her chin up as if to show him she was all right. She would make it—no matter what—even though that's not what she felt in the deepest pit of her stomach.

"This is Diana Cole," Gregory Cottrell reported to the desk sergeant, a large woman whose physical demeanor reminded Diana of a Russian discus thrower she had seen at the Olympics. "She's the one just brought in the shipment of coke. Thought she was cute hiding it in antique vases and shit." He sneered.

"I didn't . . ." Catching herself before completing the sentence, Diana turned away, her black hair falling over her face.

"What'd you say. Miss Cole?" The sergeant turned her sweaty face toward Diana, open dislike in her brusque voice.

"Nothing. 1 said nothing." Her stomach turned as she thought of how stupid, how naive, she had been. The indefatigable, independent, brilliant Diana Colucci ... so damn brilliant that she had jeopardized everything she had worked toward in the past ten years. For what? For *what?* She took a deep breath to fight the panic which began to rise in her bowels, rushed haphazardly through her stomach, and ended with an immense lump in her throat. She must not lose control. She *could* not.

There were too many things to do, too much to explain, and this was just the beginning.

"Fill this out, Cottrell. You know the procedure." The sweaty sergeant stood, her huge body almost as wide as the counter behind which she worked. Cottrell motioned for Diana to follow him through a doorway into a room full of gray steel desks lined up like those in a classroom.

"Give me your license and some other kind of identification. A credit card or something." He motioned her to sit in the chair across from him. Without another word, he cleared a space by pushing a pile of files aside and began filling in the form the sergeant had handed him.

She fumbled through her purse with fingers which refused her brain's commands, finally coming up with the required documents. She passed them to him, her hand shaking like a heroin addicts.

"Wait a minute. This license says Colucci. Hey, Deluca, this woman isn't *too* stupid. She's got two names. Which one is it, lady: Colucci or Cole?"

Diana gritted her teeth. Can't you see I don't want to be here? she wanted to scream. Can't you at least *try* to understand what this feels like? "It's Colucci. Cole is my business name. And it's not illegal," she added quietly.

"Listen, lady. I don't have to take your shit." He flipped her license back across the desk. It landed in her lap with a smack.

"That's enough, Greg." Detective Deluca stood behind his partner and placed his hand on his shoulder, almost as if he were warning him. "Why don't you let me do this? You two don't seem to like each other very much."

Cottrell looked up, then brushed a thick strand of dirty blond hair off his face. "Yeah, I guess you're right. We don't like each other too much, do we, lady? Take over, Steve. I need a cup of coffee, anyway."

Deluca waited for Cottrell to leave the room before turning back to Diana with a half-smile. "1 knew you looked familiar," he began, "but didn't know why until I heard your name. Coined, huh? Haven't heard that name in years."

Diana shifted uncomfortably in the chair and found there was no place to put her hands. Would she have to explain about her name now? Using Cole as a business name had never been a problem before. Even her checks were made out that way.

"Here, let me take those cuffs off for you. I'm sure you're not going anywhere."

"How do you know my name?" Diana asked, rubbing the red circles around her wrists.

"Your brother was Robert Colucci, right? The big football hero?" When she nodded, he smiled reassuringly, as if they were having the conversation at a cocktail party. "I remember you when you were growing up. My Dad owned the store at the end of Orleans Street. You used to come in all the time when I was working. But you probably don't remember me. You were just a kid. Your dad was the one who died in the crane accident, right?" Not now, she thought. Why couldn't I have been arrested by someone from New Hampshire or New Jersey? Why someone from home? "Yes, he did," she answered quietly. "He died when I was twelve." She flipped her hair back over her shoulder and stared him down. "Now, can we get on with this?"

Deluca's expression changed from sympathetic to guarded. Though she felt sorry to have snubbed him, he *had* to stop asking questions about her past. She had managed to forget about East Boston, and she certainly didn't want to remember it now. Not now.

"I never would've thought you, of all people, would be from Eastie. It's always nice to see someone from the old neighborhood, isn't it?" he asked.

"Not under these circumstances." Diana turned her head.

"Guess you're too far beyond East Boston now, huh? You've got a big fancy shop, can afford to bring in shipments from South America . . ."

"Listen, I don't want to argue with you, too," Diana said, a pleading in her voice. "Let's just do what we have to do. I'm not in the mood to talk about the good old days right now."

"That's understandable." He pulled his forms back in front of them and for the next fifteen minutes, was all business. When they finished, he stood up, motioning her to do the same. "The Sarge'll take care of you now." He cocked his head to the side, gazing at her as if trying to figure you out but having no luck at all. "I always thought you were such a nice girl," he said, smiling tentatively.

"Maybe I still am." Diana tried to smile back, but her lips stuck to her teeth.

"Your jewelry," the matron murmured in a monotone voice.

Stunned, Diana looked down at her hands, at the nails she'd had polished weekly at the hairdresser's, at the two rings she never took off. Suddenly, she felt an urge to chew at those perfect nails as she had as a child, before she had the money to take care of them. She closed her fingers into tight fists, then opened them and started to inch off the simple gold band on her right pinky, her mother's wedding band, the only piece of jewelry Rose Coined had ever owned. The jeweler had marveled at the tiny ring, surprised that she wanted it enlarged just a hair, just the least bit, so that she could wear it on her little finger.

The other ring also held memories. A perfect pearl, surrounded by tiny diamonds. As she slipped it off, she heard Gene Monroe's voice wishing her a Merry Christmas. Tears began to sting her bottom lids. She blinked them back quickly, slipped off her watch and the simple gold chain she wore around her neck, then handed the small pile to the matron without meeting the other woman's eyes.

"Shoes, too."

"Excuse me?"

"Shoes, honey. They're a lethal weapon."

The matron smiled, her lips an almost imperceptible line across the bottom half of her face.

When she slipped out of her heels, her feet touched the cold cement floor. She winced. From behind her, the matron gave a small cough, finally out of conversation. The woman ambled down the hall a bit, waving to Diana to follow.

"We've decided to put you in one all your own," she said, unlocking the door to a room no bigger than Diana's extra bathroom. "They'd probably bother you if we put youse both together." She nodded toward the cell across the hall. Half a dozen women of all ages and varying descriptions stood there, faces through the bars, eyeing them. "You're too fancy-shmancy for them," she said, then added quietly: "You can thank Deluca for this one."

Diana's breath caught in her throat, and a surprised, warm feeling spread through the knots in her stomach. So, she had been right; he *was* compassionate and kind. Perhaps somewhere along the line that would make a difference. Right now, all it did was make her feel like someone in this godforsaken place cared. And maybe, just maybe, someone would believe her when it came time for her to tell her story.

Standing in the center of the cell for a few moments after the door closed, she shut her eyes and rocked back and forth on her heels, the prison cell floor damp under her bare feet. She tried not to breathe, not to smell the stench of the damp and hot jail.

It was impossible not to hear the women across the hall calling her "rich bitch" and "fuckin' cunt." Though her mouth was dry, she whispered, "Please, don't." By then it was impossible to try to stop the tears from welling up in her eyes and rolling freely down her cheeks. No sobs came from her chest, no tightness choked her throat. The tears came from someplace else, someplace over which she had no control, someplace she thought she had shut off a long time ago.

It would be against her nature to curl up in the corner, to wail and beat her hands against the wall, but it was the only thing she wanted to do. Finally, no longer able to stand upright, she took the two steps necessary to reach the tiny cot which took up one side of the cell. Gingerly, she sat on the thin mattress, feeling the hard iron bar of the frame against her hip bone. For another few moments, she balanced on the edge of the bed, both hands gripping the bar beneath her, her teeth chattering noisily, her cheeks wet and cold. She was unable to put thoughts together in any coherent order for the first time in her life.

She didn't know how long she sat there, but when she found the confidence to lie back on the cot, the women across the hall had quieted and the sunlight, which had been streaming through the small window near the ceiling, had changed to moonlight.

Alone and no longer able to think or feel, she stared blankly up at the peeling ceiling.

Arnie slid behind the seat of his Saab, a grim look on his face. Loosening his tie, he turned to Diana. "Why didn't you tell me?"

"Tell you what?"

"About Luis de la Maria Quintana. He got you, too, didn't he? And how do you expect me to get you out of this? They've got *your* shipment of antiques with coca paste and/or high-quality cocaine filling every vessel." He shook his head and blew through his teeth. "Why haven't you been honest with me? Why didn't you tell me you were working with him? You know better, Diana. I can't defend you against a rap like this. Christ, don't you know my career is on the line just for bailing you out?" Pulling the car onto the expressway, he gunned the motor, the tires squealing slightly.

"Calm down, Arnie. Do you think I'd seriously be involved with dealing coke?"

"I asked myself that same question and I don't know anymore. I didn't think Robert would do it, either, but we both know how that turned out." Diana stared out the window at the Boston skyline in the distance. The hot summer sun gleamed off the Prudential tower like a beacon, like a mirror reflecting her own fear directly back to her. She took a deep breath to calm herself and felt the need for a shower and the comfort of her own home more than she ever had at any other time in her life. Fifty thousand dollars' bail—the price of a fairly decent painting or a period piece of furniture. But she had needed to get out of jail, no matter what the cost.

She felt Arnie's eyes scrutinizing her. Exasperated, she met his look. "Goddammit, Arnie, I've been framed! How the hell am I going to get out of this?"

It was the most difficult thing he had ever had to do in his whole career, yet Attorney General Arnold Goldstein knew he had to simply sit by and watch Diana suffer. It's the only way we're going to get the bastard, he reminded himself. Yet, as he studied Diana's usually lovely face, now furrowed with worry, dark circles under her eyes, he began to wonder whether he would be able to keep up the facade. She had spent more than twelve hours in jail and even that short period of time had taken its toll. Would she be able to deal with the days— maybe weeks—until this was all over? Could *he* continue to sit by and watch her suffer? He felt the familiar paternal urge to reach out and hug her, but stifled it.

Late at night, when the kids were asleep, he would turn over in his king-size bed and wrap his arms around his wife's ample body. Patiently, she would listen to his halting explanations of what was going on. And though she didn't understand all of the implications, she would rub the middle of his back affectionately, reassuring him that everything would turn out okay. He'd made the right decision, she would say. Diana would understand when everything was over.

Looking at Diana now, he wondered if Estelle was right. Somehow, in the back of his mind, he questioned whether anything would ever be right again and cursed himself for not warning her a long time ago. But would she listen? Nah. She was stubborn, "so stubborn. And, in a lot of ways, smarter than he was. She wouldn't have listened then and she wouldn't listen now. Better to keep his mouth shut. "And your eyes wide open," he could hear Estelle echoing in his mind.

"She's out? Whaddaya mean? The bail was fifty thousand bucks. Who raised it?" Black, burly, and belligerent. Captain Calvin Thompson was the most feared cop in the division. And he was Deluca and Cottrell's boss. Shaking a threatening finger in their direction, he continued, "This broad brings in millions of dollars' worth of coke, we get a phone tip that nails her to the wall, and she's back out on the street in a little less than a day. Queen's shit! I want the bitch followed. I don't give a good crap if she's all over creation twenty- four hours a day. Follow her! And Deluca—make sure she doesn't leave the state. Get it? If she does, it's *your* ass!"

Cottrell opened his mouth as if to say something but had no time to force the words out when Thompson stepped nose to nose with him. "And you, you dumb bastard, where the hell's the shipping papers I asked you to get five hours ago?" "The company said someone else . . ."

"And since when do you take 'no' for an answer? Get them! Now! No fucking excuses, asswipe!" "But what about following the woman . . ." "Deluca's capable of putting a tail on someone by himself. Besides, I don't exactly have people sitting around here twiddling their thumbs waiting for something to do. Now go, like a good little detective. I want those frigging shipping papers or we have no case at all. Now, go. Both of you! Out of my sight until you do something right for a change!"

. The door slammed behind them. Cottrell swore under his breath. Deluca lit a cigarette with shaking hands, then blew out the match with a puff of smoke. "Guess I'll see you sometime Monday," he said as Cottrell shuffled some papers on their shared desk.

"Yeah, if I can find the damn things. If I can't, it's been nice knowing you." He threw Deluca a half-hearted salute as he walked out the door and headed for the parking garage.

Arnie double-parked the Saab on Joy Street, then turned to Diana, took his half-glasses off, and mopped his face with a monogrammed silk handkerchief. He had spent the last fifteen minutes trying to convince Diana he could help her without letting her know how much he already knew. Every inch of him wanted to warn her of the danger she was in, to remind her to take care of herself, not to let the bastard kill her as he had her brother, but he knew without a vestige of a doubt that to warn her would most assuredly be to sign her death warrant. Keep her angry, he reminded himself. Her fury will keep her going. "We can't nail the asshole until he admits to pulling you into this," he said. "Somehow you've got to get him to talk to you, get him to admit he had access to the shipment." "Right. You think he's even going to answer my calls now that he knows what happened? This is what he wanted! He's gotten me back for embarrassing him, for hurting his male pride. He wanted me years ago, wanted to destroy me any way he could, even threatened the kids, and I never took him seriously. Remember? Now what? I have nothing left to give. He's got me over the coals, Arnie. He has!"

"Not quite." Using his soaked handkerchief to wipe the moisture off his glasses, he swore under his breath as the lenses smeared. "There's always ways to get around guys like this. Let me sleep on it. We'll think of something. In the meantime, I'll get a tap on your phone so when . . . and if . . . you talk to him, we'll have him on tape. Okay?" Slipping his glasses back on his nose, he looked at her affectionately. "I knew you wouldn't do something like this, sweetheart. Guess I was just scared that / had done something wrong. You know, I felt like I had let your father down, broke my promise."

"Oh, Arnie, how could you think that? You've been so good to us. To me. You're family." "Speaking of family, Mama wants you over for dinner on Sunday. Bring Maryann and the kids." "If I'm not back in jail by then."

They hugged for a long moment, both of them forgetting the heat and the perspiration they shared, and breaking apart regretfully.

"I'll call you tonight," Arnie called as she slipped out the passenger door. "And be careful."

Standing on the doorstep for a moment, listening to the sounds of the city, she watched the Saab pull out of sight. Brown swallows flitted in and out of the gardens behind the houses on Joy Street, challenging the pigeons who took up residence on every free rooftop. The wrought iron balustrades adorning the fronts of the street's townhouses reflected light like fanciful sculptures, reminding her, as always, of tiny Parisian boulevards. In the distance, she could hear traffic but here, at least momentarily, it was quiet. Almost peaceful.

She pulled open the double glass doors to the hallway and kicked yesterday's *Boston Globe* out of the way while she checked the mailbox. Gathering her mail, she barely looked at the pile until the front page of the newspaper caught her eye: CUBAN DEALER OUT ON BAIL.

The grinning, dark-skinned face in the photograph nagged at her, reminding her of another foreigner, another dealer. She gritted her teeth, fighting an urge to hurl the paper through the window and out into the street where the hot breeze would tear the headline off, flinging it into the gutter where it belonged. Where they all belonged.

"Why do they always manage to get out, the bastards?" she asked, though no one was there to answer.

Angrily, she turned off the alarm system and walked into the still heat of her apartment. The message light on her answering machine blinked with a pulsing ferocity. Later, she thought. Too much to do now. Dumping her mail and the newspaper on the kitchen table, she reached for the wall phone and called Terence.

His clipped English voice, a soothing balm to her ear, changed to a whisper when he discovered who was on the other end of the line. For a few moments, they spoke in niceties—"How are you?" "Are you sure you're all right?" "Is there anything I can do to help?" "What's going to happen?"—but Diana had little time for chitchat.

"I won't be in the shop for a while," she said, "maybe a couple of weeks. I need you to take over. Make sure the other shops are stocked. Calm everyone down. Make sure everything goes smoothly. I'll be around—you'll be able to get me at Maryann's or here-and I'll make sure we get stock for the
London shop. I just want to lie low, do some thinking, stay out of the limelight and away from reporters."

"Certainly can understand that, but what will I say if you-know-who calls?"

Tell him to go to hell, she thought, as her fingernails bit into her palms. Tell him to go back to fucking Colombia.

"Tell him . . . tell him I'll call *him*. But I don't think we'll have that problem, Terence. I think Luis has finally gotten the revenge he wanted: he'll quietly disappear, leaving me holding the bag." Her chest convulsed with the sharp pains she'd felt in the jail cell. She took deep, quick breaths, thinking of the Valium in the bathroom closet, the pills Gene had been using before his death. Would they still work? Did she want to be calmed down or was this nervousness something she could use for motivation?

"Diana ... I don't know what to say. What can I do to help you? I can't let you take this punishment . . ."

"Don't worry about me. I can take care of myself. Just do as I asked." Hard and unrelenting, her voice betrayed little of her. emotional turmoil. That's the way it has to be, she thought.

"You'll be at Maryann's?"

"Maybe. I don't really want to stay in Saugus. Luis knows the house. But she wouldn't leave when I called her . . . maybe I can talk her into taking off for a while. I'll let you know." She hung up, gathered some clothes and left, never listening to her messages.

The red Porsche slipped into traffic behind an overloaded garbage truck belching black smoke like a wheezing chimney. Steve Deluca waited patiently until he could ease his vintage Mustang into line, two cars behind Diana, without being spotted. For a long moment, he stared at the back of her head, wondering what she was thinking, how she felt, and where she was going.

To his left, the Charles River teemed with multicolored sailboats, most at full mast, all taking advantage of the hot summer weather and the breeze which had picked up since lunchtime. He pulled away from the seat, his T-shirt soaked and stuck to his back, and envied the people wealthy enough to be able to dock their playthings at the Yacht Club. When he looked toward the Porsche, he saw that Diana's eyes seemed to be following the sailboats, too; then she turned her head abruptly as traffic began moving forward. Slipping the Mustang into gear, he followed.

Traffic crawled all the way over the Mystic Bridge to the Charlestown toll booth. He had no problem keeping up with the Porsche until she took the Chelsea exit, weaving her way down back streets at speeds he could hardly negotiate. Finally, it was just the two of them, taking the long stretch of road leading between Chelsea's vacant junkyards to the Revere Beach Parkway. Deluca pulled back, letting her get enough distance on him so he wouldn't arouse her suspicions. She turned onto the Parkway and disappeared into the light midafternoon traffic.

"Shit!" He poked his head out of the car window, searching frantically while he beeped his horn at a slow-moving station wagon. Its driver gave him the finger, continuing at the same snail's pace. Frustrated, he pulled onto the meridian strip, ripping up pieces of grass and tar as he passed the station wagon and flashed his badge at them. The frazzled driver-a woman, busy yelling at four kids who were scrambling back and forth over the seat—appeared terrified that he intended to arrest her and immediately put on her brakes.

"Thank you," Deluca mouthed. Pulling in front of her, he immediately spotted the red Porsche climbing the curve beyond the next set of traffic lights. When the light turned yellow, traffic slowed on all sides of the intersection. He pressed the accelerator and skidded through before it turned red.

Following this woman wasn't going to be as easy as he thought. Maybe she had already spotted him. No, she looked preoccupied. Totally preoccupied. But she sure had a heavy foot on the gas pedal. If I was still on traffic, he thought. I'd arrest her in a New York second.

At the next traffic light, Diana took a left, baffling him. He thought she'd been heading for her sister-in-law's place in Saugus. In Everett, she slowed for a group of children crossing the street, pausing momentarily to watch them get safely to the other side, then proceeded through a quiet residential section. Within moments, she slowed and put on her blinker one more time, taking a left into the Woodlawn Cemetery.

And what if I end up in jail permanently? she wondered, downshifting to pull through the cemetery's familiar iron gates. Maryann will have to explain to the boys. They'll never understand.

Tony would want to come rescue me, acting out his favorite Rambo movie, while Chris would withdraw even more than he already has in the past couple of years. He's a teenager. I'm going to be "the enemy" for the next five or six years, anyway. Why not start now?

I could buy a ticket to Tokyo, look up Ling Chan, and stay with his family for a while. Surely he could get me a job appraising antiques. Can they extradite me from a foreign country? Or maybe Merry would hide me for a while until I can get Luis . . . No, that wouldn't do.

Her shoulders slumped. She felt exhausted. Defeated. Beaten up. Backed into a corner. Her mind rushed through other scenarios in the time it took to wind slowly down the skinny roads, between overgrown oak trees, past the gazebo where Robert and she used to sit quietly on Sunday afternoons. But nothing worked.

The first time they came here, Rob had held onto her hand tightly, though he was almost ten. A train ride and two buses, more than three hours to get here, only to realize she didn't know where they buried Papa. With Rob sniveling and complaining all the way, they had walked up and down every cemetery road until they found the gazebo and the gravestone. "Anthony Coined, Born April 1, 1931, Died September 11, 1967." For hours, they sat and stared, unseeing, at the gray marble until the sky darkened and Robbie said quietly, "Di, I'm hungry. Let's go home."

Now it was over. All she had worked for. Everything she had planned. Her whole life. Over. All because of a man who couldn't accept defeat, one man whose need for revenge was so consuming he didn't know when or how to stop, one man so obsessed with possessing her that . . . She'd never understand him, would never get away from him. In a ferocious burst of anger, she wished him dead.

If I go to the cops, he'll find out and have me killed, she thought. Or worse, the kids. If I don't go to the cops, they'll take me to court and I'll end up in some jail, someplace even worse than Framingham. My name will be ruined. All of Gene's money will be lost. They'll close all the Amaryllis shops. Everyone will lose their jobs. Goddamn that sonofabitch!

She leaned against the steering wheel and breathed heavily for a few moments while the car idled. Finally, she pulled the door open and, leaving her pocketbook on the seat, the engine still idling, she slowly walked to her parents' grave.

What the hell was she doing now? Steve pulled the binoculars out of his glove compartment and spotted Diana. He could see the Porsche, its door open. Was she meeting someone? Making a drop? Picking something up? He moved the binoculars to the right and spotted her head. There she was, kneeling on the ground in front of a gravestone. He focused in a little tighter. Who was she talking to? Strange. No one anywhere near. Only the two of them in the whole cemetery. Was she talking to herself?

"Move your head, Diana. Let me see the name on the stone," he mumbled, frantically focusing and refocusing the glasses. Finally, she leaned back on her heels, lowering her head into her hands. The names on the stone were Anthony and Rose Colucci.

"Her parents," he whispered, lowering the glasses slowly. He felt like he shouldn't be watching this very private moment, yet he had his orders. With a heavy feeling, he lifted the glasses once more.,

On her feet now, she straightened her dress, brushing away the grass still clinging to her knees. Then, head lowered, she walked back to the car, got in, and drove to the exit without looking back. This time, she turned in a general northerly direction, and Steve knew, as he followed h^, that she was heading for her sister4n4aw's house.

He had a sudden urge to protect her, though he had no idea from what.

Chapter Thirty-one

Boston, September, 1991

Sotheby's. Christie's. Skinner's. Butterworth's. The quietly-glossy auction catalogs spread across Diana's dining room table glared at her. Auction season began today, yet she hadn't been to a single preview, and wasn't even sure what she wanted to buy. She felt disconnected. Ostracized. Out of control.

Sotheby's/London offered a collection of French estate jewelry, some articles which had belonged to the Countess Maria—expensive, one-of-a-kind baubles for which Diana's clients in New York and Beverly Hills hungered. She flipped the catalog pages, pausing when a seventeenth century, diamond-studded gold bracelet caught her eye. Circling the item with a purple pen, she scanned a few more pages and took a sip of her coffee, lines of concentration creasing her forehead. How could she buy when she hadn't seen what they were selling? She knew too well how many imperfections the auction catalogs often failed to mention. Even the best of them-Christie's, Sotheby's, Phillips- made mistakes every now and then-How could she trust them? How could she possibly buy confidently over the phone?

Throwing the catalog down on the table, she walked away.

For a moment, she stared out her dining room window, frustrated and irritable. She felt like a caged animal, unable to fully participate in the business which had once brought her so much pleasure. Running the shops from her apartment provided no satisfaction at all, even though an additional three telephone lines had been installed and a FAX machine filled the alcove which had once been home to a five-foot-tall fifth century Chinese vase. Her computer, normally silent at this time of day, quietly breathed in the corner, its empty green screen reminding her of the work yet to be done.

When setting up for business earlier this morning, she had flung open the curtains to the picture window, hoping that the incoming sunlight and traffic noises would help ease her claustrophobia. They had somewhat, but now she struggled to concentrate on the business at hand instead of watching the bright blue sky above the townhouses across the street. How could she work when bits and pieces of strangers' conversations wafted through the half-open window?

The phone —her lifeline, her link to all the shops, her most important business companion — had begun ringing insistently at 8 a.m. It rang again, bringing her back to the table to face the catalogs and her problems.

After spending five minutes with Terence, answering his questions and assuring him she was all right, she picked up a catalog and quickly made some marginal notes. If the Tiffany diamond bracelet was from the Twenties, Cassandra Lord would love it. The Amish quilt would be perfect for Martha Rothcart out in Santa Fe — must be top shelf, though. She only bought stunners. And the period Queen Anne highboy looked just the right shape and size for Isadora Stern's guest bedroom. The blond Century Oil heiress had recently sent photos of her newly-built Newport boathouse, along with room plans and dimensions so that Amaryllis could furnish the whole house.

Diana punched a few keys in the adding machine to her right, figured in her buyer's premium, then her profit. There. She felt better. At least *some* work was done. She checked her watch. Another ten minutes before Sotheby's London offices would open. Time for another cup of coffee.

Deluca lowered the binoculars and sat back in the straight-backed metal chair. It was the only piece of furniture in the empty apartment the department had rented across the street from Diana Cole's building. It had been home to the detective for the past two weeks.

Occasionally, Cottrell came by to check on the progress of Deluca's surveillance or to relieve his partner, but no one else interrupted the quiet. The rest of the force was involved with a serial murder case, a huge drug bust, and the assassination attempt on Boston's mayor. Enough to keep four police forces busy, Deluca thought idly. He lifted the binoculars again, watching as Diana got up from her chair and left the room.

There had been plenty of time to review the notes on Diana "Cole" Coined, born in East Boston, January 17, 1955. That made her thirty-six. Six years younger than he. Father: Anthony Colucci, steelworker. Died: September 11, 1967, accident on job. Mother: Rose Colucci, housewife. Died: February 21, 1981, natural death in nursing home. Siblings; Robert Colucci, assistant manager, First National Stores, Winthrop, Massachusetts. Died: March 12, 1985, cocaine overdose.

She had had a tough life, at least in her younger years. No wonder she seemed so aloof. Must be just as hard for her to get close, he thought, as it is for me.

She'd had only one job in the past ten years, other than running her business, but the thing that surprised him most was how she had made her money: a *very* large inheritance from Gene Pen- chance Monroe, III, of the Boston Monroes, a distinguished family with a history back to the Revolution. He arched his eyebrows as he read. And the life insurance from her mother. Surely that had been what lifted her out of East Boston, enabling her to move to Joy Street, to the fancy brick townhouse he now overlooked.

And that wasn't the only place she owned. His eyes widened when he read of the mansion in London, the apartment in New York City's Trump Towers. Donald Trump may have lost money, but it didn't look like Diana Cole was following in his footsteps. There was the ultra-modern hillside home in Beverly Hills—complete with kidney-shaped pool, hot tub, and five bedrooms, each with its own bathroom, complete with whirlpool. How could one person live in four places? He barely saw his own apartment and it was less than fifteen minutes from the precinct.

Then there were the shops—one on King's Row in London; the second in New York City; the third on Rodeo Drive in Beverly Hills; and, of course, the Newbury Street location. All carried topnotch antique and art, catering to the wealthiest collectors.

She had made wise investments: stocks, bonds, more real estate, and her own art and antique collections, bringing her net worth to $565 million, according to the accounting firm's calculations. A half billion! A low whistle escaped his lips.

He had heard about people—millionaires—who never looked like they had that much money, but this was the first time he had actually met one. Yeah, she looked rich, but not THAT rich. Yet, somehow he knew that a woman like Diana wouldn't be comfortable flaunting her wealth, that she would be satisfied with a few luxuries, never needing to gild the lily any more than necessary. And the simple statement that she was *worth* $565 million didn't mean she had it hanging around in her bureau drawers. He flipped to the next page: the annual report for AMARYLLIS, Inc. There it was. Millions of dollars in stock and investments. Looked good on paper, but only gave her a yearly salary of $1.5 million. Only $1.5, he snickered, and turned another page. With widened eyes, he read more financials and noticed that she had invested nearly half of her yearly salary in accounts for her nephews and her sister-in-law. No other family. Now her reaction when they first picked her up made sense. She was their caretaker—in more ways than one.

No boyfriends of record. All known acquaintances were antiques and art dealers or her employees. No marriages or divorces.

Maybe it added up that she turned to cocaine. But why? Not the mon^. She had plenty of that. Maybe she was hooked like her brother, looking for that ultimate high like so many of the addicts Deluca knew. Yet, he had seen no evidence of addiction. No midnight trips for a fix. No hiding behind closed shades. Everything she did was out in the open. Maybe there was no need of doing it any other way. God knows she had enough money to turn herself and the rest of the people in Boston on to a cocaine high. It wouldn't even make a dent. But, no, somehow he knew that wasn't it.

The pieces didn't fit. Nothing made sense.

Lifting his eyes, he looked toward the building valued at over $2.75 million. She had done him a favor, leaving the curtains open. There would have been no other way he could see inside; no other way to monitor her actions. Yet for the last few days, all she did was sit at that table, flipping through catalogs, making phone calls to auction houses and dealers which he listened to surreptitiously thanks to the BPD's tapping equipment. The only time she left the apartment was to get groceries. Even her choice of food didn't smack of someone who did drugs. No midnight munchies, no bottles of champagne or gourmet lunches. Most of what she ate seemed like what he would eat if he went home. Tortellini. Artichokes. Apples. Everything was familiar, except for the designer drinking water.

And she seemed a different person now. Gone were the finely-tailored outfits, the stiletto heels, and monogrammed leather briefcase. Instead, jeans and men's shirts clothed her slim figure throughout the day. She looked like a real person—someone he might even date.

He loved watching her when she jogged down the street. Same time every night—7:35 p.m. like clockwork. Her long strides and softly swaying ass tempted him into thoughts he knew, as a police officer, he shouldn't have. But what else could he do? It got boring sitting here hour after hour. And she certainly wasn't helping him to put her story together. He felt as much a stranger to the enigma of Diana Cole as he had the first day he walked into the Newbury Street shop.

He watched her sit down at the table again and pull all three phones toward her. Settling back into the chair, he heard her go into action, listening to her conversations with the help of an earphone. Her voice, clipped and businesslike, told a veddy-propah English chap to bid "to three thousand pounds, not a penny more, on the bracelet—and number 342. Give me the final bid. I don't care what it is. . . ." Steve raised his eyebrows. Did they really work like that? Yet, the English voice was polite, deferring to her clipped tones almost reverently. Impressive.

The line to London remained intact as Diana switched to the second phone. "Miles, have you gotten the Manship sculpture in place? Make sure you call James to look at it . . . Yes, he's at Knopf . . . Chairman . . . Yup, first shot to him. If he doesn't want it, call Cary. Tell him I'm in Antigua or something interesting . . . No, don't tell *anyone* where I am. . . . How's Sarah? She home from the hospital yet? . . . Oh, tell her not to worry about work. She should stay out and recuperate. Don't you dare let her come back early. Thank God it wasn't worse than just appendicitis, huh? And, Miles, send more flowers. Orchids this time . . . No, don't worry about me. I'll be fine. Just keep everything together, okay? And Miles? Thanks. I really appreciate everything you've done. You've been fantastic. I'm lucky to have you." Her voice changed, becoming softer toward the end of the conversation. Steve was certain he'd heard a catch, a sigh, right before she hung up.

Diana pressed the digit connecting her directly to the New Hampshire cottage. Tony answered, out of breath.

"Hi, sweetie. Is Mom there?"

In the background, splashing sounds and childish screams filled the air. Tony answered; then she heard his feet pounding across the kitchen floor. The screen door slammed. Tony yelled. It was a few seconds before the screen door slammed again and Maryann, also out of breath, said hello. "Maryann? How's it going?"

"Not bad, but I'm really getting tired of vacationing—and this guy you hire^ to stay with us is a real pain in the ass. Won't even let us go shopping. The kids need school clothes, Di, and you know how I hate leaving things till the last minute." For a moment, there was a muffled silence. Maryann always managed to carry on simultaneous conversations by simply placing her hand over the receiver. Sometimes it was irritating. Like now.

"Just a little longer. I promise," Diana said. "Plus, how do you think / feel? I have to stay in this apartment while the world goes on around me. I even feel nervous jogging these days." Through the phone against her other ear, she overheard the London auctioneer sell the emerald earrings scheduled to be on the block shortly before the diamond bracelet. "Listen, hon. I've got to make this quick— London's on the other line. You're all right? Nothing from Luis?"

"Not a word."

"Okay, I'll call again later. Make sure you're careful and keep the boys close to you. Okay? I promise we won't have to go through this much longer. Amie's going to get back to me tonight."

"Yeah, all right."

"I love you."

Pause. Sigh. "1 love you, too, Di."

"And give the boys a hug."

"I will." Maryann yelled at the boys once more to quit splashing each other. "Di?"

"Yes?"

"I'm sorry I'm so snappy. Guess this is just getting to me. Take care of yourself, okay?"

For a moment, Diana allowed herself the luxury of sitting back and ignoring the phones. She rubbed her temples with two fingers, wondering how all of this would look ten years from now.

Where will I be? she mused. In a jail somewhere? In an old house, alone and poor? In another shop?

Alone. That's the word that scared her most. And it certainly seemed to ring true.

She felt a velvety wave of calm creep over her body. Whatever was going to happen *would* happen. No matter how much she worried or pondered over the situation. What was that slogan alcoholics used? One day at a time. Well, mine will be one *moment* at a time, she decided. Minute by minute. No slower. No faster.

She pulled her chair back into the table and reevaluated what she had to do.

"The show must go on," she muttered and picked the phone up again.

Diana went into high speed, shooting bids at the London auctioneer while pacing back and forth in front of the window. Steve trained his binoculars on her face, watching the pull of her lips, the fierce intensity in her eyes nibbled at her fingernails, she talked about with her friend the department had missed in their report? Another antiques bigwig?

He concentrated on ills earphones and her conversation. "Yes," she said. "All right. I'll bid again. What the hell are they doing? The bracelets not worth that much ... All right, one more time . . . What's the price? . . . Yes ... We done? . . . Okay. Keep me on hold for the rings, numbers 410 and 415. Then I want the jeweled opera glasses and the gold bureau set . . . Okay, David. I'll hold. If I fall asleep, you might have to yell. . ., This is costing me a mint, you *bet* I'm going to get those pieces!"

She stopped pacing, bending over the table to reach for the other ringing phone. Her jeans drew tightly across her ass. Deluca focused the binoculars in tighter, feeling the familiar pain in his groin. God, the woman was nearly perfect. Take all her features separately and they'd seem strange—the slightly large nose, dark round lips, wide shoulders—all might seem too much on someone else, but put them together to build Diana Cole and they somehow fell into place as neatly as pieces in a jigsaw puzzle.

A noise, like the whistle of a passing airplane, made him snap to attention. He pulled the glasses away.

"Shit!" He couldn't believe it. Diana's dining room window had shattered. Her still form lay across the table. "Shit! Shit! Shit!"

Loading his revolver, he raced down the stairs to the street. "Fuck!" Why hadn't he noticed anyone on the street? Too busy looking at her ass to spot someone trying to pick her off. "Stupid fuck!" He'd be fired for this one, sure as hell. Someone must have been in the apartment below. He looked up quickly at the window. An elderly woman pulled at a white net curtain. No. Must have been from the street. No one in sight.

He flew across the quiet street, gun in hand, sneakers slapping against the brick sidewalk. The door was locked. With a swift movement, he shot the lock and pushed his way into the hallway. Another shot and the interior door swung open. Within seconds, he was in the apartment and at Diana's side.

"Diana! Ms. Cole! Are you all right?"

A groan and a slight movement. No blood anywhere. Broken glass all over the floor. He slid down to crouch beneath the window. Looked up the street and down. No one in sight. Of course. Why should they hang around? Reaching for one of the phones on the table, he called the precinct, ordering an ambulance and a couple of squad cars. Immediately!

In the moments it took for help to get there, he lifted Diana gently off the table and into a chair in the living room. A small patch of blood stained her shirt right beneath her shoulder, but it seemed a scratch from a piece of glass, not a bullet hole. He exhaled, not realizing he'd been holding his breath.

With his left hand, he pushed her black hair away from her face. "Ms. Cole? Diana? Are you all right?" Her eyes flew open. They were bluer than he remembered. For a second, they gazed straight into his. Neither of them spoke. Then she pulled away.

"Who . . . ? What . . . ?"

"It's okay. It's okay! I'm a cop. Remember me? Steve Deluca?" Awkwardly, he pulled his badge out and flashed it in front of her.

The wail of a siren filled the room. She looked back at him questioningly. "You're going to be all right," he reassured her. It was all he could manage before the room filled with police officers and ambulance personnel.

"Are you sure you're all right?" the officer asked again.

"I'm fine. Really, I'm okay," Diana replied, though she still wasn't sure what had happened.

The last person she expected to see was the detective who had arrested her. In fact, when she first opened her eyes and looked into his, she thought she was back in jail, that none of the past two weeks had happened, and she hadn't even been released. Bewildered, she thought of reaching up to him, of pulling his arms down around her, of leaning against his chest. Somehow she felt that would make her feel safe.

"What was it?" she asked.

"Sniper. Guess they must have been in the street. You're not hit. Just knocked to the table by a piece of the window."

"Where were you?" Had she been unconscious long enough for the police to be called?

He smiled sheepishly, appeared ashamed, and lowered his head like a little boy. "Across the street. In that apartment." He gestured to the second floor apartment above Mrs. Myers's.

"Why?"

"Orders to watch you."

"Me?" Oh God, they really thought I was involved and they were watching to see if I'd make a move to pick up another shipment, she thought. Why won't they leave me alone? Arnie, when are you going to get me out of this? She lowered her head into her hands.

"You sure you're okay?"

"Yeah, but I guess I wouldn't be if I hadn't . . . if the glass hadn't hit me, if the bullet had . . . ." An uncontrollable tremor overtook her body and her voice. Teeth clacking, hands shaking, she pulled the blanket someone had given her closer around her shoulders and looked at the blue-uniformed people sorting through the broken glass on the floor.

"Here it is!" A young, blond officer raised his hand triumphantly. Between his fingers was a grayish-black bullet. "Looks like a Magnum."

"Listen, I think we should get you out of here," Deluca said, putting one arm around her and lifting her out of the chair.

Suddenly weak-kneed, she leaned against him, grateful for his strength. "My catalogs. London." "Forget about that right now. Whoever it is that's trying to get you is going to know you're not dead and they might come back. You've got to get the hell out of here. Let the boys do their job. You can worry about the auctions later."

As they were heading out the door, the telephone rang. All activity stopped. "Want me to get it?" the blond officer nearest the phone asked.

"No. It's my phone. *I* will." Diana pulled the blanket behind her and walked to the table. "Hello?"

"Did you get my message, *mi cara?*"

She closed her eyes, her shoulders stiffening. "What are you talking about?"

"My message, *cara* ... to shut your mouth. Did you get it?" Luis's voice, as calm as if he called simply to inquire about her health, purred ingratiatingly over the line.

"Listen, Luis," she whispered, aware of the eyes watching her from every corner of the room. "Haven't you had enough? Do you have to continue haunting me? Leave me alone! I've been punished enough!"

From behind her, a hand pulled the phone away. "Who's this?" Detective Deluca demanded. She could tell by his face that Luis had hung up. She brushed past him toward the door, not wanting her eyes to relay her fear.

As the rest of the officers went back to their assignments, Deluca caught up with her, taking hold of her elbow to propel her into the hall. "Okay, what's going on? Who was that?"

"Just a customer . . ."

"A customer you tell to leave you alone? C'mon, Ms. Cole, why don't you tell me? Maybe I can help."

Nicholson swiftly jotted the time and noted the digits on the tape recorder before picking up the phone. When the Attorney General answered, he said, "He's called. He's made contact with her." "Did you trace it?" Arnie Goldstein asked. - "Not enough time."

"Shit! He *must* be at the Nahant house."

"Not that we know of, sir. We've had an agent over there for the past couple of weeks and there's been no sign of him."

Arnie muttered again, under his breath this time. "Okay," he said. "Who's with her now?"

"Deluca of the BPD. He was there when they shot at her and he called the ambulance . . ." "What! Goddammit, I told you this was too dangerous. We should tell the BPD what's going on. I *knew* this would happen!"

The agent pulled back from the headphones. "Not to worry, sir. She's fine. The bullet just broke the window. Deluca's presence must have scared them. Besides, we already have the sniper in custody."

Goldstein wasn't listening. "She's not to get hurt! You hear me?"

"Yes, sir. Loud and clear."

"Keep me informed," the Attorney barked before slamming down the phone.

Steve watched her turquoise eyes narrow suspiciously, then she turned abruptly and marched down the stairs, out the door onto Joy Street. Feeling more perplexed than he had before, he followed her. "Where're you going?"

"To my car," she replied without turning around. "Uh-uh. A red Porsche sticks out on these city streets. You'll go with me."

She stopped, the blanket whirling as she turned to face him. "How the hell do you know so much about me?"

"I'm a cop."

"How long have you been following me?"

He shrugged, relishing the indignant look in her eyes, and the delicate way she placed her hands on her hips.

"Goddammit! When are you people going to realize I'm not the one you wa . . ." Suddenly aware she had said too much, she spun around, striding briskly away.

"Hey, Diana!"

"What?"

"I'm parked *up* the street."

She stopped, pulling the blanket off and balling it around her fist. Not turning. Not speaking. Her shoulders heaved as her dark head shook back and forth in amazement. He waited for her to join him.

"You know, l really don't know why you're fighting me so much. I'm only trying to help," he said as they walked slowly up the street. "What was it you were trying to say before? You're not telling me something, huh? There's been something you've been holding back from the very beginning."

Sliding behind the wheel, he turned to study her profile. "You can talk to me, you know. I won't bite you."

"Where are we going?" She turned her head, looking out the window as he executed a perfect, illegal U-turn.

"I'm not telling you until you answer my questions."

"I don't intend to."

"It'd be easier to talk to me than somebody else at the station."

"Why?"

"You're going to have to talk to someone sometime." They stopped at a light. He turned to her once more and swore there was a dewiness to her eyes.

"Take me to New Hampshire."

"I can't." Putting the car into gear, he felt her eyes still on him.

"Why?"

"It's over the state line. You can't go out of the state until after you've been to court. Besides, you're my responsibility now. You may not realize it, but you could've been killed a little while ago." He shifted into third. "Why does someone want you out of the way, Diana? Did you piss someone off? Do they want their shipment? Do you know something about someone that they don't want you to tell? You know, you could probably protect yourself a lot better—and Maryann and the kids, too—if you talked to me about it. I might just be able to help."

She balled the blanket up further on her lap, hugging it to her tightly. Her lips pursed and her eyes flitted from side to side, as if she desperately wanted to make a decision but hadn't weighed all the options.

"I want to talk to my lawyer," she finally mumbled.

Chapter Thirty-two

Boston, September, 1991

"Listen, I didn't know what you wanted. Never seen so many closets full of clothes with the tags still on them. Here." Steve laid the suitcase on one of the beds in the hotel room he had rented for her.

While Diana opened the case, pulling out what he had packed, he walked over to the window to check the parking lot. "Keep these drapes closed, okay?"

She nodded.

"We have to talk." He sat on one of the beds, a sneakered foot crossed over the knee of his jeans. "If my boss finds out I've offered you protection. I'm screwed. The only way we can do this is if you cooperate. I know there's something going on. Why don't you tell me about it?"

Diana stopped, folding a white angora sweater over her arm and smoothing its errant fur thoughtfully. "If I say something, will you protect Maryann and the boys? Will you make sure they're someplace where *no one* can get at them?" "I'll do my best. Can't promise anything. That's up to the Department. But if this is as big as I get the feeling it is, we can do something."

"Let me call Arnie again."

"You've talked to him twice today."

"Yeah, I know, but I don't know what to do right now and I need to talk to him again." She paused, staring at Deluca beseechingly. "Please?" "Go ahead. But make it fast."

Clenching his fingers into a fist, Arnie found himself inordinately happy that Diana had called him instead of storming into his office as she had so many times in the past. However, if she'd been able to see his face, she surely would have been able to tell he was lying.

"Listen, sweetheart, just pay attention to what the detective tells you," he said in a tone he hoped sounded soothing. "I'm doing everything I can on this end. We'll get Quintana somehow. Just be patient."

"How can I be patient, Arnie? I've been in jail! I've been shot at. I'm terrified he's going to go after Maryann and the boys. God, Arnie, this has been going on for almost ten years. I'm getting really tired of playing games . . ." Her hoarse whisper was tight. Agitated. Scared. Arnie knew she didn't want the police officer—what was his name? Dellicato? Laduca? No, Deluca. That was it—to hear what she was saying. If she knew that every phone call she made was being taped, would she forgive him for using her as bait when this was all over?

"Don't worry, hon," he said again, hating himself for what he was doing. "We won't let him get away with this."

As he hung up, he realized that last comment was the only true one he had made during the entire conversation.

He stared at the phone for one long, hard moment, watching the incoming lines blink on and off. Though he willed his mind to slow down, no amount of control could stop the stream of plans, meetings, appointments, and conversations he confronted on a daily basis. And to add all of this made everything else insignificant.

Out of habit, he checked his watch and quickly glanced at the calendar. Five minutes until his appointment with Senator Kennedy.

Thank God Ted's coming *here* today, he thought, as he straightened a few piles on his desk. For a moment, his eyes strayed to the window and the stream of never-ending traffic on the street below. A woman wheeled a toddler in a stroller. She looked remarkably like Diana, except her shining black hair was chin-length instead of shoulder. While she waited for the light, a man came up behind her and reached his arms around her waist. Surprised, she turned, then kissed him. The man was bending toward the toddler when the buzzer on Arnie's desk sounded. He was still watching the family when his secretary announced Kennedy's arrival.

"Send the Senator in," Arnie answered, and he wiped the moistness from his eyes before standing to welcome his old friend. Maybe Ted would help, he found himself thinking as they exchanged slaps on the back and jibes. The Kennedys always understood about family . . .

Ten minutes later, Diana came out of the bathroom, dressed in one of her silk suits, as impeccably as Deluca expected. She belonged on the cover of *Town & Country*. Suddenly, he felt like a total slob. He pushed the sleeves of his sweatshirt up to his elbows.

"Ready?" he asked.

"As ready as I'll- ever be. You're certain I'll be safe? Arnie said to make sure I get protection. If I don't, I'm not going to do this." She took a deep breath and fidgeted with one of the gold hoop earrings beneath her raven hair. Her hand shook like an addict's.

"Don't worry. I already called the station. They're waiting for us, and Cottrell will be in the hotel lobby by the time we ride down in the elevator."

Reaching for her elbow, he held her away from the door as he poked his head out, revolver cocked and ready. When she brushed past him into the hallway, he got an intoxicating whiff of perfume. Struck by the urge to bury his head in that smell, he forced himself to concentrate. "Stay behind me', now. Don't get more than a foot or two away from me," he whispered.

In the hallway, her breathing seemed magnified. Could anyone else hear it? Each room's door was a menace, a threat, a portal which could be opened as soon as they passed, a hole through which a rifle could be pointed. He moved as silently as possible, glad she had worn flats and a skirt which allowed movement.

The call to the precinct had brought more unwelcome news than he wanted to deal with at this moment. The plainclothes cops assigned to watch Diana's apartment had spotted snipers on the rooftop opposite her building for two nights in a row. Yet, no one was caught, no witnesses were willing to give descriptions, and no positive evidence had been collected. Though he couldn't tell her such news, Deluca had a feeling she knew, perhaps better than he, what she was up against.

' When the elevator door slid open, he shoved her against the wall outside and waited a few seconds before inspecting the cab and motioning her to come in. Muzak purred over the elevator's whir like a hazy cloud over a summer day. After a while, it ceased to become a distraction. Diana had a line of moisture on her upper lip as she watched the numbers blink by.

"You know," she said tremulously, "this is the first time I've been in the Airport Hilton. Don't know how many times I've gone to Logan Airport and I've never been in this hotel. Kind of ironic, don't you think?"

First floor. The door slid open. Deluca poked his head out, immediately spotting Cottrell pacing near the registration desk.

"Hey, Deluca. You okay? Station's buzzing with the . . . Ms. Cole. Didn't think we'd see each other again, did you?"

Diana nodded, lifting her chin to look slightly askance at Deluca's partner. Steve, amazed at how quickly her mood had changed from one of fear to one of supreme self-confidence, pulled her to his side. Cottrell fell into step on her right.

"Miss me?" Greg shot at Steve, past Diana's haughty profile.

"Not really." Steve, his eyes moving constantly, began to wish Cottrell had learned some manners at the Academy instead of just police procedure. "The Lieutenant waiting for us?"

"Yeah. Him and the DEA and a bunch of guys from Treasury. We've had the press up our asses since they got wind of the shooting. You realize what an expensive piece of cheesecake you have

here?" He lifted his eyebrows, indicating Diana.

She stopped mid-lobby and faced Cottrell, clenched fists at her side. "Detective Cottrell. I would appreciate it very much if you would refer to me by a pronoun or by my name. Your cute little phrases are derogatory and unnecessary. I don't appreciate them nor will I tolerate them. Is that clear?"

"Who the hell do you think you are, lady? Damn it, why do I always have to take shit from the people we pull in?"

"Maybe because you dish it out, Greg." Deluca took Diana's elbow, shooting his partner a warning look. "Just do your job and shut up. I don't like listening to your crap either."

They left him muttering to himself in front of the entrance to the hotel.

"Tell us again what you expected to be on the shipment from

Colombia, Ms. Cole." Her interviewer, a tall, thin man with sparse gray hair combed haphazardly across his forehead, leaned forward on the table. In front of him was a three- hour-old cup of coffee, an ashtray overflowing with Marlboro cigarette butts, and a legal-sized yellow pad upon which he wrote briskly in pencil. His name was Dave B r a d f o r d — D a v i d Bradford—and she had already pegged him as a man on his second wife and well aware of the importance of his job. A tape recorder whirred noisily to her right.

"If I remember correctly, I had bought a few Mayan vases, a few Peruvian rugs, some twelfth century Chilean jewelry, some larger Colombian furniture, and odds and ends which I don't really remember," she replied.

"Why, Ms. Cole? Because you knew it would be filled with cocaine? Is that why you buy vases and vessels which are easily opened?"

"No, I buy them for resale. I already told you, I don't have anything to do with cocaine. I never see the container until after it's unloaded when they go through customs in Miami. And I can't remember some of the stuff because I'm *always* on the road buying antiques. I bought some of the items on the most recent shipment months ago. Remember: I only get these shipments twice or three times a year."

"And you don't know how much cocaine was on board?"

She sighed, glancing at Arnie. His half-glasses were on the tip of his nose, his eyes on the pad in front of him. He, too, scribbled busily, unaware she was looking to him for comfort.

He had met them at the station, his appearance causing a few raised eyebrows. The gossip columnists were probably already creating rumors that the Attorney General and the wealthy antique magnate were having an affair; or that they were secretly related; or, worse, that he had been involved in the cocaine shipment. The press had already contacted him at his office, he reported to her *sotto voce* before the police began interrogating her. The story of her arrest and the shipment was hitting all the papers. There'd be no peace now. No way to keep her clients from knowing what had happened.

"Ms. Cole, I asked you if you knew how much cocaine . . . "

"And I've told you time and time again that I don't know what's on the shipment until it enters the country in Miami," she interrupted heatedly.
"I never know what's in it, never have any contact, never even see the shipment until it gets to Bos-"

"One hundred and five pounds, Ms. Cole. That's how much was there. Street value of approximately $5.5 million. More than your antiques are worth?"

She held the arms of the chair tightly, her fingernails boring into the plastic armrests, and shook her head. She had no idea Luis's shipments of coke were worth so much. Five million dollars' worth of coke . . . God, how many kids had died or been hooked by now?

How many lives did that much cocaine ruin? How much money had Luis made from that one shipment? She found herself quickly trying to multiply that profit times the hundreds of other shipments he must have arranged every year. The amount was staggering. It was enough to buy a whole country. Probably enough to get the United States out of debt.

"Di, are you all right?" Arnie put his hand protectively on her shoulder. "Diana. You're awfully white."

"I'm okay." No, I'm not, she thought. I'm as guilty as that Colombian son-of-a-bitch. Pulling her shoulders back, she pushed her hair behind her ears, then placed both hands on the table and leaned forward a little. Her body felt suffused with adrenaline. "What else do you want to know, gentlemen? I don't know *how* I can help, but I'll tell you whatever you want to know. I want this bastard caught as badly as you do."

Bradford smiled at his partner, a darker, younger man who stood behind Diana. "Good. We've been waiting a long time to get this guy. Maybe we can get him out of Boston now. Out of the country."

Five hours later, Amie walked out of the windowless room with his arm over Diana's shoulder. "I won't see you for a while," he said. "You're going to have to go completely underground after what you said in that room."

"Maryann and the . . ."

"Already taken care of. I'll get them to my sister's in Maine. She's in a completely remote section, on a lake. They'll love it. And I'll get them some protection. Don't worry about them. Right now, we have to worry about you."

"Deluca?"

"Yes, he and his partner will be offering a twenty-four-hour surveillance. Meanwhile, I have some phone calls to make. Now that I know what we're dealing with, I think there are a few people on the other side of the law who might be willing to testify against him. He's rubbed a lot of people the wrong way, your Mr. Quintana." He smiled sadistically at her, as if harboring a wonderfully evil secret.

"He's not *my* . . . "

"I know, sweetheart." He kissed her on the forehead, then absent-mindedly pushed the long strands of hair barely covering his bald spot to one side. For the first time today, he looked tired. Her heart went out to the man who had been father, uncle, brother, and friend for the better part of her life. In that split second, she realized he was putting his own career on the line to help her, probably putting politics and family on hold as well. Just as her father had asked him to do so many years ago. He had never failed her and she often wondered why. Surely he still didn't feel responsible for her.

"Thank you, Arnie. I love you, you know." She reached to give him a one-armed hug.

"I know. And you know I feel the same way, so you just take care of yourself, okay? I'll see you when this is all over." As he walked away, he yelled over his shoulder, "I'll have Maryann call you as soon as she's settled."

"How will you know where 1 am?"

"I'll know. Don't worry."

Deluca couldn't believe his luck. To be with her twenty-four hours a day, to be able to see her wake up, to talk her to sleep. To talk to her. To simply *talk* to her. No other assignment had ever made him so giddy. He found himself frequently reminding himself to slow down, that this was a job, that she was still on the wrong side of the law and that protecting her was an *assignment,* not a privilege.

"So, now we get serious," he said and turned to her, wondering what she was thinking as she stared blindly out the window. She nodded, glancing at him for a second with a distracted half smile.

In the back seat, Cottrell smoked incessantly. He definitely *wasn't* happy, Steve thought. In fact, his earlier comment about Diana had been, "She doesn't make *my* pants dance. Doesn't make *my* thermometer rise." Too bad the department couldn't have assigned someone else, but they were partners. And partners they'd remain until one of them quit or transferred or, worse—no, he wouldn't think about that. No matter how much he couldn't stomach Gregory Cottrell, he'd never wish him the same fate as Pete Sheldon.

Without warning, a gunshot and Pete's warning groan thundered through his brain. Even after all this time, the memory aroused a cold chill and beads of sweat popped out on his forehead. He shook his head, unwilling to let the flashback into his mind. Yet, he still saw the blood streaming over Pete's face, the disbelieving look in Pete's eyes, the momentary sensation of wanting to plug the hole in Pete's forehead, yet of being fascinated by the pump, pump, pump of blood. Everything stopped. Street sounds, even the yell for an ambulance seemed far away. The blue light from the squad car illuminated Pete's frozen features. The promise Steve had made to him: "Be the one to tell Gloria, Steve. Please don't let someone else do it"—had been the hardest thing he'd ever done. No, he didn't want that to happen again.

His fingers fell into the *Wipeout* rhythm.

"Cut it out, willya Deluca?" Cottrell shoved the driver's seat with his knee. "Christ, don't you ever get tired of that song? Shit, it wasn't even one of the greats!"

"I don't know." Diana's voice was quiet, thoughtful, as if coming from a well of her own memories. "Kind of liked *Wipeout* myself. Reminds me of junior high. All the guys who played drums learned how to do that solo."

"The Sixties. What's so goddamn great about the Sixties?" Cottrell continued, "Vietnam. No one has good memories about that. Kent State. The Army shooting at college kids. Everyone getting so blitzed on acid and bad drugs they still have flashbacks. That friggin' era was like a bad dream."

"Maybe, but I remember other things, too," Diana answered. "Carnaby Street. The Beatles. The Stones. Herman's Hermits."

"The Beach Boys," Steve added, snapping his fingers, rattling off more names. "Woodstock. Arnie 'Woo-Woo' Ginsberg."

Jumping a little in her seat, she pointed at him, chuckling delightedly. "The Night Train. WMEX." In the back seat, Cottrell groaned again. "So where we going, anyway? Anybody got any idea? Or is this the flower train to San Francisco?" "Cool your jets, Greg." Deluca winked at her. She was even more beautiful when she smiled and he wanted to be the one who had the power to put that look on her face. "We've got a place lined up in Marblehead. Right on the beach. Nice and quiet. We should be able to see anyone coming from any direction."

"On the beach, huh?" For the first time, the voice from the back seat was lighter, more optimistic. "Maybe this ain't so bad after all." Within moments, Cottrell was humming the chorus to *Wipeout's* guitar solo, while Deluca drummed and Diana did a comic imitation of the "Pony" in the front passenger seat.

Marblehead

The summer crowds had dissipated. Marblehead, quiet once more, proved the perfect hiding spot, Diana thought as she stood looking out of the safe house's glass doors to the deck overlooking the ocean. She longed to be on the beach, to jog from one end to the other, perhaps to collect a few rocks and shells, to breathe the salty air, to feel the spray on her face, I'll be outside.

"Just for a little while?" she pleaded with Steve, who stood behind her in the tiny kitchen whipping up another of his so-called "Italian delights." Their official cook, he had astounded her night after night with new dishes. Lasagna. Chicken *a la pesto. Zuppa di pecce.* She'd put on at least seven pounds.

"Di, you know better. You shouldn't even be near that door. Get away from there and sit down. C'mon. Supper's almost ready."

Despite the dangerous situation, the guns Steve and Greg always carried, the Drug Enforcement Agency guys roaming the beach outside, arid the constant communication with the Boston Police Department, Diana was having a good time.

Cottrell and Deluca were supposed to be sharing the "babysitting," as they called it, with the two DEA agents, but Deluca talked the captain into letting the BPD, meaning Cottrell and him, protect Diana inside the house, while the DEA took care of the outer perimeter. It made her feel much safer.

Remarkably relaxed, she had gotten used to their low-key conversations and evening chess games. Steve was a formidable partner; Cottrell was barely able to remember which piece moved in which direction.

It had been a long time since she'd shared so much of her past with anyone, but Deluca made it easy, often telling stories of his own childhood and of his large, noisy brood of brothers and sisters. After a while, even Cottrell joined in, though his tales paled next to Steve's. Still, it was easier to understand Greg after learning his father had left the family when the children were very young.

In spite of earlier misgivings, she found herself liking him. And Deluca. Well, he was a different story. When he took his shirt off to sleep on the couch at night, she had to close her fingers tightly into her palm in order to keep from touching the dark, curling chest hairs which reminded her of puppy fur. And she caught herself staring at him while he cooked. He sang to himself, happy in the kitchen, making a mess she would later clean up. She liked watching him when he wasn't looking as he pretended to croon into a pan or taste his latest creation. He was kind of cute. Thoughtful. His nice, white smile spread slowly across the bottom half of his face, then worked its way up to his eyes, until it appeared every feature worked equally to make the smile complete. It was one of the most engaging smiles she'd ever seen. And certainly the sexiest.

"Supper!" he yelled, banging on a pan for emphasis.

Cottrell came from one end of the parlor, she from the other. The three of them joined around the small, glass-topped dining room table, none of them speaking until the chicken scampi with linguine was almost gone.

"I've been thinking," Diana began, wiping her mouth with one of the linen napkins she had found in the sideboard. "Nahant isn't that far away. Just a couple of miles. What makes you guys think Luis won't find us?"

"The closer the better." Gregory buttered another piece of bread, talking through what he already had in his mouth. "I'd rather we were right under his nose, right, Steve-O?"

Steve nodded, leaning back in his chair. "I don't think he'd come looking for us out here. He probably thinks we're holed up in some Boston hotel or even farther away. Besides, the department said he's not in Nahant right now anyway. He's on a yacht somewhere in the Caribbean." Diana looked at her plate, briefly remembering the Mediterranean surrounding Sicily. That sea was so much bluer than the Atlantic, so much warmer and more romantic. She suppressed an urge to tell Steve about her trip, her aunt, the rest of her family. Instead, she rose, taking her plate as well as the other two to the kitchen sink. "Hear anything else lately? Anything else you're not telling me?"

Outside, a heavy rain pounded on the deck, almost drowning out Steve's answer. "We had to close down the Newbury Street shop. Sent your manager home."

"Why?" The dishes slid out of her hands, breaking loudly against the edge of the stainless steel sink. "What happened?"

Steve rose out of his chair, crossed the kitchen floor, and put his hands on her shoulders. "Don't get nervous. Nothing happened. Nobody's hurt. Your guy there-the English guy-what's his name?"

"Terence Pellican."

"Yeah, Terence. Weird name. Well, he was getting some pretty strange calls about bombs and such. Seems Luis knew you went to the cops, and we just wanted to make sure no one got hurt. Terence just took an early vacation, that's all." "You sure he's all right?"

"Yeah, of course. Just had to close down for a while."

"What about the other shops? London? Beverly Hills? New York?"

"They're okay. All the other managers now check in at least once a day. We got protection for them. Besides, the DBA is keeping an eye on them, too. So don't worry. Now, c'mon. I got spumoni for dessert."

"I don't want dessert."

She ran upstairs and slammed the door to her room, wishing she could lock it, though they'd made sure she couldn't. So she wouldn't be trapped inside. Bullshit. She was already trapped. She'd been trapped from the first moment she'd laid eyes on Luis de la Maria Quintana. That bastard. What had she done to him that was so horrible he felt he had to totally ruin her life?

Pulling herself into a fetal position, she wrapped the pillow around her face and soundlessly screamed her frustration into it.

"Diana? Diana?"

Two hours later, the storm still raged. Steve had left Greg snoring in the armchair downstairs and quietly took the stairs two at a time to the second floor. He pushed the door open a few inches, just far enough to see her slender form stretched out on the bed. "Diana? Listen, I didn't want you to be upset. It wasn't my decision. But I'm sure you can understand why . . ."

"Get out." Her muffled response came from beneath the pillow.

"Can you let me explain, please?" One leg, sans shoe, twitched as though she were going to get up. He reached a hand down to touch it, then pulled back. Business, he reminded himself. This is business.

"I don't want an explanation. I just want you to leave."

"Well, you're going to hear it whether you like it or not. I know this is hard for you. I'd be having a tough time with it, too, but you have to understand we're only doing our job. We have to make sure you and your people have protection."

Her head turned, revealing red-rimmed eyes. Had she been crying? Surprised, he looked at his hands, not knowing what to say.

"I don't want to *need* protection," she said. "I don't want anyone else I know in any danger. I don't want to be afraid anymore. Can you understand that? Do any of you understand how this feels? I feel *totally* helpless! *Totally* alone! And I'm tired of being cooped up in this fucking house!" She flung the pillow across the floor and sat up straight, pulling her knees to her chest. "I need to get out of here or I'm going to go nuts."

Biting his lower lip, he thought for a moment. "It's too dangerous . . ."

"Bullshit. How can it be dangerous if he's not even around?"

"He's got plenty of workers. Plenty of *corporales.*" Steve lifted one eyebrow, pronouncing the word in Italian. "He's not the one going to sit on lookout. They are. And it's safer for *him* if he's not around. Then he won't get blamed if anything happens."

"I know that." She shook her head from side to side and gave a little laugh. "You think I'm stupid?"

"No, I don't . . ."

"I just need some fresh air. Let me walk on the beach. Take me to the store for a Coke. Something. Anything."

"Well, maybe I can . . . if you promise not to take off. Maybe . . ." Pushing a hand through his thick, curly hair, he was sorry he had offered, aware that he could be fired for what he was about to promise. At that moment, she raised her head and the sight of that perfect face, mouth moist and slightly open, hair rumpled and eyes glittering like a trusting child's, caused all of his senses to go into overload.

"My cousin, Marion, is getting married tomorrow. 1 really wanted to go to the wedding. Maybe I can . . ."

"Oh, take me, Steve. Please. I'll wear a wig. 1 1 1 stuff my shirt so I look fat. I'll put on glasses. I'll wear a complete disguise. Anything. Just take me."

"Okay." Cottrell's going to kill me, he thought, and then I'm going to lose my job.

Chapter Thirty-three

Marblehead, September 15, 1991

Feeling like a schoolgirl on her first date, Diana wriggled into the pink silk cocktail dress she had bought on her last trip to Rome. A little bit tight, but it would do. Now for the wig. She pulled the long blond fall over her head, then flipped it back and stared in the mirror. The effect made her laugh so hard her legs buckled under her. Black eyebrows, olive skin, and blond hair. This wouldn't fool anyone! Great disguise.

She was still laughing when Steve opened the door.

"Ready?" He stood in the entryway looking like a totally different person in his tailored black suit, white shirt, and businessman's striped tie. His hair was combed back and before he stepped further into the room, she got a strong whiff of Canoe. She reeled, remembering the smell as the one Robbie had used in high school.

"Wow! Look at you!" she said, settling into letting the scent bring back good memories instead of bad.

"No, I'm too busy looking at *you*. You know, maybe with a little bit of makeup and some long dangly earrings . . ." A wry smile tugged at the corners of his mouth. "You're not really the blond type, are you?"

Together they joked a little more, adjusting the wig, then finally deciding a hat would work just as well.

"God, Di, if I get caught. I'm screwed," he said as he slipped behind the wheel of his Mustang.

"But just think of how much fun we'll have." She grinned and gave him an impish wink, arranging her long legs in a way that forced him to look at them. She was being coy and she knew it. But she didn't care. For the first time in a long time, the old flutters were back. The kind that made her love just being with a man.

For a few moments they waited in an uncomfortable silence, smiling at each other and nodding, but not speaking, until Greg finally ran out the door, pushing his arms into the sleeves of his sports coat.

"I don't believe we're doing this," he said, squeezing into the back seat. "We're going to be deballed if the captain finds out."

"And who's going to tell him?" Steve backed out of the driveway carefully, his windshield washers doing double-time.

The autumn rain, which had fallen for the past two days, continued throughout their ride along the back streets of Marblehead, through the small, quiet towns of Lynn and Saugus, into the suburb of Revere, then the dark, close streets of East Boston. Diana watched the fleeting shadows on the dashboard, actually enjoying the gray cast of the sky and the muggy way her skin felt in such weather. She could barely believe how elated she felt just being out of the house and found herself taking pleasure in studying the streets she'd seen a million times before. Occasionally, she stole a glance at Steve, still marveling at how different he looked and inhaling the fragrance of his cologne. But he concentrated on driving.

He and Greg scrutinized every passing car, especially the ones behind them. But nothing happened and they heaved a collective sigh of relief when they reached the small hall where the wedding reception was being held.

"Are you sure this is such a great idea?" Greg asked, leaning forward into the front seat.

"It'll be fine. I know everyone here. They're family. Couldn't be safer." Steve motioned for Diana to stay put until he got around to her side of the car. "Madame . . . " he smiled, gallantly opening the door and crooking his arm for her. "I hope you appreciate this."

Boston

"I can't believe you let her get out of the house!" Arnie held the phone tightly against his ear and rubbed the upper part of his stomach with his other hand. An ulcer. That's all he needed. In a way, he wished it would all end as soon as possible. He could take Estelle to the Caribbean after explaining everything to Diana, and putting the Colombian in jail ... but he couldn't begin to plan anything—not yet. Patience, he chided himself. I have to be patient. "You guys are supposed to be protecting her. I've been counting on you."

"We've been listening to the conversations inside the house, sir," Nicholson reported. Patiently. "Evidently, she talked Deluca into taking her out. Seems she was going stir crazy. If we had stepped in, they would have put two and two together. I don't think you'd want that to happen."

Despite his aggravation, Arnie smiled. If Diana was anything, she was convincing. He wasn't surprised she'd gotten through to the cop. "You *do* have someone shadowing them . . ."

"Of course, sir."

"And Quintana?"

"He's not due back until tomorrow."

"Are you sure?"

"That's what we've heard, sir."

Arnie paused to rub his stomach once more. "I want her protected, Nicholson. Don't let *anything* happen to her."

When he hung up, Arnie reached into his desk drawer for the bottle of Rolaids. Somehow he wasn't convinced that *anyone* would ever be able to keep tabs on Diana Cole.

And he wondered if that would be her success. Or her downfall.

East Boston

The street was littered with broken bottles and bits of paper flattened with the rain. Diana walked on tiptoe, not wanting to get mired in the muck piled ankle-high along the gutter.

Typical East Boston, she thought. Forgot how dirty it is. Whatever made me think this would be fun? Her nose wrinkled as she vainly tried to smile at Steve and Greg. Well, this is what I wanted. At least I'm out. Doesn't even matter that it's raining or that the air smells of car and truck fumes. I'm out.

She remembered another wedding, in another part of the city, a long time ago, when the orchestra played "Sunrise, Sunset," Maryann danced with her father, and Robert disappeared into the men's room. Diana went after him, standing at the door, knocking softly, smiling innocently at the people who looked at her strangely as they went by. She thought Rob might have been overwhelmed by emotion, but when he came out, smiling that broad, devil-may-care smile, and throwing an arm around her shoulder, she conceded she might have been wrong.

"Are you okay?" she asked.

"Whaddaya mean? Why wouldn't I be? You think this sappy music does me in? Naw . . . c'mon, Di, you know me better than that." And he was gone, melting into the crowd, making his way toward his bride, yelling at the orchestra to play something fast. "Hey! How about some rock 'n roll? Don't you know anything by the Stones?" The moment was forgotten.

Home. The streets down which she had walked to school, to the store, to Santarpio's Pizza House. It had been a long time. It was still dirty, still smelled like old gas fumes and Italian food, but it was home.

Within seconds after entering the hall, Diana was introduced to "Mama" Deluca, who gave Greg a smacking kiss and dragged all three of them to the head table where they were introduced in both Italian and English. The family told the band to stop playing and crowded around the three newcomers, hugging and kissing Steve as though he had been absent for more than ten years. When all was back to normal, the music resumed, the waitress was summoned to bring food, and they sat at a large table to eat and listen to news of the Deluca clan.

"You know this guy?" One of Steve's uncles sat next to Diana, fat cigar in his equally cigar like fingers. "This guy, he's the best nephew in the world. He is! Don't you just love him?" With a hearty laugh, he pulled Steve's ear and mussed his hair. Diana, amazed at Steve's patience, suppressed a smile,

"Never thought you were the family type," she said, when the confusion died down a little.

"Ah, Christ, don't you know this group would like nothing better than to see this guy married? Shackle him to an expensive house, give him 6.5 kids, and his mother would be ecstatic." Greg shoveled another forkful of lasagna into his already overloaded mouth as he spoke. "And he wouldn't mind it, either."

"Someday. Maybe one of my kids will be out on the dance floor having a ball like those two." Steve nodded toward his nephews doing clumsy break- dance imitations for a jubilant, clapping crowd.

"Looks like what *my* nephews would do." Laughing a little, she remembered Tony and Chris at the same age. "They're pretty crazy, too."

'They kind of get under your skin, don't they?"

"Nothing like being an aunt. You get to spoil them rotten, then you can take them back to their parents."

"I know what you mean."

The softly-spoken comment made Diana turn to look at the detective who had spent the last week protecting her. His features were undoubtedly tranquil. A slight smile played around the edges of his full mouth and his eyes, normally sharp and sliding from side to side, were actually dewy.

He loves them, she thought, just like I love Chris and Tony. An unanticipated feeling of camaraderie took her by surprise. Maybe they had more in common than she was willing to admit. After all, he wasn't half bad at chess, he came from the same town, had the same kind of family, knew some of the same people and even had some of the same values she had. An uncomfortable flush colored her cheeks. She turned her head away.

"Hey, Diana! Let's dance. I've got to work off some of this food." Steve stood, reaching a hand out to her. With his jacket off, his tie loosened, and his hair rumpled, he looked like a high school boy. She stood up and stepped into his arms.

Without warning, the lights dimmed to the point where they could barely see where they were going. Diana stumbled. From the far comer of the h^ came a barely-controlled, childish shriek.

"The boys are at it again," Steve said with a chuckle. Pulling her closer, his face grew serious and by the time the lights came back to normal, they stared into each other's eyes. "Haven't danced slow in a long time." She forced herself to keep him at arm's length and nodded, keeping her arms stiff, trying to quash the feeling of contentment she got from being close to him. No doubt he was attractive, and she admitted feeling "that" urge. But not for a cop, she reminded herself. Especially not a cop from East Boston.

Their bodies sway^ as if they were one, and she relaxed into the feeling, closing her eyes for a moment. She felt his head move back and his chin press against her forehead, inching her face up to meet his.

Yes, she wanted him to kiss her. There was no doubt in her mind. Knowing she had lost control, she swallowed his lips with hers. Eagerly. Anxiously. They stopped dancing, and concentrated on exploring each other's mouths, totally forgetting where they were and who was watching. Mentally, she fought the feeling enveloping her, devouring her senses, but her body would not agree, until finally, she pushed against his shoulders, shoving him away from her. Her last glimpse of his astonished eyes remained in front of her, blinding her, as she groped for the door to the street.

Once outside, she leaned against the building, breathing heavily, letting the rain wash over her burning cheeks while she tried to regroup. This was wrong. How could she keep herself in check? In all her adult life she had never even *tried* not to respond to her sexual urges. Yet, now it felt important, almost imperative, to do so. Why? Was it because he was special?

Within seconds, the door opened. Steve stood there, a baffled look on his face, as if he was seeing her for the first time.

"Why . . ."

"Don't ask^," she said, shaking her head and moving away. "Just don't ask. It isn't right and you know it. Why you even *thought* you could kiss me is beyond me. We're not supposed to be lovers or even friends. This is business. Off limits . . ." "Who. says?"

"I say." Folding her arms over her chest, she looked down the street, watching the gray rain fall against the car hoods and onto the metal grates covering the shop windows.

"You can't tell me you didn't want to kiss me as much as I wanted . . ."

"Let's not talk about it anymore, okay?"

He stood in front of her; his black curls were shining, the mist on his face made him appear flushed. "Listen, come back inside. It's too dangerous to be out on the street."

"I can't go back in there!"

"Well, then, talk to me!"

"I can't . . ."

"You can't what?"

"Can't get close to you."

"Why?"

"Because . . ."

"C'mon, Diana, what the hell are we playing here? Twenty questions? We're both adults. You know as well as I do that something's been going on between us since we met. Why don't you just let it happen? It doesn't mean I still can't do my job. In fact, I'll do it even better. I'd protect you with my life!"

"That's just the problem! I don't want you to protect me with your life! I've had enough people die on me. I don't want you to join them!"

"So, that's it." Steve took her closed fists and brought them to his mouth, kissing every finger, then opening them gently to kiss her moist palms. "Honey, I'm not going to die on you. I've got a lot more living to do."

"Not if you stay with me, you won't. Now let's just stop this." Pulling her hands away, she breathed shakily, avoiding his eyes, fighting for control. "This is business, Steve. It's damn serious business. I can't involve you. I just can't be responsible."

"Hey! Listen to me!" He took her face in his hands. "I'm responsible for my own life. I'm a big boy. I can make my own choices. And if I choose to fall in love with you . . ."

His words delved deep into her heart. Terrified, Diana tore his hands from her and started running up the sidewalk, aware that the dress was getting ruined. It would never be the same. *She* would never be the same. Behind her, she heard him start to come after her, then stop.

"Diana!" His shoes made a clip-clop sound against the wet sidewalk, and she knew even before he caught her that she wouldn't make it very far.

"Don't ever run away from me again . . ." he said as he came up beside her and blocked her path.

"Please, don't . . ."

"Diana, listen to me. If you want some space, if you want me to leave you alone until this is over, I will. But just remember this . . ."

"No! You're a cop, damn it! You risk your life every day. I'm not willing to go through that again, so stay away from me, Deluca, okay?"

"If that's the way you want it . . ."

"Yeah, that's the way I want it."

"You got it." He stepped away and raised both hands, palms up. As she walked by, he turned his face from her, and through a storefront window, she could see him still standing in the same position as she went back into the hall.

Chapter Thirty-four

Marblehead, September 15, 1991

The solid click of the heavy oak front door reminded Diana anew of the fact that she was captive in a strange house. She found that a depressing thought, one which made her shoulders droop and caused her feet to drag. Perhaps under different circumstances or at a different time, she and Steve might have been able to be friends, but not this way, not under these circumstances.

Greg busied himself turning on the alarm, an invisible, high-tech laser system which protected the house's whole perimeter twenty-four hours a day. Installed by the Department, it sent a silent signal to the local police station as well as to the occupants if anyone stepped onto the three-sided porch or attempted to open a window or door. Outside, a heat-sensitive light system only went into service when the laser beams detected a warm body within 200 feet of the house. Without warning, strong floodlights would switch on, illuminating all sides for a full ten minutes, or until they were physically turned off.

"Your watch. The DBA guys will be back pretty soon, too," Steve said to Greg, ignoring Diana as he had for the past couple of hours. "I'm going to take a nap for a little while."

"No problem. I'll get you up at midnight. You can take the early morning shift." As Greg went toward the kitchen, she headed upstairs, determined to get out of her fancy clothes and into a warm sweatshirt and pants. Amazing how easy it had been to get used to wearing comfortable clothing during the past couple of weeks. No longer did her designer clothes mean anything. There was no one to impress, no meetings to attend, no auctions to peruse. Nothing to do but wait.

The dress slid easily over her hips, slithering to the floor in a pink mess. She kicked it across the room, then sent her pumps in the same direction. They landed in a scarlet pile against the wall.

Why couldn't he understand what she meant? Why didn't he see the logic in her refusal to be with him? She was only trying to protect him, only trying to show him he'd get hurt if he stayed with her, if he cared for her. It was the only fair thing to do. But during the rest of the time they spent in the hall he sullenly sat in his chair, speaking only when spoken to and trying to avoid her eyes. Feeling guilty, she'd made little effort to talk to him, had danced a couple of fast songs with Greg, and played with the children who visited the table. She'd even had a long conversation with Mama Deluca, who, she decided, reminded her of her Aunt Cecile.

They had talked of Italy, of her visits to Europe, of her business. Mama Deluca finally leaned over to Steve, telling him to "snatch this one up. She's a smart girl. Make a good wife for a crazy boy like you." It was the only time Steve had met her eyes, yet the look was a challenge—one which she lost, for she had been the first to turn away.

It wasn't fair. But what really was? Had the past twenty years been fair? Had losing Papa and
Mama, Gene and Vito, and Robert been fair? Was what was happening now *fair?* She shook her head, unused to feeling sorry for herself. Perhaps she'd just never given herself time before. She didn't like this—too much time on her hands. Too much to think about. She longed to be busy, to pick up the phone and put together a deal, to call the airlines and make reservations to Japan so she could pick up new merchandise, find out what was happening with the shops. Talk to someone besides cops.

Luis. The bastard. She grabbed a comb and pulled it through her wet hair, hardly wincing when she tore out large chunks. If he hadn't come into her life, she wouldn't be thinking this way. She watched the comb pull through another strand of hair and didn't stop when a large tangle came out in the comb. She didn't like the way she looked these days. Angry. Always angry. All because of that dope-dealing bastard . . .

Yet, I wouldn't have met Steve if it hadn't been for Luis, she mused. Guess there was always something positive . . . not positive. It couldn't happen. I won't let it.

She pulled the comb through her hair once more and tried to focus her thoughts on optimistic outcomes, but she knew she had ruined the one good thing she'd been given in the last couple of years.

Pulling the black sweatshirt over her head, she thought of Steve's crestfallen face, of their dance, and of the moment their lips met. Abruptly, she sat down on the edge of the bed, clutching her stomach.

Never thought I'd feel like this again. It's like . . . it's like . . . Vito. The first time. Love. No. Can't be.

She pulled the matching black sweatpants over her thighs, amazed to find them a little loose about her waist. Black. The color of mourning. Well, maybe she was. It certainly felt like grief. And, heaven knows, I know what that feels like. She laughed sardonically, biting back the urge to scream and kick, to curse God.

Despite her scattered thoughts, the action of pulling on her sweat suit made her automatically think of jogging. Her leg muscles tensed up and the adrenaline pumped through her veins.

Just like Pavlov's dog, she thought with a wry smile. I'm programmed.

She missed running, missed being out in the weather, missed the feeling of rhythm and strength when she fell into an easy stride. Often she had classical music running through her mind as she ran and somehow it helped make it easier to think of that now.

In the last couple of days, she had come to the shocking realization that all she had accomplished in the past ten years had been done woodenly. She had woodenly gone through life, amassing goods— things—chasing from one end of the globe to the other, from one man to another, from one possession to another. Woodenly accepting affection. Woodenly rejecting any intimacy. Only to come to this, to come to the point where she might lose everything. At first, the thought that she might lose her social status had been important. Devastating. But now, after seeing Steve with his family, she realized that what she had been searching for, what she had been trying to build, was only a panacea for what she had lost long ago. Family.

Maybe Robert pinpointed her mistake when he told her she should have spent more time with him, Maryann, and the kids than with Gene. But Gene was family, too. She couldn't have let him die alone. And she couldn't hold herself responsible for Robert's death, either. She had come to terms with that long ago.

Maryann was right. Rob had been on a collision course with suicide from the time Papa died and it had gotten even worse after they lost Marcus. How many times had Diana rescued him after he'd crashed his bike into a brick wall? How many nosebleeds had she stopped with wads of toilet paper after he'd come home from a fight? How many times had he played football without protection, driven his car thirty or forty miles above the speed limit, taken so many chances that, sooner or later, he was sure to lose the gamble?

So much wasted time to find out what she should have known long ago. And the person who taught her all of this was downstairs, believing she hated him. He had no idea how he'd ripped the blinders off her eyes and opened her life to the possibility that passion might still become a permanent resident. She tied her black Nikes and slipped out the bedroom door, wondering what she would say to him.

The rain continued to pound on the roof and against the doors, sometimes so hard she thought the glass would break; in the past few days it had fallen so quietly, it had been the perfect lullaby. For a moment, she paused, looking out the stairway window, watching the angry ocean's waves slam against the two-lane road leading to the house. Only one way in and one way out.

She remembered coming out to this peninsula in the wintertime. She'd been in her last year of high school. Marcus/Vito, Robert, and she were going to try the new Mexican restaurant in Marblehead Center and they had driven up this road, looking for a quiet place to watch the snow fall against the sea. The road had been closed, washed out by small icebergs thrown onto the highway by the ocean's magnificent force. They wondered how the **peninsula's** residents were able to survive being cut off from the world, but through the snow they saw a dimly flickering light, proof that someone was out there. She remembered thinking the home might have a fireplace. Maybe the family was roasting marshmallows and telling ghost stories. A family. Mother and father, a couple of kids. Safe in the storm, laughing and enjoying the haven they had made against the rest of the world. For a moment she'd been jealous, then Marcus reached for her hand, Robert started complaining about being hungry, and she realized that everyone's haven was a different place with different people inside. Marcus and Robert had been hers.

Engrossed in her memory and still looking out the window, she bumped into another warm body.

"Excuse me," Steve said, trying to go around her.

"No, wait a minute." Did she dare? Yes, it was time to go the extra mile, to stop acting woodenly and to admit how she was feeling. She put her hand on his arm and felt the tenseness she could see in his face. "I'm sorry about before. I mean ... I didn't . . ."

"It's okay," he said. "I can understand how you really don't want to take a step backwards. You're too far beyond this Guinea from East Boston."

"We're not Guineas. Don't ever use that word." She hadn't meant her voice to be so sharp. His eyes widened with confusion. "I may have moved out of East Boston," she continued, "but I never stopped being Italian."

"Then why did you change your name?"

"It seemed easier at the time. It just kind of happened because most people found it hard to pronounce." Diana shrugged. "Good for business, I guess."

For a moment, conversation stopped. The light through the window made wavering patterns across Steve's face. She reached out tentatively to stroke his cheek and took a deep breath, wondering where to begin. "I'm really sorry I hurt you. You're the first one I've cared about in a long, long time and it's pretty . . . it's pretty scary." To her amazement, her voice caught and a choked sob escaped.

Steve caught her hand and brought it to his mouth, kissing the palm lightly. She shuddered as a rippling of butterflies went through her stomach. Taking the two steps to bring them together, he wrapped his arms around her and gently pressed her head into his shoulder.

"This is scary for me, too," he whispered. "I don't usually fall for the women I arrest."

She felt the rumble of his low laugh and spread her fingers on his chest as if to catch it. The familiar warmth in her loins slowly forced her to forget reality. She wanted Steve Deluca, his naked body against hers, as soon as possible. The feeling was almost desperate.

His breath began to quicken as he spread his fingers against her back. She could feel each digit as clearly as if they had been imprinted like a brand. Once again, she shuddered and pushed her body into his, pulling his shirt out of his pants and running her hands under it, reveling in the warmth of his skin. His answer was a long, deep sigh. With another unhesitating move, she slid her fingers around to his groin, slipping his pants' zipper down and reaching inside to caress the stiff hairs.

Moaning, Steve lowered his head and caught her mouth, devouring it, thrusting his tongue inside, then pulling back as quickly as he had begun. "Not here," he whispered. "Greg's just outside. He could come back any minute."

But she wouldn't stop. *Couldn't* stop. Holding him tightly to her, she wiggled her sweatshirt up and placed his hand on her breast. His touch, no longer tentative, instantly brought her nipple to life. She felt as if she was swimming under water. Slowly. Laboriously. She knew her passion had overtaken her and that, essentially, she was raping him. Right on the staircase. But Steve wasn't resisting. No, he wasn't resisting at all.

She didn't care. For the first time, she was the seductress instead of the seduced, and she found a primal pleasure in hearing his soft moans, found herself even more excited when she pushed his hands away from her pants so she could bend to caress him with her mouth.

"Oh, Diana," he whispered. His hands wound tightly in her hair as he lifted her to press against him once more. Biting her lips, he finally got his fingers under the waistband of her pants, and she was amazed at his soft, delicate touch.

After kicking one pant leg free, she wound her legs around him. With a smooth, gliding motion; he entered. Her head fell back, all strength left her limbs, but she met his motion. Again and again and again. And found herself repeating the same phrase he whispered in her ear. Over and over and over.

"I love you. I love you so much. Don't ever leave me."

Clinking cups brought her back to reality. She had gone back upstairs, straightened her clothes, and brushed her hair, still feeling as though her muscles had turned to liquid.

"I'll go downstairs," Steve had whispered, before pulling away. "Greg will think something's weird otherwise."

Greg was in the kitchen, fixing coffee. The smell wafted toward her nostrils, beckoning her, promising her warmth. A cup of strong coffee would be good right now. Coffee and conversation.

On silent sneakers, she stepped into the parlor. Steve had fallen asleep on the couch, stretched out to fill it completely, feet dangling over one end, fully clothed except for jacket and tie. His mouth was slightly open, his hand under his head. A soft snore escaped his lips.

Opening the closet, she took out a blanket, opened it completely, and covered him with it, standing over him for a moment just watching him sleep. Why did people always look like children while they slept? Even grown men seemed innocent, the cares of the world temporarily erased, the lines around their eyes and across their foreheads softened. She tucked the blanket in around his neck, suppressing the urge to drop a kiss on his forehead.

"Want some coffee?" Greg stood in the kitchen doorway, two cups in his hand. "I made some for Steve, but I guess he was serious about taking a snooze."

She nodded, grateful for the distraction, and moved away from

Steve's slumbering body. A week ago, Greg would have had some kind of comment to make, some sarcasm to which she would have bitterly replied, but they had come to a sort of agreement lately. Though he still wasn't one of her favorite people, she accepted him. And he seemed - to feel the same.

"Here, put your own cream and sugar in. I've got to call the station. If they tried to get hold of
US while we were out, we're fucked." He picked up the kitchen phone and punched the numbers while she feed her coffee. She leaned against the doorway, sipping the hot brew, half-listening to his conversation, then drifting back to the hurried tryst on the staircase. Feeling warm. Safe. Loved.

When Greg's voice became louder, briskly asking half-questions, she listened more closely.

"When? ... It just happened, then . . . Both kids? . . . Where's the mother? . . . Get the Staties to make a report . . . Anyone see the car? . . . Yeah, I'll get her to call ... Let us know . . . Yeah, we'll be on alert . . . The DBA guys aren't back yet . . . Another hour . . . Yeah, I'll let them know when they get here."

He hung up and rushed past her, bending over Steve and roughly shaking his partner's shoulder. "Hey, buddy. Wake up. Naptime's over. We got ourselves a crisis."

"Hmmm? What?"

"The Colombian's got Diana's nephews." ^

Steve's eyes immediately shifted to Diana. All senses came alert as if someone had thrown a switch. Though she looked shocked, she appeared calm, as though the abduction was expected, as though she had been waiting for it—and was almost relieved it had finally happened. Before, he would have thought such a reaction was cold, but now he knew differently. Her mind worked double-time, just like his. He could imagine what she was thinking, how quickly she'd be skipping over possibilities, solutions, rescue plans, and how much she'd blame herself for putting the boys in danger.

"What're they doing?" he asked Greg.

"Whatever they can. Guess the A.G.'s office is involved and they know . .

"Is Maryann okay? Where is she?" Diana asked. Greg turned. "They took her to the Saugus house. Figured that'd be the first place Quintana would call if he wanted to get in touch. You know a kidnapper usually tries to make some sort of deal and the house in Maine didn't have a phone. Besides, she was left on a highway someplace after he had his goonies take the three of them out of the house. Guess he wanted someone to know what he'd done. Wants to flush you out, probably. Must have figured out that since he didn't succeed in killing you, you went to us. Not difficult to guess, even for an asshole like him. Wonder how many grams he snorted to make him so intelligent."

He turned back to Steve. "The A.G.'s office found out some

pretty interesting stuff about Quintana. Guess he's not too well-liked around these here parts. Made some enemies in the Mafia." Steve was sitting up now. "Oh?"

"Yeah, might even be able to get some help from them in nailing him. But we're dealing with a full-blown war. These guys aren't armed with cap pistols."

"Figures." On his feet now, Steve paced back and forth in front of the couch, wanting to be on the street, wanting to be part of the team that would bust the son-of-a-bitch. "What're we supposed to do?"

"Sit tight. Wait, the captain says. Do nothing. Just be aware of what's going on."

"Does Quintana know where . . ."

"No. He has no idea we're here."

"You sure?"

"Nothing's ever sure, Steve-o, my boy." Greg walked toward the sideboard where he kept his ammunition. "Bring anything stronger than your nine millimeter?"

Steve mumbled his answer, determined not to let Diana hear. Though she remained quiet, listening, her fingers were white-knuckled around her coffee cup.

"Are they hurt?" Her voice sounded tiny, feeble, in the charged tension of the room.

Greg glanced quickly at Steve, then continued loading his Magnum. "No. As far as we know..."

"As far as you know! Can't you guys find out if the boys are okay? Can't you check somehow?" She strode toward them, reaching her cup to the table as if to leave it there, when the lights suddenly went out. In the dark, the cup crashed to the floor.

"Shit!"

"Goddammit, what next?"

"Diana, get to the floor!"

Steve heard a thump and, satisfied she had done what he told her, slid his own belly against the rug and crawled to the curtained window. Behind him, Greg whispered, "How come the alarm . . ."

"Maybe it's cut off, too. Listen, I'll take the front of the house, you head around back. Give me three minutes before you go, okay?"

"Wait!" Greg grabbed his partner's leg. "Let's check this out before we go out there. It's dark and it's still raining. If we kill the alarm before checking whether it's still working, we're fucked. It's our only line of defense until the DBA. guys get back."

He was right. "Okay. Check it out. I'll check the windows down here."

Through each downstairs window, all he could see was pelting rain and crashing surf. No cars. No dark figures. He heard Greg's stealthy steps move across the porch, the boards creaking beneath him. The outside lights should have gone on by now, the alarm should have been blinking, but there was nothing. Shit! This house was supposedly protected. Safe. How the hell could Quintana have found it so easily?

The front door opened, and Steve heard the sound of wet shoes coming into the parlor. "I think it's safe." Greg's voice sounded relieved, normal. "Looks like the power line is down and the road's washed out. No one's getting in or out for a while. I'm going downstairs to see if 1 can figure out how to hook up the generator. It'll give us something, anyway."

"Okay. But, just to be safe. I'm going to stay at the windows. And Diana, you stay down."

Boston

"I've got to go," Arnie said to his wife as he snapped on the light. "They've got the kids." "Good Lord," Estelle whispered as she picked up the last of the supper dishes. "What're you going to do?"

Goldstein slipped his arms into his jacket after reaching for his tie and deciding against it. "I don't know. Maybe I'll stay at the station. Maybe I'll go out to Marblehead and be with Diana. I don't know. If they had listened to me, if they hadn't gotten Diana into this, maybe we would've been able to catch him a long time ago. But no . . . now look at what's happening."

"Calm down, honey. You know what the doctor said. . ." She reached around his neck and straightened his collar with a maternal pat. She smelled like Ivory soap, and, for some strange reason, that calmed him a bit.

"Yeah, I know what he said, but how the hell am I supposed to stay calm when shit like this happens?" He popped three Rolaids into his mouth, hesitated, then popped in a fourth.

"Maybe you should resign. Being Attorney General has been nothing but aggravation . . ."

"Not now, Estelle. 1 really don't need to be nagged right at this moment." Reaching for the door, he caught a last glimpse of her worried face and went back to drop a quick peck on her cheek. "Don't wait up for me," he said as he closed the door behind him.

As he started the car, he swore under his breath. At Luis Quintana. At the ineptness of the DBA officers. At the stupid BPD detectives "protecting" Diana. At the rain. At his life. At ever getting involved with the Colucci family.

Then he caught himself. The Mercedes warmed up and he switched on the windshield wipers and headlights. He could see Estelle at the kitchen window, the curtain pulled back, watching for him to pull out of the driveway. He waved to her, though he knew she couldn't see him, and found himself wondering if the lines of worry across her forehead were for him or for Diana's nephews.

With the wipers slapping time, he considered his life, his marriage, the commitment he'd made to give both his clients and the State of Massachusetts the best he had, the fairest decisions, trust and faith in his ability. It hadn't always been easy, especially in the early years. His career was in its infancy when Estelle showed up in his life, a quiet, intelligent girl who considered him the most handsome and dynamic man she'd ever met. She made him feel important and, in feeling that way, he *became* important. She gave him everything he needed—patience, understanding, love. Even when he hadn't deserved it. And she'd been at his side through the worst and the best of it. There had been many times he'd turned away from her, forgetting her feelings, leaving her lonely at night so he could chase his ambitions, but she'd ^ways been there waiting for him—no matter when he chose to come home.

He knew she'd be there after this latest crisis, too.

This time I'll show her how much I appreciate her, he thought as he waited for the red light on the corner of Beacon Street. I'll take her on vacation as soon as this is all over. Just the two of us. Maybe she's right. Maybe that's all I need to calm this damn volcano in my stomach.

Before heading into the downtown parking garage, he popped a few more Rolaids and wondered if Rambo ever had to deal with bleeding ulcers.

Marblehead

More than half an hour later, the generator hummed noisily, powering the alarm system and giving them serviceable, though dim, lights.

"There. That ought to do it for a while." Greg wiped his hands on his jeans. "I'm going to change my clothes. You okay done for a couple of minutes?"

Steve nodded, then looked toward the parlor floor. "Diana, you okay?" Thinking she had crawled under the couch or behind a chair, he walked into the room. "Diana? Diana! Greg! She's gone, damn it! Diana's gone!"

Chapter Thirty-five

Marblehead, September 15, 1991. 9:07 p.m.

Diana could barely see two feet in front of her. The rain pummeled her face relentlessly like little frozen icepicks, and cold sea water circled around her ankles. Pushing her way through the water, each step became harder than the last. Within moments of leaving the house, each Nike felt like it weighed more than a cement block; her jogging suit was soaked and sagging, her hair plastered against her head causing freezing drops of salt water to burn her eyes.

She ignored it all, the vision of her nephews facing Luis's anger forcing her onwards. Again and again she saw their faces, heard their voices urging her to share a game, to sit beside them at dinner, to read them a bedtime story.

I'm special to them, she reminded herself when it felt she would be unable to take another step. I have to be there for them.

And another face wavered in front of her. She shut her eyes, begging Robbie's ghost to leave her alone, but it wouldn't. After a while, she realized he just wanted to help. Perhaps she'd been forgiven, after all. When she finally looked back to the beach house, she had reached the other side of the causeway. Rain still stung her face, but she had gone past the sea water; her sodden sneakers now slapped against solid pavement. For a moment, she stood staring at the light in the distance, catching her breath.

The light. That meant the power was back on. They'd be out after her soon. With a chuckle, she realized she'd gotten past the DEA agents with no trouble. The rest should be easy. She turned and walked toward Atlantic Avenue, hoping someone would take pity on her and give her a ride toward Saugus.

Saugus, September 15, 1991. 10:14 p.m.

"What the hell?" Maryann took an automatic step backwards. Her hand flew to her throat as if the action would take away the apparition in front of her. Diana sent a silent prayer of thanks that Maryann hadn't let loose with a scream,

"It's okay, Mare. It's me." Diana stood in the cellar doorway of the Saugus house, her sweat suit dripping all over the floor.

"God, look at you! How did you get in?" Maryann ran for the bathroom, coming out with an armful of towels. Pushing Diana back down the cellar stairs, she turned on the washing machine, then draped one of the towels over Diana's head and wrapped another around her shoulders. "You're soaked."

"Came in through the bulkhead. Good thing I wore black. Cops didn't even see me. Lot of good they'd do you if Quintana decided to come over." Diana shivered uncontrollably.

"Listen, get that wet stuff off and we'll talk. Okay?" Maryann pulled the sodden sweatshirt over Diana's head. 'The patrol will be back again soon. They just went to get supper, but there's someone outside, isn't there?"

"Yeah. Two squad cars. They got someone in here, too?" she whispered as if suddenly realizing she might have to hide.

Maryann nodded as she squeezed the rain out of Diana's pants. "Have had since I got home. That's why I made you come back down here. I was heading down to do the laundry, anyway. The cop thinks I'm nuts. I should be pacing the floor or crying hysterically, or something schlocky . . . but you know me," she laughed nervously, "give me a crisis and I get the uncontrollable urge to clean the house." She paused a moment. "You know what happened, obviously."

"Yeah. Greg, one of the cops who's supposedly protecting me called the station and they told him everything. We don't have much time, do we?" They kept their voices down, both of them anxiously looking toward the cellar stairs.

"No, but that doesn't matter. You can stay here."

"I'm not supposed to be here. Supposed to still be in Marblehead."

"Well, then, what the hell are you doing here? No, don't answer. I can tell by your face you're up to something." Maryann's eyes narrowed.

"The cops aren't going to get to the kids in time," Diana replied, wrapping her arms around her still-cold body. "Besides, they'll probably end up having an out-and-out war with Quintana. That would put the boys directly into the line of fire . . ."

"So what do *you* intend to do? Or rather what are *we* going to do?" Maryann briskly rubbed the towel over Diana's shoulders, bringing back some of the warmth. Diana relaxed into her hands.

"No, not *us*

"What do you mean *not us*'? They're *my* kids, Di! Whatever harebrained scheme you've cooked up—I'm going to be part of it!" She stopped moving the towel and Diana immediately shivered again.

For a moment, the women looked straight into each other's eyes, deriving the strength they needed from each other, as they always had. Diana remembered Maryann's words of sympathy when she first put Mama into the nursing home. And her encouragement when Diana went to work for Gene. If not for Maryann—the spunky redhead who could out swear Robert, the determined mother of her two favorite people in the world—Diana knew she would not have been able to hold on. She would never have made it through the pain of splitting up Mama's belongings, the dull throbbing depression after Gene's death, or the absolute shock of Robert's. Maryann had been her strength, her pillar, the one who held the family together. Now it was time to return the favor.

"Where's the gun Rob bought a couple of years after Chris was born?" she asked.

A dazed expression spread over Maryann's features; her eyes wandered to the ceiling, then down to the cement cellar floor. "Jeez, I don't know. I put it away . . . somewhere . . . don't remember where."

With both hands on Maryann's slim shoulders, Diana begged, "Think! You've got to think!"

"In the attic. Maybe. Maybe in that old trunk up there."

"Go! Find it! And get something comfortable on. We're going for a ride."

"What's the plan?" Maryann handed the towel to Diana, a determined, fierce expression on her face.

"We're going there ourselves," Diana answered. "We've got a better chance of getting in and getting the boys than a bunch of cops with flashing blue lights. I know Luis's property. I've been thinking about it and there's a way to get in. That is, if you're willing to take a chance ... a big chance." One eyebrow cocked, Maryann laughed. "You really have to ask me that? They're all I have left. I'd die for them."

Diana felt a grim smile twist her face. "Then we're even, hon, 'cause I feel the same way."

While Maryann went upstairs, Diana took off her jogging suit, squeezed more of the rainwater out, turned the dryer on high, and stuck the suit in. Better damp than soaked. The sneakers would have to do as is, wet or not.

With a large towel wrapped sarong-like around her body, she waited impatiently for Maryann to come back. From upstairs, she heard a mumbled conversation, then the door opened and Maryann returned, carrying a laundry basket.

"Did he see you get the gun?" Diana asked. "No," whispered Maryann. "I told him I was getting dirty clothes from the kids' room." She nodded toward the gun as if it were a coiling snake. "Don't know where the bullets are. Maybe there's some still in it."

Diana groaned and flipped through the chambers. Fully loaded. "God, Rob. Didn't you even know enough to unload the frigging thing?" She put the revolver down on top of the dryer, then unloaded her clothes. "We'll leave through the bulkhead. There's no sense waiting around. We've got to get out of here before the patrol gets back."

As Maryann pulled a raincoat off the coat hook, Diana shrugged into her still-wet suit. "Oh, by the way, where's the Volvo?"

Maryann smiled apologetically. "In the shop."

"Where?"

"Down the Center."

"You have an extra set of keys?"

"You know I always have extras."

"Bring them. We'll take the car, fixed or not."

"I hope to hell it is. The transmission was gone. We wouldn't get anywhere . . ."

"Cross your fingers," Diana said as they headed outside. They stopped at the bulkhead. Diana lifted one of the doors carefully and peered outside. "I don't see anyone," she whispered. A stray spider web caught against her eyelashes and went into her mouth. She resisted the urge to sneeze.

"The cop was out front before." Behind her, Maryann's head popped up and she looked anxiously around the yard with jerky, birdlike motions. "I don't think they can see us back here. Listen, you think I should call my dad?"

"No! No more cops! They only screw things up." Flipping the gun's hammer, Diana fully opened the bulkhead's lid and slipped out into the dark yard. "You with me?"

Maryann nodded, her eyes filled with the fire Diana was used to seeing. "You bet your sweet ass! You know how to use that thing?" She gestured toward the gun.

"Yup. And you'll never guess where I learned how."

10:38 p.m.

The Volvo started right up, though the muffler sounded a bit loose. "That wasn't even the problem," Maryann mumbled, after listening to the car for a moment. "It was the damn transmission . . ." Guiltily, she glanced around the station's parking lot, looking in shadows for mechanics who might come out yelling at her for taking her own vehicle. She'd pay for the car when everything was all over. Martin, the Mobil station's owner, was sure to understand. He had kids of his own, didn't he? Somehow it didn't occur to her to worry about anything besides paying for the car. She knew, in the back of her mind, that if she concentrated on the big problem instead of the little ones, she'd lose it.

"What the hell are you waiting for? Let's go." In the passenger seat, Diana sat with the silver revolver in her lap, her lips pressed tightly together like a praying nun's. Maryann could practically hear her mind buzzing.

They pulled out of the station onto an almost- empty street. Shoving the car into first, she whispered, "Wait a minute. Cop car."

"Duck down. Make believe you're fixing something on the dash," Diana said.

The car passed by. Both breathed a deep sigh. "Okay, let's go."

Maneuvering the car around the rotary in the middle of the square, Maryann glanced at Diana. "Now where?"

"Luis's house. Where else?"

"How can you be so sure that's where they are?" "Only safe place in Massachusetts at this point. He's got the whole estate rigged with a million different alarm systems, armed guards, plus all his goons. No way anyone's going to get in."

"Then how are we . . . "

In the dark, she swore Diana's teeth flashed like neon. "You seem to forget. I'm the one who decorated that place. I know all its faults and how everything works. And I don't forget anything. I could walk around those grounds in my sleep. I know where all the men are stationed and where the doorways are that lead inside. Hopefully, that'll help us."

For a moment, the car's engine and the slushing sounds it made as they sped down the almost- flooded back streets were all Maryann heard. She'd always hated the rain. It made her feel achy and old; she didn't like being wet. Chris shared her dislike—he was the easiest kid in the world to keep inside when the weather was lousy. She wiped her eyes with the back of her hand. And Tony, even at eleven, was still afraid of thunder and lightning. How must they feel now? Would they think she'd forgotten about them? Would they be able to comfort each other until Diana and she got there? God, that sicko better not do anything to them.

Her boys. They'd grown up so fast. Almost teenagers now. Girlfriends soon, then high school graduation. Her own high school days were still so clear—how could her babies be old enough for that already? They were good kids, she thought. Good grades. Helped around the house. Maybe a little sloppy sometimes, but that's normal.

"Turn here," Diana said. Maryann turned left as Diana commanded, toward the super-huge, twelve- screen cinema where, just a month ago, she and the boys had seen some horror movie—*Freddie #10* or *Halloween #7*—she couldn't remember now. They drove in silence, past the well-lit New England shopping mall, down the two-mile strip where garish McDonald's and Burger King signs competed for business with the New England Clam Box and Louise's Ravioli. The car followed the curve of the rotary, past the Rising Sun Chinese restaurant where she and Rob went after the movies, down the straight slice of highway called the Lynn Marsh Road, the dark, quiet thoroughfare where high school students still raced their cars. Eerie at this time of night to be driving pell-mell past five-foot-tall swamp grass and sand dunes as big as her house, she thought.

The house. Diana.

"How did you get to my house? I never did ask you."

As if jolted out of deep thought, Diana's eyes blinked rapidly. She told Maryann the story in fits and starts, as though she didn't remember some of the pieces or her mind was elsewhere. When she finished, they had reached Lynn and Maryann could smell the ocean.

"There's something else I've wanted to ask since we left the house," she said. "I know you have a plan, but you really haven't told me yet. Do you think you might want to let me in on it?"

Looking out the window, Diana described how the alarm system worked, where the transformer was located, what Maryann should say when the guards come to the gate and how long to wait, stalling as much as possible before driving away, leaving her there with the boys.

"Just ram into the gate, that's all? What about the car?" Maryann envisioned a Dirty Harry movie where the cop drove right through a plate-glass store window. Would she be able to walk away as he did?

"Just do it. Don't worry about the car. It's got the strongest frame of any car on the market. Besides, I'll buy you a new one when this is all over. Just think about the kids. Just concentrate on them and you'll be able to do anything. Don't worry about being afraid or of what they're going to do if . . . just remember the kids are counting on us." Diana took a breath and continued.

"If you hit the box just right, you'll kill the whole alarm system. Then pull the injured woman routine, you might even want to pretend to be a little drunk—we can stop and get a nip at the liquor store on the end of the beach—and the guards'll probably buy it. They're pretty stupid and won't be expecting a woman alone. They've *got* to buy it."

"What if they don't?" All Maryann could think of was how she'd feel if she lost the boys.

Don't think about it, she warned herself. Don't even imagine it. I'd go nuts. Definitely.

"You've got to *make sure* they do or we're *all* dead. There's a lot of firepower in that house. A hell of a lot more than *we* have." She patted the revolver to make her point.

"And what are *you* going to do after you get into the library?"

Diana's fingers clenched around the gun she still held in her lap. "Hopefully, confront Luis. Then I'll get the boys and get out of there. I know the cops are probably following us by now—or, at the very least, keeping an eye on Luis's place. Maybe they'll come in like the cavalry. But we have to get there first. He'll be watching for the cops, but not for us. We're the only ones who have a chance."

Slowing down for a light, Maryann watched her sister-in-law's face in the shadows. "Just hope it's that easy," she said quietly.

Chapter Thirty-six

Marblehead, 10:35 p.m.

The high-bodied four-wheel-drive truck waded gleefully over the flooded highway like a child allowed to play in the rain, pushing aside rivers of sea water easily, effortlessly. When it finally found dry land, its tires spun for a brief second. Steve felt a line of sweat break out on his upper lip.

"C'mon," he urged through clenched teeth. "C'mon!"

In the passenger seat, Greg fumed like a volcano about to erupt. "So much for your sweet-and-innocent Diana. Had to make it harder on us. Couldn't simply let us do our job. Had to be Wonder Woman and go out and save the day . . ."

"Can it, Cottrell. Let's just do without the announcer bullshit, okay?"

The truck's tires caught and squealed on dry pavement. Both cops were purposefully silent as the borrowed vehicle maneuvered down the road and into the center of town.

Only moments before, they had been forced to call the station, admitting to the captain and the DEA officers who came to relieve them that Diana had slipped away. Even Steve felt a bit foolish. How could two professionals lose one witness so easily? He had been proud of his record—up until now-and knew that Cottrell was blaming everything on him. He had a perfect right to. If he hadn't gotten so involved ...

"You'd better find her!" the captain had screamed. "And fast. She's going to get caught right in the middle of the bust that's going down at Quintana's house. And, goddammit to hell, we've waited too long to get this guy for some society dame to fuck it up! Find her, Deluca, or I'll have your motherfucking Italian ass in a sling!"

The truck's muffler burped impatiently as they waited for a red light to change, but its engine growled to life when Steve pressed the accelerator and forced the shift into second gear.

"She's not too smart, is she?" Greg's voice had a razor-sharp edge to it, his animosity toward Diana back in full force.

"She's smarter than we give her credit. Probably doesn't have too much faith in *us*. Can't say as I blame her. She gets arrested for bringing in someone else's coke, her brother was killed by the asshole, her nephews are abducted ... I'd be pretty pissed off myself, at this point."

"Pissed enough to take the whole thing on yourself? To blow it for us? Just makes it worse when Mary Q. Citizen gets into the act.

You, of all people, know that, Steve-o."

"She doesn't know what's going down. Take it easy, Cottrell. We'll get there in time to stop W." Somehow, he thought, if I have to die making the effort. I'll get there. Not to stop her though, but to make sure she gets those boys back—and that Quintana gets what's due him.

"Yeah, right. We're going to make great time in this rain. Should've brought the Ark. Would've been quicker."

Steve shot him a look, then decided against answering.

The cab was quiet again, except for the patter of rain on the hood, as they raced toward Quintana's Nahant mansion.

Boston, 10:40 p.m.

Special Agent Nicholson's gray jacket rippled with frustration as he leaned across the seat and lit another cigarette. "Yes, I think you're right," he said to Arnie Goldstein. "It's definitely time to let the cops in on what's going down."

Arnie sputtered like a brewing teakettle. He felt small and insignificant in the van's passenger seat. Why wasn't the agent driving faster? Why didn't he seem the least bit perturbed? "Yeah, it's about time," he finally answered, "especially since the Boston cops are going to be out of their jurisdiction. I don't know how you guys let this all get so fucked up, but I can tell you *one* thing—we're getting Quintana if 1 have to go in there and get him myself!"

"Don't worry, sir. We've got the best men on the force. The canine unit is on their way and there's no way he's going to escape with all of us there." "Why doesn't that make me feel better?" Arnie yelled, feeling the veins in his temples throb. "For years these goddamn Colombians have been getting away with murder. You've got a sting set up months in advance and moments before it comes down, they escape. Why is this one any different?" The agent's lips made a thin line across his face. He looked as if he might finally lose his cool. "I don't know, sir. I'm just doing my job, sir."

"Well, then, get the lead out of it, motherfucker! We're going to be the last ones there!"

As the speedometer reached sixty, Arnie dug in his pocket for yet another Rolaid. Was it only fifteen minutes ago that he'd been safe and warn, in bed with Estelle? The chill in his bones felt as though it had settled in twenty years ago. He studied the agent's hawk like expression in the dim light. Maybe he ought to give the guy a break. After all, he was doing his job and, according to Kennedy, was supposed to be one of the best.

"Anything I can do to help, I will," the Senator had told him. And Amie knew Ted wasn't interested in any publicity. In fact, he wanted his involvement kept quiet. "We're in this together," he'd said when shaking Amie's hand at the office door. His light eyes crinkled as he cuffed Amie on the shoulder. "God knows there've been times I've leaned on you."

"Ah, Ted, don't even worry about it . . ."

"My mother's always said 'God only gives problems to those who can handle them,' Goldstein. Think of this latest one as d challenge."

A challenge. Ha! Such a challenge I'll probably end up in the hospital, Arnie mused.

The car's radio cracked with messages from the other units closing in on the Nahant mansion. He leaned forward as they started up the incline to the Mystic River Bridge, trying to quell his all-too-familiar fear of heights. His throat tightened and his mouth grew dry. He kept his eyes straight forward, too afraid to look to the side, toward the black sky he knew dropped straight down into the murky Mystic River's waters.

The agent reached for the microphone and spoke briefly into it, relaying his position to the unit coming in from Andover.

"Are we going to get there first?" Amie asked, swallowing hard.

"Looks like the officers in Marblehead have a jump on us," Nicholson answered in his typical tight-lipped, droning style. "Only problem is no one seems to know where they are. They can't raise them on their beepers."

Nahant, 10:48 p.m.

Diana's sneakered foot tapped impatiently. The liquor store manager was certainly taking his time with the customer before her. Obviously, they were friends who had spent the previous evening playing cards, but she didn't care.

"Listen," she finally said. "Can I pay for this? I'm late for an appointment."

The men looked at her, giving her the once-over as if appraising *her* for purchase instead of the liquor. Then the burly cashier gave her a half-grin, his cigar still stuck between his teeth, and took the money she handed him. "Sure, honey. Need a little fortifier before your date?" Both men laughed as he bagged the nip of Jack Daniels and passed her change across the counter.

"I'd need about a gallon if I was dating the guy I'm going to see," she replied and laughed back at them, her patience gone. Bewildered, the men shrugged their shoulders and went back to their conversation about the poker game.

Getting into the car, she threw the little bag onto Maryann's lap. "Here, have a drink, then sprinkle the rest on your clothes. Eau de Whiskey cologne . . ."

By the time they reached the general store which serviced the tiny peninsula, the Volvo reeked as though someone had been on a binge and gotten sick in the back seat. "Thank God I don't have to stay in this car," Diana murmured, trying to get Maryann to laugh.

But her comments fell on deaf ears. Maryann's face was white, determined, her eyes wide as the Volvo made the long hill past the grammar school and into the neighborhood where the houses were larger, more ostentatious, some encircled by high iron fences and ancient oak trees. "God, Di, I hope to hell the boys are here. I hope we're doing the right thing."

As Diana's fingers encircled the cold steel of the gun, she, too, had a momentary lapse of courage. Maybe they weren't. Maybe this little brainstorm was one of her worst ideas. Then Tony's and Chris's faces flashed into her mind and she took a deep breath. "Yeah, we're doing the right thing. Just think of the boys, Mare. And trust me . . ."

For a few moments, neither woman spoke. Diana thought about everything that happened during the past ten years. Isn't this what happens when people are about to die? she wondered. Your whole life in a flash.

Newspaper clippings of drug busts involving the Medellin cartel flipped through her mind as though photographed specifically for her to remember at this particular moment. The belt Rob wore around his arm the day he died. The smell that filled the tiny house—the acrid, nauseating odor of death. Moments at auctions when she experienced the thrill of capturing a new piece of art. The feel of the Riviera sun on her face. The half-decorated California house. Will I get a chance to finish it? she asked herself with a barely controlled feeling of nostalgia.

Every little detail became crystal clear. Every sound the car made going through the rain, every tree that lined the road, every shingle on every house was as distinct as if someone had suddenly held a giant magnifying glass before them. She felt her breath leaving her body, could envision her veins receiving the blood her heart pumped out, knew that every single hair on each inch of her skin stood at complete attention. This must be what it's like to be high, she thought, and half waited for a vision or some hallucinogenic experience to occur.

Her thoughts were as orderly and lucid as if her brain had miraculously turned into a high-tech computer. She knew exactly what she needed to do. And, surprisingly, was no longer afraid. A strange calm, a sense of ecstasy, spread throughout her body, and at that particular moment she could have sworn she was invincible.

Swampscott, 10:55 p.m.

"Why didn't you ask if this frigging thing had gas before we borrowed it?" Cottrell stood outside the truck, next to the gas pump of the well-lit Mobil station. Though he flashed his badge at the attendant inside in order to get quick service, he couldn't force the gas out of the pump any faster.

"Christ! What the hell do you want from me? At least I got us out of there. How was I supposed to know this goddamn thing was on empty!" Steve slapped the hood with an open hand, promising himself he wouldn't get any more upset, he wouldn't get nervous, he wouldn't allow Cottrell's impatience to creep into his own mind. If I get nervous. I'll start fucking up, he thought. Can't do that. No. Have to stop.

"The least you can do is call the station and find out what's going on," Cottrell was saying. "You know we can't do a damn thing until the DEA gets there—we have no jurisdiction in yuppie towns like this."

Deluca flipped Cottrell the finger as he strode angrily past him and into the garishly-lit service station office. Without asking permission, he lifted the desk phone and dialed.

"Hey!" A redheaded attendant holding a greasy rag reached for the phone, but was not quick enough. Steve brushed away his hand, then pulled his badge out of his pocket. With a sheepish grin, the boy backed off.

"What's happening?" Deluca asked when the captain answered.

"Aren't you there yet?" He imagined the captain's face, darker than ever, a permanent line reaching across his forehead and dipping into a ravine between his eyes. "DEA boys left a long time ago. Seems like they knew about this all along. They set the Cole broad up in order to catch Quintana and now she's going to blow the whole thing. How come you're calling on the phone? Why aren't you using the . . ."

"Don't have our own car. We had to borrow a truck and we're in a gas station." Through the window, he saw Cottrell waving madly, obviously finished pumping gas. "Listen, Cap, I've got to go. I'll check in later." Without waiting for a reply, he hung up the phone and raced outside.

"They set her up!" he yelled as he bounced into the driver's seat. "They fucking set her up! I can^ believe it! And she walked right into their trap. Damn it!"

"Who? What the hell are you talking about?" Cottrell barely had time to get into the truck before Deluca pulled away from the curb, leaving a strip of rubber and an open-mouthed attendant with a handful of change.

"The Federal Drug Enforcement Agency, that's who. The big boys." Steve couldn't keep the derision from his voice. "How can they send someone
like her in with a bunch of sharks?"

"Maybe because she knows Quintana. Y'know, she might not be as innocent as you'd like to think."

Without hesitation, Steve reached over and grabbed his partner's shirt, bringing them only inches away from each other. "Who the fuck do you think you are?"

"Hey! Hey! I'm in this with you, partner. Cool your jets!"

Reluctantly, Steve released him. "If we didn't have other things to do. I'd beat the shit out of you right here and right now. I've had just about enough of your crap."

Cottrell straightened his shirt. "Well, I'd save that attitude for the enemy, if I were you. Besides, what makes you think you're so easy to get along with? Y'know, you don't have to keep on carrying around Sheldon's ghost. It kind of makes it hard for those of us who'd like to count on your loyalty."

That hurts, Steve thought, though he couldn't tell Cottrell that. He concentrated on the road for a minute, letting his partner's words sink in. "Have I really been that out of it?"

"Think about it," Cottrell answered, his head turned toward the window.

"Hey, I'm sorry, man . . ."

"Forget it. Just get the job done and stop letting your emotions get the best of you."

Though Deluca knew he was right, he wondered how he could possibly disassociate his emotions where Diana Cole was concerned. *Nahant, 10:59 p.m.*

"Okay, let me off here." Lifting the gun to the light, Diana flipped through the chambers once more, then stuck it into the elastic waistband of her jogging pants. "Be careful," she admonished Maryann. "And remember what I said—jam the car into the third rail on the left of the gate. Hard! You won't have a second chance. If it works, you'll know it because all the lights will go out and people will come running from every direction. Just stay with the car and act really dazed. Don't make any quick moves or they'll kill you without thinking twice. And do whatever you need to do to keep them busy, Mare. I need as much time as you can buy me."

She looked over at her sister-in-law. Illuminated by the single streetlight, Maryann's face looked younger than her sons'. To their right, the end of the peninsula dropped over fifty feet into the Atlantic Ocean. On their left, a small community of exclusive houses sat quietly in the rain, like dignified old ladies. No lights burned in any of their windows. Yet, in front of them, the Quintana mansion was ablaze, shining like fireworks on the Fourth of July. Each window was illuminated and all the searchlights were on, streaking back and forth across the sky. Even the paths down to the ocean were lit. Obviously, Senor Quintana expected company. Yet all the lights made the house a perfect target.

Reaching across the seat, she gave Maryann a quick squeeze and smiled. "I love you, hon. Take care of yourself."

"You, too. And tell the boys ... I don't know what to tell them. Just get them, Di. And be careful."

"I will. You be careful, too," she paused a moment and found herself wondering whether either of them would make it through alive. "You'd better go. I can't stay in this car any longer. You stink."

Forcing a grin, Diana got out and walked away, rapidly blending in with the night.

With shaking hands and trembling legs, Maryann sat in the car for a few seconds, letting the motor rev, her lights off and her heart pounding so hard she could hear it above the ocean's roar. The rain had momentarily stopped. That's good, she thought. Then again, maybe it's not. Maybe Diana would have more cover in the rain. One more minute. Give her time to get to the fence and I've got to go.

Her nervousness changed to a rush of adrenaline when an image of Rob popped unexpectedly into her mind. He seemed to be telling her to be strong, to be angry, to get back at that asshole Quintana for what he'd done.

A surge of unbelievable strength welled through her as she felt the car beneath her respond. Seat belt tight, she padded her sweatshirt up and stuck it under the shoulder harness, thinking it might give her a little extra protection during impact. Looking straight ahead, she thought of her boys, of Rob, of the chance to finally have a normal life. She turned on the Volvo's lights. As she pushed the car through first gear and into second, she whispered, "This one's for you, Robbie. For what we could have had. For what we *did* have."

The gate came closer and closer. The Volvo was racing now, picking up speed with every passing second. What would Chris and Tony say at a time like this? As metal hit metal, she found herself screaming, "Cowabunga, dudes!"

Chapter Thirty-seven

Nahant, 11:02 p.m.

Diana reached the left hand corner of Quintana's property at precisely the same moment Maryann's Volvo knocked out the power. She heard the crash and cringed; then a groan, like a giant's sigh, split the night air as all power systems in the estate went down.

It's Howdy Doody time, she thought, scanning the grounds furtively for Quintana's dogs.

Flipping one leg over the fence, then the other, she was on her feet, running for the patio doors leading to the library. The grass beneath her felt like ice. Her sneakers gripped, then slid, gripped again and slid out from under her. The gun flew out of her hands into the darkness.

"Shit!" she whispered, crawling on her knees in the direction she thought it had fallen. When her fingers closed around the steel, she could hear excited voices down by the gate and the sound of a couple of shots. Please, God, she begged. Let them be warning shots. Don't let them be shooting at Maryann.

From behind her came the unmistakable growl of a large dog. Remembering Luis's fondness for his specially-trained Rottweilers and pit bulls, she scrambled to her feet and ran, pushing her legs unmercifully, running faster and harder than she ever had before. Glancing over her shoulder, she could see the dog having the same problem with the wet grass that she had had only seconds before. Thankfully, the rain covered her scent and her years of running had kept her in top condition. She hesitated to think what might have happened if she had spent all her waking hours behind a desk.

Ducking behind a large fir tree, one of many which encircled the house's perimeter, she took a deep breath and readied the gun.

Please don't come near me, she thought. I don't want to kill an animal.

But the dog kept going on past, barking madly, unsuccessfully seeking her out in the dark.

She couldn't believe her luck and took a second to catch her breath, to calm herself before glancing up toward the house. Only about a hundred feet more. Dim lights in the downstairs windows. Probably candles. Perfect. Now she could see where she was going, but they couldn't see her coming.

She could hear the dog in the distance now, his barks becoming fainter as he rounded the other side of the house. He'd be back soon. They weren't trained to give up. No time to waste. She wiped her hand on her wet pants and balanced the gun in her palm. Lady Smith, the imprint on its handle had said. Ironic that Rob would have bought a lady's pistol. Maybe it wasn't his after all. Maybe he'd bought it for Maryann. She gripped it tightly, finding an odd reassurance in its solid weight.

Spotting the library doors, she noted that more candles were being lit. The more light they had, the less time she'd have, she realized and braced herself for the last sprint across the lawn. Though she reached the doors in seconds, it seemed hours. Everything felt like it was going in slow motion. She could still hear noises down by the gate. No more gunshots. Good. That meant Maryann was probably safe. Oh God, she prayed, please keep her that way.

Flattening her back up against the brick wall, she held the gun in front of her with both hands. A furtive glance inside revealed nothing. Tentatively, she tried the door, surprised when it swung open easily. Two quick steps and she was inside.

11:05 p.m.

"There they are. Slow down." Greg leaned out the window, rapidly speaking with the plainclothes DBA men parked less than two blocks from Quintana's.

"So?" Steve's foot, still on the accelerator, itched to push it to the floor.

"He says there's two more cars on their way. The locals are already there because of an alarm foul- up. Somebody's already fired some shots. They're as screwed up as a monkey fucking a football."

Without hesitation, the truck raced up the road. Steve's only thought was a guilty one—for not taking better care of the woman he now knew he loved more completely than anyone else he had ever met.

11:06 p.m.

Arnie could hardly believe his eyes. The mansion was surrounded by cars with blue lights flashing and those pops he heard weren't firecrackers.

We're too late, he thought.

"What the hell's going on?" he yelled over the din. 'This wasn't supposed to happen until we got here!"

Nicholson, busy checking his gun for ammunition, gave Arnie a cursory glance. "This is no time for hysterics, Mr. Goldstein. We have a job to do and the best way you can help us is to stay out of the way."

"Nick, this is Caspar," the radio crackled. "Do you read?"

"This is Nick. What's the situation?"

"Somehow the local gendarmes were alerted and they're the ones causing the gunfire. Seems there was an accident, a brown Volvo, Mass, plate #HE56Y, ran into the gates . . ."

Though the agent continued, all Arnie heard was the reference to the Volvo. Why did that plate number ring a bell? Opening the van's door, he stepped out, craning his head to see beyond the police cars. The Volvo, momentarily illuminated by a flash—was it gunfire or a searchlight? — looked familiar.

"Get down, Goldstein!" Nicholson barked, the radio receiver still held to his mouth.

Arnie dropped behind the nearest vehicle, still determined to see the action at the gate. There was a woman up there . . . the red hair . . . Maryann! That meant Diana was . . . another shot, this one from the house.

He groaned. That meant Diana was on the property . . .

11:07 p.m.

Slowly, Diana's eyes adjusted to the dim light. She scanned the room, spotting candles on the desk and on the table next to the door, but no people. The flames threw eerie designs on the walls, making everything look out of proportion. Big things were small; small things grotesque. The shouts and gunfire outside seemed very far away.

Suddenly, the large leather chair behind the desk swung around. The man sitting in it leaned forward, noisily sniffing something into a long silver tube. She took a few steps toward him, certain she'd found Luis alone and marveling, once again, at her luck. In the silence, her sneakers sloshed. The figure behind the desk paused.

"Who is there?" Luis's distinct accent was slurred, almost to the point of being unrecognizable.

"Just me, Luis," Diana said. A few more steps and she was away from the windows, where he could see her.

Though she couldn't distinguish his features, his teeth gleamed in the candlelight as he gave a dry, hoarse laugh. "You have finally come for your nephews, eh, *mi cara?* I knew you would. *Si,* they have been bad boys, Diana. You ought to tell them how to behave."

Her throat constricted. "Luis, if you've done anything to those kids. I'll . . ."

"You will what, *mi cara?* Kill me? I doubt it." This time Quintana's laugh ripped through the room like a madman's. "You know, Diana . . ." Pushing back the chair, he rose unsteadily and came around the desk. She could no longer see his face, nor whether he held anything in his hands. ". . . since I have had your nephews here, I have done a lot of thinking."

"Oh? About what?" Thinking quickly, she slid behind a high-backed wing chair and lowered the gun so the silver barrel would not reflect in the candlelight. No need to reveal she was armed. It might be just the thing to set him off.

"Do you really want to know?" He stopped, holding on to the front of the desk. Even in the dim light, she could tell he was disheveled and, in spite of her hate for him, she was shocked. Luis had never looked anything but immaculate. "I will tell you." He coughed loudly, then spat onto the floor. She recoiled, remembering the Oriental beneath their feet. He raised his head and sniffed. "I have been thinking of my childhood, Diana. Remember when I told you the story of how my mother died?"

Outside she could hear yelling and the sound of running feet. His goons were starting to come toward the house. More gunfire. Sirens. Were they bringing Maryann inside? She had no time, yet the wrong move would blow her chances completely.

"Yes, Luis. What about it?"

"Well, I was thinking how much that affected me. Our childhoods formed all of us, *mi cara*. That is why you are you and I am . . . well ... I am Luis de la Maria Quintana, richest cocaine dealer in Colombia, Massachusetts, New York, Spain, Florida, Portugal . . ." Again, insane laughter tore the air. He took another step toward her.

"Stay right where you are. No more fucking around, Luis. I didn't come here to listen to you. I came to get the kids."

"What is that in your hand? A gun?" He laughed once more. "You forget that I know you, Diana. You told me once you could never shoot a living thing, remember?"

Straightening her arms, she levelled the revolver at his shadowy figure. From upstairs, she heard the unmistakable yell of a teenaged boy . . . Chris! "You're not alive, Luis," she said, amazed her voice sounded so calm. So cold. "You haven't been for a long, long time . . ."

"You're not going to fire that gun at me, are you, Diana?"

"I don't want to, Luis. Don't force me. Just give me the kids."

"So, why would you want to kill me? Because of Robert? Because of your nephews? Hear them, Diana? They have been very, very naughty." He took a couple more steps, then suddenly was running directly toward her with the full force of a bull elephant.

11:08 p.m.

Arnie ran toward Maryann. Though Nicholson yelled at him, he kept going, unsure of anything except he had to be at her side, he had to let someone know he was there, he was trying to help. More gunshots. He fell, only feet short of his destination, and felt the sudden sting of tears against his eyelids.

"What's happening?" he asked, flattening himself on the ground next to a dark-haired man he suspected was a cop. The man had arrived in a four- wheel-drive truck at the same instant Nicholson's van had, and though he was in plainclothes, there was a BPD badge attached to his belt.

"Quintana's men just realized what's going on. They're moving the car away from the gates, using the woman as a shield. Wait a minute, who are . . . Attorney General Goldstein! What're you doing here?"

"Same thing you are. I've wanted this guy for years." Arnie pushed his glasses up on his nose. "Where's Diana Cole?"

"We think she's inside. I'm going after her."

"You? No, you can't. Wait for the task force."

"No way. It'd be too late. I'm going . . ." The cop slid to a kneeling position and laid his gun open on his hand to load it. Arnie watched him for a split second, impressed by the man's agility.

My hands are shaking so bad, I don't think I could hold my dick to take a piss, he thought, and this guy looks like he could easily thread a needle. "Listen, Detective . . ."

"Deluca."

"Deluca. You can't go in there alone."

Deluca looked at Arnie briefly. There was an intensity to the cop's eyes that somehow mirrored Diana's when she informed Arnie so long ago that she had decided to take care of her family. "Watch me," Deluca replied defiantly.

11:09 p.m.

Without thinking twice, Diana steadied her hands, aimed, and squeezed the trigger. Once. 1\vice; Luis kept coming at her, his bulky form swaying as though he was drunk. When he was less than a foot away, he teetered and her finger started squeezing the trigger once more, then he fell against her, his weight pushing her to the floor and knocking the gun out of her hand. A soft thud next to her made her flick her *eyes* to the right. The table had fallen and the candle's flames spread over the rug, igniting the wool fibers. An acrid smell filled her nostrils.

She stretched her fingers toward the gun while trying to free herself of Luis's incredible weight. Was he dead? Probably only knocked out. He had enough coke in his system to fool his brain into thinking he was still alive. Yet, he wasn't moving. And he seemed to weigh a thousand pounds. Beads of sweat broke out on her forehead and above her lip as she finally pulled one leg free.

Luis stirred. A drop of something wet slipped from his face down her neck. She kept still as he groaned something unintelligible. He moved again.

Frantically, she pulled her other arm free and pushed at his dead weight, trying to roll out from under him. The gun was only inches away. If only she could reach it!

The circle of fire grew larger and seemed to be rejuvenating him. She gave one last Herculean push and reached for the revolver.

"No, Diana," Luis's harsh voice whispered in her ear. "You are not leaving me now. We are going together."

Her fingers closed around the gun. She turned, put it to Luis's head, and pulled the trigger once more.

"Cover me, Greg!" Steve ran for the house as blinking blue lights surrounded a dark-colored Volvo. On the ground next to it lay a redheaded female. Unconscious, it looked like. They must have dumped her there when they realize they were surrounded. Gunfire rang from all comers of the property. He squeezed in through the fence and sprinted up the front lawn. Less than a hundred feet away, an Uzi's scattered shots lit up the night. He lowered his SIG-Sauer, sighted, and shot. The man fell.

Getting up, he ran again, keeping his eye on the house and wondering where Diana could be. Damn, it was a big house. She could be anywhere. A single shot rang out—inside the house. Then another. Heading in the direction of the sound, he saw the front door of the mansion suddenly illuminated. On the steps stood a large blond man, pointing a broom-handled Mauser in his direction.

Steve dropped, rolled, lifted his arm, and shot. The man disappeared into the house. "Shit. I missed," he whispered.

This is crazy, he thought. No one uses Mausers anymore. No one except madmen.

He watched the door, waiting to see if it would open again and realized the man had probably retreated now that he knew this exit was covered. Tb the right of the door, orange flames caught Steve's attention. Fire! On top of everything else! And Diana was inside.

Do I follow him? he wondered. Without another second's hesitation, he was on his feet, his legs pumping. Behind him, the gunfire was now punctuated by the sounds of nine millimeters and Magnums. Good. That meant the DBA was in place. About time. Maybe they could be some help for a change.

Out of breath, he reached the door and leaned against the wall, unsure whether the blond man had gone further into the house or was waiting right inside the hallway. Crouched and ready to move, he caught a glimpse of skin and flattened himself into the bushes. The blond man came out once more, right above him, the Mauser ready. No time to think. Steve raised the SIG and shot without aiming. The blond man fell to his knees and lowered the Mauser. Before he tumbled, he stared at Steve with unblinking ice blue eyes and swore something in German.

Behind him, the fire raced to the left-hand side of the door, totally out of control. Steve took a deep breath and dove to the right, screaming, "Diana!"

11:15 p.m.

"C'mon, boys. Don't waste any time. We've got to get out of here." Diana looked without pity at Luis's guard lying in a pool of blood on the bedroom floor. She'd had no choice. He had gotten in her way. It was either him or her nephews.

"Where's that other guy? The one you knew." Chris ran down the stairs ahead of her, yelling back over his shoulder.

"Dead. Let's go! You've got to run like you never have before. We're not out of here yet." She ran down the hall, trying to ignore the sounds of chaos outside and the crackle of fire below. She dismissed the thought that all the antiques and works of art she had spent over a year collecting would soon be ashes. Nothing else mattered now. Nothing but Chris and Tony.

"Hey! Over here!" she called to them. "The back way." She guided them to the servants' stairway, silently praying no one would be at the other end. In the dark, they bumped against each other and she shushed them. She found herself counting the stairs, then they reached the door leading into the kitchen.

"I'm going to open it," she whispered into the inky mustiness of the stairwell, knowing that if the fire had reached that part of the house, they were all goners. She put her palm fiat against it. Cool. "If I say it's okay, we run. If it's not. I'll keep them busy and you guys take off out the back door. It'll be right on our left past the pantry. It's just about six or seven steps from this stairway, okay?"

"But, Auntie Di, what about you?" Tony asked.

"Don't worry about me. You just run. Run faster than you ever have before, understand?" Silence. "Understand?"

Two scared voices acquiesced.

She held her breath as she tinned the knob. The click of the tumblers falling into place sounded louder than all the gunshots still echoing outside.

She pushed the door open an inch and sniffed. The smoke burned her nostrils, but she felt no heat and the kitchen was quiet. Everything was dark. She pushed it open a little further. Still no sign of Luis's men.

"C'mon," she whispered. "Go for it!"

Tony and Chris exploded through the door, their young legs pumping faster than Diana's. Turning once more to glance over her shoulder, she satisfied herself no one was coming and followed them, holding the gun ready though she wasn't sure how many bullets were left.

Finally, they were on the beach, the rattle of gunfire behind them. She breathed hard and tried to push back the plastered mess of her hair. Her hand smelled like pennies and she realized with a start that she was covered with Luis's blood.

"We've got to go back around the building. Your mother's back there," she said as she leaned against a wet rock to scan the grounds.

"Mom? Mom's here too?" Chris's blue eyes were incredulous.

"What'd you think-that we'd leave you here?"

"You and Mom did all this?"

"Well, I think we had *some* help. But, yeah, we did most of it." She grinned, hoping her feeling that Maryann was all right was correct.

Tony and Chris exchanged amazed glances, then reached for Diana. "Let's get going. Superwoman," Tony said, a beatific smile on his face.

"Awesome," Chris breathed.

Behind them, branches crackled. All three ducked. Diana brought the revolver even with her body once more, hoping she had enough bullets left. Had she used four? Or was it five? It was too late to reload, and she couldn't remember. Dear God, don't force me to find out, she thought.

"Diana!" The shrill whisper echoed in the night air.

"Who's that?" Chris asked.

"Don't know. Wait a minute. I think it might be . . ."

Out of the darkness came a familiar dark-haired figure, his gun at his side. "You okay?" Steve asked.

Without thinking, Diana ran straight into his arms, covered his face with kisses and held him as tightly as though she hadn't seen him in years. "God, am I glad you're here!"

"Why? You didn't need me. You're a heroine! It's all over. They're loading Quintana's boys into the cruisers."

She paused and listened. The only sound was the ocean's roar. It seemed the most beautiful sound she had ever heard. "Thank God," she whispered.

Steve beamed, then lifted his chin toward the boys. "Your nephews?"

Nodding, she walked with him to where the boys still crouched behind some bushes. "Chris. Tony. Meet Detective Steve Deluca of the Boston Police Department. He was one of the ones who arrested me . . . then kept me captive in Marblehead." Looking up into Steve's face, she laughed lovingly.

11:30 p.m.

Arnie watched with relief as Diana walked across the estate's lawn toward the gate, her arm around Deluca's waist. It was over, he told himself. All over. Now, maybe the ulcer would calm down, Estelle will get off my back, and things would get back to normal. Tomorrow I'll call the travel agent . . .

With a look of surprise, Diana spotted him and headed his way.

No, he thought. It's still not done. I have to tell her.

Looking skyward, he muttered, "Hey, Tony. You mind if I wait until tomorrow?"

11:38 p.m.

"Promise me you'll never try something like this again?" Steve, his arm still around Diana's waist, looked calmly toward the flashing blue lights into the crowd which had gathered. The rain had stopped. Quintana's men had all been rounded up, their bales of cocaine seized along with their money and guns. As the DBA officers made their report, the many police radios buzzed with calls. Chris and Tony sat near the Volvo with their mother, talking excitedly among themselves. A full, yellow moon appeared behind swiftly moving clouds. The rain had finally stopped.

Shivering, Diana looked toward her family. "The nightmare's over."

"Not yet, babe," Steve squeezed her. "You still have to testify."

She lowered her head, looking at the revolver still in her hand. "You're wrong. It *is* over. The nightmare's finished. Luis is dead. He can't hurt us anymore." She nodded toward the house where orange and red flames leaped through the roof. Though the fire department had been called, they still weren't able to get through the barricades the cops had set up. Somehow she thought it appropriate that everything should just burn to the ground.

As the ambulances disappeared down the road, Steve leaned toward her and pressed his warm lips against her cold ones. The gun dropped to the ground as she wound her arms around his neck. For what seemed like a century, she held him tight, wishing the moment would never end, that she would never have to give up the full and completely alive feeling encompassing her body. Now she knew she'd never truly been in love before. And she wanted to relish that feeling as long as humanly possible.

"Listen, I hate to break this up . . ." Strolling toward them, Greg held a clipboard in his hand. "Think you might want to sign this, partner?" Steve reached for the pen and scrawled a signature on the form, never taking his other arm from her shoulders. "I think you two ought to connect back to earth. There's plenty of time for this romantic stuff later," Greg said with a begrudging smile.

With a chuckle, Steve lowered his head to hers once again. "Hey, lady," he whispered against her neck, "do you think we might be able to have a real date one of these days?"

"How about tomorrow night?" she whispered back.

Epilogue

The Riviera's sun blazed in full force, warming her near-naked body and making all movement totally unnecessary. All around her children laughed, kicking sand at their sisters or brothers, while motorboats pulled skiing vacationers through the blue Mediterranean like knives through buttercream frosting. Lazily, Diana turned over, luxuriating in the feel of the cocoa butter against her skin, and sighed.

"You don't want to go back, do you, *cherie?*" Meredith, clad in a bright pink chiffon caftan, sat next to her, leafing through an Italian fashion magazine.

"Oh, I do. It's just that I'm feeling rather . . ." "Pampered?"

"Umhmmmmm . . ."

"A year is a long enough vacation, my dear." Diana turned her dark head toward her old friend. "Some vacation. I've opened three more shops and filled them with marvelously decadent things, taught four managers how to treat Amaryllis's customers, gone to one wedding . . ."

"Maryann made a beautiful bride, didn't she?" "She'd never have gotten married again if I hadn't pushed her and Terence together. You don't know what it took."

"Such a nice man." Merry gave a little sigh and lifted a plump arm to wave at Chris and Tony down the beach. They struggled with windsurfers, their bronze bodies muscular and healthy.

Soon the boys would be in college, Diana thought with a grin, then shook her head at the fact that so much time had passed so quickly.

"I've got to get back to the villa," she said. On her feet, she brushed the sand from her legs and shaded her eyes with one hand. "The boys'll be all right, don't you think?"

"Be serious, *cherie*. Those darling children will never even notice you're gone. They're no longer babes, you know." Merry lowered her sunglasses. "Calling Steve again? Didn't you just call him last night?';

Folding her blanket, she nodded, a twinkle in her bright blue eyes. "He's supposed to be picking up the Silver Ghost and the '32 Rolls today. Should be back in his hotel room by now."

"Yet another specialty for Amaryllis. Will you ever stop?"

"Why should I? This is my life, what I love to do."

"What about children?"

Diana stopped and turned, faking an exasperated look on her

tanned face. "Merry!"

"Well . . . I'll never have grandchildren, you know. Just thought I might borrow yours."

With a laugh, she continued up the beach, only stopping when she recognized a familiar body striding toward her. It couldn't be! He was supposed to be in Houston, an ocean and half a continent away.

"Steve! What are you doing here?"

Enfolding her in his arms, he answered her with a long, searching kiss. "Came back a day early. Missed you."

"And the cars?"

"Who wants to talk about cars? Let's go to the villa. We've got more important things to do." His warm brown eyes looked down into hers, reflecting the love he had confessed long ago and which continued to multiply every day.

Giving up the force was one of the first things he, had done once the trial was over. He had realized he was eager to leave his work, that Diana was far more important than the Boston Police Department, and he had followed her to Paris to live with her there.

Within a few months, he was bored and began going with her to auctions. Diana had tapped his interest in antique cars, introducing him to others in the field, teaching him how to sell and buy, feeding him books on the subject; then she sat back and watched his addiction grow. Three months ago, she asked him to help her add classic automobiles to her inventory and opened Amaryllis of Dallas with him in mind.

"I'm going to work, though," he warned her and added his police force pension to the money it took to begin supplying the branch with vintage automobiles of all prices and descriptions. She nodded, as if they had made an important deal, realizing that his male ego still needed to be stroked even though his small pension was barely enough to pay the secretarial staff.

"Did you think about what I asked you?" he said-

She nodded, unable to speak.

"And your answer?"

"Yes. On one condition."

A slight scowl darkened his face, but his strong arms grew tighter around her waist. "What's that?"

"1 keep my name, we only have two children, and there's no Amaryllis of Omaha."

Throwing back his head, Steve Deluca laughed from a deep place in his chest. "God, I love you, Diana Colucci."

"I love you, too," she whispered. Linking arms, they head^ up the road to the villa on the hill.

"Know what?" she said.

"What?"

"1 just heard Sotheby's is opening an office in Australia and 1 thought . . ."

About the Author

Dawn Reno Langley is the author of 29 books, including novels, children's books, nonfiction guides on antiques and art, and time management.

She reviews theater, dance, and music in the Raleigh-Durham area, where she also rehabs houses as part of The Rehab Crew.

Currently, she is working on a collection of essays and several new novels.

You can contact her through her website: http://dawnrenolangley.com

Photo by Rick Crank Photography

Other Books by
Dawn Reno Langley
CHILDREN'S BOOKS

EDMONIA LEWIS: The Sculptor They Called Wildfire

middle grade reader

REVIEWS: Dawn Reno has given a heart wrenching account of Edmonia Lewis: The Sculptor They Called Wildfire. Life was terribly difficult for the young woman known as Wildfire. She finds herself taken from her Indian Reservation and delivered to Oberlin College, knowing no one. Edmonia knows she has a destiny to fulfill, but not quite sure what it is. After being beaten and charged for murder, Edmonia discovers her desire for sculpting. She doesn't allow prejudices to stand in her way and continues to succeed, becoming one of the world's most acclaimed Women Sculptors. Edmonia Lewis is truly an inspiration to all women. -- *Kim Gaona Kim's Reviews*

In EDMONIA LEWIS: THE SCULPTOR THEY CALLED WILDFIRE, Dawn E. Reno writes about the extraordinary life of Edmonia Lewis, a child of the mixed races of African American and Chippewa. In the 1800s, the time of her birth, a woman was not highly educated, nor was she a sculptor. But Edmonia Lewis was both. In this nonfiction short story, artist Harriet Hosmer gives voice to the life of her extraordinary friend. Edmonia, who retained her native American name of Wildfire, lived a life seldom dreamed of in her era. She attended college at Oberlin College, something a woman, particularly of mixed blood, just didn't do back then. While in college she was accused of poisoning her two best friends. She even introduced herself to Lloyd Garrison, the editor of The Liberator, a well-known newspaper which led to her career of a sculptor. As a student of art history, I was enchanted by this brief look into the life of such an exceptional woman, a role model woman may yet wish to follow for her vision and strength. -- *Cindy Penn, WordWeaving*

A TALE FROM LAVALLAH

early reader picture book/coloring book

Klorinda, a young girl who longs to be a wizard but is forbidden because wizards are only--and always—male, belongs to a community of females led by her mother. Always a bit of a rebel, Klorinda breaks the rules and longs to leave her home, but she cannot.

When her world is threatened by the sinister Netaz, she breaks the rules once again and travels with her trusted pet, Chuczka, to the distant land where her father, Geo, a Master Wizard, lives. Though her father wants to help, this is a battle Klorinda must fight alone. She hesitates, but when Chuczka is kidnapped, she is forced to enter an adventure far beyond anything she has ever expected.

THE GOOD LION

early reader

Beryl Markham, the first female aviator to fly alone from east to west, grew up wild and free in the savannahs of Kenya. As a child, she ran barefoot through the Kenyan wilderness, played with native Kikuyu children, rode her father's thoroughbred race horses, and learned how difficult it is to grow up without a mother.

YOUNG ADULT

AFTER ALWAYS

coming of age novel

Coming of age is never easy, but Ralph Waldo (R.W. to his friends) Carpenito has more to deal with than the average adolescent.

When his father is accused of sexual harassment and the kids in school start bullying him, R.W. struggles to rely on his own inner strength to understand what's happening around him and to fight for what he knows is true: his father's innocence.

NOVELS

FOXGLOVE

suspense

Strong women and dramatic situations combine to make FOXGLOVE by Dawn Reno Langley, a suspenseful, action-packed, and romance driven novel. From the tragedy of Tiananmen Square to the fall of the Berlin Wall in Germany to the dangers of war-torn Africa, Dakota Rabinowitz and Iris Bell battle everything from stray bullets to discrimination, and rise above it all, not only to solve a mystery but to also rescue their friendship and their powerful belief in life . . . and love.

FOXGLOVE is the story of a forbidden romance between a wealthy German banker suspected of being an arms dealer, Nicholas Ellison/a.k.a. Nicholas Ellsberg, and American photo-journalist, Dakota Rabinowitz, and how their relationship disrupts their lives and their futures.

FOXGLOVE is a suspenseful adventure which takes two long-time journalists--Dakota (Frances) Rabinowitz, photographer, and Iris Bell, writer--around the world, through a web of intrigue woven by a man who changes their lives in more ways than they could possibly imagine.

And, lastly, FOXGLOVE is about the friendship between two very different women, a friendship that must rise above race, religion, and the changes caused by the passage of time, and how that friendship still remains strong in spite of everything the world throws in its way.

LOVING MARIE

women's fiction

When Krista Bordon-Hathaway travels to Colorado to find the peace she thought her best friend Marie had found there, she instead discovers that Marie had another life, a life she never chose to share with Krista. Unwillingly, Krista falls into that life and begins a relationship with Peter, the man with whom Marie had an affair.

As Krista reads Marie's journal and discovers the amazing power of love, she struggles with her own life and the mistakes she made leaving her daughter with her husband, an abusive man.

LOVING MARIE is about what happens to Krista when she meets Peter and how she almost loses him—all because they both love Marie.

LISTENING TO THE SUN

paranormal romance

Christina Angela Giannelli is too traumatized to remember what happened to her one night three years ago at Belvedere Pond. But Jesse Harkinson hasn't been able to forget what that night meant to <u>his</u> life. For three long years, he's wondered why the police found her car and belongings, but no sign of her.

After spending years hiding from her past in Canada, Christina is determined to find out who attempted to kill her that evening, and makes the long trip back to Vermont and her past. In order to protect herself while she attempts to ferret out her attacker, she's decided to lie and say she has total amnesia. The truth is she has psychogenic fugue, a type of partial amnesia brought on by a traumatic event which causes the victim to flee--and to forget, as a means of protecting him/herself. Though she remembers everything about her life before the night at Belvedere Pond, all she can remember of that actual evening is the nightmare of being hunted down and set afire by someone whose face she cannot conjure up.

LISTENING TO THE SUN is a suspenseful, paranormal romance about a couple trying to find their way back to each other in spite of otherworldly influences.

ALL THAT GLITTERS

women's fiction

Diana Colucci had what it took to get to the very top: the dream of making a name for herself in the world of international antiques--and the beauty and brains to turn her fantasies into breathtaking reality. Leaving the crowded tenements of her girlhood far behind, she became the protégé of a fabulously wealthy Boston Brahmin-moving from the high society of Beacon Hill to the jet setting royalty of Europe. Transformed into a woman of power and extraordinary passion, Diana was swept off her feet by a dashing South American prince charming... Until her fairy tale romance exploded in devastating heartbreak --and she was plunged into a deadly web of hate and revenge.

From Malibu and Rodeo Drive to Paris, London and Rome, she carved out a magnificent empire--only to risk losing it all before she found the love she'd been searching for a love beyond the dream...beyond the fantasy...and beyond her heart's desire.

Originally published by Kensington Publishers and finalist for Romantic Times' *Best Glitz Novel of 1994.*

THE SILVER DOLPHIN

women's fiction

Originally published by Kensington Publishers under the pseudonym Diana Lord, THE SILVER DOLPHIN is Dawn Reno Langley's tale of heiress Carrie Debary, a story of romantic suspense, set on the sundrenched Hawaiian Islands.

When Carrie abandons Houston high society for a simpler life in Hawaii, she never dreams she'll find love with marine biologist Alex Madison. Then an accident leaves her new husband badly injured, and Carrie is bereft and confused. In her grief, she falls prey to a dangerous gang, as well as an affair that's sure to break her heart.

Her world splinters and threatens to shatter, forcing her to make one of the toughest decisions of her life: save herself or save her husband.

Check Dawn Reno Langley's website [http://dawnrenolangley.com] for a full list of publications and blogs. Dawn Reno Langley is available for discussions with book clubs, writing workshops, interviews, and other speaking engagements. She blogs on Goodreads. For more information on current activities and appearances, subscribe to her newsletter (link on her website) and get a FREE book!

Made in the USA
Columbia, SC
28 July 2024

39000602R00174